SALEM CROSSING BOOK FIVE

A Day at the Beach

ANTONIA CHURCH

A Day at the Beach

ISBN: 979-8-88653-463-4

Published by Satin Romance
An Imprint of Melange Books, LLC
White Bear Lake, MN 55110
www.satinromance.com

Published in the United States of America.

Cover Design by Caroline Andrus

Dramatis personae

The Noble family

- Maggie (Jacquelyn Salem), 40—Neve's adopted mother
- Mark (Gilbert Graham), 40—Neve's adopted father
- Nevada "Neve", 23—moved from Iowa to Florida to start a new life, engaged to Bryce Graham
- Cyprus, 22—Neve's adopted brother, twin to Willow
- Willow, 22—Neve's adopted sister, twin to Cyprus

The Graham family

- Tomás—original founder, immigrated from Puerto Rico
- Grandame Mavis, 96—remained in SX after the rest of her family left
- Amanda, 46—Bryce's mother
- Bryce, 26*—returns to SX after a long absence
- Zephyr, 25—Bryce's sister
- Tom, 28—Bryce's cousin, FBI agent

The Salem family

- Nathaniel—original founder, immigrated from England

- Alexander, 89—father to Tessa, Nolan, and Mariposa
- Tessa, 60—powerful matriarch of the Salem clan, mother of Domino, Makenna, Micah, and Sean
- Domino [deceased]—former candidate for mayor, murdered
- Makenna, 26—scandalized progeny ostracized from the family
- Sweetheart "Sweetie", 6—child born of Makenna's illicit relationship with Martin Montgomery
- Micah, 25**—playboy scion
- Sean [deceased]**—tragic victim
- Nolan, 57—father of Jacquelyn, Juliet, Naomi, Alistair, and Britney Iblīs
- Daphne, 55—mother of Juliet, Naomi, and Alistair
- Juliet, 26*—Naomi's twin sister, popular and rich
- Naomi, 26*—Juliet's twin sister, black sheep of family
- Alistair, 25—ambitious and charismatic
- Simmeron, 25—cousin, publishes local gossip in *Simmer Salem's Scandal Sheet*

The Zhang family

- Sun—original founder, immigrated from China
- Lula [deceased]—mother to Millie and Kevin
- Kevin, 50—chief of police
- Millie, 52—head of powerful political dynasty, mother to Juliet, Dalton, and Owen
- Corden, 54—Millie's husband, biological father to Nevada Noble, Juliet, Dalton, and Owen

- Juliet, 26*—presumed dead
- Owen, 28—former co-mayor of SX, ex-husband of Britney Iblīs
- Dalton, 25**—prodigal son who studied abroad for year

The Montgomery family

- Samuel—original founder, emancipated slave from the North
- Martin, 56—influential but shady business leader, father to Carver, Jax, Sammy, Riley, Bryce, Sweetie, and Damien
- Amaya [deceased]—Martin's sister, mother to Clover
- Magdalene, 56—Martin's wife
- Carver, 27**—troubled offspring, frequently incarcerated
- Sammy, 26*—food truck entrepreneur
- Jackson "Jax", 25—bad boy with a heart of gold
- Riley, 23—spoiled brat troublemaker

The Ryan family

- Constance—original founder, immigrated from Ireland
- Helen, 69—retired municipal worker who preceded Neve in her position
- Solomon, 75, and Judith, 75—moral leaders in SX
- Rebecca, 48—owns the cottages along the cape as Neve's landlord
- David, 46—runs a nonprofit SX homeless shelter
- Rob, 25**—estranged husband to Ariel Álvarez
- Saul, 55—reverend, once married to Mariposa (Álvarez), who ran off when their daughter Mariah was a baby
- Mariah, 27—ambitious and independent
- John, 50—quiet, loner, morose ever since his wife died in childbirth, father to Delilah and Caleb

- Delilah, 26*—quirky oddball who offends most people
- Caleb, 27—overprotective brother, socially strange

The Álvarez family

- Dominga—original founder, immigrated from Cuba
- Ramón "Ram", 25**—big badass biker
- Isabel, 77—a woman with many mystery lovers, none of whom she married, mother to Carlos, Maria, and Mariposa
- Carlos, 55—proprietor of cafe/bar called Laverne's
- Anna, 27**—transitioned from Angelo ten years ago
- Maria, 53—advocate against the subjugation of the Álvarez family in SX, mother to Ariel and Acindina
- Ariel, 26*—self-centered drama queen, engaged to Rob Ryan
- Acindina "Cin", 22—spitfire waitress at Laverne's
- Mariposa, 50—former wife to Saul Ryan, mother to Mariah Ryan and Nevada Noble, left SX for Boston for 20+ years

The Iblīs family

- Ebrahim—original founder, immigrated from Persia
- Neil Iblīs (Halloweather) [deceased]—co-

conspirator behind the Dark Summer kidnappings, father to Clover Black

- Elizabeth Iblīs (Halloweather), 49—sister to Neil, mother to Britney and Damien
- Britney Iblīs (Halloweather), 28—ex-wife of Owen Zhang, daughter to Nolan Salem and Liz Iblīs
- Damien Iblīs (Halloweather), 26—murdered Domino Salem, son to Martin Montgomery and Liz Iblīs
- Clover Iblīs (Black), 23—raised in Boston by Mariposa Álvarez, biological offspring of Neil Iblīs and Amaya Montgomery

The Miccosukee tribe

- Andre Mascolo [deceased]—kidnapper who abducted the Dark Summer captives
- Anthony Mascolo [deceased]—Andre's twin brother
- Auberon Fox— true love of Naomi Salem

**a Caesar sibling, born on the Ides of March*
***a Dark Summer captive*

Previously in Salem Crossing...

Nevada "Neve" Noble moved from Horton, Iowa, to the beautiful Florida coast, working as a social worker for the City of Salem Crossing, otherwise known to the residents as SX. After a brief fling with local bad boy Jackson Montgomery, she fell in love with Bryce Graham, a doctor originally from SX who had returned home after a ten-year absence. After the "death" of the mayor, Juliet Zhang, Bryce ran for office and won. He also discovered his father, Martin Montgomery, was one of the disreputable citizens of SX. After a tumultuous campaign and seismic familial revelations, Neve and Bryce became engaged. Shortly thereafter, Neve discovered she was secretly born in Salem Crossing. After analyzing historical records and chasing leads around SX, Nevada found that she was Corden Zhang's daughter. Her mother was a descendant of Salems and Álvarezes. As a hurricane approached SX, Bryce learned Neve had been lying to him. The deception nearly destroyed their relationship. But even as the storm tore Salem Crossing apart, it brought Neve and Bryce back together.

Meanwhile, elsewhere in SX...

Six families rule Salem Crossing, descendants of the founding settlers embroiled in drama and romance for over a hundred years. The animosity between members of the different clans existed for generations until seven siblings were born on the same day on the Ides of March. Twenty-six years ago, a member of each family gave birth on the same night during a violent tropical storm—Bryce Graham, Delilah Ryan, Ariel Álvarez, Sammy Montgomery, Juliet Zhang, Juliet Salem, and Naomi Salem. These pseudo-siblings, dubbed "the Caesars," became fast friends and remained inseparable for sixteen years until Bryce moved away. Bryce recently returned, ten years later, and Salem Crossing will never be the same.

A hurricane recently struck Central Florida, causing extensive damage along Salem Shores and crippling the resort industry in SX, bringing financial peril to the Salem family. Among the casualties were Anna Álvarez and Auberon Fox. As the city reels from the devastating blow from Hurricane Marlena, the citizens must pick up the pieces and work together to rebuild their beloved Salem Crossing.

Drama permeated SX after the storm. Fifteen years before, a madman named Andre Mascolo kidnapped seven youths during the Dark Summer—Micah and Sean Salem, Dalton Zhang, Rob Ryan, Anna and Ram Álvarez, and Carver Montgomery. Recent answers about what really happened have generated more questions. A seventh founding family—the Iblīs clan—sold their claim to the land in a dubious deal with the Salems during the nineteenth century. The descendants of the original Iblīs immigrants to Florida—Britney, Damien, and Elizabeth Halloweather—prepare to reclaim the rights to their portion of land as SX focuses on recovery.

The runoff election for SX's co-mayor approaches after being postponed until after the holidays. After the death of Auberon Fox, Martin Montgomery faces off with Mariah

Ryan in a contentious head-to-head competition. Jackson Montgomery and Acindina Álvarez grow closer as new dangers threaten any future together. Jackie Salem searches for a way to save the family fortune while dealing with the fallout of her extramarital affair with Martin Montgomery. Ariel Álvarez investigates the suspicious activity of some of her fellow Caesars—will she discover an impostor replaced Juliet Zhang and the real Caesar is being held captive off the coast of Salem Shores, while SX prepares for the holiday season amidst the aftermath of a natural disaster?

Meanwhile, Nevada Noble decides to face the many mysteries that plague SX proactively while her fiancé is busy coordinating recovery efforts after the storm. She assembles a task force to tackle the lingering mysteries—Why did Damien Halloweather kill Domino Salem? Are there really pieces to an ancient treasure map hidden among the six founding families of SX? Who kidnapped the Juliets and why? What is the Iblīs family up to? Why did Helen Ryan switch Neve with Clover at birth?

It's Christmastime in Salem Crossing. Will Santa deliver joy and peace to SX, or will the holidays bring more danger to a town already plagued with turmoil?

Prologue

JULIET ZHANG

Juliet Zhang woke up on the beach.

She had been dreaming of her wife. Juliet was beside her in the sand, tanning topless. Any other method was a sin in her book. Sunglasses covered her dreamy blue eyes, and a smirk curled the edges of her luscious lips. Men slowed and stared as they passed, but Juliet Zhang wasn't jealous.

Those dicks could look as much as they wanted because Juliet Salem was going home with her tonight.

The occasional female companions of the ogling males became envious and wandered by with a scowl, unsuccessfully attempting to avert the eyes of their companions. The husbands and boyfriends are unable to avoid gawking at the perfect pair of tits. The Juliets were tanning on a restricted stretch on private Salem property with no rules about proper beach attire. Trespassing tourists passed along the shore at their own risk. Sharks and riptides might pose a danger in the water, but the female tourists worried more about the maneater sunbathing in the sand. Disgruntled wives and girlfriends simply picked up the pace, speeding through the surf as their men soaked up the sight of the beautiful topless blonde on the beach.

Juliet Zhang, out in public with Juliet Salem. Years ago, as teens, the Caesars could sneak around together, and the beach was a popular destination. Although bold as a teen, Juliet Salem had become less brazen as an adult. But this afternoon, nothing bothered her. Let them see. Let them look. No one could do a thing to stop her.

"Wouldn't this be nice," Juliet Salem asked, sliding her shades down her perfect, pert nose and giving her wife a wink, "if this wasn't a dream?"

Juliet Zhang sprang to an upright position. She wasn't wearing beach attire, but a strange, mustard-colored jumpsuit that resembled a prison uniform. The smell of Juliet Salem's coconut lotion transformed into the dank stench of rotting seaweed. The soft, elegant sands of Salem Shores turned hard and rough. As Juliet watched her wife, now asleep beside her, she grew older and grayer, her skin darkening, and her features changed. She mimicked a mirror image of Juliet Zhang. Soon, she was staring not at a beautiful blonde Salem, but an aged ancestor Juliet had long thought dead.

"Grandmother," Juliet whispered.

The older woman in the sand beside Juliet stirred. Her eyes fluttered open. Gray brows furrowed over dark eyes. She struggled to get herself up on her knees. "Where are we?" her grandmother asked in a tired, hopeless tone.

Juliet stood. She ached all over. She scoured the beach in both directions and found only the sea in either direction, trying to figure out where they were. Staring at the ocean, she attempted to mark something to reference their location, but all she saw was the endless expanse of the Atlantic. The sun peeked over the lip of the liquid world. Brilliant pools of orange and bright red striations painted the coastal waters. It would've been beautiful if Juliet hadn't feared for her and her grandmother's lives.

From the lack of any sign of civilization, discernible watercraft moving along the horizon, or even a jet contrail in the distance, Juliet decided they'd washed up on one of the islands along the chain far offshore the Florida peninsula. They hadn't made it back to the mainland. Juliet didn't know the islands around Salem Crossing like her pseudo-sister/sister-in-law, Naomi, who made these waters more of a home than the opulent Salem compound where she grew up.

"I don't think we made it home," Juliet said, cursing under her breath.

Juliet recounted the events of the previous night. She'd plotted the daring escape for days. She broke herself and her grandmother out of the cells located on the deserted island where her backstabbing fellow Caesar, Delilah Ryan, held them captive. Her grandmother had been presumed dead and stuck in that prison for ten years. After releasing them from their adjacent cells, Juliet stopped by the third prisoner's cell, offering him escape. The other prisoner sat in the darkness, unmoving. He did not reply. Juliet pleaded for a minute, to no avail. Finally, her grandmother advised her to leave him behind.

"We can send the authorities back for him," her grandmother said. "He's been here longer than I. He's too afraid to try."

"You're not staying behind, though," Juliet stated, searching her grandmother's face for signs of giving up.

Her grandmother put a thin hand on her shoulder. "I have something to live for right in front of me, Juliet."

They commandeered a canoe in a small bay, a little boat likely used to paddle across the quarter-mile expanse of the cove. Instead, Juliet pushed off and paddled out to sea, hoping she had chosen the right direction. A chance at freedom was worth the uncertainty of success. The possibility of death didn't dissuade Juliet from trying to get back to her wife and friends. Juliet Zhang would never give up.

Juliet paddled through the night and was spent by the time the silhouette of land appeared, framed by an endless starry sky. Her grandmother had passed out from exhaustion. Juliet dragged their craft ashore and managed to get her grandmother into the sand, covering her with a couple of blankets she'd brought from the prison cell. Juliet promptly passed out, not remembering snuggling beside her grandmother on the beach.

"Let's move inland," Juliet said as the bright morning sun offered hope. "Maybe the island is big enough to show signs of civilization."

Some islands along the coast, like the resort where Alistair Salem constructed an expensive hotel and vacation destination, were sporadically occupied. Maybe they could find someone who could be of help or have a way to communicate with the mainland. She headed inland, navigating thick vegetation slowly enough to allow her grandmother to keep pace.

The overgrown foliage proved nearly unnavigable. No one had been through this bramble since the dawn of humanity. Juliet started feeling disheartened when they came across a clearing under a high canopy of trees. Something didn't belong. A clue like one of those Agatha Christie mysteries she'd watch with her grandmother on occasional afternoons when Juliet and her brothers needed a sitter. She glanced at her grandmother to see if it elicited the same response. But the woman Juliet remembered from her youth seemed to have vanished. A shell remained. Her grandmother's spirit was broken and lost.

A tarp piled with firewood lay in the clearing. Someone had left it behind. It was the first sign that the island may be inhabited. Juliet looked closer. The standing water from the recent downpours left shallow puddles in the shape of shoeprints in the muddy soil. All the puddles pointed in one direction. She followed, keeping her pace slow enough for her grandmother to keep up. Cancer and captivity had left her a weak and withered shadow of her former self.

The directions of the footprints led to a cold campfire at the center of another clearing, which appeared to have been recently used. The hurricane had scrubbed the area of most evidence, but near the campsite was a wet, gray char and a couple of soggy cigarette butts. In the distance, empty crates as ominous as a pool of blood on a kitchen floor. One of the wooden pens appeared refurbished, while the others were rotted and broken. In one tangle of brush, a yellow ribbon of police tape fluttered in the soft breeze.

"Hahkv Island," Juliet whispered under her breath.

"The Dark Summer?" Her grandmother swept her eyes across the scene. "It looks like someone was here more recently."

"I heard about it in Iowa," Juliet said. "Acindina Álvarez kept an eye on things in SX for me. She said the original abductor tricked Dalton and the other survivors into returning to Nightmare Island."

"Dalton got abducted? Again?"

"He's okay," Juliet said, walking among the rotted crates where the devil had once corralled her brother like a pig for weeks and weeks. "Neil Halloweather happened to be in the right place at the right time and rescued them, killing the kidnapper in the process."

"That's a bullshit story. No way in Hell those boys would ever let someone wrangle them back here ever again," her grandmother muttered. "Dalton would rather die than be dragged back here."

"Yeah," Juliet agreed. She thought the same thing when Acindina reported the story. Carver Montgomery was big as fuck, and Ram Álvarez was larger still. No old man could force any of those men, or Anna Álvarez either, for that matter, back to Nightmare Island.

"So, now we're stuck in this godforsaken place," her grandmother said. "Out of the shark tank into the gator pond."

Juliet leaned against one of the wooden crates. She imagined her brother stuck in the small box made of sun-bleached planks, captive here for weeks and weeks. Juliet recalled the Dark Summer when the whole town banded together in search of the seven missing kids in SX, Dalton Zhang, Carver Montgomery, Angelo and Ram Álvarez, Sean and Micah Salem, and Rob Ryan. Those kids had endured agony. Juliet had been captive for only about a week so far. Her moxie consisted of sterner stuff than Dalton's, and he woke up and faced every day, although usually drunk and depressed. Juliet would survive this situation. She would get back to SX and reunite with her wife.

Juliet stopped at the eighth crate, which no one had ever occupied. Most people believed that Andre Mascolo intended Bryce Graham to be his next victim. Bryce was more of a brother to her than Dalton ever was. How would a summer in captivity have affected Bryce if the kidnapper had abducted him? Would Bryce have met the same fate as Sean? Sean Salem was the sole fatality of the Dark Summer. One kid out of the seven never woke up from the nightmare.

His murderer was dead. Neil Halloweather had gunned down the man responsible for the terror that horrific summer.

Or had he? Acindina's last report before Juliet's abduction suggested something about the whole story stunk like rotten fish.

Naomi Salem had found the captives fifteen years ago. She had sailed the routes along the outer islands countless times through the summer. One day, Naomi spotted signs of movement on Hahkv Island. She reported suspicious activity and saved the lives of six kids. And she probably prevented Bryce from becoming the next victim.

"It took a whole town searching for those kids the entire summer to find them the last time." No one would accuse Lula Zhang of acting optimistically after ten years of captivity. "No one is even looking for us. I'm presumed dead, and they probably think you are, too."

"Juliet wouldn't give up on me," Juliet Zhang said. She had updated her grandmother on many events over the last decade since everyone believed Lula had died. They'd had a week to discuss many different things as the hurricane locked down the island, and recovery efforts had directed their captors' attention elsewhere. "She's looking for me."

"We wanted to find those missing kids. We thought we had turned over every rock and checked every corner of SX. And yet, we never looked here."

Lula Zhang was co-mayor at the time and instrumental in the search and rescue mission. Careful planning ended up being upstaged by pure luck.

"Juliet might not consider searching Nightmare Island, but Naomi thought of it once before. We're Caesar sisters, Grandmother. The Salem twins won't rest until they find me."

"That hurricane made a direct hit on SX. The last thing anyone will be thinking about is a woman who was hiding in Iowa, and someone who died ten years ago. Who knows what sort of devastation SX is currently dealing with? I'm afraid we're not at the top of the list of concerns, Juliet."

She was right, damn it. Juliet couldn't accept escaping one prison to simply become marooned somewhere else, where she couldn't escape. She needed to get to SX and warn everyone that Delilah Ryan was an evil bitch. That was a twist she never saw coming. Her Caesar sister was as crazy as the mad hatter, but she never struck Juliet as an evil mastermind. Now, if it had been Ariel, then Juliet would understand. In fact, as they were growing up, Delilah had always said the logical, cool, and calculating Juliet Zhang was the one who reminded her of a James Bond villain.

"Then we find our own way off this cursed island," Juliet said, scouring the area for...what? A helicopter with a full tank that somehow survived the hurricane? She didn't know how to fly a chopper. A discarded cell phone with a full battery? Deus ex machina was a foolish fantasy, and the practical Juliet Zhang wouldn't put her faith in phony miracles. Her grandmother had been a woman of faith before she disappeared ten years ago, and Juliet hadn't seen her praying since her unexpected resurrection.

"You still believe in God, Grandmother?"

"Faith is finite, Juliet, and my tank ran dry years ago."

"Yeah." Juliet looked at the sky, empty and endless, no sign of a miracle, neither a search drone nor divine intervention. "God helps those who help themselves, right?"

Her grandmother stared at her feet, not even glancing up. "Not in my experience. We're damned no matter what."

How had it come to this? Juliet had followed in her grandmother's footsteps. Lula had been the mayor when she disappeared. How had such a strong leader turned into a hopeless mess? Juliet had also served in City Hall. Was she destined to lose faith eventually?

Juliet glared at her grandmother, "I'm not going to give up so easily."

"Neither did I for the first few years. Then, for a few more years, I would occasionally get a flash of hope. Now, it's a good day when I don't wish the cancer would finish the job someone started ten years ago."

Who was that someone? Juliet's captors had primarily

remained masked. Only Delilah had revealed herself, throwing it in her pseudo-sister's face. Who was the mastermind behind the prison on the remote island off Salem Shores? Delilah Ryan didn't have the financial means or the architectural intellect to construct an evil lair. Why did someone kidnap Juliet and her grandmother? Who was the guy in the end cell? Her grandmother said she'd seen an Álvarez in the clinic before they transported her back to her cell. Which Álvarez? Juliet was fighting not only for her freedom but to rescue all of them.

"We still have the canoe," Juliet said, unconvinced the small raft could make it across the open ocean between Hahkv Island and Salem Shores.

"Sea's too rough," her grandmother said. "The waves will capsize us."

Juliet turned and started walking to the shore they'd washed up on. "I'll swim back to SX if I have to."

"You won't have to swim, Juliet," came a voice from within the tangled undergrowth. "We've got a boat."

Britney Halloweather emerged from the thick foliage. Contrary to her usual glamorous, designer outfits, she wore a fashionable khaki ensemble that resembled what a wealthy person would wear on safari. Britney had been her sister-in-law until lately, the mother of Juliet's nephews, and first lady of SX for many years while Juliet and Owen Zhang served as co-mayors. They'd spent holidays and a hundred other family functions together. Juliet knew her as well as she knew anyone outside her own Caesar siblings.

"Thank God, Britney," Juliet said, stumbling toward her unexpected rescuer. "We were kidna—"

She came close enough to see that Britney wasn't alone. Britney's brother stood at her elbow. Damien Halloweather aimed a pistol at the Zhangs. The look on his face didn't suggest he intended to help reunite the Juliets. She thought about the man in the mask who'd brought them food and water through the hurricane. His build and posture matched Damien's.

The Halloweathers were in cahoots with Delilah Ryan.

"You've got to be kidding me, Brit," Juliet said.

"Have you ever known me to have a sense of humor, Juliet?"

"Hell, no," Juliet said, turning to her grandmother. "This bitch has been keeping you locked up, Grandmother?"

Juliet's grandmother squinted, as if trying to focus on a blurry image. "Is this the slutty little Britney who used to run around with Owen? I never imagined she was smart enough to be involved with a criminal mastermind. I haven't seen her on the island before. The other one usually wears a mask. I never guessed he was a Halloweather."

"We're not Halloweathers," Britney said.

"Well, you're fucking certainly not a Zhang anymore, either," Juliet snapped.

"We're descended from one of the original settlers of SX, Ebrahim Iblīs. We are going to take back what's ours."

"Ibli-wha?" Juliet muttered. "What are you talking about, Brit?"

Britney approached with Damien in lockstep like a loyal pet. "Your grandmother knows. She'll have plenty of time to fill you in. Come with us."

Damien jabbed his gun at the Zhangs. Juliet considered running, preferring a chance at escape to further incarceration, willing to chance a bullet in the back before she started to suffer the slow descent into hopelessness like her grandmother. But Juliet realized by the evil in Damien's eye that he wouldn't shoot Juliet first. He'd aim for her grandmother. He'd make Juliet lose her again.

She couldn't go through the pain.

There had to be another way.

Juliet followed the Hallowe—the Iblīs sibs. They had a boat waiting. Somehow, the psycho siblings had tracked Juliet's escape from the prison to Nightmare Island. They were going to take Juliet and Lula Zhang back. Juliet made herself a solemn promise: she would find a way back to her wife or die trying. She couldn't let ten years go by until another prisoner arrived and explained how Juliet Salem found a new love, not long after Juliet Zhang went missing, and everyone presumed her dead.

No.

That wasn't how this story ended.

Chapter One

HOLIDAYS WITH THE GRAHAMS

It had been decades since Mavis Graham last hosted a Thanksgiving meal at the Graham Manor. In the aftermath of the most devastating disaster to ever hit Salem Crossing, Mavis hosted more Grahams under one roof than had gathered in two generations. She stood at the head of the table and listened as the mayor of SX, her great-grandson, Bryce Graham, said words of thanks for the last year, highlighting his election to City Hall and segueing into his future with his fiancée, Nevada Noble.

Nevada would soon be married into the family, and any offspring they produced would add to the official bloodline in Salem Crossing. Bryce and Nevada showed great promise in restoring the Graham family to prominence in Salem Crossing.

How long did Mavis attend annual SX events like the Snow Ball alone, representing the family when no other Graham remained? How many church services had she experienced as the solo member of the sixth original family of SX? She lost track of the funerals she attended unaccompanied, as she survived, yet someone else younger than her died.

Now, her cup runneth over. Grahams started coming out

of the woodwork. A decade ago, Bryce had lived here for sixteen years with his mother, Amanda, and his sister, Zephyr. They had been the only members to spend more than a brief visit in SX since the rest of the Grahams left in a mass exodus decades ago. Zephyr had returned a few months ago when her brother came back, and their mother followed more recently. Mavis was glad to have them back in the fold.

Other Grahams, less familiar with SX, had come home and decided to stay a while. Her great-grandson, Tomás, had returned to investigate the awful events at Hahkv Island during the Dark Summer, an FBI agent with an aspiring career. He extended his visit, the investigation necessitating further examination, while a smitten Delilah Ryan required more of his personal attention.

Gilbert Graham spent some time in SX a couple of decades ago and ran off with the Salem girl to Iowa. He returned with a whole entourage. Two new members of the Graham bloodline and an adopted daughter were added to the family fold. Nevada would soon have double ties to the family after she married Bryce.

Mavis was suspicious of the young Conner Graham, who arrived shortly before the hurricane hit SX. Conner was the offspring of her son Julian, a grandson she'd never met before, and someone Julian never mentioned. Obviously, the kid wasn't an impersonator, as he could've been Bryce's long-lost twin brother. Mavis tasked Conner's sister, Amanda, with contacting their father and learning more about this mysterious newcomer, but Julian was notorious for disappearing for months at a time. Mavis had known many rabble-rousers in her time, and this kid smelled like trouble.

Her entire family in Salem Crossing gathered for Thanksgiving at the Graham Manor, and she felt like her old self for the first time in a long time. She hadn't realized how lonely she'd been for so long until loved ones once again filled the family home. Mavis Graham managed ninety-five years in this town, longer than anyone else in SX, and most of the last forty years had been lonesome. Now, as conversation filled the halls and the scent of a holiday meal permeated the mansion, Mavis was more alive and energetic than she had been in decades.

"Grandame, would you bless the food?" Bryce addressed, concluding his speech, already as windy as a seasoned politician.

Mavis gave thanks like a good Christian and finished with a hearty "Amen." The family members along the long table followed her lead and proceeded to eat. They broke bread together. Mavis remembered when her parents were alive, and her siblings shared spots up and down the great table intermixed with cousins, aunts, and uncles during the holidays.

Many decades ago, before the great exodus, Grahams gathered in numbers too great to be accommodated here in the great hall. Lower-ranking Grahams occupied the auxiliary dining room, while anyone under eighteen sat at the kids' table in the family room. The Grahams were as numerous as Salems or Montgomerys back then. Over the course of a single year, half of them exited Salem Crossing. Within another two Thanksgivings, Mavis remained alone at the head of the table.

Mavis lost her beloved Archie thirty-eight years ago, the last Graham to pass and the one who left her alone. She loved him dearly, but she still felt bitter about his abandonment of her. Mavis endured almost four decades solitarily representing a family against the many wolves surrounding her in SX. She'd wanted someone to stand beside her, but Archie was lying six feet under for these last years. Mavis managed alone.

"I bet things are different this year, Grandame," said Tomás. "How did you spend last Thanksgiving?"

Mavis thought back to a year ago. She had spent many holidays alone over the last century. More by herself than with someone else during the previous forty years, but she had company last Thanksgiving. Someone she hadn't seen in a very long time. He'd arrived with surprising news and grand plans. He wanted Mavis to hear him out. She listened, her attention riveted by every single shocking turn.

Mavis focused on the present lest the past whirl her thoughts away. "I had someone over. A quiet evening swapping stories. You know how the old folks can ramble."

"I remember Grandma Mary going on and on whenever we spent the holidays in New England. She would tell stories for hours without taking a breath," Zephyr said.

"Our mother was a talker," Gilbert conceded, looking at Amanda, who nodded in agreement. "She often said that's why our father left her."

"And why she thought Gilbert stayed away from her for the last twenty years," Amanda added.

Gilbert recoiled, stung. He'd abandoned his family for a Salem tart, and Mavis knew the harlot had slept with the diabolical Martin Montgomery all those years ago before she disappeared with Mavis's grandson. Gilbert was a naïve fool who would never suspect his wife of cheating, but Mavis had been around long enough to know a Salem never changes. Mavis saw the way Jacquelyn had been acting since she returned to SX, and she noted the furtive looks between her great-grandchildren whenever their mother acted more like a Salem than a Noble. They saw she was still the same woman who had once fit right in with Tessa, Domino, Simmer, and the rest of those pompous Salem bitches.

The tryptophan in the turkey kicked in, mellowing the conversation for a while. Mavis picked up threads of discussions regarding the rebuilding of SX, the funeral arrangements for those lost in the hurricane, the return of Juliet

Zhang as soon as the storm blew over, and the murmurs of rumors of the kind of scandals that have pervaded this town for all of Mavis's nine decades.

Most in-laws acted timidly around Mavis, but Nevada Noble boldly spoke in any social situation. "Where's Delilah, Tom? I thought she might spend Thanksgiving with us."

"She doesn't want to leave Naomi alone. And Naomi isn't ready to be sociable quite yet," Tom stated.

"I'm glad Delilah has risen to the occasion," Bryce said. "I've been so busy. Juliet is reeling from her wife's miraculous return. Ariel is dealing with her marriage problems." Bryce glared at Conner, who'd slept with the wedded Ariel during the hurricane. Mavis thought that Álvarez girl had always been a bad egg. "Samantha's getting her business back up and running, dealing with insurance."

Tom was always trying to do the right thing. He said, "Delilah asked me to stop at the docks to see Naomi on Evvie's Explorer after this. You and Neve should come along. Naomi would be glad to see you."

Bryce nodded.

"We should check on Jackie, too," Gilbert suggested, maybe feeling pressured by Tom's supportive gesture toward Delilah. "She's staying at the Salem compound to oversee recovery efforts." Gilbert looked almost apologetically at Mavis, as if he needed to make some excuse for his absent wife. "Tessa has a lot on her plate and depends on Jackie as her right-hand woman."

"I'm glad you were able to take some time away from recovery efforts, Bryce," said Amanda. "You've been working so hard since the hurricane."

"There's so much to do. No end in sight," Bryce said, shoveling food into his mouth like he expected someone to need the mayor at any moment.

Amanda said while adding more food to his plate, "So

much stress and sadness. We need a little sun to break through the clouds sometime soon."

"The Snow Ball will give everyone something to look forward to in the coming weeks," Mavis stated sagely from the head of the table.

Bryce said in a tender scolding voice, "Grandame, you can't think we're still going through with the Ball. Hurricane Marlena destroyed half the venue. It'll take months to execute the proper repairs on the Lillian Graham Center for the Arts."

If Mavis were a few years younger, she would have smacked Bryce upside the head for such a tone. His mother ought to do it, but she never took a firm hand against her children. And Lord knows Bryce never had a father figure around.

"The Snow Ball has been held every year since the inception of Salem Crossing," Mavis said. "This year will be no exception."

Bryce shook his head like he was telling a toddler she couldn't have candy. "Logistically, it would be impossible, Grandame. I have to consider public safe—"

"This year will be no exception," Mavis firmly repeated.

A remembrance flickered in young Bryce's eyes. He had lived here as a boy until he was sixteen, a charismatic kid running around SX with his six pseudo-sisters. He and his biological sister, Zephyr, brought energy and youth into a mansion that had long been quiet. How Mavis loved those sixteen years. Then they left ten years ago, and she suffered a lonely decade in their absence. Now, they were back, and she had Grahams pouring out of her ears.

Bryce had lived with her long enough to know that she meant business. If Mavis ever had to repeat herself, the discussion ended then and there. She hadn't survived ninety-five years by giving in. Mavis Graham made her way for almost a century. It wasn't going to change with Bryce.

Bryce inevitably conceded. "Maybe you're right. After so much has fallen apart, Salem Crossing needs a reason to unite as a community."

"The venue will have to change," Amanda said. "If we can't get the repairs to the LGCA completed in the next few weeks, then we'll have to switch location."

"The Snow Ball has altered the venue several times over the decades," Mavis said.

"We can't hold the event anywhere along Salem Shores," Gilbert said cautiously, taking care not to appear against Mavis's decision. "The devastation along the whole coastline is extensive. It'll take the Salems years to rebuild."

The Salems suffered the greatest losses of any family in SX. They had lost two family members to the storm. The properties along the coastline had borne the brunt of the hurricane. Mavis had seen pictures of entire resorts in ruins. A rogue tornado had razed the main Salem compound.

"Graham real estate weathered the storm better than most of SX," Conner added insensitively. "Initial assessments indicate minimal property damage and negligible loss of assets."

"Now's not the time to gloat about our good luck, Conner," Amanda scolded.

"I'm just saying we could host the ball here at the house. We weren't so foolish as the Salems to build our house upon the sand," Conner said.

Zephyr built on her mother's comment. "Will you quit with the negative vibes, dude? We have Salems in this room who lost family members in the storm."

Conner didn't back down. Argumentative like his father. "Am I supposed to feel sorry that some rich and powerful assholes died in their billion-dollar seaside resorts? Those sanctimonious SOBs were headed to hell long before I rolled into town. Hurricane Marlena simply gave them the fast track to eternal damnation."

Bryce stood and pounded his fist on the table. "That's enough, Conner. I won't have you badmouth all the Salems in one breath. Two of the Salems are like sisters to me. My fiancée is a Salem, and so are my future in-laws. You've been here for a few weeks and already wreaked havoc on Salem Crossing. I have enough on my plate with Marlena's aftermath without worrying about trouble in my own house."

"Don't worry, Bryce." Tom eyed the young rascal across the table. "Conner offends Neve, Willow, or Cyprus again, and I'll have the FBI on his ass in a heartbeat. No way he showed up in SX out of nowhere without a checkered past."

Conner closed his mouth and remained silent.

"That settles it. We will have the Snow Ball at the Graham Manor. The ballroom will accommodate the festivities," Mavis announced, her decree the last word on any subject.

Thanksgiving dinner resumed.

Mavis eyed Gilbert's children. Mavis thought Gilbert's little family was more Nobles than Grahams or Salems. None of them appeared upset at the loss of Francine or Krystal. She suspected no one had ever introduced the two young Nobles to the marginalized Salems.

Zephyr was offended that young Conner put the importance of Graham properties over the value of the lives of two smarmy Salems. Mavis considered Zephyr an unredeemable hippie who believed that peace and love would ultimately prevail. Mavis agreed that anything Graham—person, place, or thing—was more important than any Salem.

A new year was approaching. More Grahams occupied SX than at any time since the great exodus. Mavis had been planning this moment for most of her life. The fates finally aligned for the Grahams to regain power in Salem Crossing.

Schemes that had been unfolding for decades teetered on the cusp of fruition. Mavis had a lot to be thankful for this year. She would bear witness to the rise to power of the Graham dynasty.

The Grahams might remain neutral in the feud between families, but that was only because Mavis Graham hated all the other bloodlines in SX equally.

Chapter Two

Nevada Noble had seen little of her fiancé since the hurricane. Bryce had been working day and night on reconstruction efforts. The bureaucratic red tape was terrible enough, but the fighting between the families of SX had increased tenfold since Marlena tore through the town. All sides pressured the mayor to make major decisions that would affect every family and shape the city's future. Bryce had meetings, conversations, and conference calls. He provided updates to the press, escorted dignitaries touring the devastation, met concerned citizens during town halls, and Dr. Graham even performed some medical consultations for Salem General on the side as the hospital staff remained overwhelmed after the storm.

Neve took little moments here and there when she could. They spent Thanksgiving together for a few hours at Graham Manor before some emergency pulled Bryce away from the dinner table. She would drive to work with him in the morning on the nights he didn't sleep at the office and pick him up from work if he called it a day before she'd fallen asleep, so they could talk on the commute back and forth. They took showers together on the mornings he slept at home. She would catch a quick lunch or dinner when he had time. Somehow, after sporadic breaks in their physical intimacy due to "potential ancestral conflicts" and "lying to her fiancé about his dead sisters," Neve and Bryce found time to catch up on lovemaking.

Today, she joined Bryce on his twice-weekly tour of SX. Rico Álvarez had become something of Bryce's right-hand man. Chief Zhang didn't appreciate the appropriation of one of his officers, but Bryce's influence in SX had increased significantly due to his effective leadership following the hurricane crisis. He required constant police escorts, as important people were coming in and out of town due to the storm. The police force was mostly loyal to Chief Zhang in his dislike for Bryce Graham, but Rico had proven himself time and again during the hurricane.

"Same route as before?" Rico asked from the front seat of the SXPD SUV, exclusively reserved for Bryce's official duties.

"Yes," Bryce replied. "Take us through Old Mat first, tour the outlying neighborhoods, then wind back to finish along Salem Shores. We'll have to survey progress more closely when we get to the coast."

"Roger, sir."

Neve looked at her fiancé. He was burning the candle at both ends. His eyes had become sunken, and his brown-toned skin appeared paler than usual by three shades. He needed a haircut and a shave—and a long damn vacation. However, the recovery effort from Hurricane Marlena would last for the foreseeable future. How long before Bryce crashed and burned? Neve wouldn't let him. She reached over and took his hand, offering him strength.

Neve leaned over and kissed his cheek. "It should be better after the runoff election. You'll have a co-mayor you can lean on."

"That's not until the new year," Bryce said.

They'd had to postpone the election after the hurricane to allow for community recovery. Some places in Old Mat were still without electricity. Many roads remained impassable. Insurance auditors and property assessors continued to inspect the incalculable devastation along Salem Shores. Many citizens commuted between SX and other living arrangements as their homes remained uninhabitable. An election would be impossible for weeks to come.

With Auberon Fox dead, only Martin Montgomery and Mariah Ryan ran for the open seat to serve with Bryce. Dalton had come in third place, and his mother petitioned to get him back in the race in place of Auberon. However, the rules of SX only allowed a candidate to renege on a resignation from the race and return to the ballot. Thus, the courts ruled Auberon would remain on the ballot as a posthumous candidate to fill the three-contender requirement.

Bryce had pressured his fellow Caesar sister, Juliet Zhang, to return to the mayoral office. Technically, she was legally dead, undergoing a lengthy legal process to reverse the declaration. Since Juliet had faked her demise, the penal ramifications still needed to be sorted out. Certainly, she was a long way from everything returning to normal. Bryce even offered to resign if she became re-eligible to serve legally. Juliet didn't commit. She told Bryce she wanted to first focus on getting her life in SX back on track.

Neve's hopes that Juliet Zhang's return would alleviate some of Bryce's stress proved to be futile. After days of worrying whether the other Juliet was alive or dead, JZ showed up unhurt after the hurricane and offered only vague explanations as to what had happened to the two Juliets—an inexplicable boat trip off the coast of Salem Shores before an encounter with an aggressive whale capsized them, resulting in an amnesiac Juliet Salem washing ashore before the hurricane and an unlucky Juliet Zhang became stranded on a deserted island farther south along the Treasure Coast. After surviving the storm as a castaway, locals finally rescued her. Brought to shore thirty miles south near Vero Beach, Juliet traded her wedding ring for a motorcycle and rode back into SX in style.

"Why didn't you call?" Bryce had asked shortly after her return. "I would've come to get you."

Juliet Zhang wasn't the type to ever ask for help. "SX had enough shit to deal with. I can replace a ring. I can't substitute friends and family."

JZ retreated after the brief exchange, claiming exhaustion. She'd rested a lot since returning. After reuniting with Juliet Salem and making her rounds to apologize to the Caesars and her Zhang family, she'd avoided most acquaintances since her return. Neve remembered the active, no-nonsense Mayor Zhang she'd worked under when she first arrived in SX, and she thought Juliet had changed.

Bryce agreed when Neve asked. "Something's off. Both of the Juliets are different."

"Maybe the Caesars need to sit down and hash it all out," Neve suggested.

Bryce nodded, but his duties had precluded a Caesar get-together since the idea came up.

As they drove through the residential neighborhood after surveying repairs at Manny's Motel, Neve asked Bryce if they could make a quick stop. Bryce instructed Rico to pull into an empty driveway.

Since arriving in Salem Crossing, Neve had attempted to cultivate a cordial relationship with Isabel Álvarez. The cantankerous woman pushed Neve away whenever she attempted to make a social call. Then, it turned out Isabel was Neve's grandmother. Had Neve's biological mother, Mariposa, told Isabel that Neve had been switched at birth and was a biological Álvarez? Or maybe the rumors around SX reached Isabel?

Neve didn't bother knocking on the front door. She knew she'd find the old woman in the garden behind the house, tending her plants and culling weeds. The backyard scene was very different than the idyllic garden Neve had visited not so long ago. The weather had wreaked devastation in small doses along Old Mat. Isabel's plants were as much victims as the hotels and condos along Salem Shores.

The charming décor arranged around the yard had been tossed around and overturned. The wind had strewn repurposed antique garden tools across the yard. Weathered planks of driftwood embossed with the family name lay broken into pieces throughout the yard. The once whimsical garden gnomes now lie scattered, battered, and broken. The storm had uprooted and ruined plants by the dozens.

Isabel Álvarez knelt on the ground in the center of the backyard, moving with the quick and grim determination of a doctor performing triage to save a patient. She may be approaching eighty years old, but she had the verve of someone a third her age. A stack of withered plants grew taller as she collected the dead into a funereal pile. The look on her face suggested a military leader who had lost good men in battle.

"We can help," Neve said, kneeling in the dirt near her grandmother.

"The time for help passed days ago. I grieve alone," Isabel snapped.

"At least you can salvage a great percentage of the garden, ma'am," Bryce offered.

Isabel scowled at Bryce and said, "If I wanted irksome optimistic bullshit, I'd get a Ryan over here. You don't lose one out of four children and celebrate that it could've been worse, Mr. Sunshine-and-Roses."

"Mr. Mayor will do," Bryce stated simply.

"Mr. Mayor didn't do a damn thing to save my garden," Isabel huffed. "Too busy worrying over Graham properties and Salem real estate, I suppose."

"I was focused on infrastructure and evacuation, Isabel. As you recall, I stopped personally to try and get you to find safe shelter from the hurricane."

Neve watched as her grandmother's eyes flickered with confusion. She didn't remember. Acindina Álvarez had explained that their grandmother suffered from the early stages of dementia. Neve observed confusion cross the old woman's face, searching her thoughts for an event that happened only days ago. Nothing.

Isabel got angrier. "Fucking politicians. Want everyone to run and hide. I didn't go anywhere during the storm. I stand and face adversity instead of retreating like a coward."

"You're lucky you didn't get hurt. Your home sustained damage, and you could've been injured," Bryce said with compassion rather than being argumentative.

Isabel had been staying with her daughter, Maria, Neve's aunt, for the last few days while a small group of locals repaired part of Isabel's roof. Instead of waiting on a long list for a local contractor or an opportunistic handyman from another town to fix the damage, the Álvarezes of Old Mat took care of their own. A crew of locals with the necessary tools and skills had been going around the community, repairing homes one by one. Today, Isabel returned to her place after the neighbors finished patching her roof.

Bryce was too nice, so Isabel turned her ire on Neve instead. "What are you doing here, Yuma? Shouldn't you be collecting insurance money for some Salem properties with your substitute mamá?"

"Then you know I'm an Álvarez?"

Isabel stood, sturdy and quick for a woman her age. She

looked Neve in the eye without hinting at the fog of confusion that had affected her moments before. The lines on her face traced a bitterness cultivated over the years as carefully and thoroughly as the plants in her garden. The furrows tilled across her forehead and into her cheeks suggested a life that had seen its share of uprooted plants and sustained damage.

Isabel shrugged dismissively. "A name doesn't mean a damn thing. I have three offspring, Mariposa, Maria, and Carlos, and not one with their father's last name. Because it doesn't count for shit if there isn't a connection. Like a stray kitten lost from its litter and raised by squirrels, you are no more an Álvarez than Mr. Sunshine-and-Roses Mayor here."

"The Nobles aren't squirrels. They're good people." Neve inwardly chuckled at how silly she sounded

Isabel spat on the pile of uprooted plants. "They are cowards, like the spineless citizens who evacuated SX during the storm. They ran off with a baby that wasn't theirs and hid for decades away from their families."

"They didn't know I was your granddaughter. They thought I was someone else."

"*You* are not my granddaughter. You *are* someone else." Isabel's words cut Neve like a knife.

Neve glared, wanting to say all kinds of hurtful things to the bitter old woman, but she held her tongue. She had spent countless hours since learning about her true origins, imagining what she had lost because Helen Ryan switched two babies at birth. Neve ended up in Horton, Iowa, instead of somewhere else. But she realized the duplicity had been a blessing. Mark and Maggie Noble were better-suited parents than Mariposa and Corden would've been. Neve would rather have grown up with Willow and Cyprus than any local Zhang, Álvarez, or Salem.

They left the old woman in her floral fiasco and continued making calls in Old Mat. They circled the rest of the neighborhoods before ending up along Salem Shores. The rest of SX was spared more than the devastation along the coastline. Isabel Álvarez's plants were nothing compared to demolished high-rises and eroded beaches. The uprooted vegetation within the Salem properties was palm trees and centuries-old oaks.

Rico Álvarez parked in the SX Club lot. The building had withstood the storm better than most other Salem properties. It had become a de facto headquarters for Jacquelyn Salem as she spearheaded efforts to rebuild the resort properties, which are crucial to the local tourist industry and vital to the Salem family's bottom line. Neve detested the place. During the hurricane, she had walked in on her mother committing adultery with Martin Montgomery.

"Flashbacks," she stated to Bryce as they approached the entrance.

Bryce, who had witnessed his illegitimate father cheating with Neve's mother, grimaced and shook his head. They'd both rather forget about that awful image.

The main lobby had become a regular meeting place for the Salems to address the challenges of rebuilding dozens of properties and handling billions in repairs. On previous visits, they'd met Nolan, Alistair, Tessa, and even Neve's grandfather, Alexander, wandering around the club. Mom had set up a war room in Tessa Salem's upstairs office. They ascended the spiral staircase and found Mom huddled with Juliet Salem, poring over stacks of contractor quotes and insurance documents.

"...doesn't jive with the policy small print over here. Something's wro—"

Neve and Bryce appeared at the top of the stairs. Juliet broke away from helping Jacquelyn and ran to give Bryce a big hug. The Caesars moved off to the side, their convo quickly following the familiar pattern between pseudo-siblings. A different language Neve was beginning to understand in bits and pieces.

Things had been awkward between mother and daughter since Neve walked in on her mom in the arms of a man who wasn't her father. They hadn't talked about the incident yet, and the conversation ranked as about the last thing on planet Earth that Neve wanted to discuss with her mother. However, Neve didn't want to keep the secret from her dad. She had learned her lesson about keeping secrets after Bryce almost called off their wedding because she hadn't told him the Juliets had faked their deaths.

"We're checking up on the rebuilding efforts," Neve said, filling the silence.

Her mom shuffled some of the papers on her desktop, almost as if trying to conceal something. One more clandestine operation in the ever-expanding oeuvre of Jacquelyn Salem.

"It's a lot of work," her mother said. "I've been a teacher for the last twenty years. This is something of a learning curve. Red tape knots around this whole thing. I need to coordinate endless moving pieces every step of the way."

"Anything I can do to assist the rebuilding effort?" Bryce asked.

Jacquelyn bared a huge yawn before replying, "Can you add more hours to the day? I need like an extra forty to keep up with the paperwork."

"Federal and state aid are pouring in. I have people at City Hall who can help process funds," Bryce offered.

Her mother looked skeptical. "Are you really that naïve, Bryce? Plenty of people in the SX bureaucracy are actively working toward the demise of the Salem dynasty. Any assistance from City Hall would only be in servicing the fall from grace of my family name."

Bryce frowned. "Everyone knows that the Salems are integral to the local economy. We don't have Salem Crossing without your family."

"Plenty of people disagree with you, Mayor. They believe Montgomery Crossing or Zhang Crossing would be just as successful," Jacquelyn remarked.

"The community has set aside those animosities and will work together to rebuild this town."

Her mother scoffed. "Your foolish optimism isn't going to help me, Bryce. Hopefully, whoever becomes co-mayor won't wander around the ruins with their head in the clouds. You need someone with balls to keep you in check." Neve considered the remaining two candidates to co-mayor with Bryce. One had balls, and she didn't want her talking about Martin Montgomery's junk. "Until then, you don't have the moxie to be of any help to me. Enemies surrounded us, yet you're wasting time chasing rainbows."

Neve wondered if she looked forward to working one-on-one with Martin Montgomery if he won the special election. Their affair could continue amid stacks of paperwork among the ruins of Salem Shores. Owen Zhang and Riley Montgomery had carried on a secret rendezvous in the Fallout Shelter for months. Neve imagined her sneaking off to the secure location with Bryce's father. Imagining her mother spending her extra forty hours a day with Martin sickened Neve.

"Mom—" Neve was unable to avoid the topic of her mother's adultery anymore.

"Not now. I'm focused 100% on getting my family back on its feet. I don't have time for personal drama." She wore a no-nonsense expression that warned Neve not to push her another inch.

Her mom's statement had a double meaning. She warned Neve away from the topic, declaring she didn't have time to deal with relationship problems. But Mom's words also suggested that she wouldn't become entangled in further romantic distractions with Martin Montgomery. She had work to do, and she wouldn't let her daughter or a paramour distract her.

Neve and Bryce left without any further information about the progress of the rebuilding efforts along Salem Shores than they had before. Her mother had attempted to reassure Neve that her affair was short-lived and over, but Neve remained unconvinced. She also concealed part of the story regarding the Salems' rebuilding efforts. Enemies surround us. Bryce believed SX would come together after the tragedy and support each other in rebuilding, but her mother thought the other families were like sharks in the sea, sensing blood in the water. Neve glanced at her fiancé as they exited the SX Club. Jacquelyn was right about one thing: Bryce was optimistic and naïve. The hostility among the six families of SX would be worse than ever.

Chapter Three

ARIEL ÁLVAREZ

Ariel Álvarez gazed in the mirror. Everything was backward. The things she once found normal had flip-flopped, leaving her disoriented and lost. Like trying to read words upside down on a page, her mind struggled to make sense of a world transformed into something familiar but foreign. Her expectations had all been twisted, and she could hardly tell left from right.

Her wedding ring was on her right hand in the mirror, an unwed woman. Ariel didn't know the exact status of her marriage. Rob had caught her cheating with Conner Graham during the hurricane and hadn't spoken to her since. She didn't know if she could repair the relationship. She didn't know if she wanted to fix her marriage. The woman in the reflection didn't look like anyone's wife.

The world had gone backward. Salem Crossing suffered extensive damage during the storm, and many of the coastal properties were in ruin. The hometown that had gone chiefly unchanged for her twenty-six years had transformed into a broken version that needed significant work to rebuild. Sometimes, a thing had to be razed rather than rescued, and one had to start from scratch.

Even the people she once knew, including herself, had become mirror images of themselves. Cin was sneaking around with a Montgomery. The Juliets had faked their deaths and returned, both different than before they "died." Conner Graham, who could have been a reflection of her true love, Bryce, arrived to shake things up and rock her world. Delilah was actually dating someone who wasn't her brother. And Bryce had become engaged to that little Noble bitch.

"Regretting your recent life choices?"

Speak of the devil...Delilah Ryan appeared over Ariel's shoulder in the mirror. Before Bryce left SX in their youth, the Caesars had been as close as real siblings. Ariel knew Bryce, Sammy, Naomi, and the Juliets better than Cin, her own sister. But Delilah and Ariel never got along like the others. Ariel never had the patience for Delilah's loony personality and lack of filter between her batty brain and vulgar mouth.

Ariel answered Delilah's reflection. "Just thinking it could always be worse. At least I'm not in some weird, incestuous relationship with my brother."

"You wish," Delilah quipped back without missing a beat. "You've been in love with Bryce since you were old enough to toddle around after him on playdates."

"Bryce is not our brother."

"That's always been your problem, Ary," Delilah said. "You're the only one who thought so."

Ariel turned, and Delilah looked no more ordinary without being backward than she did in the mirror. She wore a rainbow-striped blouse with vertical lines, but her pants featured only the three primary colors with wider bands running horizontally. For some reason, Delilah decided to pair the atrocious outfit with a sun visor, one with the translucent neon bills in bright pink, although they were indoors.

"What the hell do you want?"

Delilah glanced around as if it were apparent. "I'm not here to order sushi."

They were standing in the public bathroom at City Hall. Bryce had called a meeting between the Caesars. Ariel had arrived first, hoping to catch Bryce alone, but Neve was at his side. The conniving cunt had lied to Bryce and all the Caesars about the Juliets being dead. Ariel had believed for a short while that the betrayal might be enough to ruin the relationship between Bryce and Neve, but the events of the hurricane had inspired Bryce to take her back. The other Caesars may have forgiven Nevada for her lies, but Ariel used the excuse to further express hatred toward the deceitful bitch.

"You still chasing that Bryce lookalike, or did you let Rob back into your viper's nest?"

"Don't pretend to show interest in my personal life, Lilah. You only want to enjoy my pain."

Delilah's expression shifted from one of superiority to one of concern. Ariel liked that less than her acidic arrogance. Delilah was about as crazy as Ariel's grandmother, Isabel, on one of her bad days. She didn't need pity from someone whose previous love life consisted solely of Caleb Ryan.

"I don't get any pleasure from your fucked-up life, Ary. I want you to get your shit straightened out."

Ariel glared at her pseudo-sister. "Remember the À La Moo?"

The À La Moo restaurant had been an upscale steakhouse run by Stewart Salem when the Caesars were young. The pseudo-siblings were thirteen, and Bryce's mother had invited all the Caesars out to the À La Moo for Zephyr's birthday. Ariel had been incredibly aggressive in trying to get Bryce to kiss her near a statue of an Angus bull dancing with a Jersey cow. Young Ariel thought the scene romantic and pursued Bryce more overtly than usual. Delilah had confronted Ariel about her flirtation in the restroom of the À La Moo, and a catfight ensued. Delilah ended up with her head in a toilet with Ariel repeatedly flushing until Sammy showed up and rescued the sputtering Lilah.

"You wouldn't," Delilah sputtered.

"I don't know if I can fit that fucking visor into the bowl, but I'm willing to give it a try." Ariel threatened.

"I'm not a teenager anymore, Ary. I won't get flushed without a fight."

"If we fight, I guarantee you're getting a mouthful of toilet water, Lilah."

Delilah stepped into a stall and locked Ariel out. "You need to grow up. We're not kids anymore. The world changed."

Ariel regarded the reflection in the mirror and how everything she knew seemed reversed and wrong. Damn, she hated when Delilah Ryan made sense. It always caused her to doubt her own thoughts. She despised agreeing with her eccentric, loony Caesar sister.

Ariel exited the restroom and entered the meeting room, where the city planners had plastered prints on the walls around the room detailing rebuilding efforts in the different sectors around SX. She did bookwork for the Halloweathers on the side, and the restaurant required only minor repairs from the hurricane. The commercial district along the shoreline was otherwise owned by Salems, and Ariel noted that all the other properties in the vicinity had sustained much more significant damage.

Naomi and Sammy huddled near a coffee machine. Sammy sipped as Naomi stared at a spot on the floor. Naomi's boyfriend had died during the storm, killed saving a simpering Salem—Naomi's nosy cousin, Simmer. Sammy had been consoling the grieving Caesar since the storm wreaked havoc on Naomi's life, more so than the other pseudo-sibs. The storm hadn't caused the damage to Ariel's marriage. Her life had been a hurricane long before Marlena rolled over Florida.

Sammy gave Ariel the stink eye from across the room. Ariel could understand Delilah being upset over the cheating scandal with Rob because they were cousins, but what the hell did Ariel do to Sammy Montgomery? Ariel was always the black sheep of the Caesars. The least liked among the pseudo-sibs. Her obsession with Bryce while they were growing up alienated her sisters. She was closer to the Caesars than anyone else in her life, but she always felt like the weakest link in their unbreakable bond.

"What's her problem?" Ariel asked Bryce, ignoring the woman beside him.

Bryce and Nevada presented a united front. Their repaired and revitalized relationship stabbed Ariel like a knife to the heart. They were leaning against a table, holding hands, exuding a lovey-dovey energy that made her nauseous. Ariel couldn't believe that Bryce forgave Neve for lying about the deaths of the Juliets. In fact, all the Caesars had forgiven Neve. Ariel's pseudo-sibs treated Nevada Noble like one of the group instead of shunning her like a backstabbing Judas.

"Samantha is upset," Bryce stated. "She's taking your husband's side."

"I cheat on a guy she hasn't said two words to in twenty years, and I'm the bad guy," Ariel muttered, "but the Juliets lie about being dead for months, and everything is hunky-dory a few days later?"

Bryce sprouted one of his stunning, heart-melting smiles. "Did you say hunky-dory?"

"That's the saying," Ariel snapped.

"That's the saying your great-great grandma probably

used when Dominga Álvarez founded this town with the other original settlers," Bryce stated with a bemused grin.

"Why did you call us all together, Bryce?" Ariel asked, changing the subject. She nodded at Neve. "And what the hell is she doing here?"

Bryce's smile collapsed, and he glared at her. She didn't like pissing him off, but she didn't like Neve more than she cared about making Bryce mad. Neve didn't spout off an insult, try to defend herself, or even smirk condescendingly. The Iowa interloper simply refused to take the bait, letting Ariel's antagonism fizzle. That was worse than a zinger. Ariel really hated the bitch.

"She's my fiancée, Ariel. Get used to her being here. We're going to get married soon."

"Getting married means you don't fuck some rando tumbleweed blowing through town in a hurricane, Ary," Delilah said as she exited the restroom, drying her hands on a paper towel, but her mouth was as dirty as ever. "Just because a guy looks like Bryce doesn't mean you need to drop your pants and screw the shit out of him."

"I'm surprised your first boyfriend doesn't look exactly like Caleb, Lilah," Ariel snapped. "Or was Caleb your first?"

Ariel had had more than two decades of practice pushing Delilah Ryan's buttons. The redhead's face flushed bright red, and her freckles seemed to glow like LED lights across her face. With hair the color of flickering flames, it appeared her whole head was on fire as she came across the room at Ariel. Ariel watched and waited for her pseudo-sister to get close enough to bust out her front teeth.

"You disgusting whore," Delilah screeched, crossing the room in a clumsy sort of gallop, like a newborn fawn trying to run before it became used to new legs.

Ariel was going to knock her the fuck out.

"Whoa," Juliet Salem said, catching Delilah around the

waist as JTS entered the room. The Juliets had arrived last but entered in the nick of time to save Delilah's ass from a whoopin' like she hadn't had since she was thirteen. "Settle down, Lilah."

JZ stood to the side as her wife held the hellcat from crossing the remaining distance to Ariel. Bryce had already been on a trajectory to intercept, and he helped JTS hold the rabid Ryan back from attempted murder. They had had enough Caesars in danger lately. None wanted another. They all knew they were saving Delilah from herself. Ariel would wreck the gangly goofball.

JTS and Bryce pinned Delilah to the wall. The things coming out of her mouth were about as vile as the devil cussing out the damnedest sinner, but Ariel wasn't listening to Delilah's bile. She watched JZ. Juliet Zhang had always been the peacekeeper of their group. She would calmly and coolly tamp down chaos when fights erupted between the Caesars. Bryce could never defuse a tense situation when they were young because no one feared him. Juliet Zhang intimidated everyone. Yet, today, she watched from the sidelines as Bryce struggled to tame the wild Ryan.

Strange.

Everyone else was emotionally involved in the fracas. The melodrama didn't interest Ariel. Like any other siblings, the Caesars thrived off petty little squabbles and the minor commotion of everyday life, while Ariel only thought about Bryce. She loved her other Caesars differently, in a distant way. She didn't get tangled in the yarn like the other mewling kittens. That allowed her a unique perspective on her sibs.

Juliet Zhang has changed.

Ariel thought of the mirror image that she had considered in the bathroom. Juliet Zhang had always possessed a quiet confidence. That hadn't changed. But something in her demeanor wasn't the same. Perhaps JZ had evolved into a new version like everyone else, but something told Ariel the change wasn't natural. What had happened in the few days from finding Juliet Salem washed up on the beach to Juliet Zhang returning to SX on a motorcycle like a total badass? Ariel suspected JZ hadn't told them the whole truth, or maybe nothing but untruth.

The only other person in the room who might've considered the situation objectively was the woman who stole Bryce's heart. Ariel wasn't going to ask Neve her opinion. She'd rather punch the whore in the face. Ariel egged Lilah on until she flipped her shit because she couldn't piss off Nevada like she wanted. Bryce would rush to the helpless maiden's rescue. Thus, Delilah ended up as her punching bag by proxy.

"C'mon, guys. We haven't been all together in ten years, and this is how we start the reunion?" JTS said, cinching Delilah at the waist as Bryce restrained her by the wrists.

The feral wildcat with flaming freckles and flying red hair finally stopped struggling. Delilah huffed and puffed like she'd run a marathon. Ariel leaned against the opposite wall, arms crossed, at ease. She might run her mouth, and she could quickly end any physical altercation Delilah might try, but she didn't start this fight. Did she? Well, she wasn't trying to continue it.

"Fine," Delilah said, pacing between JTS and Bryce, remaining on the other side of the room. "Just keep her away from me." Ariel raised her hands in surrender. She hadn't budged since Delilah walked in. "And keep her quiet."

"You know damn well I'm not going to quit talking, Lilah," Ariel snorted.

"Then stop talking about each other," Bryce said firmly.

He was in brother mode, or politician mode, which didn't command the respect that JZ would when they were young, and Juliet put her foot down, but it still held enough weight. Ariel clammed up, and Delilah glowered silently.

Satisfied he'd diffused the situation, for the time being, Bryce moved to the center of the room, equidistant from Ariel against one wall, Delilah pacing along the opposite side of the room, Sammy and Naomi commiserating against a bulletin board along the east wall, and Juliet Salem rejoining Juliet Zhang near the door leading in and out. The despicable Nevada joined Bryce at his side in the center.

Bryce addressed the group. "As Juliet said, we've not all been in the same room in ten years. I'm glad we could get together for the first time in ages for such an important announcement."

"We already know you're getting married. Not new news, Bry," Delilah said, still grumbly.

The words made Ariel's stomach tie into knots. She hated the idea of Bryce and Nevada together as man and wife. She knew she had married Rob in a desperate attempt to make Bryce jealous. That was a mistake. The regret and rejection had driven her into Conner Graham's arms. Another mistake. But it had dulled the hurt for a while. That feeling returned as soon as Lilah mentioned marriage.

Bryce continued, "It's not just that, Delilah. We—"

"You're having a baby?" Sammy interjected.

Fuck. Ariel's guts heaved, and she almost puked at the news. Lightheaded, she was lucky to be leaning against the wall. She might've toppled over otherwise. Her mind swam in protest of the idea. Terrible visions of a Neve swelled up with Bryce's baby. She pictured a future kid who looked a lot like Bryce, a little like Neve, and nothing at all like Ariel.

"No," Neve said, the most glorious two letters Ariel had ever heard. "It's not that."

No one was looking at Ariel. Sometimes, it was beneficial

to be the least-loved sibling. She wiped away the tears standing in her eyes before anyone noticed.

Bryce's face lit up like fireworks on the Fourth of July. "We decided to have the wedding in January, after the Snow Ball. The Ball will be a positive affirmation of the rebuilding of Salem Crossing. We want to keep the momentum of positivity going. We'll get married in Hourglass Park the week after the Snow Ball."

The announcement finally shifted the mood in the room. Delilah's frown changed to a bright smile, and her animosity evaporated like water off Ariel's skin after a swim in the sea. She released a sigh of relief. The event was far enough away that anything could happen over the next month to derail their happily ever after.

"That's why we invited all of you here today. We want to ask you something," Neve added.

"Will you all be in our wedding party?" Bryce asked.

Immediate affirmations followed. Sammy squealed. Delilah did a strange, silly dance. Ariel saw Naomi smile for the first time since Auberon died. Juliet Salem gave the happy couple a big hug. Ariel watched JZ share accolades and considered that she looked like an actress playing a part. The smile on Juliet Zhang's face seemed to suggest something more sinister than sincere.

"How about you, Ariel?" Neve asked.

It had to be her. Bryce asking would've been too weird. It would be difficult no matter who invited Ariel. But she couldn't say no. She would never refuse Bryce. This would be the closest she'd ever get to standing at the altar with the man she'd loved her whole life. She could imagine herself facing Bryce instead of this impostor.

Ariel nodded. She couldn't form the words. She didn't trust her voice.

The Caesars started planning for the future. The recent

past had been such a disaster that they all needed something to look forward to. They deserved a brighter tomorrow than their today. But she didn't think the future would be any more pleasant than the present. More heartache. More coming in second place. More drama and turmoil in the life of Ariel Álvarez.

Ariel had no idea just how right she would be.

Chapter Four

JACKIE SALEM

"Maggie?"

Jackie was working on a mountain of documents stacked as high as a barstool. She'd been working tirelessly day and night to sort through the endless paperwork required to apply for federal and state funding for the multiple properties that had sustained devastating damage along the coastline during the hurricane. There was enough red tape to tie the Salems in knots for months unless she discovered a way to unravel the mess. Every decision could cost the family millions of dollars.

She looked up. The makeshift desk faced the window overlooking the beach. Some days, that was the only taste of the outside she had enjoyed recently. Last year at this time, she would've been grading papers for her high school class before trudging home in the snow—now, she shuffled around more money than she had ever imagined while glimpsing sporadic views of a spectacular shoreline.

The voice came from behind her inside the SX Club. The person had used her Iowa name. Neve, Willow, and Cyprus called her Mom. The only other person in SX who would identify her according to her other name was her husband. She spun the swivel chair and faced him.

"Gil," she said, using his SX name.

He had been Mark for the last twenty-three years. But Mark was married to Maggie Noble in Horton, Iowa. They were a long way from home. She considered her life there a dream, like Dorothy in Oz. This was the truth. Life with Aunt Tessa and Uncle Mason. Here, Neve had found her heart in Bryce Graham, Willow had discovered something to engage her mind as an investigator, and Cyprus had bravely stepped out on his own as an independent young man. They weren't in Kansas or Iowa anymore.

"You haven't been home in days," Gil said.

"Home?" Jackie glanced around at the disarray.

What was home anymore? She didn't feel like Graham Manor was home at all. The Salem estate didn't have Neve, Willow, or Cy around to make it feel right. Their house in Horton seemed fake, a façade like the rest of their life. They'd lived a lie for two decades, pretending to be something to protect the wrong kid. Helen Ryan had switched Neve for the baby born to Amaya Montgomery. Jackie had given up twenty years in service to a case of mistaken identity.

"I miss you, Maggie," Gil said. "You're working yourself too hard."

"This is important work," Jackie said. "The fate of this family depends on rebuilding the Salem properties damaged by the hurricane."

"You don't owe the Salems anything. Your real family needs you, too," Gil stated.

"I owe them twenty years, Gil. We left under false pretenses and abandoned our families for so long. And all for what? We kidnapped someone who wasn't who we thought she was. We lived a complete lie for all those years for no fucking reason at all."

"A complete lie?" Gil repeated, flinching. "You don't think our life in Horton was real?"

"Fake name. Fake careers. Fake past." Jackie stood and faced her husband

Gil recoiled as if she'd slapped him across the face. "Was our marriage fake? Our kids? Our family? Our love?"

The marriage was false. Fake names and birthdates were used to create an invalid marriage license. They exchanged vows before Reverend Ryan at Our Lady of Faith but never filed the legal paperwork in SX. The false documents listing Mark and Maggie Noble weren't even legal certificates. When she cheated with Martin Montgomery during the hurricane, it wasn't even technically adultery. Maybe that was why she didn't feel so guilty about being with another man. Jackie and Martin's steamy sex session felt more real than the last twenty years of her life.

"I need some air," Jackie said, turning from Gil and heading for the exit.

"Do you still love me?" His voice cracked, and his tone was tinged with the fear of what her answer might be.

Jackie paused. The question wasn't so easy. She had faked her life for so long she couldn't tell what was real and what she'd been pretending for over half her life. Did she ever truly love him, or was she simply playing a role? Jackie remembered swooning over the dashing young man in SX who had convinced her to save a baby that had no other chance. But had she ever really been in love with him?

"I don't have time to unpack all that baggage right now. It needs to wait until I get the Salem assets in order. This situation is more pressing," Jackie stated, standing tall and keeping her back straight.

"Your rich family's money is more important than our marriage?"

"If I don't get this right, this entire town is going to

implode. Thousands of SX citizens are depending on me right now."

"Please, Maggie..."

"Don't call me Maggie. That isn't my name." She walked through the door. "I'm Jackie," she declared.

She left Gil devastated in the room behind her. She had pretended to be Maggie Noble for twenty-three years. He'd been a good husband. Kind, loyal, loving, and a great father. But Jackie didn't have genuine feelings for him. Ever. She made do because she believed she was protecting Neve. It turned out she'd wasted all those years. The thought of so much of her life lost to a mistake pissed her off. She directed that anger toward Gil. He'd brought her into this cockamamie scheme and been wrong about it the whole damn time.

She walked onto Salem Shores and stomped through the sand along the coastline. She'd been working and sleeping in the SX Club since the hurricane, one of the few structures along the coastline that suffered only minor damage. She set up a temporary workstation with a pub table and a bar stool, with top-shelf liquor close at hand, on the main floor of the nightclub while she slept upstairs in Tessa's penthouse suite above the barroom.

The club had been closed since the storm. No one in SX was in a partying mood, and tourists were barred from the city until Mayor Graham could get a handle on safety concerns as emergency management services surveyed the city's properties one by one. Jackie had the place to herself ever since the hurricane. The exact location where she and Martin had reconnected after all those years. Reconnected twice.

Jackie went far enough down the coast that she was sure Gil would be gone when she returned. The beaches were eerily empty of tourists. Teams of volunteer environmentalists worked on cleaning the shoreline. Jackie didn't meet a single SXer during the hour-and-a-half stroll along the shore. She didn't appreciate Gil's ambush, but she did enjoy the excuse to get away from work and catch some fresh ocean air.

She returned to the club, and Gil was gone. Too exhausted to resume work, she ascended the spiral staircase in the center of the club in a tired twirl. Before Gil's interruption, Jackie had been poring over paperwork for twenty-four hours straight. If she hadn't been so sluggish, she might have noticed a change in the suite as she walked into the top-level area. Instead, she zombie-shuffled into a room already occupied by someone else.

The trespasser spoke. "Private hot tub? Pretty damn posh for a schoolteacher from Iowa."

"I was posh before I was a teacher," Jackie proclaimed.

"I remember."

"I know Montgomerys aren't exactly model citizens when it comes to law and order, but breaking and entering by overriding a pretty sophisticated alarm system is fucking ballsy for a candidate for SX mayor."

"I was fuckin' ballsy before I ever ran for mayor."

"I remember," Jackie said.

Martin Montgomery soaked in her hot tub. Aunt Tessa's suite over the SX Club spared no amenities. This place was as luxurious as any penthouse in the premier hotels along Salem Shores. A Rembrandt hung in the living space, the meditation room featured a replica beach and waterfall, and the bedroom showcased one of the best views along the Atlantic coast. Jackie never thought she'd see Martin Montgomery sitting in her hot tub.

Jackie was sure he was naked.

Martin wore that devilish grin that had gotten her in trouble before. "There's room for one more."

"There's room for a basketball team," Jackie said, one blonde brow raised curiously.

He leaned forward as if imparting a juicy secret. "I'm not here to play hoops."

"You look like you're ready to score," she quipped with a playful smirk.

Jackie didn't hesitate for a moment. She had spent her adult life pretending to be someone else. Jackie Salem had left SX at eighteen with Gilbert Graham and played housewife and teacher for twenty-three years. Nevada might have been disappointed when she discovered her mother's affair. Gil couldn't accept that Jackie didn't act like Maggie Noble anymore. Aunt Tessa would be furious if she knew Jackie was sleeping with the enemy. But Jacquelyn Salem didn't give a single fuck what anyone else thought anymore. It was long past time that she lived her own goddamn life.

Jackie unbuttoned her blouse, shedding the business attire top she'd been wearing for twenty-four hours straight. She sloughed the professional skirt over her hips and stepped free from the confines of fabric. Unprepared for a surprise visitor in her hot tub after long hours at the office, Jackie wore a plain white bra and beige panties purchased at a discount store in Horton a couple of years ago. Martin stared at her as if she were wearing luxurious, high-end lingerie from Agent Provocateur. Jackie stepped to the edge of the sunken tub and reached behind her, unclasping her bra. Her fulsome breasts burst free, and Martin looked like a wolf who'd found worthy prey. Jackie planned to give him something to hunt. She sloughed off her underwear and slipped into the steaming water.

Jackie sat directly across from Martin. If she extended her foot, she could verify he wasn't wearing any swim trunks under the swirling water, but she didn't need confirmation. He wouldn't sneak into her private quarters for anything that required clothes. His hungry gaze never wavered from her location across the hot tub.

"We've got to stop meeting like this," Martin teased.

"Maybe if you quit stalking me." Jackie licked her lips. "You don't see me creeping around Montgomery, Inc. offices."

"We treat trespassing differently on Montgomery properties, Jackie. You might end up in handcuffs."

"It wouldn't be the first time," she said with a wink.

Jackie recalled the passionate weekend with Martin before she disappeared with Gil, taking Neve to Iowa with a mistaken agenda to keep the baby safe from a nonexistent threat. Martin was older than she was, nearly twice her age, yet more vigorous and adventurous than the eighteen-year-old Gil Graham ever managed. He had handcuffed her to the headrail of the bed for one mind-blowing fuck session during their forty-eight-hour marathon affair.

"Is it the last time?" he asked, clearly wanting reassurances that this affair would be ongoing.

"I've just returned to Salem Crossing after being gone for half my life, Martin. I'm not thinking about last times just yet."

"Any of these moments could be the last, Jacquelyn," Martin said. She loved hearing her real name during these intimate moments. She'd spent the last twenty years being called Maggie in the bedroom. Mark and Maggie Noble had been on a two-decade stretch of endless roleplaying. "Auberon Fox. Frannie and Krystal Salem. Anna Álvarez. None of them thought it was their last time before Marlena changed everything."

"They haven't found Anna's body. She could still be alive."

"Hope." Martin's eyes lost their lasciviousness and became serious. "You wouldn't be so optimistic if you hadn't been away from SX all these years. This place would've broken and buried your enthusiasm for the future long ago. In many ways, Iowa saved you from becoming like the other Salems."

Jackie hadn't thought about that. She considered her family. Tessa was cold and selfish. Dad was a whore. Makenna was a mess. Something about Alistair rubbed her the wrong way. Sean was dead. Domino was dead. Juliet had faked her death to escape. Naomi was devastated with grief. She couldn't name a single happy ending for anyone with the last name Salem. Maybe she was better off as a Noble.

Jackie pushed all those thoughts aside. She wasn't Mrs. Noble, the schoolteacher, at this moment. She wasn't Mrs. Noble, the wife of Mark. Jackie Salem was still the woman who had once disappeared for two days and rocked Martin Montgomery's world so hard that he had come crawling back as soon as Jackie returned to SX. She moved across the hot tub, erasing the space between them. After long minutes of foreplay, she confirmed Martin was wearing nothing.

She wrapped her fingers around his shaft and stared him in the eye as his hunger turned to bliss. He groaned as she squeezed. He might not be the vigorous man in his early thirties who could keep up with an eighteen-year-old ingenue for a forty-eight-hour marathon of sex anymore. However, he was still a fit and energetic man of fifty-six who could keep pace with a schoolmarm who was a little bit rusty.

Jackie kissed him, her mouth exploring his. He wasn't the only one with a ravenous streak. They had enjoyed two steamy sessions during the hurricane, and Jackie had been ready for another round ever since. The first couple of times had been like an appetizer or a reminder of their long weekend together all those years ago. Jackie wanted a repeat of the two-day sextravaganza of her youth.

His hands found her large, slick breasts, fondling,

squeezing urgently, and pinching her swollen nipples. She bit her lip to keep from crying out, a habit gleaned from twenty-three years of quiet orgasms in a house full of kids and a husband working in his office in the next room while she got off with the help of a battery-powered accessory. But no one would overhear anything, so she could scream tonight.

"Oh, that feels so fucking good," she said aloud.

She had her knees planted on either side of the submerged seat, lifting out of the water enough to raise her chest to the level of Martin's face. He suckled one breast and massaged the other. His other hand traveled to her ass beneath the water, squeezing her right cheek as bubbles tickled her taint. She could feel the length of his impressive erection along the inside of her thigh.

The hot tub wasn't deep enough to tread water, but her head was swimming in an ocean of pleasure. Martin moved his hand so that his pinky brushed against her pussy, sending all thought right out the door. She disengaged her nipple from his mouth and started kissing him again, a burning passion unbridled by any caution. She wiggled her hips until she positioned herself just right. She moved her slit up the entire length of his cock, waves of desire making them moan in an erotic duet.

"My God," Jackie groaned. "Oh, shit, shit, shit."

The water in the hot tub wasn't the only thing bubbling. Jackie's cunt was starting to pop and fizz before she even had a chance to mount him properly. She held her climax at bay as she aligned herself with his amazing dick. She gazed into his eyes and recognized a reflection of her own need and passion. And something underneath? Feelings that she didn't want to consider? The effervescence of her pussy scrubbed all logical thought as she lowered herself onto his erection.

"Fffuck," she cried, a caterwaul equal to the squawk of gulls along the seashore. "Fucking fuck!" Waves of orgasm crashed over her like the surf on the beach. "Oh God, oh God, oh God, oh God!" Her voice carried throughout the suite, down the spiral stairs, and echoed across the entire abandoned club downstairs. Jackie didn't have to mute one goddamned word.

Jackie rode Martin hard, moving up and down, splashing water everywhere. They caused a veritable flood in the ensuite bathroom. Jackie contributed to the tsunami with her own deluge, coming for what seemed like an eternity. Her bucking hips slowed as she came down from her climactic high. Jackie leaned back, floating in the hot tub, bobbing like a small boat bouncing freely on the open sea. She experienced complete bliss.

Then Jackie realized Martin was still rock hard inside her pussy.

He wasn't done yet.

"You want to finish this in bed?" he asked.

Jackie had her arms spread out, still floating, Martin's rigid member filling her with comfortable completeness. She wasn't ready to disengage. Impossibly, Jackie felt she still had some fuel left in the tank. She smiled at the ceiling for another few seconds, then let him scoop her up in his strong arms. Jackie had believed he might not have the stamina of his youth, but maybe Martin could last for another forty-right-hour interlude.

As he carried her to the bed, Jackie was eager to find out.

Chapter Five

JACKSON MONTGOMERY

Jax had been running errands for his father nonstop since the hurricane. The Montgomerys suffered less damage to their properties than the Salems and Zhangs. Still, enough warehouses and secondary businesses around town required insurance claims to keep Jax with a to-do list as long as Santa's naughty and nice list. Every morning, his father tasked him with a dozen things he needed to complete that day, and Jax never finished until long past sunset.

Carver continued his recovery after Neil Halloweather shot him a few weeks ago. They sent him home after the hurricane and arranged for a nurse to check on him every day. Still, Jax made daily stops to ensure his brother didn't need groceries, someone to wash the dishes, or a willing ear to hear one of Carver's many conspiracy theories about who was really behind the Dark Summer kidnappings. Someone different masterminded the whole affair every time Jax stopped by.

Jax's father had grown increasingly distant after the storm, preoccupied with something unrelated to the Montgomerys' professional affairs. Jax could recognize when his father had stressful business on his mind, but he often seemed almost pleased with whatever distraction diverted his attention elsewhere. Jax wondered if his father was creeping around with a new mistress. Considering the recent reveal that Damien Halloweather was their brother from an affair with Liz Halloweather, or Elizabeth Iblīs, to use her real name, maybe Martin Montgomery had rekindled an old flame.

This morning, Jax woke up and checked his phone. Cin had messaged him a good morning with a kissy-face emoji. They'd decided to take things slow. Old-fashioned romances used to be about an extended courtship and waiting until marriage for sex. Jax and Cin chose to emulate this archaic dating style, but Jax often wondered if the choice was a mistake. He didn't know if he could wait until a wedding to consummate things or if this relationship was even headed toward marriage. They both knew that sex wasn't going to make their already complicated relationship any easier.

Jax stared at the picture of her that popped up with her message. He'd snapped it a few days ago when they met at Copper Cove after dark. He'd started a campfire on a remote section of the beach, and they cuddled by the firelight until late. The picture caught Cin staring at him, lit by the glow of the campfire, with the strap of her tank top slipping down her arm, looking as sexy as hell. The reflection in her bright brown irises captured the flicker of the orange flames. Her smile was subtle and alluring, full lips shaped for kissing. He loved the dimple between her brows that suggested she was thinking something dirty. Jax groaned as he stared at the image, his boxers tenting beneath the blanket, aching for release.

Not right now.

He hadn't received any message from his father. It was eight a.m., and nothing. That hadn't happened since the hurricane changed SX forever. Riley ran a few errands for their father, but Jax acted as the Montgomerys' primary right-hand, while Carver remained out of commission. Luckily, the family business was currently focused on the legitimate task of collecting insurance, rather than dealing with illegal shit that could get him in serious trouble. He couldn't go to jail when things were only starting to heat up with Cin.

He sat at the edge of his bed and dialed his father. He wasn't going to make plans to be rerouted by Martin on a Montgomery agenda that would last all day.

"Jackson," his father said in a way of answering. Couldn't say hello. That would be too personal for a convo with his son.

"I didn't see an itinerary for the day. Maybe I didn't get your text?" Jax questioned.

"No list today."

Jax frowned. His father sounded out of breath, like he had interrupted him while he was working out. He knew better than to ask what Martin was up to. Jax's mind circled back to his father's habitual cheating on his mother. Jax suddenly thought about Millie Zhang and his years-long affair with the nasty woman. Nolan Salem infamously fathered multiple children out of wedlock. Did every middle-aged SXer find satisfaction outside their marriage?

"I'm sorry, I have the day off?" Jax asked, checking if he had heard his father correctly.

Jax overheard sounds that could have been the splashes from the beach, a swimming pool, or a tub, but certainly not places where Martin Montgomery could be working in an office.

"You've been working hard lately, Jackson," his father said, still sounding winded even though he was in as good shape as Jax. The words were as close to a compliment as Jax might have ever heard from the man. "Take the day. A few, actually. You need a little vacation. Check on your brother. Otherwise, don't bother me for a few days."

The phone disconnected.

Jax stared at the device in his hand, flabbergasted. A few days off? His mouth hung open. Cin's pretty picture popped up with another message. Jax had texted her back before calling his father, and she replied with a few flirty words. The message ended with:

CIN

Will I cu 2nite?

JAX

How about sooner?

She replied immediately.

CIN

Really? Or teasing?

Jax called. She picked up in a split second. "My father gave me the next few days off. He said I needed a vacation."

"Is he sick?" Cin asked sincerely, concerned.

"He's something," Jax said, leaving the question of what exactly ailed the old son of a bitch til later. "I need to stop by and check on Carver. Meet you after?"

"Absolutely," Cin said excitedly. Then she followed with a long "Ummmmmm."

"You thinking what I'm thinking?"

Cin's voice dripped with excitement. "They hired my cousin Aliyah when I was running from the law and pretending to be sick. They gave me my hours back after they cleared me as a murder suspect and made Aliyah part-time.

She's always begging me for hours. I can see if she'll take my shifts for a few days."

"We're going to drive inland until we find a little town bordered by orange orchards where no one knows the last name Montgomery or Álvarez," Jax said.

It was a date. A getaway. Jax and Cin had promised not to take things to the physical level until they both agreed they were ready. Tonight, they would be staying in a motel room together for the first time since Neil Halloweather's confession to the murder of Domino Salem exonerated Cin. Could they control themselves? They'd spent a lot of nights together while Cin was on the run. Jax and Cin could barely control themselves then, and that was when they thought they were enemies.

Abstinence might prove impossible.

A subject for discussion later in the day.

Jax stopped to visit his brother before he left town with Acindina. Carver was the only one in the family who knew Jax was seeing Cin—his father would kill him if he ever found out Jax was in love with an Álvarez. As much as Jax hated the thought of his father cheating on his mom, he hoped that some slutty coed out for a good time with a rich man would distract Martin for a while. His father wouldn't wonder about Jax's whereabouts if a gold digger bedded him down in some hotel room.

Carver was in bed, propped up with pillows, watching a reality show where they attempted to solve local unsolved mysteries from cold cases that had gone untouched for many years. Jax wondered what the serious, sonorous host of the program would uncover if his crack team of sleuths shone a spotlight on the events of the Dark Summer. Were there clues on Nightmare Island that the SXPD had never discovered or evidence they covered up? The confession they'd elicited from Neil Halloweather before his untimely death had only created more questions than answers. The central mystery remained unsolved. Why had Mascolo and Halloweather conspired to kidnap those boys fifteen years ago?

"You don't have enough damn mysteries in your life, bro? You need to know what happened to the retired science teacher thirty years ago in Grand Rapids, Michigan?" Jax taunted.

"At least these shows have a resolution before the credits roll. I'm sick of questions without answers," Carver grumbled, his voice thick from meds and gravelly from disuse.

"The Dark Summer isn't a television show, Carver."

"This episode deals with a double murder involving two neighbors," Carver said, overly invested in tabloid TV. "This really happened."

Jax watched two unskilled performers reenact a scene where the neighbors argued over trimming the hedges between their properties. The PG-rated dialogue included "tarnation" and "shenanigans." No one who killed anyone, even in Michigan, used language like that. The events of this show were no more accurate than the story Carver had told Anthony Mascolo to get him back on Hahkv Island.

"Neil confessed to masterminding the whole thing. Maybe you should leave it at that," Jax said.

Carver ignored Jax's plea to leave it be. "Neil Halloweather also confessed to killing Domino Salem, but we know damn well his nephew did it. What else did he lie about?"

Neil's nephew. Carver was talking about Damien Halloweather. Their half-brother. Their father's illegitimate son.

"Neil was on Hahkv Island during the Dark Summer. You said you heard Mascolo talking to someone else. It had to be him. He killed Sean Salem," Jax said.

"There's more to the story, Jax. I don't think either one

of those assholes was smart enough to execute a mass abduction."

"Not everything is a conspiracy, bro," Jax said, nodding at the television. "Sometimes it's just neighbors killing neighbors."

Carver shrugged. Jax wondered if he'd ever be satisfied with the answers about the Dark Summer. In the end, nothing would adequately explain how anyone could kidnap seven young boys and keep them in cages for weeks. Jax worried his brother might never find peace from the horrors of that experience.

"I'm going out of town for a few days," Jax said.

"Romeo, you sly mother-fucka. You taking that little Capulet to Disney like you're newlyweds or some shit?"

"This isn't a Shakespearean tragedy, Carver. Just a couple of people trying to figure it out in a world that doesn't think it should work."

Carver chuckled derisively. "You ever read Romeo and Juliet, dipshit? Even the cheat sheet for the test? That's the exact fucking plot of the play, bro."

"I'm not going to kill myself at the end."

"If our father finds out you're screwing an Álvarez, you'd better hope you can drink some poison before Martin gets his hands on you."

"We're not screwing," Jax said as if that was the part that needed correcting. "We decided to take it slow."

"Holy shit. Jackson Montgomery, taking it slow? I remember you dumped Kylie Meeks after she didn't put out on the second date."

"Kylie?" Jax repeated, thinking back. "That was like a lifetime ago."

"Yeah. Seems like yesterday," Carver said, his voice changing, quieter, sadder.

Jax observed his brother. He was muscular, with tattoos

covering his arms, scars crisscrossing his flesh from endless fights in his youth and compounded during his years behind bars. If there were ever a bigger badass to grace the shores of SX, Jax hadn't met him. Yet, Carver, who had taken no prisoners, now bedridden, stitched up, and searching for answers to unsolvable mysteries, was unable to get up and take his trash out to the curb.

"Need anything before I go?" Jax asked.

"You could bring Britney Halloweather over to play nurse for me," Carver said. "I could use a sponge bath."

"You'd pop your stitches if she decided to rock your world, bro."

"Worth it."

Jax punched his brother lightly on the arm. "You know she's a Salem. Nolan's illegitimate daughter. If you think our father has problems with the Álvarezes, imagine what he'd do about a Salem."

"You've been with Brit. You drool over Nevada. You've been having an affair with Millie Zhang for years. Now, you're chasing after some cute little Álvarez ass. Who are you to question me about women?"

"Because I wasn't the one locked up with a bunch of other men for the last few years. The only women you've been with lately are the imaginary kind. No actual partner is going to measure up to that kind of expectation. So, start with someone you don't care about because the reality of your situational abstinence will ruin your next experience with Britney Halloweather or any other babe. Heal up a little, then find a bored housewife on vacation in Cocoa Beach who will appreciate it if you throw her a fuck, no matter how bad it is. Get disappointed first, then work your way up to Britney-level."

Carver threw a pillow at Jax's head. "Get the hell outta here."

Jax gave him a one-fingered salute with a jackass smirk on his face. "In the meantime, I left you a fresh tissue box on your nightstand. Lotion is in the drawer."

The words, "Fuck you," followed Jax out the door.

He was free. His Carver errand finished, Jax drove his red Jag to where Cin agreed to meet. Cin lived in Old Mat, and other than getting a beer at Laverne's or renting a room at Manny's Motel, there wasn't a place in the Álvarez neighborhood where a Montgomery wouldn't stick out like a sore thumb. The doom Carver predicted, regarding Jax and Cin's relationship, might be inevitable, but Jax wouldn't sabotage it earlier than its natural conclusion. He had to believe they could avoid fate.

Our Lady of Faith was the oldest church in Salem Crossing, nestled in the neutral neighborhood populated by Ryans. All sorts of SX citizens attended church, so seeing an Álvarez or a Montgomery around wasn't strange. Jax himself attended services regularly and was friendly with Reverend Ryan. He circled the cathedral once and spied no vehicle in the wrap-around parking lot. Jax pulled up to the back door, where Acindina Álvarez exited. He didn't know who had brought her or how long she was waiting, but she sprinted across the gap between the church and the car and ducked inside the Jag, instantly camouflaged by the dark-tinted windows.

Cin looked like she wanted him to peel out of the parking lot, lay rubber, and make a hasty exit before anyone spotted them. But Jax kept his foot on the brake, leaned over, and kissed her luscious lips. He hadn't seen her in several hours, and it felt like weeks or months. After a lingering kiss, he reluctantly disengaged and exited the lot.

"Do you think we'll get to the point where we don't have to sneak around like this?"

Jax considered putting a bullshit spin on their longshot

chances, but they had wallowed in denial for too long. "The Juliets faked their deaths to get a chance at being together. Juliet Zhang seems pretty smart, and she couldn't figure out another way."

"They're together now. Their families seem willing to overlook the animosity between the Salems and the Zhangs," Cin said.

Jax turned out of town and left SX behind. "The hurricane interrupted the retribution that Tessa Salem and Millie Zhang are cooking up. You can bet there will be hell to pay after the dust from Marlena finally settles."

Cin sighed sadly. Did she really still believe in happy endings? "After all they've been through? You don't think the families will let it go?"

"The families of SX never let anything go."

Cin preferred a different answer. She sought a more hopeful reply to her question. They both wanted this relationship to work. But Jax wasn't into fairy tales. No noble king would override the local decree and make peace across the lands. The dragons ruled SX, and they'd rather burn the place down than allow a happily ever after they didn't approve of.

"You think we'll ever become enemies, Jax? Will our families eventually turn us against each other?"

"Not necessarily. Carver thinks we're both going to end up dead."

"Jesus," she whispered, taken aback. "Prison made him a major bummer."

"His only happy place is daydreaming about Britney Halloweather."

Cin wrinkled her nose. "He couldn't have had a thing for Chastity Ryan or Raven Zhang?"

He shrugged. "I don't think we have to end up enemies, Cin. Or dead."

She smiled. "You know how to make our ending a happy one?"

He nodded. "You still have that map? The one Bryce gave you a long time ago?"

She furrowed her brow, confused about what Bryce Graham had to do with this. Bryce had given Cin the answer ten years ago. He left her a map of where to find him if Ariel Álvarez ever came looking. But the map wasn't the key to finding Bryce anymore. It was the way to get out of SX. The map symbolized escape.

Cin realized what Jax was getting at, and her eyes lit up. She leaned against his arm as Jax kept driving. This time, it would be a three-day getaway. As soon as Carver completely healed, Jax would turn over his family responsibilities to his brother, and Jax would be free. He would take Cin, and they would run away.

The only way for their love to survive was to escape SX.

Chapter Six

Neve was busier than ever fulfilling her official duties—she accompanied Bryce on his SX rounds; she worked with Reverend Ryan at Our Lady of Faith to facilitate an outreach program for the underprivileged citizens affected by the hurricane; Neve resumed weekly visits around SX to follow-up on the social services visits arranged before Marlena; between responsibilities and extracurriculars, Neve visited City Hall to bring Bryce food, give him a back rub, or take some precious time for romance.

Despite her overfull agenda, Bryce was even more occupied. His long hours at City Hall left Neve with enough free time to focus on the community's many unresolved mysteries. She couldn't investigate the multiple individual threads of inquiries alone. Neve made a mental list of people who could contribute their unique skills to her investigations.

After reaching out to several individuals, Neve finally organized the first meeting of a group of select allies. Willow affectionately called the assembled acquaintances "the Crossing Guard." Neve hosted the inaugural gathering at her bungalow, which had sustained minor damage in the storm. A few shingles were missing from the roof, some parts of the gutter and a downspout were ripped off, and a window was broken. Her dad, who was handy with minor home repairs, patched her up shortly after the storm passed. She fared better than most people along the beach line. In fact, her father was working a little farther down the Point at Rebecca Ryan's home, which suffered more extensive damage.

Nevada worked in her kitchen putting together some hors d'oeuvres while Willow greeted the guests and entertained them. Willow popped her head through the doorway as Neve arranged the last of the charcuterie board. Her sister was a perfectly capable hostess, which worked out because Will didn't know her havarti from her burrata, capricola from her soppressata, or cornichons from her pepperoncini. Yet didn't she appear a bit frazzled as she peeked around the door jamb?

"We have any Stella?" Willow asked.

"I thought you were a wine kind of gal," Neve said.

Willow gave Neve the stink eye. "The Dark Summer guys all drink Stella. You know that."

The survivors of the Dark Summer were like shadowy counterparts to the Caesars—united by a mutual event, like the Caesars, but without the happy connotations of a shared birthday. Kidnapped and held hostage on a deserted island for weeks, the common trauma among the group who endured the Dark Summer bonded them like veterans of a particularly bloody battle.

Neve didn't know any of the Dark Summer survivors well. Carver helped them get Neil Halloweather to confess to aiding and abetting the kidnapping all those years ago, and he was Bryce's half-brother, although a few select people knew. Neve had crossed paths with Dalton Zhang when he was running to be co-mayor with Bryce, but that was before she learned Dalton was her half-brother. She attended Rob Ryan's wedding to Ariel Álvarez, but Neve had hardly known the guy, and that marriage was already on the rocks. Anna had been lost in the hurricane and was presumed dead. Ram Álvarez was a stranger. Micah Salem, her cousin, was rarely around. But every one of the survivors liked their Stella. Neve had a six-pack in the fridge.

"You seem eager to keep our guest content. Ulterior motive?" Neve teased, handing her sister the cold brew.

"I know you know what I did, Neve. You don't need to play coy," Willow muttered.

Neve gave her sister a wink. "A threesome with Ram and Cin. That's a helluva Cuban sandwich."

Willow blushed. "You're devious."

"You're devilish," Neve replied.

The sisters exchanged a knowing smile. Ram Álvarez was a massive man. He arrived early and parked his Harley in front of Neve's bungalow. He said two words, both polite. He might've smashed the hell out of Willow during a one-night stand, but he still treated her like a lady. Tattooed and muscled from scalp to sole, he was the consummate gentleman.

Neve followed Willow into the living room, precariously balancing her giant charcuterie board. Ram could've sat on her sofa and taken up about three-fourths of the space, but instead, he wedged into Neve's small armchair so that the other guests would have ample seating. He looked like an adult relegated to the kiddie table at Thanksgiving. The biker seemed eminently uncomfortable.

Willow handed Ram the beer, and a knock on the door interrupted any potential awkwardness.

Tom Graham arrived alone. Neve had asked him not to bring Delilah. "And don't tell her where you're going," Neve had added. "There's no way she won't tag along if she finds out what we're doing." He hadn't liked avoiding his new girlfriend, but Neve's intriguing invitation was too tantalizing to refuse.

Tom entered as Neve held the door open.

"I wish you'd have let me bring Delilah. She was a big help in nabbing Neil Halloweather," Tom said.

"I have specific reasons for inviting every member of the Crossing Guard to this meeting," Neve replied.

Tom raised a dark eyebrow. "Crossing Guard? Really?"

Neve shrugged. "Willow came up with the name. I was going to call us the SX Investigators, but that sounds like we're solving perverted crimes."

"That could be what we're doing. You haven't told us what this is all about."

"It's not about that," Neve said dismissively. "How did you get away from Delilah? You two have been all over each other every time I've seen you together."

Tom looked disgusted. "Caleb has been especially creepy the last few days. I told her to spend time with him while I did some work."

"Well, this is going to be work," Neve affirmed.

Another knock at the door, and Neve answered. Naomi Salem had been mourning the loss of her boyfriend ever since the hurricane. Neve hadn't seen her without another one of the Caesars by her side, her pseudo-sibs and her twin sister Juliet taking turns supporting her through her grief. Now, she stood alone in Neve's doorway. Sadness hung over her like a cloud, but her steely temerity made an umbrella against utter desolation. Naomi was as badass as Ram in her own way, and a broken heart wouldn't keep her down for long.

"You ready to get back into the hunt, Naomi?" Neve asked.

Still standing outside Neve's front door, Naomi gazed into the sky as if searching the heavens for a sign from Auberon Fox that it was okay to move on. Despite a disheveled appearance indicating she hadn't slept in weeks, Naomi was still gorgeous. Her sunshine-blonde hair had an envy-inducing color, and her bright blue eyes contrasted with skin tanned from a lifetime at sea. She carried perfect genes, which Neve shared by twenty-five percent.

"You ever lost someone close, Neve?' Naomi asked, still staring at the sky.

"Not really, no."

"You're never ready," Naomi said, tearing her eyes away. Neve stared into the blue orbs, and worlds of pain tinted those brilliant irises. "You ever heard that some sharks need to keep moving or they drown? They must continually force water through their gills, or they won't get the oxygen they need to survive. Doesn't matter if they're hurt or tired or if the world's turned to shit all around them. They move or die."

Naomi walked inside, found Willow, and followed her on a mission to retrieve an adult beverage. Neve stood in her doorway, watching Naomi disappear into the kitchen, hoping she would never suffer a loss like that.

"The quaint charm of a beachside cottage," came a voice behind Neve.

Neve turned to the person standing on her doorstep. Simmer Salem wore one of her signature cloaks, this one in a bright red that nearly blinded Neve. The woman was a pioneer in clandestine couture, making sneaky-as-fuck look fashionable. Lois Lane meets Little Red Riding Hood. Only Simmer was like the Big Bad Wolf, ready to huff and puff and blow anyone's reputation down with her scandalous hot air.

"What's she doing here?" Naomi asked, returning from the kitchen with a goblet of wine.

"Neve invited me. Apparently, this club needed a little flair." Simmer stepped inside, looking around as if she were making mental notes about Neve's interior decorating choices.

"I don't want her here," Naomi said through gritted teeth.

"Bad blood, cousin?" Simmer asked, calm in the face of the storm. "We're family."

"We might be cousins, but we're not family, Simmeron. I disowned a lot of Salems, and you're on the shitty list," Naomi retorted.

Simmer's shoulders slumped, and her eyes revealed weakness. "I've been on that list my whole life, Naomi. I'm here to make up for some of it."

"You're the reason he's dead," Naomi snapped with her voice raised.

Auberon had been trying to save Simmer during the hurricane when the section of the building collapsed around them. Auberon Fox sacrificed his life protecting Simmer from the crushing debris.

"I know," Simmer said. "I owe him. I owe you. This is my way of paying tribute to his sacrifice, Naomi. I can't bring him back. Neve asked for my help. I'm here to give it."

Naomi stared across the room at Simmer. Tom, Willow, and Ram were between them, but no one would try to stop Naomi if she rushed across the room to attack Simmer. If Naomi wanted to kick Simmer's ass, not even the hulking Ram could stop the fiery hellcat. But Naomi didn't resort to violence. She nodded, still scowling, and looked away as tears rolled down her cheeks.

"Welcome, everyone, to the first meeting of the Crossing Guard," Neve said, turning the subject away from recently deceased boyfriends.

"Strange group you've put together, Neve," Naomi slurred, with an empty wine glass in hand.

"Neve, I don't know about the name," Tom said.

"We need a name," Neve insisted. "This one fits."

"How does it fit? What do the six of us have in common?" Simmer asked.

Neve navigated the discussion back to the meeting's purpose. "There are a lot of loose ends around SX. I think this team can work together to figure out what's going on."

"Most of us have no mutual interests," Simmer stated.

"The Caesars are bonded by a random date of birth. A different kind of shared event binds the survivors of the Dark Summer. Our particular individual talents bring us together to aid in finding the truth," Neve explained.

"I don't know if that's enough of a reason to all get along," Naomi muttered as Willow handed her a fresh, full goblet of wine. Full enough to possibly overflow.

Neve walked over to the wall, which featured two windows with open blinds, a view of the dunes outside her backyard, and the sea beyond. A set of drawn curtains covered a third space between the windows. She pulled back the drapes and revealed a whiteboard featuring a list of topics. She and Willow had already aggregated the burning questions haunting Salem Crossing since she arrived in town.

1. *Why did Damien Halloweather kill Domino Salem?*
2. *What is the real reason behind the Dark Summer kidnappings?*
3. *Who kidnapped the Juliets and why?*
4. *What is the Iblīs family up to?*
5. *Who is Conner Graham?*
6. *Why did Helen Ryan switch the babies at birth?*
7. *Is there an ancient map to lost treasure?*

Neve paced in front of the whiteboard, reading the list aloud one by one. She had everyone's attention in the room.

They might not understand why Neve assembled this eclectic group of Salem Crossing citizens, but they were all riveted by the subject matter as she detailed the agenda. Their rapt attention proved that Neve had chosen the right people to investigate the various shenanigans in SX.

Naomi leaned forward, mesmerized by Neve's list. "I didn't realize the full extent of intrigue. Auby and I were looking into the treasure map before he died."

The words caused her pain, but Neve watched Naomi focus on the question rather than the context.

"You think there really was a map?" Tom asked curiously.

Naomi looked around the room, measuring if she could trust the people gathered there. Her gaze settled particularly on Simmer Salem. Naomi exhaled, as if lifting a heavy weight off her chest. "Auby and I found the Salem piece of the map during the hurricane. Ripped into sections just like the legend. One part of the original document. It's real, alright."

Surprised murmurs traveled around the room. Naomi's revelation lent credence to Neve's desire to get this group together. Naomi had provided legitimacy for the Crossing Guard.

Simmer's eyes lit up as she scanned the scandalous headlines. "Babies switched at birth? That sounds like a headline on a special edition of my Scandal Sheet."

Tom frowned at the list. "And you're suspicious of Conner Graham? Plus, you want everyone here to get involved in investigating Domino's murder?"

"You think the rest of the Iblīs clan is up to no good? Including Elizabeth? And Britney?" Naomi asked.

The members of the Crossing Guard shared a cacophony of whispers. Neve suddenly wasn't sure she could get them to all work together on topics that might be more gossip than crime.

"Why us?" Ram spoke up for the first time since Neve

convened the meeting. His deep voice reverberated through Neve's tiled room. He rarely spoke and used few words when he did, so his contribution to the conversation seemed to convey more importance than if Simmer had started rambling. Willow's lips curled into a smirk at his words, the bass shaking through their bones. Neve imagined her sister had some pretty steamy memories of Ram shaking her bones.

"You each have unique assets you bring to the team," Neve stated.

"The Crossing Guard," Tom interjected, walking to the board, studying it like a detective examining a set of clues.

"Agent Graham can use his FBI clout to get information behind the scenes on some of our suspects," Neve said. "He's also proved himself as someone who can get the job done. He busted Neil Halloweather."

"He had his part in the kidnappings during the Dark Summer, but there's no way he killed Domino Salem, even if he confessed to it," Tom said, tapping the first item on Neve's list. "We need to prove Damien did it. The little bastard should be behind bars."

Neve nodded. She strolled around the room, pausing by each of her guests.

"Simmer knows more secrets about SX than anyone who's ever lived. She can help with the connections between our citizens that maybe no one else knows about."

"I do know where a lot of the bodies are buried," Simmer said proudly, then realized that death wasn't a laughing matter in Naomi's presence, or maybe anyone's, and clammed up immediately.

Neve paused next to her sister. "Willow has proven to be a crack investigator. She's already helped me uncover my true parentage. She's spent the last couple of weeks following some leads."

Naomi, finished with her second glass of wine, sat cross-legged on Neve's plush rug. Her eyelids drooped, and some of the pinched sorrow melted away. She looked more like Juliet than Neve had ever noticed before.

Neve put a hand on the Caesar's shoulder. "Naomi has proven to be an intrepid adventurer. She found the Dark Summer boys all those years ago. Now, she's found the first real clue to the map of the secret treasure. Juliet Salem washed up on Salem Shores, the legends of sunken treasure happened off the coast of SX, and Hahkv Island still hides some of the answers we're looking for. We need someone who can focus on the mysteries at sea."

"Evvie's Explorer is at your service," Naomi slurred.

"And me?" Ram asked.

"Besides being a mountain of muscle in case we find ourselves in a bit of trouble, and trust me, Willow's especially good at stumbling into dangerous situations, we need someone brave and trustworthy who knows the ins and outs of Old Mat."

Ram glanced at Willow, who looked away and tried to play innocent. Ram nodded. Neve knew how protective he had been of Cin, but Cin now had Jax to watch over her. Ram needed a new protégé. Neve couldn't think of anyone better than Ram to keep an eye on Willow. This was a dangerous mission, after all. Some answers would expose information that people would do anything to keep secret. Damien was a killer, and they would be snooping around his family. Their enemies had kidnapped and killed to preserve the secret behind the Dark Summer abductions and the lost treasure map. Helen Ryan had upended Neve and Clover's lives to protect Clover from Neil. Or was there something else going on?

Neve assembled the Crossing Guard to catch the bad guys around SX. But she didn't even know all the opponents they were playing against. Their enemies might be dangerous.

Neve surveyed the room. She trusted most of the people she invited in, but she might have also invited a viper into the group. Would Simmer betray them? Was Tom secretly the enemy? Or was it someone she least expected who might be working against solving these mysteries to keep something on her list a secret?

Neve was riding a pretty intense wave, ready for it to crash at any moment. She would hang ten as long as she could. Maybe she could reach solid ground before she wiped out. Neve kept a smile on her face while the group discussed the mysteries plaguing the Crossing Guard, but she wondered why she used a surfing metaphor when she'd never been on a board before. She didn't have the first clue how to stay on top of the wave.

Chapter Seven

HOLIDAYS WITH THE ZHANGS

Millie Zhang gathered the family for the holidays shortly after Thanksgiving. The Zhangs always held their annual holiday party early to avoid the other Christmas soirées around SX. A less festive vibe than usual permeated the crowd this year. The last few months had been devastating for the political standing of the Zhang dynasty, and the yuletide may be the only time the whole family could be together without animosity bubbling into fisticuffs. Everyone was pissed at everyone. Millie herself could strangle any one of her kids right about now.

Juliet's fake death and subsequent resurrection caused Millie a huge headache. First, she considered her daughter's treachery a significant betrayal. Her daughter's supposed death had devastated Millie, a rare emotion that dragged her into deep grief for long weeks. It turned out to be a hoax. Juliet put her through hell to be with one of those fucking Salems. Millie's sorrow turned into blazing anger after her daughter returned. Everyone else in the family was also extremely pissed at Juliet. The lovesick fool had given up her powerful mayoral position for romance. Millie had always pictured her daughter following in her fierce footsteps, but the influence of those godforsaken Caesars had been too powerful to overcome.

Dalton was supposed to be the prodigal son returning from abroad, but he proved to be a disappointing mess. He had buried the trauma of his ordeal during the Dark Summer for years, and the shit came bubbling up when she needed him to be at his best. Dalton assaulted an old man for kidnapping him fifteen years ago. Her son failed to win the mayoral election, marking the first time in eons that a Zhang occupied neither of the co-mayoral positions. Ever since, Dalton wandered around town drunk as a skunk.

Owen was a train wreck that kept on crashing. He'd been lured into an affair by a conniving young woman. A Montgomery, no less! The backlash of his adultery resulted in his resignation from City Hall. His estranged wife publicly embarrassed him over and over before finally divorcing him. Britney intended to ruin him financially, so he had to take a job at Restful Meadows retirement home wiping senior citizens' asses. Millie's connections to the rumor mill around SX suggested Owen had become Mariah's latest sub in her kinky dominatrix dungeon. Owen was such a fucking disappointment.

Millie would have to do what she always did—take charge and regain the upper hand.

The holiday party was more of a mixer than a traditional feast, where everyone sat at a long table and discussed their personal lives. Millie's private business would blow the socks off anyone else at the Zhang gathering. Most of her time focused on professional concerns. She worked from when she got out of bed until she hit the mattress at night. The only leisure she enjoyed was between the sheets in the guest house, where she hooked up with a rotating harem of young studs.

The party occurred in the ballroom, a large area past the front foyer dedicated to social functions. The room was inaccessible to the rest of the house, with one entrance and exit, so Millie wouldn't have to worry about guests meandering through her personal space. She didn't even like her offspring wandering through the halls of her home. The three of them moved out long ago. Only Corden and the waitstaff visited anywhere beyond the ballroom, not even during private visits from her sons or daughter.

"Lovely party, Mother."

Owen had dusted off one of his old suits. Millie looked him over, wondering how she had ever birthed such a colossal fuckup. She certainly understood having a predilection for extramarital sex, but one could easily manage desire and compartmentalize liaisons. Millie had been cheating on Corden for decades, and he'd never caught her once. Her doltish husband never suspected a thing.

"It's droll, Owen," Millie said witheringly. "Just like the company."

Owen gritted his teeth, wisely biting back a retort. "Sounds like you're feeling festive. Want another eggnog?"

"Like I'm mixing anything with my brandy, dear boy."

Owen surveyed the crowd of aunts, uncles, cousins, and in-laws around the room as if searching for another topic of conversation to provoke Millie's ire and divert her focus from him. Corden visited with Millie's brother, Kevin, who was more of a source of monotony than melodrama. Millie's father was already drunk and playing grab ass with his much-younger girlfriend. Owen didn't dare criticize his grandfather. Margo berated her daughter, Nora, for her unfortunate holiday attire—a dress resembling a Christmas tree, complete with lights. Nora had wound her long black hair into a halo around her head and topped it with a glowing angel, looking like the tree topper was taking a shit on her head. Owen would know he couldn't do a better job of mocking Nora than Margo managed. Chuck and Dora Reed stood alone in a corner, the party the highlight of their year, despite everyone ignoring them because their average annual salary was less than most Álvarezes. Ripe for ridicule, yet unworthy of attention. Corden's sister, Esther, wore a silver-and-gold muumuu. Millie disliked her eternal geniality, but Owen loved her and would never say a bad thing about her. Dudley Zhang leaned on the counter at the open bar, wobbling to the live piano music. The drunkard was too pathetic for derision. Greg and Raven Dean were dancing and handsy, making Millie's body warm. Greg was one of her regular consorts.

Millie offered her son a lifeline before he made fun of Greg and pissed her off, changing the topic before Owen could bungle it.

"Where's your sister?" Millie asked.

"Probably off with Juliet Salem," Owen said, relishing another target for Millie's indignation. "Her wife."

Millie flashed him a loathsome glare. "I know the story, Owen Orville Zhang."

"Hey, I'm as pissed as you that Juliet faked her death, married the enemy, and now acts like nothing is wrong."

"If the rumors are true, it seems that Britney Halloweather is the illegitimate daughter of Nolan Salem. Juliet isn't the only one married to a Salem," Millie said with venom dripping from her tongue.

"Divorced," Owen said.

"And you had children with the bitch. My grandchildren are one-quarter Salems."

Millie turned and walked away. Greg and Raven had taken a break from dancing, sitting at a table with Raven on Greg's lap, wriggling that tight little ass against his crotch. Millie would never humiliate herself by giving the young stud a lap dance. He was more like a lapdog in their relationship, his tongue wagging until Millie told him to stop. The couple made eye contact with Millie as she passed, but her expression never wavered from a complete poker face.

Dalton wandered in with some tourist floozy on his arm, already drunk or high. Millie thought the deaths of the men responsible for his kidnapping during the Dark Summer would set things right, but he was more out of control than ever. She folded her arms over her chest as he staggered up, trying to look as sober as he could manage.

"Mother, this is Anastasia," Dalton introduced.

"My name is Carly," the girl said in a British accent.

"She's Egyptian. Certainly not a Salem," Dalton slurred.

"I'm from Liverpool," Carly corrected. "And I don't know what a Salem is."

Millie stepped up to her youngest child and adjusted his crooked tie. She brushed a blush of white powder from the shoulder of his suit jacket. She tucked a lock of his mussed hair behind his ear in the place where it had stuck up since he was an infant. Millie caught Carly's look of disgust. This grown man was more of a baby. Being rich and bringing Carly to a fancy party wouldn't make up for Mommy straightening his trousers.

"You don't need to stay at this boring ole party, Dalton. You made an appearance and showed your familial affiliation. You young kids ought to be out having fun around town rather than staying cooped up with a bunch of stuffy Zhangs." Millie slipped a handful of hundreds into Carly's hand. "Go, have a good time."

Millie watched Carly drag Dalton out of the door they'd entered. She had no doubt Carly would take him to Laverne's and buy him cheap drinks until he passed out. Carly would then leave him there and pocket whatever remained of the cash Millie had given her. That was fine with Millie. She merely needed Dalton not to make an embarrassment of her at this party. She had people on the payroll at Laverne's who would see he'd make it home safely.

Raven Dean was back on the dance floor with her husband. Millie watched Raven grinding on Greg as she passed. Martin stopped her to share a few words, but Millie only had eyes for the sexual energy wafting off the man she mounted on a regular basis. Millie was getting hot. Millie's phone vibrated in her pocket as her brother's conversation turned toward the Zhangs' political future. She checked the message. What opportune timing.

Millie cut off her twin brother in the middle of a droll story. "Excuse me, Martin. There's a bit of business I must take care of."

Millie slipped out to the foyer and made sure no one was following before heading into the private residential wing using her passcode on an electronic lock. She went down the hall to her main bedroom, where she kept a private bathroom separate from Corden's. The linen closet wasn't only for storage; the shelves folded in and slid to the side, revealing a door that led to the exterior. A short path from the house wound down to the guest bungalow.

Recent upgrades enhanced the building's security, and Greg Dean himself added a video feed to show Millie who was coming and going. Millie had suspected for the last few years that Jackson Montgomery smuggled young women into her private sex retreat when she wasn't aware, but since she discontinued their carnal relationship a few weeks ago, he wasn't the one she'd catch sneaking around. However, the security features now alerted Millie when one of her concubines entered the suite, and video surveillance let her know which one was present.

"How did you know I desperately needed to get away from that awful party?" Millie asked as she entered the bedroom.

"I know dealing with those ungrateful children of yours is stressful. And sex is a great outlet for pent-up energy."

Damien Halloweather was sitting on her bed without a stitch of clothes on. His lean, magnificent body showcased his incredible dedication to the gym. He ostensibly worked for his mother and uncle at their restaurant, but Millie also funded him with a stipend that included full membership to the SX Fitness Center. The toned body was merely the garnish for the main event, a dick that was the envy of nearly every other lover in her stable of suitors. Only Jax compares in magnificence—physical evidence that they were half-brothers from different mothers. Yes, Millie knew all about that little SX secret.

Millie shed her clothes as she crossed the room. She stopped a few feet from him. Millie was all business twenty-four/seven. Before she fucked this stud half silly, she had official matters to get out of the way first. She used Damien as more than merely a good lay when she needed some big dick. He also performed odd jobs around SX that were more unsavory.

"Do those bothersome interlopers still suspect you of having something to do with Domino's murder? Or have they let it go and left your uncle Neil to take the blame?"

Damien's lust wafted off him in waves, but he remained still like an obedient dog waiting for a command. "That Noble bitch still shoots me glares whenever she and her pretentious prick boyfriend stop in at Halloweather's to check on the progress of the remodel."

Millie watched his cock twitch as he caught a whiff of her pheromones. She wanted him buried in her so badly. Intercourse was imminent, but first, she had a few questions.

"What about the FBI agent? The little Graham bastard? Is he still poking around?"

"He hasn't come by since the hurricane. No one can

prove a thing. I'm not going to jail, Ms. Zhang," Damien said, trying to put the conversation to bed so Millie could get bouncing on the mattress.

"I'm not worried about you, Damien. I can't have Domino's death come back to me."

"I'd never tell anyone who wanted her out of the way. Or why. I promise."

Millie leaned forward, almost daring him to come over and fondle her. He didn't move. "I know you wouldn't dare. But what if you talk in your sleep? Or try to impress some sweet young thing from out of town?"

"I sleep alone. And I'm not into sweet. I don't want anyone from somewhere else." Damien roamed his eyes over her chest. "I prefer sultry, spicy, and near."

Millie stepped close enough to touch him. She guided Damien's face to her left breast and leaned in as he nibbled. She slipped off her underwear as his hand found her pussy, already melting from anticipation. His fingers worked at her clit, and his tongue worked her nipple. He pushed her gas pedal into the redline, shifting gears like a man who knows how to drive a luxury vehicle.

Millie knew her way around a stick shift.

She pushed him back and mounted him. If he had anything to say about foreplay, the words never passed his lips. Millie herself never made a sensual sound when she was fucking these guys. She remained silent and deliberate, pushing herself toward a climax with efficiency and precision. She took his impressive, engorged member inside of her in one smooth descent, her pussy lips smashed against the muscle at the base of his cock. She almost made a sound as he filled her. Almost.

Millie worked out twice a day, and that didn't include fucking someone half her age on a regular basis. She could keep up with the most athletic of lovers. A few years ago,

Millie bedded a Navy SEAL who was a distant Ryan relative back in SX for a visit. Before he left, he told Millie that she was more badass than any man he'd served with in the military.

She rode Damien Halloweather hard. His cock was sublime, but Millie really got off knowing he was a stone-cold killer. She had ordered him to kill Domino and frame Acindina Álvarez. She hadn't forgiven that little bitch for making her chop down her azaleas all those years ago. And Damien had executed the mission efficiently and admirably. Only by sheer luck had some sneaky meddlers traced the murder back to the Halloweathers, but Neil had taken the blame for the Dark Summer incident, as well as Domino Salem's murder, before Tom Graham gunned him down. His confession wrapped everything up perfectly.

She had groomed Jax Montgomery for years to graduate from lover to weapon, but he had never risen to the occasion. Damien had achieved greater success than even Jackson. He had become her most valuable asset and her favorite piece of ass.

Millie started to come, the massive dick inside her shuddering at the same time she quivered in climax. His magnum condom caught every ounce of ejaculate. Millie Zhang abided by no mess in her coupling with any man. She finished a protracted orgasm while he was still hard inside her, then did a dismount equal to an Olympic gymnast. If they were giving out medals for fucking, she'd be accepting the gold.

Damien waited in bed like a loyal hound while Millie cleaned herself up. He wouldn't take care of himself until she left. He watched her get dressed and check herself in the mirror. A little flushed but otherwise ready to rejoin the party. Millie turned back and faced the naked man in her bed before she exited. He was still glorious, even after she came down from her hormonal high.

"I might have another job for you soon. Stay tuned."

"You know I can get it done," Damien said assertively.

Millie reentered her home through the secret passageway behind the linen closet and retraced her steps through the residential halls. She rejoined the party in progress. Greg and Raven acted even more explicitly in their groping. Her father was making out with his girlfriend. Owen settled for visiting with Chuck and Dora Reed. Corden laughed at something his sister in the muumuu said, and her brothers had their heads together in the corner.

"Where have you been?"

Millie didn't startle. If she did, she'd have jumped out of her skin and given Juliet cause for suspicion. But Millie had tempered all quick reaction decades ago, as cool as the coldest cucumber. She simply turned and faced her daughter. Juliet must've been watching when Millie reentered the room.

"I needed some air," Millie said.

"You look warm. You'd think the December night would have cooled you off," Juliet said.

"I'm cool enough to freeze this conversation in its course, Juliet Zhang," Millie replied sternly.

The Juliet who dealt with her mother before she disappeared, would've heeded that tone and retreated. Juliet could be as stubborn and defiant as Millie ever was, but a fight with Millie was a losing proposition. The Juliet who returned after faking her death to spend the rest of her life in Iowa with her one true love didn't take heed of Millie's tenor. In fact, Juliet boldly smiled and took a step forward.

"You don't scare me. I was dead once. I can be dead again," Juliet confidently stated.

"I'm not trying to scare you." The hell she wasn't. Millie didn't like that she couldn't intimidate her daughter. The selfish brat had put her through misery for a little Salem bitch, and now Juliet had grown some balls. "We're on a level playing field, Juliet. We want the same thing."

"You want to blow this party so you can fuck Juliet Salem tonight too?"

"Vulgarity is not going to get you back into City Hall, young lady," Millie said with a clenched jaw. "If you want to get back into the mayor's office, you'd better start acting like it again."

"The election is too far gone for me to jump into the race."

"Owen quit, triggering the special election that got Bryce into City Hall. You...'died' to trigger a second special election. We wait until after Martin Montgomery or Mariah Ryan wins the race. Then, something might just happen to prompt another special election."

"Another," Juliet repeated, savoring the idea. "I can get back into the mayor's office."

Millie knew she had her daughter on the hook. "The Zhangs will return to power. It's inevitable."

Dalton was hopeless. Owen was a fool. The only hope was Juliet. Her daughter was the Zhangs' only chance to reclaim their former glory in SX politics.

Chapter Eight

Neve had a lot on her plate. She coordinated the investigative efforts of the Crossing Guard and received regular reports from the members about dead ends and possible leads. All the partners seemed invested in solving the outstanding mysteries plaguing SX. Naomi was back on the Evvie's Explorer, sailing offshore and focusing on the area near Hahkv Island to see if the partial map she'd found could yield any clues. Tom used his FBI credentials to outline the history of the Iblīs family over many decades since founding father Nathanial Salem screwed Ebrahim Iblīs out of the family's claim on the original settlement that became SX. Willow was undercover in Old Mat, and Neve wondered if Willow spent any time under the covers with the badass biker. With Cin seemingly inseparable from Jax since Domino's murder, Neve couldn't imagine another third wheel in Willow and Ram's bed. She worried Willow would never settle for any situation that could turn into a serious relationship. Simmer spent several afternoons at Restful Meadows, allegedly to turn a page on her gossipy ways and start serious journalism in the form of a memoir of the early days of Salem Crossing, interviewing senior citizens to gain insight into some of the old-time origins of the mysteries plaguing present-day SX.

Neve also partnered with Bryce to oversee the progress on the Snow Ball celebration that Grandame Graham had pushed forward despite the devastating storm damage, arguing that the city needed an event focused on positivity. Grandame wasn't wrong, but the timing definitely sucked. Mariah Ryan volunteered to head the committee organizing the event to gain political points in the upcoming election, but she spent as much time campaigning for mayor as coordinating the ball. Somehow, she had avoided Martin Montgomery's threats of forcing her out of the race using blackmail about the sex tape Riley had recorded of Mariah and Jax. Neve still couldn't believe Jax had slept with Mariah Ryan.

Luckily, Mariah had enlisted Delilah and Caleb, who, despite bickering like an old married couple, booked the entertainment, arranged caterers, and designed the decorations. The oddball sibs were actually very good at the task. Between Delilah's quirky eye for design and Caleb's obsessive attention to detail, the event was on schedule, under budget, and, according to Mariah, was "the biggest, snowiest, balliest Snow Ball ever."

Christmas was approaching, and Neve did not attend the Zhang pre-holiday festivities because she had not yet revealed Corden as her biological father. Mariposa's stark fear about Millie Zhang's reaction fueled Neve's reasoning to keep her paternal parentage secret for a little longer. However, she'd already attended the Grahams' gathering, committed to the Salem shindig, and would go to the Ryan Christmas extravaganza because Mariah had invited her. She would only visit the Álvarez celebration if Mariposa returned to SX for the holidays, which sounded unlikely. Neve would attend more of the founding family festivities than any other citizen of SX.

The rescheduled special election to fill the second mayor's seat was set for the Tuesday after New Year's. Neve had expected Martin Montgomery to publicly criticize Mariah's lies about being repentant for her wanton ways by exposing her sex tape with Jax, but thus far, both campaigns had resisted character assassination in the wake of the hurricane. They both promised rejuvenation for the city upon election. As Bryce pushed himself to the limit, trying to keep everything in the devastated town moving forward and gradually healing, he no longer cared which would win. He needed help at City Hall. Running everything solo for much longer would lead him to a breakdown.

And then Neve had to plan the wedding. Neve and Bryce decided to get married in January, a little over a month away. Since Bryce was already overwhelmed with making decisions and coordinating efforts as agencies from all over the country offered assistance to SX, the main responsibility for their impending wedding fell on Neve. Luckily, they had decided on a simple affair. Bryce seemed to enjoy talking about the small details late at night when he and Neve settled down and grabbed a few hours of sleep. Such as what kind of flowers to use, choosing their songs, the color of the bridesmaid dresses, the menu for the reception, etc.

"Jesus Christ, Caleb, I don't need you up my ass all day," Delilah swore, interrupting Neve's thoughts.

"My Lord, Delilah. Language," Caleb huffed.

Neve smiled to herself. The Caesars teased Delilah endlessly about her creepy relationship with her brother, yet she would so often inadvertently open herself up to ridicule. Delilah's word choices were regularly regrettable. Neve watched as Caleb puttered around the Graham ballroom, fixing labels. Delilah capriciously indicated where the décor should go. Delilah's regular tirades never dissuaded Caleb. He diligently continued to follow, straightening and smoothing every decoration she placed across the room until her next outburst.

The Snow Ball usually occurred at the Lillian Graham Center for the Arts, but they had to relocate to the Graham Manor because of storm damage. The house had been mostly empty over the last half-century, only occupied by more than Mavis Graham for the brief sixteen years when Bryce was a boy. The home hadn't hosted a community event in half a century. Grandame Graham instructed Delilah and Caleb to spare no expense on the opulent extravaganza.

"Those two haven't changed a bit in ten years."

Neve turned around at the sound of a voice she didn't recognize, but she knew who it would be before she even laid eyes on the woman. Willow had told her about the newcomer in town who had spent a summer in SX when the Caesars were teens. Someone who had once dated Bryce.

Leira wasn't what Neve had pictured. Bryce was a clean-cut, upstanding professional who looked the part of a doctor and a mayor. Even as a young man, Neve imagined him as a buttoned-up preppy Graham in a stiff collar and starched khakis. More nerd than jock in his youth, his popularity originated from being a Caesar and constantly surrounded by his six beautiful pseudo-sisters. He even graduated from high school two years early. She'd seen pictures of a young Bryce with his hair styled like he was the class president. Not exactly the bad boy of SXHS.

Yet Leira was a punk rock biker bitch from head to toe. She wore a short neon pink mohawk down her shaved head. Neve counted piercings through her nostril, an eyebrow, multiple metals in each ear, and a stud through her bottom lip. Neve imagined the piercings didn't end where she could see them. A tattoo of a snowflake decorated the left side of her face. The Latina woman looked like she could kick ass.

"You must be Leira."

"And you're Nevada Noble. Bryce's fiancée." Leira licked her lips. "I've met your sister."

"Yes. So she said." Willow had had a threesome with Leira and her companion during post-hurricane cleanup, and Will had immediately run to Neve and Bryce to report. Juliet Zhang's surprising return had sidelined the Caesars' attention ever since, but the reunion of Leira and her childhood cohorts was inevitable. "I've heard a lot about you."

"I'm sure Bryce told you some wild stories," Leira said.

Neve hadn't heard Bryce say a word about her since Willow informed the Caesars that Leira was back in town. With everything else happening, catching up with an old flame seemed very low on Bryce's list of priorities. Maybe that's why Leira didn't trigger any pangs of jealousy as Neve considered her and Bryce's mutual past.

"He never mentioned you at all, but Sammy had a lot to say," Neve reported honestly, with a bit of a savage twist. If Leira were still interested in Bryce, it would be good to let her know he wasn't even thinking about her.

"Sammy always had a lot to say," Leira said, her brows crinkling in loathing.

So, Leira didn't like Sammy. From Sammy's account of Bryce's last summer in SX, Leira was an interloper who had taken time away from the Caesars' last weeks together. In the end, Leira left before the end of summer. Bryce stayed a few more days until school started, then left for college and didn't return for a decade. Leira was barely an afterthought in the Caesars' lives.

Yet here she was again.

"Look what the fucking cat dragged in. Leira Gemini. Back from the dead," Delilah said, noticing the woman talking to Neve and striding over like an arrow loose from a quiver. Caleb bobbed behind her in her wake.

"I wasn't dead, Delilah. There's life outside SX, you know."

"Yet you came crawling back like some weird deep-sea creature hauling her ass out of the surf."

"I'm here to help the recovery efforts. I heard Hurricane Marlena hit the community hard and wanted to help. I have fond memories of this place." Leira's luscious lips curved into a lascivious smile. "Some people more than others."

It took some effort to look more outrageous than Delilah Ryan. Today, Delilah wore a bright yellow sundress resembling a lemon, mimicking the same rough, scaly texture. Neve kind of wanted to peel, zest, or squeeze her for lemonade. Delilah had applied matching lipstick, a neon yellow color that Neve didn't even know existed. Her boots were as red as maraschino cherries, with big hoop earrings to match. A top hat completed the wild outfit, the vibrant green of fresh melon. Delilah resembled a fruit salad.

Yet Leira looked like she'd stepped out of a time machine from the Eighties, with the result being if Madonna and Cyndi Lauper had a baby. Dad was obsessed with everything from the 1980s, from music to movies. Neve had watched cult hits like *Ghostbusters* and *Goonies* a hundred times. He had a room over the garage with posters of featured icons of the era on the wall. She was raised on music from Janet Jackson to Boy George.

Leira wore a top made of netted material that cut off midriff, revealing her pink bra beneath. Her ripped jeans had enough holes to prove she wasn't wearing any underwear beneath her pants. Her shoes were vintage high-top sneakers with Velcro straps. If someone handed her a guitar, she would be fit for induction as an official Bangle.

Neve could cut the animosity between the two women with a knife. Whatever had happened all those years ago, Delilah had held a grudge against Leira ever since. Delilah was usually the one getting under someone's skin, so Neve watched the shoe on the other foot with amusement. Caleb fluttered at Delilah's elbow as if worried the grudge match would turn into a brawl.

"Leira?"

Neve turned at the sound of the voice, and the person who recognized Leira hadn't been around ten years ago when Leira dated Bryce. Tom Graham crossed the ballroom floor toward Delilah. That meant Tom knew Leira from somewhere else. This was another twist in a day full of surprises.

"Tommy," Leira purred. "What the hell are you doing here?"

"You know my family is from Salem Crossing," Tom said, frowning. He had an expression of someone who saw their history teacher at a rave. The two things didn't belong together. "I didn't expect to see you...again."

Delilah turned her gaze from her boyfriend to Leira. "How do you two know each other?"

"We dated for a while last year," Leira said. She looked from Delilah to Neve. "That means I've kissed both your boyfriends and one of your sisters."

Delilah took a step toward Leira with her hands balled into fists.

"You come here to stir up trouble?" Delilah asked, her face inches from Leira's.

"Back off, bitch," Leira warned.

Neve watched Delilah's face shift from pasty to red without a flashing yellow warning between colors. Her fist shot out so fast that Leira, obviously fit and badass, didn't have time to duck. Leira ate Delilah's knuckles, the pierced lip cutting into both face and fist alike, blood spraying from the impact in an arc that stained Caleb's lily-white shirt.

"Holy shit," Neve said, retreating before she ended up in the middle of a catfight.

Tom stepped toward the women, but Caleb had already leaped to his sister's defense, swinging his fists like a mime in battle against a circus clown. Caleb was in more danger of hitting himself than anyone else. Tom grabbed Caleb before he came close enough that Leira could knock him the hell out. He held back the spastic wildcat as Caleb punted an invisible football and threw his arms like a kid having a tantrum in a candy store.

"I should've beat your ass ten years ago," Delilah said, kicking at Leira like an angry goat.

"You'd still be in a wheelchair if you'd tried," Leira sneered, punching Delilah in the boob.

"I'm going to rip every piercing out of your body and make you eat them," Delilah cried, elbowing Leira in the stomach and doubling her over.

"Crazy psycho," Leira said, knocking off Delilah's green top hat, grabbing a handful of red hair, and pulling her head toward the floor.

"Evil cunt," Delilah called back, getting her arm around Leira's neck and putting her in a chokehold.

"Cunt this," Leira hollered, punching Delilah in the crotch.

Delilah doubled over and exhaled, losing her grip on Leira's head. The two women staggered away from each other, huffing and puffing, and Neve guessed the altercation was over. She took a step toward the women, thinking she could broker peace. Instead, Delilah charged at Leira and headbutted her right in the chest, knocking her backward into the big snowball decoration and sending it rolling against the wall.

"Knock that cocksucker out," Caleb cried.

Delilah stood over Leira, who was lying at her feet. She was so stunned by her brother's language that she paused to look at him. Leira swept her feet around and kicked Delilah's shin, bringing her to the floor. They rolled onto each other, swinging fists, clawing at each other's faces.

Delilah and Leira staggered to their feet and faced one another with scratches and tears, trying to catch their breath. Tom pleaded with them to stop, but both still had their hands balled into fists. Neve had been in enough scrapes with her sister, Willow, when they were young, to know better than to get between two hellcats when the claws were out. They had to finish this.

"I fucked your boyfriend, bitch," Leira taunted, landing an uppercut that made Delilah spit blood. "I bet you haven't."

"He didn't even mention it. Must've been forgettable," Delilah countered, visibly stung, lashing out with a lucky punch to Leira's nose, making it gush twin jets of red.

"The memory of my pussy is probably the only thing that keeps him sane on those nights when you're polishing your chastity belt," Leira said, spraying blood as it ran into her mouth, landing a fist that would leave Delilah with a black eye.

"But you let him go, and I'm fighting for him," Delilah said, swinging and missing.

"You're going to lose this fight, you loony asshole, and next, you'll lose Tom." Leira grabbed the front of Delilah's wild outfit and pulled her face into hers.

Defiant and struggling against Leira's grip, Delilah managed to say, "I won't. I love him."

That made Leira pause. She hadn't expected that from the crude Delilah Ryan. She recovered after a second, winding up to pop Delilah right in the mouth when a strong hand grabbed Leira by the wrist.

"That's enough. Both of you," Tom said.

Tom had cuffed Caleb to a large metal snowflake decoration suspended over the table for the punch bowl. Caleb had a manacled hand in the air, as if he had a question or was trying to fist-bump God in Heaven. Tom stepped between the fighting women as Leira let go of Delilah. The place was a disaster. The two women were a mess. But Tom Graham looked at Delilah Ryan like she was the most beautiful thing he'd ever seen.

"You love me?" he asked.

Delilah smiled ear to ear, beautiful despite the scratches, bruises, and blood everywhere. "Sure feels like something more than mild irritation."

Neve smiled. Getting through Delilah's defenses was an impressive feat. Tom kissed her, and Delilah winced, aching in any number of places. Leira skulked away as the happy couple cuddled in the middle of the empty dance floor. Neve looked at Caleb, looking miserable with his hand in the air. She turned and left.

Neve needed to add one more item to her list of mysteries for the Crossing Guard.

Who the hell was Leira Gemini? And what was she doing back in SX?

Chapter Nine

ARIEL ÁLVAREZ

Ariel agreed to meet Rob at Kenny's Koffee to discuss their crumbling marriage. Rob wanted them to try counseling. His uncle, Reverend Saul Ryan, had the resources to facilitate regular meetings with a professional through the church. Ariel was hesitant. She wasn't sure there was anything to salvage after her whirlwind affair with Conner Graham. Right now, she couldn't guarantee that it wouldn't happen again.

She arrived early to survey the battlefield. She wouldn't put it past Rob to ambush her with an intervention, maybe bringing Bryce to convince her to fight for their marriage or recruiting Ariel's mother to guilt her into attempting reconciliation. Ariel needed to secure the high ground in case Rob launched a sneak attack.

Ariel ordered a latte and chose a corner table obscured behind a fake potted palm, where she could sit with her back against an emergency exit in case she needed a quick escape. She brought her laptop and pretended to be working. She wore an overcoat and a fedora pulled down over her ears to conceal herself from customers in case Rob arrived with reinforcements. It might buy her enough time to slip away if Rob didn't immediately recognize her. Ariel watched locals coming and going as she pretended to be working at her table.

Not everyone was a local. Ariel was surprised when she recognized the woman who had entered five minutes after she had settled in. The other Caesars had teased her that summer long ago when Leira Gemini spent a few weeks in SX, all of them saying how Ariel looked a lot like the stranger from out of town. "You sure your dad didn't have a love child in another state, Ary?" Sammy had taunted. She couldn't be sure since Ariel had never met her father and didn't know his name. Her mother had told Ariel he was a tourist passing through town who never knew he'd fathered a daughter, so Ariel couldn't say Sammy was wrong. Ten years later, the woman no longer looked like Ariel. Leira wore a pink mohawk with piercings everywhere. Cuts and bruises covered her face. Had someone beaten the hell out of her lately?

Ariel had heard she was in town, but their paths hadn't crossed. This was the first time she'd seen the interloping bitch in a decade. Ariel loathed the woman. Leira arrived in SX during Bryce's last summer and stole precious moments with him away from all the other Caesars. Ariel had been in love with Bryce for years, and Leira managed to start a romance with the teen boy in a matter of weeks. How many summer nights had Ariel fallen asleep while plotting ways to get rid of Leira Gemini?

Ariel blended into the shadows, wanting to avoid a confrontation with the ghost from the Caesars' past. Enough drama would ensue once Rob arrived, and she didn't need to start with an appetizer of age-old animosity. Instead, Ariel spied on the woman as Leira talked with her companion, a handsome Black man wearing a tank top displaying delectable, defined biceps and tight gym shorts accentuating a perfect ass. The conversation appeared one-sided as Leira talked while the yummy man listened.

Leira studied the menu. "We need to get him something for his birthday. He bought you that nice red velvet cake last week. And it isn't like we turn twenty-six every year, is it, Booker?"

Booker shook his head.

"You think he'd like a croissant?" Leira asked. "Caid is bougie like that sometimes."

"Get the poppyseed muffin. He likes those damn things," Booker said.

Leira gave her companion a flirty wink with her swollen eye. "I'd rather you get my muffin. Being back in SX makes me horny as hell."

"We could hit up Willow again. That was fun," Booker suggested after the barista took their order.

Leira rolled her eyes. "I'm not wasting my time on some Salem brat. I want one of the Grahams. Bryce, if I can get him. Tommy, if I can't."

Booker scowled. "Why are we bothering with the Grahams? The Salems have the power in this town. Or the Zhangs."

"That's the mission, bro. We have our orders," Leira said.

The barista handed them their drinks and a small paper bag with a poppyseed muffin. They exited. Ariel watched them go, ducking behind a menu that covered her face. What the hell was that about? When she heard Leira was back in SX, she figured it was for cleanup or vacation. But Leira apparently had an agenda. She had totally ruined Ariel's plans for her last summer with Bryce. Ariel might have gotten Bryce to fall in love with her before he left for college if Leira Gemini hadn't distracted him. Now, Ariel sure as hell wouldn't let her come in and steal Bryce from Neve when Ariel couldn't manage to do it.

What did Leira want with a Graham? Ariel had bedded Conner Graham during the storm, a virtual lookalike of Bryce. Leira must not know about Conner because she was focused only on Bryce or Tom.

"Ariel?" Leira might not have noticed the person in the corner she hadn't seen in ten years, but Ariel couldn't hide from her husband so easily. Rob eyed her attire. "You look like Carmen Sandiego."

She'd been trying to evade Rob if he came in with Reverend Ryan and a pair of marriage therapists, but Leira's unexpected appearance distracted her. Lucky for her, Rob was alone. Maybe he wasn't entirely certain he wanted reconciliation. Ariel wasn't sure she'd ever wanted to marry him in the first place. She'd wanted Bryce to get jealous and stop the union before things got to this point.

"I didn't want you to get the wrong idea," Ariel said.

"I've had nothing but wrong ideas about you all along, Ariel." Rob's reply cut.

He sat across from her. He wore a nice shirt and an average pair of slacks, nothing to indicate an attempt to woo her or make her jealous. Rob maybe understood the status of their relationship better than Ariel gave him credit for. He didn't look like a man ready to beg her to come back. Rob appeared as unsure as Ariel about whether they could save their relationship. Ariel wondered if there was anything worth fighting for.

"You're the one who wanted to meet. I've got places to be," Ariel said, unnecessarily combative. She might be the one who cheated on Rob, but she preferred more time to figure out what she wanted before he backed her into a corner. Ariel started getting up.

"Sit down," Rob demanded, his tone rattling her.

Rob never acted assertively toward her in his whole life. They began dating in high school when Ariel was a teenager in love with Bryce. She'd believed she would marry Bryce since the day she was old enough to understand what it meant. Ariel only dated Rob because everyone made it seem like she would never get Bryce Graham. But Ariel was always in love with Bryce. Rob probably knew that at some level.

Rob never rocked the boat. He was madly in love with Ariel, but Ariel was in love with Bryce. There was enough unrequited love going around for a dozen country songs. Rob remained careful never to piss Ariel off because he knew there was another contender for Ariel's affection. He was a desperate pet, afraid of rejection.

"You're angry. That isn't a good mindset for a civil conversation about our marriage," Ariel said, but she sat again.

Rob's gaze softened, and she thought he would crumble, yet he remained resolute. She expected begging, but he looked ready for negotiation. Had Rob somehow grown a spine after she ripped out his heart?

"Do we even have a marriage, Ariel? Or was this all a scam to make Bryce jealous?"

Ariel froze. She thought she'd been so clever about her scheme. Honestly, she never considered what Rob was thinking or feeling, or if he suspected her true intention. Does one consider the emotions of a rook or a pawn when playing chess? Ariel had never wondered whether Rob ever suspected a thing.

"You think it's all a lie?" she asked.

"Is it?" Rob challenged, sounding genuinely unsure. "When we were kids, it was Bryce this and Bryce that. He left for ten years, but it never felt like he was really gone. Like a ghost between us. Then he came back, but he fell for Nevada Noble. You acted like a jealous schoolgirl, but I thought you were maybe processing some lingering emotions. Unpacking baggage from when you were a teen. Bryce was with Neve, and I didn't believe he was a threat.

"Then, you suddenly wanted to get married. I was relieved. I thought you dealt with your shit, and all was good. But you brought Bryce along on our wedding day, and you were more interested in him than me at the ceremony. We didn't even get a proper honeymoon. I had to deal with Dark Summer b.s. Then a hurricane blows through town, and I find you fucking a Bryce lookalike."

He looked both exasperated and undeterred. Rob appeared ready to see this conversation through to the end.

"So, tell me, Ariel, was it all a load of crap?"

His insightfulness stunned her into silence. She had played Rob for a fool all these years, but he understood exactly the whole time. She thought she was so clever, leading him around on a leash. Instead, it turned out the dog knew his station in life all along. And remained at her side.

Until Ariel broke her marriage vows. "I'm not ready to make any decisions on going forward, Rob. I need time." After being the alpha in this relationship their whole life, she suddenly felt vulnerable.

"I do, too. But I didn't want you to decide before you had all the facts."

"What's that supposed to mean?" She hated being on the defensive.

"There's something you don't know," Rob said.

Ariel didn't like this new dynamic. Suddenly, Rob acted like someone awakened after stumbling around sleepwalking his whole life. She had pegged him for a gullible stooge, but he proved he possessed mettle equal to Ariel Álvarez.

Ariel considered Robert Ryan for perhaps the first time in her life. Had she ever seen him as a person before, or had she always used him as a convenient placeholder until Bryce Graham pulled his head out of his ass and realized he loved

Ariel? Obviously, Bryce was never going to come around. A convenient doppelgänger named Conner Graham provided her with an irresistible distraction during the storm. A man who looked like a near-perfect facsimile of Bryce, ready to fulfill a fantasy twenty years in the making.

But Rob was a real man with a tragic story. He had been kidnapped as a ten-year-old boy and held hostage on Nightmare Island for a summer. Trapped in a crate for weeks, he didn't know if he would ever see his family again. Sean Salem died out there on Hahkv Island. Rob had been in mortal danger. He survived a trauma that Ariel couldn't imagine. Yet how many times had Ariel asked him about his harrowing ordeal?

Not once.

It had always been about her—Ariel Álvarez.

She realized there was probably a lot she didn't know about Rob.

"Lay it all on the table," Ariel said. Rob winced. He had spied Ariel fucking Conner on a picnic table outside Laverne's in the middle of the hurricane. Poor choice of words. "Let's get it all out, Rob."

"I slept with someone else," Rob confessed.

Ariel wasn't sure she heard right. One thing she had never questioned in her life was Rob's loyalty. She had treated him like shit for so many years, but his dedication to her never wavered. Rob was a Ryan, faithful and true. Ariel never worried about him cheating on her, flirting behind her back, or even checking out another bikini-clad tourist at the beach. Rob would never, ever, ever.

"You cheated on me?" Her voice rose two octaves higher —more than she intended.

The woman at the next table looked up from her laptop, the click of keys pausing at the juicy context of Ariel's exclamation. Ariel shot her a glare that would make most people quake in their shorts, and the woman grabbed her device and her coffee and scurried out of Kenny's Koffee.

Rob kept his voice low. "You don't get to take that tone with me. You slept with Conner Graham first."

"You went out and got your revenge, huh?"

Rob had tears in his eyes. "I was shattered, Ariel. Broken into a million pieces. Someone was there to pick up the scattered fragments. It just happened."

Ariel felt a strange mix of jealousy and anger. Why? If she never had real feelings for Rob, then why should she care if he fucked someone else after she's already done the same? Because she never in a million years imagined Rob would ever cheat on her. Yet here they were.

"Who was it?" she asked through gritted teeth.

"Doesn't matter," Rob stated.

"It does to me."

Rob betrayed some satisfaction that he'd hurt her. She recognized the faint curl at the corner of his mouth, the one he wore when Ariel's temper started to percolate. He liked it when Ariel got riled up, as long as it was at someone else. This time, her anger showed she cared enough to be pissed.

Ariel was surprised. She did care enough to be pissed.

"Leave me alone," Ariel said.

Rob stood. "For now," he said and left.

Ariel stewed angrily for a few minutes. Why was she so upset? Rob cheated on her because she slept with Conner. Ariel was in love with Bryce Graham, not Rob Ryan. Rob might be her husband, but it was only in name. A game. He was a stooge to make Bryce jealous. And now it backfired, and she was the one wondering who had bedded her spouse.

Juliet Zhang walked in. Ariel was still glowering in the corner, hiding her pouting face behind the menu to avoid local customers. JZ didn't notice her Caesar sister sitting there. Juliet went to the front counter, and the barista approached as if JZ were the holy ghost resurrected from the tomb. Everyone in town knew the legend. The Juliets' funerals had been the biggest story in SX in ages. Now, Juliet had returned from her own staged death.

"May I help you, ma'am?" the barista asked, like she was trying to get a celebrity to sign an autograph.

"Do you sell muffins?" JZ asked, scanning the menu over the barista's head.

"We do, yes, all kinds," the barista replied, starry-eyed and stuttering. She handed JZ a laminated menu with shaky hands. "We have twenty varieties."

"Poppyseed," Juliet said without scanning the list.

"Popular flavor today," the barista said. "Here, or to go?"

"I'll take it with me. Can you put it in a bag? It's not for me."

"Of course. Right away, ma'am."

The young woman retrieved Juliet's order. JZ took the sack and left without noticing Ariel.

Ariel exhaled after Juliet was gone. What the hell was going on? Leira came in with a strange man and ordered a poppyseed muffin for someone's birthday, then Juliet Zhang came in and ordered the same oddball muffin that wasn't for her. That couldn't be a goddamned coincidence. What did JZ have in common with Leira and her friend? Did it relate to the weeks she hid in Iowa with Juliet Salem? Or was it connected to the stretch of days JZ was missing after JTS washed up on Salem Shores? JZ had been acting weird ever since she came back to life. Hadn't Juliet learned her lesson about keeping secrets after she and her wife almost died?

Apparently not.

Something strange was happening in SX, and Ariel wanted to know what was going on.

Chapter Ten

JACKIE SALEM

Jackie buried herself in work. She didn't want to consider Gil and her fake marriage over the last twenty-three years. Thoughts of Martin Montgomery would only get her into serious trouble. She avoided Neve because she didn't need her sanctimonious daughter giving her another guilt trip about cheating on her husband. Dealing with insurance company bullshit and gold-digging contractors and federal agency motherfuckers proved to be less stressful than anything going on in her personal life.

It had to be bad when she'd rather deal with Tessa Salem than anyone in her immediate family.

"Quit pacing like a goddamned cougar, Jacquelyn. You're making me dizzy," Tessa snapped as Jackie went back and forth in front of Tessa's giant desk.

"Pissed-off energy," Jackie muttered. "These FEMA bastards have red tape wrapped around every federal dollar available to rebuild the shoreline."

"You need to get to the gym. Beat the hell out of a punching bag before you lose your shit on one of the employees."

"It'd more likely be one of the cousins. Makenna drives me mad. Or maybe Ravenna Baudelaire."

"Leave Makenna out of it. I'm running out of offspring."

Jackie raised a blonde eyebrow at her aunt's dark humor, but Tessa pored over a stack of paperwork as high as the bottle of wine beside the documents. The two spent the last few hours camped in Tessa's office inside the Salem estate. The room smelled musty, and there were spiderweb cracks in the walls. A framed portrait of their ancestor, Nathaniel Salem, hung over Aunt Tessa's desk, slightly askew. Jackie straightened it out.

Half of the building had collapsed during the tornado that accompanied Hurricane Marlena, and the inspectors would've condemned this place if Tessa hadn't pulled some strings. She ought to have saved her favors to ease the process of rebuilding the Salem resorts instead.

Despite the storm blowing half of it out to sea, Tessa refused to leave her home. Her relatives, Francine and Krystal, had died right here. Auberon Fox perished while saving Simmer Salem's life a mere twenty yards away. Yet Tessa considered the home a lifeline to everything the family had built over the past decades. Their legacy is inexorably entwined with Salem Shores. Tessa would never retreat inland.

"How's Alistair doing on insurance claims?" Jackie asked.

"You think we have a lot of paperwork? Alistair can barely walk through his office. He's got stacks as high as Sweetheart," Tessa said.

Sweetheart Salem was three and a half feet tall.

Tessa had assigned Jackie the task of tracking the free money available through the governor's disaster declaration. The government offered grant funds, zero-interest loans, and borrowing relief for properties affected by the hurricane. No other family in Florida had lost more in the devastating storms than the Salems. Jackie had spent countless hours applying for every program available, and the denials started arriving a few days ago. The bureaucrats approved nothing. The government kept requiring more forms, financial statements, estimates, and documents.

With most of the remaining resorts closed for repairs, the Salem funds began drying up fast. Bill collectors had already begun demanding payments after only a few days of being late. Like sharks sensing blood in the water, creditors circled the Salem debts, eager to repossess at the first sign of trouble. Jackie needed the feds to approve protections for their properties against lenders until they could open the Salem businesses and generate profit.

Tessa shoved a pile of paperwork away, frustrated. "We need to move money around. We can liquidate assets to fortify our funds against the vultures."

"Our valuation is in the toilet, Aunt Tessa. Our resorts all look like this house. Damaged, dilapidated, and potentially condemned. We can't open any of the hotels right now. If they start failing inspections, the authorities will shut them down for weeks or even months. We need people spending money on Salem properties pronto."

"This paperwork is going to bury us. We need reinforcements."

"One step ahead of you. Everyone should be here by now," Jackie said, checking the time on her phone.

Tessa looked intrigued. Jackie needed to do something to impress her aunt. Alistair had purposely locked up the effort regarding the insurance to ingratiate himself with their aunt. He had been the go-to guy for years before Jackie returned to SX. Alistair hated that Jackie wandered in like the prodigal Salem and pissed in his pool. Jackie had lost too much time to worry about her little brother's wittle feelings. No more pools. Jackie was preparing to take over the whole damn ocean.

Jackie led Tessa down the hall, where a thick tarpaulin served as the roof over a damaged section, past the ruined library and a lounge to a corner still relatively intact called the billiard room. Jackie sometimes wondered if one of her ancestors had remodeled the mansion using the game of Clue as inspiration. A sheet of plywood covered the single window, but the billiard room otherwise remained unscathed.

"This place?" Tessa grumbled, stopping in the hallway before entering.

The billiard room featured a large pool table in the center, a bar along one wall, and a décor more masculine than the other rooms in the house. The area featured an undertone of mustiness like the rest of the mansion, but the smell didn't overpower the reek of cigar smoke from a century of Salem men puffing away within these walls. Tessa had stopped that practice decades ago, but the stink of the past wouldn't come out despite a dozen layers of new paint.

"There aren't any other larger gathering areas without a gaping hole in a wall or the reek of mold," Jackie said.

Tessa made a face, indicating she wasn't breathing through her nose, and followed Jackie inside.

The others had already arrived. Willow and Cyprus stood in one corner, their expressions neutral. Thankfully, Neve hadn't ratted out her infidelity to the twins yet. Jackie didn't invite Neve, since she didn't want to suffer her daughter's pious scowl right now. Makenna sat in a chair, her arms folded and her head down, not as high as Jackie feared. Makenna appeared somewhat sober for the meeting. Micah stood behind her, guarding his sister against evil mojo. Juliet and Naomi looked no more like twins than Willow and Cyprus, although the blondes were identical rather than fraternal.

Besides those expected attendees, Jackie had called in some surprising reinforcements. Jackie's father, Nolan, was known for being a notorious cheat and had fathered several illegitimate children. One such bastard, a member of the Miccosukee tribe named Mutt, had arrived in SX many years ago, and the Salems paid him off to remain silent about his true parentage. Jackie had known about her half-brother for a few weeks. Now, she'd invited him to be a part of the Salem family.

"What's he doing here?" Tessa hissed.

"He's willing to lend a hand. We need all the help we can get," Jackie said.

"I'm not entirely convinced yet," came a voice behind Tessa, the last guest to arrive.

Mariposa Black, formerly known as Mariposa Ryan and never Mariposa Salem, although she was Tessa's biological sister and another illegitimate offspring—since Nolan inherited his predilection for mistresses from his father, Alexander—stood inside the Salem estate for the first time in her life. The family had never accepted her as a Salem when she lived in SX, and she had disappeared twenty-three years ago, around the same time Jackie left. Jackie had accidentally raised Mariposa's daughter, Neve, after Helen Ryan switched Mariposa's baby at birth.

What a tangled web these black widow spiders had spun.

The sisters couldn't be more different. Tessa wore a sophisticated business suit and featured gemstones from her ears to her fingers, with her blonde hair formed into the modern style of influential female figureheads and fair skin as perfectly toned as her svelte figure. Mariposa had chosen a polka-dotted dress in wild red and yellow on a field of blue like a kaleidoscope of summer suns against the background of a cloudless sky. Her hair-sprayed mane was black, streaked with silver, as majestic as a lion's. Mariposa's figure was broader and curvier, with a warm brown complexion more like Neve's than Jackie's.

"Oh, hell no. She's not welcome here," Tessa said, stepping away from Mariposa.

Mariposa folded her arms and remained in place. "I have as much right to be here as you, Tessa. We have the same father."

"You are an Álvarez through and through," Tessa sneered.

"My last name is actually Black," Mariposa corrected.

"And Ryan before that. And Álvarez before that. Never Salem," Tessa retorted derisively.

"She's half Salem. As much as anyone else here," Jackie interjected.

"She's not welcome in my house," Tessa said, raising her voice.

"It won't be your house much longer, Aunt Tessa, unless we marshal every single troop that we can manage in the war against the enemy coming to take everything," Jackie stated.

The two half-sisters glared at each other as seconds turned into years. Ages of animosity built up over decades. Jackie had only recently realized Mariposa Black, whom she'd known as Mariposa Ryan growing up, was her illegitimate aunt. This made Neve her cousin in addition to being her adopted daughter. Jackie would never voluntarily return to Horton, Iowa, but life had undoubtedly been much simpler there over the last twenty-three years.

"I thought you left Salem Crossing because you were afraid Millie Zhang would kill you when she found out about your dirty secret?" Tessa asked.

Mariposa recoiled as if someone had slapped her. Jackie knew Neve was Mariposa's biological offspring with Corden Zhang, but most people in the room didn't. Would Tessa reveal the truth so Mariposa would skitter back to Boston, or would she blackmail her sister to keep Mariposa away from the Salems? Or was this simply Tessa's way to goad her outlandish sibling?

"If Millie Zhang finds out I had her husband's love child, then I guess I'm ready to fight the bitch," Mariposa said to gasps across the room. "She can't be any worse than you."

Tessa sized up Mariposa, from her six-inch stilettos to her dress featuring more polka dots than a hundred and one Dalmatians.

"She's not worse than me," Tessa warned.

Then Tessa extended a hand as a peace offering. Mariposa joined the other Salems inside the billiard room. Jackie was shocked that it worked. Tessa must be really worried about the creditors coming for their property if she willingly mended fences with an Álvarez. The storm had created an opportunity for some truly surprising allegiances. The truce gave Jackie some hope that they might make it through this.

"What was that about having an affair with Corden Zhang?" Naomi asked.

Mariposa looked at Jackie. Jackie looked at Willow and Cyprus. An agreement was passed between the four attendees who knew the whole truth.

Jackie sighed, so tired of the drama in SX that had been absent all these years in Iowa. Maybe not *everything* was better in Florida. "Nevada Noble is Mariposa's biological daughter. Gilbert and I thought we were taking Neil Halloweather and Amara Montgomery's baby away from Salem Crossing to keep her safe, but Helen Ryan had switched the two infants at birth."

"I took Amara's infant with me to Boston, thinking I was running away to protect my baby from Millie's wrath if she found out Corden had an illegitimate child," Mariposa added.

"I brought Mariposa's daughter to Iowa and raised her

with my family. I didn't know until recently about the switch," Jackie said.

"Why?" Micah asked. "What did Helen Ryan get out of switching babies?"

Jackie shrugged, dismissing the question, though she also wanted answers. "A mystery for another day. First, the wolves are hungry for the Salem fortune. The hurricane devastated our properties along the coastline. Alistair is working with the insurance companies, but it takes time to collect on our policies. In the meantime, the lenders are coming at us hard. We qualify for emergency funds from the state and federal governments, but the red tape is tying us in knots. We want trustworthy people to advocate for our money and sort through mountains of paperwork. We need every trustworthy Salem to help save the legacy our family has built over all these long years."

Jackie received nods as she surveyed the room. Her rousing speech had succeeded. Everyone seemed inspired to take action. The discussion delved next into the more technical aspects of securing volunteers to commit hours aiding Jackie and Tessa sort through reams of paperwork and coordinate efforts to complete applications for the various programs available through emergency management. The guests slowly exited the billiard room as Jackie created a schedule for every Salem willing to help save the estate.

Soon, Jackie was the last one remaining. She felt like the belle of the ball, staring at a full dance card. She'd created a schedule that went all the way through the holidays, staffing a small army to help process documents. After starting the day overwhelmed, she now felt like her team could manage the daunting effort to cut through the endless red tape.

"Jackie Salem rides back to SX on her high horse and saves the day."

Jackie looked up from her makeshift desk at the small

bistro table where men of the past had enjoyed a cigar, sipped expensive whiskey, and talked shit about women. Alistair stood in the doorway with his arms crossed, looking like the jealous child after his sibling had managed to win points with Mom for good behavior.

"It's not a competition, Alistair. We're both trying to save the family from financial ruin."

"One of us has dedicated their whole life to making sure this family stays on track. While the other was playing happy housewife in Bumfuck, Iowa, for the last two decades."

The words stung. Alistair was trying to relegate Jackie's whole life to being Mrs. Noble. There was more to the story than that.

"I taught history for twenty years, Alistair, so I don't need a lesson from the likes of you. Yesterday is behind us. I want to focus on the future."

"There's no destination without making the journey, Mrs. Noble."

"I'm as much a Salem as you," she said with a bitter tone.

"You're an imposter," Alistair accused. "You lived so long as Maggie Noble that you don't know what it takes to be Jackie Salem anymore."

Jackie stood. She used to spend time right here in this house long before Alistair was ever born. She'd put in fifteen years as a Salem by the time Alistair took his first breath. Jackie faced Alistair, eye to eye, glaring at him with inches between their similar Salem noses. Neither blinked.

"I'm not here to fight." Jackie used a threatening tone rather than attempting to de-escalate the situation. "You work the insurance companies. I work the government programs. Win-win."

"We win when we make sure the game favors our family," Alistair said. "Do you remember that the Salems set the rules?"

"Are you saying the insurance companies are ready to disburse billions to bail our ass out?"

"I'm saying I have everything working toward a specific goal, and I'll be damned if I don't succeed. Plus, I'm going to manage it without recruiting the likes of Mariposa Álvarez."

"She's a Salem, Alistair. It's time to bring in every relation willing to lend a hand."

"You sound like someone who isn't in control of the situation. You're still standing in the storm and trying to keep your world from blowing away," Alistair said, turning and starting down the damaged hallway.

Jackie watched her brother turn the corner at the end of the corridor and disappear. Damn it, but he wasn't wrong. She felt like a storm still raged, wreaking continued havoc on her family. Her entire world threatened to blow away. After being away for so long, Jackie wasn't used to fighting a hurricane. She would have to prove herself. Jackie would need to earn her right to return to the family fold.

Chapter Eleven

JACKSON MONTGOMERY

Two days had gone by too damn fast. They spent forty-eight hours tamping down their lust for one another and focusing on an old-fashioned romance, like something out of a time when SX wasn't even a town. They walked among the orange orchards outside a small village called Snowy Pines. Holding hands was as much physical contact as they allowed themselves during their entire getaway. The local theater was showing *The Princess Bride*, and Cin begged Jax to take her, but she didn't try very hard because it was one of Jax's favorite movies. They sipped on coffee at a small cafe called The Small Coffee Shoppe, and they took a midnight stroll along the quaint cobblestone streets circling the historic downtown.

They loved the local restaurant called Lovebirds. It wasn't very romantic, as it resembled one of those roadside diners referred to as a "dive" on a cable TV show. They claimed their favorite booth in the back, private and perfect. The food was wonderfully kitschy, with onion rings to die for and a burger bigger than Cin's face. Best of all, no one knew them from any other anonymous tourists and left them completely alone.

Yesterday, they played eighteen holes at Snowy Pines's miniature golf course, Ice Golf. The holes had a wintry theme with obstacles like a snowman on hole six, and hole fourteen had a surface as slippery as ice. The course was centered around a small lake with a fountain in the middle shaped like a giant snowflake. Jax won the first match, but Cin beat him the second time through the course with a hole-in-one on the last green. They spent the morning on a tiebreaker round, and Cin beat him by a single stroke. He could handle Cin beating him with a few more strokes than just one.

They'd rented a lakeside cabin and spent the evenings in a canoe. The sunsets were spectacular. They enjoyed brunch together outside at a bistro table on the backyard porch, watching the wildlife wander the shoreline. A late-season storm had rolled across the area the night before, and Cin leaned into Jax with his arms around her as they watched the thunderheads roll by, rain washing the world away.

The rental featured two bedrooms, and though it was as difficult as anything he had ever managed, they stayed in separate beds. The first night, Jax found an old episode starring a sitcom mom he'd always thought was sexy as hell and masturbated to take the edge off his hunger for Cin. Jax didn't know if he'd have been able to stay away from her room all night without the release. On night two, Jax couldn't find anything to arouse him on television, so he eventually snuck out of his bed and tiptoed across the cabin to Cin's bedroom. Her door was closed, and there were sounds of commotion inside. She was watching something pornographic in there, and it sounded like she was at the end of getting off. Jax had previously witnessed more than one Acindina orgasm, and he knew when she was finishing up. He'd arrived too late. She needed to satisfy her needs on night two like Jax had managed on night one. He skulked back to his room, unsatisfied.

Only one night remained before they had to return to SX

and resume their everyday lives and the secrets and lies of their illicit relationship. Cin had an evening shift at Laverne's tomorrow. Jax had to get back to doing his father's bidding. Their whirlwind getaway wrapped up without much physical progress in their relationship. Jax and Cin had agreed to take things slow, but the glaciers had moved faster across the continent. Jax wanted to experience a more traditional relationship with Cin, but at this rate, they'd be living in a retirement community up in Villages before they consummated things. He didn't mind being ponderous, but he did want progress.

They managed little beyond holding hands.

They exited after their meal at Lovebirds, full and happy, and Jax said, "Last evening in Snowy Pines. Anything you want to do? There's live music at the pavilion tonight. Some kind of annual holiday festival from dusk till dawn."

"I suppose the whole town will be there," Cin suggested.

Jax watched the gears turning in her mind. He recognized that lusty look in her eye when she was up to something sexy. She glanced at the sky, turning dark as twilight set in. If everyone were downtown, the rest of the town would be mostly closed for business. Everyone in a small community like Snowy Pines would attend the festival.

"I want to go to the golf course," Cin said.

"Our waiter said they were only open till two o'clock today. I think the employees at Ice Golf make up most of the band playing at the festival."

Cin flashed a sexy smirk, grabbing his hand and dragging him toward the course. "I don't want to putt. I want to swim."

Jax's mouth fell open as she pulled him along. They'd had a conversation the previous night while sitting on the back porch of their rented cabin, looking at the moonlight reflecting on the lake's placid waters. Cin had had a few beers, making her smiley and carefree. Loose enough to be a tease but not so drunk as to lose her inhibitions. Jax didn't want things to progress unless she was sober.

"You ever go skinny dipping, Jax?" Cin had asked.

Jax had inhaled at the thought of her stripping down right there and then.

"No. I've had to sneak around for most of my rendezvous in life."

Cin already knew that his only steady relationship in his adult life was with Millie Zhang, an extramarital affair that solely occurred in the guest house behind her lavish estate. Jax had been with many women, primarily tourists, besides Millie, but those had been nights of need and desperation. Neve had been the only woman he'd ever been with that involved something more than meaningless sex. Now Cin... when they finally consummated their relationship, Jax would experience something new. None of his former flings had ever involved anything as adventurous as skinny dipping.

"There are alligators out there. No way they'd be able to resist a mouthful of naked Acindina," Jax had said the previous night, looking at the lake by their cabin.

"Just the alligators, huh?"

Jax fidgeted in his seat. "You want to take it slow. Getting naked right now while we're both a little tipsy probably isn't the way to do it. Besides, I'd find you a lot less sexy if an alligator took a bite out of your top half."

Cin leaned over, moonlight illuminating her cleavage in her low-cut tank top. "You're worried about my top half?"

"Top and bottom, babe. I want everything intact when we're ready to take this further."

Cin grinned, took a swig of her beer, and stayed put. They were unwilling to risk life and limb in alligator-infested waters, nor the possibility of taking things too far when they were trying to pump the brakes on rushing into intercourse.

Speaking of courses, now, less than twenty-four hours

later, they arrived at Ice Golf. A small town like Snowy Pines didn't need high-tech security measures. Cameras were pointed at the entrance and nowhere else. Jax spotted motion-activated lights that would bathe the course in fluorescents and possibly alert someone heading to the festival. He had broken into enough places with much better security than this small-town attraction. He deactivated the breaker by picking a very simple padlock.

"You're handy to have around when I want to get into places I shouldn't."

"I have all kinds of talents," Jax teased.

"I've seen a few of your tricks," Cin murmured.

They might not have been intimate with each other, but they had watched each other have intercourse with other lovers on multiple voyeuristic occasions. Their journey from the beginning had been unique. Now, they were sneaking into a minigolf course a hundred miles from home. Despite trying for something traditional, they ended up exploring more extraordinary experiences.

"Boost me over," Cin said.

The only way to get her over the six-foot fence was to grab a handful of her delicious booty and give her a shove over the top. Cin grasped the top rail, wedged her foot between wrought iron posts, and Jax put his hand on her left cheek. He instantly got a hard-on. Her ass was firm, round, and juicy as hell. He resisted squeezing it. If he started, he might not be able to stop. And he wanted to see her naked in the lake.

He lifted her so she could swing one leg over, holding her buns in the air as she secured her position. She looked down over her shoulder at Jax with his palm against her butt cheek and smiled.

"You can let go now."

"In a moment," he said.

"Take your time."

He eventually set her delicious bun free, and Cin went over the fence, dropping down on the other side like an agile cat. Jax wasn't as tall as he wished, just shy of six feet, and the smallest Montgomery in the family besides Sammy. However, he was fit and strong and managed to scramble up the side of the exterior fence and down the other without any trouble. They were inside and landed right on the fifth hole.

The obstacle on the fifth hole was an enormous structure that Jax referred to as a window squeegee during their first visit. He was confused about how that related to a snowy theme, but then Cin said she believed it was something called an "ice scraper." The scraper was made of resin and stood six feet tall, with the handle pointing straight up into the sky. It blocked the green except for a small gap on either side of the blade. Tough hole.

Cin pointed. "There. Past the earmuffs."

The sixteenth green featured muffs of metal that created a loop-de-loop for the ball to circle before heading to the hole. Jax followed Cin past the cup that had caused him the most difficulty earlier today. He managed three over par. Cin stopped by the snowman statue on hole six, where the green followed the curve of the small round lake on this obstacle. She stared at the pond revealed by the moonlight above, the night illuminated like the view at the lake the night before. In the center of the water—no wider across at any point than maybe fifty feet—the snowflake-shaped fountain was still and silent.

"The moon and stars are so bright. You can see everything tonight," Jax said.

Cin bit her bottom lip seductively. "Good. Don't blink."

She started removing clothing. Her tank top peeled away smoothly, a movement familiar to women everywhere, like a dance of seduction akin to animals preening in the wild. Jax wasn't going to blink for the foreseeable future. Cin hung her shirt on one of the snowman statue's twig arms. She wriggled out of her capris and draped them over Frosty's other arm. Her panties were red-hot scarlet with a satiny patch over her center and two thin straps over her hips. Cin kicked off her flip-flops and left them on the green.

She turned to Jax, bathed in silvery moonlight, and popped the clasp on the front of her bra. Her bountiful breasts popped free, resplendent under the starlight. She looked so goddamn sexy standing topless beside the snowman. She draped the bra over the statue's top hat and put her arm over the snowman's shoulder. The December air, even farther inland and south than SX, was still cool after dark, and her nipples stood out from the dark circles of her areoles like twin nubs of hard candy.

"Take a picture, it'll last longer," she teased.

"I'm never going to forget this," Jax said.

One last piece. Cin did a glacial reveal of the final bits. A slow-motion tease that lasted an eternity. She slid down one side of the thin hip strap of her underwear, almost revealing the cleft of her pussy, then pulled it back up. Finally, she moved the patch of red satin covering the main event past her swollen lips, revealing her delectable opening. It had been weeks since he'd last seen her naked, but every part of her stood up to the perfection in his memory. She was smooth from scalp to toe tips, every part of her shaved to the skin. How slippery would she be when she was wet?

Cin hung the pair of panties over Frosty's carrot nose and turned away, walking toward the placid pond. He stared at her ass that had consumed his touch moments ago, now on full display—juicy, firm, and round. He wanted to touch it again, now bare and smooth. Cin glanced over her shoulder as she reached the water's edge, smiled like a woman who knew what effect she was having, and gave Jax a flirty wink.

"Coming?" she asked.

He worried he was in danger of it. He'd worn jeans today that were too tight to accommodate the iron flesh in his pants. Jax practically ripped his shirt off, kicked off his shoes, peeled off his socks, and then opened the zipper of his pants with great relief. Thank God he'd chosen boxers today, or his jockey shorts would have still been strangling his hefty erection. The shorts tented impressively as Jax shed his jeans and dropped the pants next to the sixth hole. He left his boxers over the cup like a final, kinky obstacle. Jax headed for the pond, leaving the snowman to guard their discarded attire.

Jax dipped a toe as he watched Cin grab an eyeful of his swollen dick.

"Cold," he hissed.

"It's fucking freezing."

Jax worried about his cock shriveling up like one of those balloons that's twisted into an animal shape after it deflated. His erection appeared impervious even to the cool water as he waded in up to his balls without losing an erg of stiffness. It helped that Cin waited for him in the shallows, water up to her belly button, with her breasts open to the night air. A sight like that could keep him warm through the coldest winter nights.

"This is mad," Jax said with a smile.

"We agreed to wait to make the final plunge," Cin said, referencing their current pledge of abstinence. "But I think we can have a few adventures in the meantime."

"We already had a few adventures before we got serious," Jax reminded her.

"This night is for you and me," Cin said, slipping into water deep enough to cover her chest and touch her chin. "Just me and you."

Several hot, voyeuristic nights had led to this moment—one watching while the other got thoroughly fucked, participating in a small orgy where each had another partner, and starring in fantasies inside one another's heads. But this was the first real experience between only the two of them.

They swam for a long while. It was more like a dance. The urge to fuck each other in this starlit pond under the romantic moon and the peaceful surroundings, enhanced by the public setting and the danger of being caught, revved Jax's engine so that his stiff cock never softened an iota. They would sometimes float closer and retreat before the compulsion to touch became too great. Cin's nipples would regularly pop above the surface like twin periscopes spying on Jax. She would float on her back for long seconds, her glistening body visible from face to feet, the soft moonlight playing across her flawless skin. Occasionally, Jax floated in the shallows close enough to shore so that his erection extended from the surface like a shark's fin circling prey. Cin seemed so close at times that her breasts might touch his chest, or her pussy could catch his cock. Yet, despite the overwhelming desire to take her right there, surrounded by eighteen holes, Jax managed to avoid sinking the putt.

"Jesus Christ, are you two going to fuck or not?"

The words made Jax colder than the water. His dick finally deflated at the sound of a stranger's voice. Cin moved closer, her arm wrapping around his waist. Their bare hips touched underwater, side by side, but there was no spark of desire in the nearness. Someone was out there, and Jax was defenseless. He hadn't expected his enemies to find him in Snowy Pines.

"Who the hell are you?" Jax called, trying to sound badass.

Someone stepped out from behind the snowman statue where Jax and Cin had left their clothes. It was a woman, visible only in silhouette, with the stars behind her. The shadows of the obstacles around the nearby holes otherwise hid her features. It could have been a stranger or Jax's sister. He couldn't see anything besides her outline.

"I'm bored," the stranger said. "And you two are boring and boringer. I've been waiting for you to seal the deal ever since you started stripping. I've seen old people sexier than this bullshit."

"You some kind of peeper? Or a spy for my dad?" Jax asked.

"This has nothing to do with you, Mr. Montgomery. I've been trying to get you two alone where I was sure you wouldn't pull a gun on me. I couldn't try it while you were drinking on the back porch of your cabin or canoeing on the lake. I expected Jackson Montgomery would have a weapon."

The stranger arrived at the water's edge, holding the pistol Jax had left near his pants. The reflection of moonlight off the water illuminated her face. She almost looked familiar. Why did she make Jax think of Britney Halloweather? And... someone else...

"What do you want from us? Blackmail? Or...?" Cin asked with a strong voice, as she found and squeezed Jax's hand underwater.

Neil and Damien Halloweather were murderers. Britney had ruthlessly shredded Owen Zhang's heart. If this woman were related, could she murder them both and leave them bobbing in the minigolf pond? Would the citizens of Snowy Pines find Jax and Cin's naked bodies floating under the big snowflake fountain come morning?

The stranger kept the gun leveled more toward Jax than Cin. "I want to talk. There are things you need to know. I had to talk to you outside SX because I don't dare set foot in that town."

"You could've talked to us at Lovebirds. Or when we were playing golf this morning."

"No, I think Jax would've recognized me more quickly by

daylight. And you would've noticed the resemblance, too, Cin," the stranger said.

"What resemblance?" Cin asked.

"Between you and me," the stranger said. "Acindina Álvarez, I'm your sister."

Chapter Twelve

Neve's team of investigators was spread across SX, working on their list of mysteries and trying to find answers in a world devastated by secrets and lies. If Bryce hoped to rebuild this broken town, the Crossing Guard would need to help him solve some of the lingering questions plaguing SX. He worked hard to repair the damaged property and heal the societal rifts around the community as Neve focused on uncovering what eroded the very foundation of the town—the drama between families that have lived together for more than a hundred years. Secrets and lies have been weakening the underpinning of this community since the town's origin.

Neve met Bryce for a working lunch. He'd crawled out of bed long before dawn while Neve was asleep and had enough meetings to keep him at City Hall until long after dinner. They ate in his office as Carmen Zhang, president of the city council, made the final preparations for the special election after the holidays. Bryce would soon finally get some backup in the co-mayor position and alleviate pressure from being solely responsible for SX's reconstruction.

"Martin and Mariah still insist on a debate?" Bryce asked.

Carmen nodded. "New Year's Eve. Since the special election is the first Tuesday of the new year, they want to capitalize on the holiday."

"Politics on the day before the Snow Ball? Buzzkill," Neve said.

Carmen looked impressed rather than irritated. "They intend to dominate the social conversation right before the biggest community event of the year. Everyone will be talking about it at the ball."

The discussion shifted to other matters, and Neve slipped away with a kiss, promising to return for dinner. She had arranged to meet Willow at Memorial Park at one o'clock. Arriving early across from City Hall, Neve wandered along the line of statues, pausing at each effigy of her ancestors to imagine the lineage from Nevada Noble to the first citizens of SX. She had come to this town as a stranger a few months ago, but now she stood there as the product of its long, storied history. Neve had deeper roots in Salem Crossing than nearly anyone else in town.

One-half Zhang. Neve stared at the statue of Sun Zhang, a stern woman who arrived in Florida after her husband died on the overseas trek. She fled political persecution in China for a new life in America. Every coin her family ever earned went to the Zhangs' investment in their Florida future. After suffering under oppression for centuries, the Zhang family vowed always to influence the freedoms and laws governing their community.

One-quarter Álvarez. Dominga Álvarez's statue represented a strong and handsome woman with a face weathered from decades of hard work. If she ever had a husband, no record of the relationship made the trip from Cuba. She arrived with sixteen children, all of whom worked hard to build New Matanzas into a thriving town and made the Álvarez's section of the city the most impressive of the earliest neighborhoods. Dominga's work ethic continued in the citizens of Old Mat today.

One-quarter Salem. Nathaniel Salem was instrumental in shaping modern-day SX. He invested every last British pound to buy out the Iblīs share of the city and then led negotiations with the Miccosukee tribe, sending them away with the Salems' ship filled with treasure. Dirt poor after buying out the Iblīs family, the Salems ended up with the last available land—the shoreline considered least valuable at the time. But agriculture turned less lucrative than tourism in the nineteenth century, and Nathaniel Salem's foresight turned into riches beyond anything the pioneer could've imagined.

"You think Nathaniel Salem had ever guessed what his family would make of his stretch of worthless sand?" Neve asked as Willow approached.

"Sometimes things don't turn out like you expect," Willow responded.

Willow had never thought she'd be a part of a family worth billions. Neve would never have guessed she was related to the same family, since they were both descendants of Nathaniel Salem. Willow probably didn't expect to team up one-on-one with Ram Álvarez to investigate the Dark Summer. Willow previously preferred a two-on-one situation, but Ram currently loomed over her right shoulder like a bodyguard assigned to protect a princess.

Neve turned her back on the memorial to Nathaniel Salem and faced her sister. "Anything?"

"You might be right. I think the Dark Summer ties into the legacy of this town. All the way back to Nathaniel Salem."

"The map?" Neve asked.

The Crossing Guard speculated that the purpose of the Dark Summer kidnappings was to blackmail the founding families into giving up pieces of a treasure map that had been separated and distributed back in the early days of the town. The map supposedly marked the location of the Miccosukee ship carrying the payment for the land, which had sunk somewhere off the coast of Salem Shores. Naomi had found one section of an old map at the Salem estate.

Willow nodded. "We went to see Ram's dad."

Neve glanced at the big guy hovering at Willow's elbow. He looked like he could snap any motherfucker in SX in half, but Neve knew he was as gentle as a butterfly. He rocked back and forth on his big feet, looking like a kid waiting for the team captain to pick him for the kickball team. Neve hadn't thought the mountain of a man possessed the capacity for being jittery.

"You don't have a good relationship with your father?" Neve asked Ram.

Ram shrugged shoulders that resembled a statue of Atlas more than Dominga Álvarez. His head was the size and shape of a cinder block, yet his eyes conveyed peacefulness and wisdom Neve would attribute to a kindly old grandmother. Neve couldn't think of a better protector for her sister as Willow poked her nose into the business of powerful and possibly dangerous people.

"He doesn't like to talk much," Ram said.

Neve didn't miss the irony. Those were the most words she might have ever heard Ram string together at one time.

Willow took over telling the story, bailing Ram out of having to explain the findings of their visit himself. "We asked Mr. Álvarez about the Dark Summer. Javier Álvarez was reluctant to discuss the terrible months his son went missing. He insisted that he didn't want to talk. He kept ignoring my questions, staring at the television, shrugging, or repeating that he had nothing to say."

"He likes to watch lucha libre," Ram added in a reverberating bass.

"So, you hit a dead end?" Neve asked.

Willow smiled. She showed aptitude as a crack investigator. She didn't do dead ends.

"I specifically asked about the treasure map. *That* got a reaction."

"He spilled his secrets?"

Willow looked up at Ram, who nodded for her to go on.

"Not right away. But he became agitated. Jumpy. He didn't want to talk, but Ram didn't give him a choice."

Neve noted Ram was still rocking from foot to foot. He shared his father's nervous tics.

Ram sighed. "He felt guilty for what happened." Ram looked at the statue of Dominga Álvarez. "He was supposed to keep me safe." Neve thought about Dominga's sixteen children and how she'd crossed the sea without a husband to bring them to this new place. "Nightmare Island haunts him as much as me."

A father's failure. Neve never considered what effects the kidnappings had beyond the seven boys out at Hahkv Island. The experience traumatized their families, as well as the whole town.

"I demanded answers. He owed me," Ram said.

Neve frowned. "Owed?"

Willow put a reassuring hand on Ram's massive biceps and explained, "Javier never told the cops. After the authorities arrested Mascolo, Javier thought it no longer mattered. He told us that someone had called while Ram was missing, asking for the Álvarez piece of a treasure map. The caller offered the return of his son for the piece of the map. Javier said he'd heard of such a relic in passing, something his great-grandmother had mentioned when he was a kid. Javier told the caller he didn't know where to find a piece of a treasure map. The cops were all Zhangs during the Dark Summer, and Javier didn't trust the Zhangs. For all he knew, if someone in

SX was looking for treasure, the Zhangs were as likely to be behind the kidnappings as anyone. Instead, Javier approached Miguel Álvarez, Anna's father, and asked if he knew about a map. Miguel said he also received a phone call and knew no more about a map than Javier. They agreed that the SXPD would not offer any help. They looked for the Álvarez piece of the map around Old Mat, but they found nothing."

Neve's hands closed into frustrated fists. "That's it? That corroborates that the abductions connect to the piece of the map, but it's still a dead end, Will."

"I wouldn't be skulking around a bunch of statues of dead people if I didn't have more than that, sis," Willow said with a brilliant grin.

Neve smiled back. Of course, Willow always saved the best tidbit for last.

Willow continued, "Javier pointed at the lucha libre on the television. He told us, 'I didn't realize it then, but I think Miguel was lying. Acting. Like the masked wrestlers. It looks real enough, but it isn't the truth. That's how I felt about Miguel looking for the map.' He realized years later that Miguel knew more than he'd told Javier."

"Did you talk to Miguel?"

"Miguel Álvarez is dead," Ram stated.

"He died the year after the Dark Summer," Willow explained. "But he knew something. He's the next clue."

"Dead men tell no tales, Will," Neve quoted.

Willow pointed at the sky like a detective punctuating a valuable clue. "But Miguel told somebody something when he was alive. I guarantee it. Someone told him the secret. And Miguel passed it along. I will find out who."

Neve believed it. Her sister was persistent. She would get to the truth.

Willow and Ram left. Neve checked the time. She pursued her own avenue of investigation. Neve could use her pending nuptials as a good reason to stop and see Zephyr and her future mother-in-law. She needed a good reason to spy within the walls of the family estate, and Grandame Graham was exceptionally perceptive on potential subterfuge. There wasn't a wiser woman in all of SX.

Neve drove to Graham Manor. She hadn't told Bryce about the Crossing Guard snooping behind the scenes regarding multiple avenues of investigation. Neve had different reasons for staying silent on the subject, especially after keeping the Juliets' fake deaths a secret from Bryce. This time, she would tell him as soon as the burden of further turmoil in SX passed. Right now, Bryce's plate was overflowing. Naomi agreed with the decision to keep Bryce out of this for now. Neve would tell him after the special election.

Neve expected several other family members to be there besides Grandame. Amanda, Zephyr, and hopefully one more Graham.

She knew Dad wouldn't be there. He was meeting her mom at Halloweather's to hash out some marital woes. Neve had threatened her mother by saying she would tell her father about the extramarital affair between "Jackie Salem" and Martin Montgomery. Her mom had taken reclaiming her former life to a new level. Neve wouldn't stand to see her mother make her father a cuckold any longer.

Zephyr answered the door and gave Neve a tight bear hug that squeezed the air out of her lungs. Bryce's sister was remarkably strong for a girl the size and shape of a twig. She wore a smile that practically touched each side of her poofy head of hair, shaped like a black cloud of cotton candy around her face. Her eyes glittered with her innate happiness and were glazed over with a little herbal twist.

"Can we look at dresses?" Zephyr asked, bouncing on the balls of her feet.

Neve and Bryce had decided the members of the wedding

party would be Zephyr, Willow, Cyprus, and the Caesars, but they hadn't sorted who was wearing dresses on Neve's side and who would don suits on Bryce's. Ariel would never stand up for Neve. Cy already expressed excitement about rocking a tux. Zephyr obviously wanted a dress, so she would be on Neve's side. Bryce would have to choose the best man from among the six female Caesars. Neve and Bryce had yet to sort out the rest.

"Of course! I'm here to get your advice," Neve said, which was true. But she also had other reasons for being there. "Is your mother around?"

Amanda Graham entered the room as if Neve had summoned her by name. She looked like a fairy godmother today, dressed in a costume that might have once been part of a Cinderella exhibit at one of the Orlando attractions. What might've been charming thirty years ago appeared unconventional on a woman closer to a senior citizen than a senior prom attendee. Neve raised an eyebrow, but Zephyr flashed her a rare, dark look that warned Neve not to ask.

"Nevada," Amanda said, enunciating Neve's name with a British flair. Neve had limited exposure to Bryce's mother thus far since she revealed she'd returned to SX, but her previous interactions had never indicated an accent. "My dear, are you here to make selections for the wedding ceremony?"

Neve felt like she'd accidentally time-traveled to an era of aristocracy and serfs instead of surfboards and flip-flops. Zephyr rolled her eyes behind her mother's cartoony antics. Neve had always thought Zephyr was a bit strange. Free-spirited with a hippie-chick vibe. Now, Neve understood a little where the unconventional personality came from. Bryce was very different from the two women. Had his Montgomery genes blocked the quirkiness of Amanda's influence, or did his circle of Caesar sibs counteract the effects of his oddball upbringing?

"Yes, I'd love your input," Neve said. "We're looking at dresses, flowers, and music. I need to make some decisions before the whole ceremony sneaks up on me."

The ladies reviewed a long list of possibilities, and the conversation remained fairly typical for the most part. Amanda suggested a horse and carriage deliver Neve and Bryce to the venue, but Neve tabled the idea until Bryce could officially nix it. After narrowing down selections for flowers, food, and a short list of possible bridesmaid dresses, Neve excused herself for the bathroom as Zephyr and Amanda argued over musical selections.

Neve wanted to ask Conner some questions. One of the items on her list was the strange timing of Conner's arrival. He arrived in SX during the biggest storm to ever hit Salem Shores. Why had he come to town when everyone else was evacuating? What was he up to besides ruining Ariel's marriage?

Conner sounded so much like Bryce when she heard his voice. He was talking to someone in one of the many auxiliary rooms. Neve lost track of whether it was an office, a den, or a library. She approached quietly, purposefully eavesdropping, hoping to catch a clue to what Conner was up to. Was he speaking to Grandame, or maybe Tom was trying to get information from him?

The other person in the room wasn't Grandame. It was a man. He didn't sound like Tom.

The stranger said, "Everything is going to plan. We need everyone in place if it's going to work."

Conner replied in a confident tone uncannily like Bryce's, "Most of the players are already on the board. Kennedy came back with Jackson Montgomery and Acindina Álvarez."

"We need to keep that Montgomery boy away from her. He's not a part of the plan."

"I'll take care of it. The Grahams have waited too long to return to power. This is our chance to make things right."

The stranger chuckled, pleased. "The other families have ruined this town for too damn long. We're going to put this place back together the Graham way. I trust you'll make sure nothing gets in our way."

"Nothing," Conner emphasized. "I promise, Father."

Neve's eyes grew wide. She scurried away before anyone caught her eavesdropping. Julian Graham left Salem Crossing many years ago. Now he's back?

Chapter Thirteen

HOLIDAYS WITH THE MONTGOMERYS

Every December, the Montgomery family gathered exactly twelve days before Christmas to decorate the tree. A song played in the background on a loop, and *five golden rings* stretched into eternity. The event encompassed an entire day. There would be food from morning till evening, libations after lunch, decorating in the afternoon, and usually, the get-together would descend into fighting long before midnight.

Magdalene Montgomery followed tradition. The whole of Salem Crossing was obsessed with customs. The six families of SX had been doing the same thing repeatedly in many ways since the town's inception. Animosities ran between families simply because that was how it had always been. Montgomerys versus Salems, Salems versus Zhangs, the Álvarezes against everyone. From the town's rampant rivalries to the Montgomery ritual day of decorating to Magdalene's personal practice of turning a blind eye, this place reeked of institutionalism at every level.

"Grab the box of ornaments out of the craft room, will you, Jackson?" Magdalene asked.

Jackson stared out the large picture window framing the

twelve-foot fir Martin had instructed his employees to pick up and deliver to the house. Jackson and Samantha managed to mount the tree in the stand and position it perfectly. Magdalene fussed with flocking the branches while the rest dispersed around the great living room, mostly staring at their phones. Jackson had the same vacant look on his face as everyone else in the room, but his interest focused through the window rather than on the glass of an electronic screen.

Jackson ignored her.

"Your mother asked you to do something, Jackson," Martin interjected in a booming voice without looking up from his device.

Jackson snapped out of his reverie at his father's command, like a trained dog. Tradition borne of quick retribution.

"I'm sorry, Mother. What was that?" Jackson said, turning toward her.

"The box of decorations. The one with the ornaments labeled with the family names. I was working on their restoration in the craft room. Will you get them for me?" Magdalene repeated.

"On it," Jackson said, leaving the room.

Jackson had been acting differently lately. Normally, he treated the family as a burden, doing so reluctantly. Tradition dictated that he be there every year for decoration day, but he'd always grumbled and glowered through the festivities. Magdalene had tried harder when the kids were young, attempting to make the day a fun and festive occasion, but now she accepted that most traditions were endured rather than enjoyed. Other than having his head in the clouds today, Jackson almost seemed...happy.

Damn, that meant he must be in love.

Samantha knew everything about everyone in SX. Her little food truck allowed her to intercept some juicy gossip around town. When she returned before Jackson with a plate of her homemade sugar cookies, Magdalene cornered her daughter on the opposite side of the room where the rest of the family congregated.

"What's the weird vibe about?" Magdalene whispered.

A stricken look crossed Samantha's face, and Magdalene realized Samantha thought she was talking about her. Magdalene hadn't even noticed Samantha acting oddly. Her daughter was the Montgomery who least fit in. Magdalene felt like the Caesars raised themselves and were more connected to one another than their flesh and blood. Samantha's personal life had always eluded Magdalene.

"What do you mean?" Samantha asked.

"Jackson has been acting odd lately. Is he seeing someone new?" Magdalene committed to rooting out one child's secrets before delving into another's.

Samantha looked relieved at the change of subject. What was she hiding then? Her daughter glanced at Jackson as he reentered the room and placed the box of ornaments near the tree. Samantha shook her head.

"If he is, he's sneaking around town and keeping her a secret," Samantha replied.

Magdalene looked at her son. Samantha phrased the answer obliquely. She didn't deny that she knew something. What were these two hiding?

"Are you bringing anyone to Christmas dinner this year, Samantha?" Magdalene asked, changing the topic and catching her daughter off guard.

Samantha's mouth formed a thin line, the expression of someone holding something back.

"I don't have anyone I'd want to subject to Christmas dinner with the Montgomerys," Samantha dodged.

Magdalene frowned. "What's that supposed to mean?"

"I'm saying you'd need to date someone for a couple of

years before they were ready for the big leagues. You don't start right off juggling with flaming knives, y'know."

"We're flaming knives?"

"Being too close to this family is dangerous, Mother."

Samantha walked away. None of her children intended to bring a guest for Christmas dinner. Besides Jackson and Samantha, Riley's last relationship was with a married man, and a Zhang, no less. Carter sat on a chair in the corner of the room, bandaged and healing from gunshot wounds. He hadn't had time to meet anyone since prison, and Magdalene didn't want him bringing home anyone he'd met while locked up.

Another boring holiday with only blood relatives. Well, maybe not entirely boring.

Magdalene went to the box of ornaments. The Montgomerys had a tradition going back to Martin's mother's early days. She had inscribed the names of the immediate family on big red bulbs to hang on the tree. The practice continued as the family grew. Martin and his siblings, then Martin's children.

As the inheritor of the Montgomery traditional home, Martin had become the keeper of the Montgomery family way. The original ornaments were more than half a century old, fragile glass globes that Magdalene handled carefully. The first two featured the names Jefferson and Candace, Martin's mother and father. Magdalene hung them on a lower branch. Normally, both of them would be here to dispense decorations, but their cruise wouldn't return for another week. Apparently, certain rites had an expiration date after retirement.

Magdalene pulled out the globes with her and Martin's names and asked. "Riley, can you climb the ladder and start hanging these from the top? You know how your father likes his near the star."

Jackson had already strung the lights and positioned the star. Other family heirlooms passed down through generations included ornaments in the shape of angels, snowflakes, and Baby Jesus. One special heirloom was an antique wooden manger of unknown origin. The personalized red bulbs were the last element added to the tree. Once upon a time, the kids eagerly and harrowingly hung the ornaments on the limbs. Now, Magdalene had to twist Riley's arm to get her to help.

Riley hung her parents' bulbs on the tree, where Martin liked them. Martin took time from scrolling on his screen to appreciate the position of his ornament. He liked things just the way he wanted and refused to be questioned. That was a tradition in the Montgomery household. Martin was king, and the rest obeyed his command.

Riley added a bulb for Amara, Martin's sister, who'd passed away twenty-three years ago. Magdalene handed Riley a new bulb for Clover, the illegitimate cousin no one had known existed for the past two decades. She placed it too low, and Samantha fussed after her, moving it to another bough.

Martin's brother, Malcolm, had a bulb, but he'd taken that with him decades ago when he left SX. If Malcolm did a Christmas tree, he would have the bulbs for his offspring.

"Here's me," Riley exclaimed as Magdalene handed her her own bulb.

It brought a smile to Riley's face. Doing the same things year after year could bring comfort. Nostalgia was the warm blanket on a cold December night. As Riley stared at the big red bulb, Magdalene saw the memories of the previous decorating years unlock. Riley placed it on a limb with great reverence. Riley, normally capricious and selfish, seemed to feel the weight of connection to something grander. A task repeated for half a century.

"Carter, are you up to placing your bulb on the tree?" Magdalene asked.

"I've missed enough chances," Carter said, struggling slowly to get to his feet. No one offered help. They all knew better. He shuffled across the room, accepted the bulb from her, and stood steady enough to hang it on a mid-range bough. He shuffled back and returned to his place in the chair.

Samantha and Jackson stepped up. Magdalene handed each of them their personalized ornament. Samantha studied the tree, choosing the perfect position between Magdalene's, Martin's, Carter's, and Riley's. Jackson absentmindedly dropped the hook onto the nearest branch and returned to his thoughts.

Damn it, he *is* in love, Magdalene thought.

The Montgomery name carried a curse for anyone in love. Happiness and romance were ever at odds in this family. The Montgomerys lusted after exactly the wrong partners, repeatedly. Detestable relationships full of desire turned to heartache, and then to hatred. Magdalene didn't know one goddamned happy ever after where the prince or princess bore the Montgomery moniker.

Four children and all single. The other five families in SX had recently enjoyed weddings. Ariel Álvarez and Robert Ryan were married. The Juliets had secretly tied the knot—A Salem and a Zhang. Bryce Graham was engaged to the Noble girl, who turned out to have connections to Salems and Álvarezes. Yet true love remained only a fairy tale for Samantha, Carter, Riley, and Jackson, as it had been for the Montgomerys for generations.

Tradition. Wash-rinse-repeat. Doing the same fucking thing too many times over.

Samantha stood back, admiring the decorated tree. She believed it was complete and reviewed the handiwork, moving a bulb here and an ornament there until everything became balanced to her liking. But there was no true equilibrium. There was nothing neat and tidy about the Montgomery family.

"Riley, we aren't done with the bulbs yet," Magdalene said.

They should've been. Magdalene wasn't a grandmother. Riley stared and blinked. She didn't understand her last words. Magdalene pulled another red bulb from the box. One she'd created yesterday in her craft room. The embossed name faced away from Riley.

"We don't have anyone else who needs an ornament, Mother," Riley said, perplexed.

"And yet, I'm holding this," Magdalene said, nodding at the red globe with the answer to Riley's unsaid question in her outstretched hand. "Will you do the honors?"

Riley eyed her suspiciously as she took a hesitant step forward. Riley paused. She looked at her, then over at her father, who was now paying attention. His phone dangled uselessly in his right hand. Magdalene had piqued the interest of the whole audience in the room.

Jackson arrived at Riley's side as if he could somehow protect her from the future. The future wasn't the problem. Everything in the past led to this moment.

Martin eyed Magdalene suspiciously. He searched her expression for the truth, but they had established a foundation of lies long ago. Her poker face equaled the most stoic ancestors of old. Strong, proud Samuel Montgomery, original founder and legendarily cool, would have considered Magdalene worthy of her surname despite being married into the family.

"What are you up to, Magda?" Martin murmured.

"Tradition. The names of *all* your Montgomery line go on the family tree, Martin."

Riley took the ornament and looked at the name on it. She frowned. She looked as confused as Magdalene felt when

Simmer Salem sat her down the previous night and spilled her secrets. Simmer cornered Magdalene at Kenny's Koffee. Simmer said she had an epiphany after Auberon Fox saved her life. She wanted to reveal important information she'd uncovered and told her, "There are plenty of assholes in SX, Magdalene, but you're one of the few good people. I'm trying to make some things right."

Riley turned the bulb so her family could see. "Whose sweetheart is this referring to? Jax have a new girlfriend?"

Jackson's flinching reaction confirmed Magdalene's suspicions. Jackson was sneaking around with a woman.

"It's not a pet name. It's a given name," Magdalene said.

"Sweetheart Salem?" Samantha asked with a raised eyebrow. Samantha shot a surprised and accusatory glare at Jackson. "You knocked up Makenna?"

"No. I never...I didn't..." Jackson stammered.

"It wasn't Jackson," Magdalene said.

Riley's eyes went to Carter next. "Conjugal prison visit?"

Magdalene revealed the answer. "She's your half-sister, Riley."

All four of Magdalene's offspring glared at their father. Martin sat resolutely in his seat, meeting their stares as he had faced countless enemies innumerable times across negotiating tables. Magdalene had confronted him with knowledge of a bastard child, and he shrugged it off as if it were a simple misunderstanding. Magdalene could not tell if he was angry, astonished, or plotting revenge.

The Christmas song, as old as time, played repeatedly in the background. Riley had been licking a candy cane, and the scent of peppermint floated in the air. Fake snow surrounded a manger scene on the fireplace mantle. Gifts piled five high near the tree, ready for Riley to arrange beneath the boughs as soon as someone placed the last ornament.

Magdalene took the personalized red bulb back from

Riley and hung it equidistant between Jackson and Samantha's ornaments, front and center. The family stared in stunned silence as the word "Sweetheart" took its place among the rest of the Montgomerys. Martin glared from across the room.

"That's not all. I've been very busy crafting all night. Our family keeps growing by the second," Magdalene announced.

She pulled another surprise from the box. This one represented Damien Halloweather. Jackson and Carter didn't look surprised, so they already knew, Magdalene thought angrily, and kept the truth from me, but the girls' mouths hit the floor. Samantha shook her head, as if she were living in a bad dream. Riley approached her mother as if Magdalene were holding a ticking time bomb. Judging by Martin's expression, Riley might be right.

"Damien's our...brother?" Samantha stuttered.

Samantha heard a lot of gossip around town with her food truck, and she ought not be too surprised at the secret lives of any SXers, yet she appeared gobsmacked by her father's double infidelities. If she only knew that her mother wasn't done with the surprises yet.

"A killer for a brother, I guess I'm not the worst Montgomery anymore," Carter muttered from his chair.

Magdalene shook her head. "You never were." If Martin understood that she was talking about him, he didn't show it.

"You had an affair with Elizabeth Halloweather?" Riley managed to utter.

Samantha gaped at Martin. "Is this true, Daddy?"

Daddy. As if she were eight, and Martin had just revealed there was no such thing as Santa. The truth stunned Magdalene's children into dumbfounded comments. Only Carter appeared nonplused as he had seen worse in prison.

Magdalene placed the red ornament between Carter and Clover's bulbs. Samantha didn't even bother to come over to rearrange. Magdalene didn't know if the revelations had stunned Samantha into inaction or if she waited to see how many more surprises her mother revealed before she sorted out the bulbs.

"One more," Magdalene announced, removing the last ornament from the box. She concealed the name embossed on the red globe. Everyone watched anxiously. This was the biggest event that rocked the Montgomery household since Carter left for prison. But for these crimes and misdemeanors, Martin's sentence would be life without parole.

Magdalene made sure the name faced Samantha when she revealed the last bastard. "Bryce." An audible intake of air greeted the surprise. Even Martin finally reacted. His bottom jaw unhinged as his eyes widened in utter shock. The motherfucker knew about Sweetheart, and maybe he knew about Damien, but he had no idea about Bryce.

"No." He stood and pointed at the bulb. "That's not true."

The reaction surprised Magdalene. He looked like a man who witnessed something impossible appear right before his eyes, like invading aliens or a haunting ghost.

"I've seen documentation. There's irrefutable proof," Magdalene said.

"Anyone can forge paperwork. That's a goddamned lie," Martin shouted, snatching the ornament, and threw it against the far wall, where it shattered into a million pieces. His face was sweaty, and his bulging eyes had a maniacal glint. Magdalene half-expected him to throw his head back and cackle like a madman.

Magdalene glared at him. "You admit to two and refuse the third? No matter. Two is enough."

The children backed away as Magdalene stood in front of her husband. He was usually a few inches taller than she, but she wore heels for the special occasion, as she did every year.

Tradition. She met him eye to eye. He ranked runner-up only to Tessa Salem and Millie Zhang in SX for scariest badasses, but Magdalene wasn't afraid. She was pissed.

Montgomery men had cheated on their wives since the founding of the town. Rumor suggested Samuel Montgomery fathered bastards up and down the Treasure Coast. Martin was simply the latest in a long line of lotharios. But tradition ended today. Habits were made to be broken.

"No more. You get your bitches settled, and you bring your personal business in-house. You're not doing this anymore." Magdalene pointed her finger at the tree and the shattered bulb on the floor. "You want to be mayor, then these secrets need to stay under wraps. And I won't abide one more mistress, Martin Montgomery. You have till the end of the year to get your affairs straightened out."

"Or else?" Martin asked, standing firmly in place.

"You know what I'm capable of," Magdalene said. "The Snow Ball is a rite of passage. It signifies unity and rebirth. That's the start of your second chance, Martin. Your last chance. It's an appropriate venue to start all over together. After all, it's an SX tradition."

Chapter Fourteen

Neve hadn't wanted to burden Bryce with extra crises while he was rebuilding Salem Crossing and waiting for the election for a co-mayor to help him out, but after she discovered Julian Graham was back in town and maybe up to no good, Neve needed another Graham on her side. She considered her father, but she didn't trust herself not to tell him about her mom's affair with Martin Montgomery. Neither Willow nor Cyprus knew any more about Julian Graham than Neve did. Grandame? Amanda? Tom? Zephyr? Who else might be part of Julian's plans?

She trusted Bryce. She needed his help.

Neve was nervous about revealing the Crossing Guard to Bryce and showing him her list of mysteries the group worked to solve. He agreed to arrive early and be home in time for Neve to make dinner and enjoy it on the lanai overlooking the Atlantic. The December breeze was chilly, but Neve still found the novelty of eating outside near the holidays irresistible. She picked at her dessert, and Bryce lovingly watched.

"God, I miss seeing you more than a few minutes here and there," Bryce said, a tired smile across his face.

"The special election is coming up fast. It'll be better once you have help."

"Depends on who wins. Martin might be as much trouble as he is useful."

"He's your father. It would be a good way to get to know him better."

"I might not like learning any more about Martin Montgomery than I already know."

Neve didn't want to talk about that side of Bryce's lineage. The Montgomerys weren't the ones stirring up trouble at the moment. She worried the Grahams, perpetually passive in all things Salem Crossing, suddenly sounded poised to take point in the city's reconstruction. One more mystery in an avalanche of enigmas.

"Ready to go inside?"

Bryce took it the wrong way and got that smoldering look on his face. "I'm ready for another kind of dessert."

Neve grinned back. "We'll get to that. First, I need to show you something."

She stood, grabbed her dish in one hand, and led him inside with the other. They left their dishes at the sink, and Neve took Bryce into the living area. Between two shuttered windows, drapes covered a wide section of the wall. Bryce frowned. He knew as well as Neve that the curtains didn't cover another window. Neve stood in front of the pleats like someone introducing the cast of tonight's play.

Neve took a deep breath. "I put together a team. We're following up on all the weird things around SX."

"Team? Like detectives?"

Neve shrugged. "Sort of. Willow's on the beat. She has a natural aptitude for that sort of thing. Your cousin, Tom, too. He's got sources in the FBI that can help."

Bryce didn't say anything for a moment. He stared at the drapes like they covered the prize behind curtain number one. Maybe he wanted to choose option number two instead, the door to the bedroom and uncomplicated sex with Neve. How much more before the cascade of bullshit in SX buried him? Maybe he didn't want to be any part of the Crossing Guard.

"Who else is on your team?" Bryce asked instead, neither an endorsement nor opposition.

"Ram's along for insight into the Dark Summer. And to keep his eye on Will."

"I bet he is," Bryce said, a playful smirk replacing his serious face. Neve had told him about Willow, Ram, and Cin's hot-and-heavy threesome. "I feel better with Willow poking into dark places if Ramón is along for the ride."

Neve nodded. "Naomi's also helping."

Bryce seemed pleased. "She needed to move forward. Thanks for including her."

"It's about healing as well as helping. She knows the islands offshore, and we're looking into some hinky shenanigans along the chain of islands."

"Hinky shenanigans? Is that official detective terminology?" Bryce teased, stepping closer to Neve.

"As official as my Crossing Guard badge."

"I can deputize you as a municipal officer. That comes with a badge." Bryce leaned into her personal space.

"Does it include handcuffs?" Neve winked, turning her face toward his at an angle.

"Depends on if you pass the training seminar." Bryce moved closer, his lips near enough to brush against hers, and sent shivers up her spine.

"Mr. Graham, you are dangerously close to misdirecting my mission."

"Future Mrs. Graham, I plan on taking your mission in every direction."

They kissed. This was a prelude to something that might

take them long into the night. But then they'd be too exhausted to revisit the list. With tremendous effort, Neve disengaged and stepped back. She held up a finger, panting like a dog and catching her breath. Cooling off.

"First, this," Neve said.

Bryce nodded, still smiling. Neve knew what came next would wipe that grin off his handsome face.

"The last person on the team is Simmer Salem," Neve said.

And, as predicted, Bryce's expression collapsed like a house of cards in an earthquake. His brow wrinkled, not in anger but concern.

"You can't trust Simmeron."

"She's trying to redeem herself, Bryce. After Auberon sacrificed his life to save her, she decided to use everything she knows to do some good."

Bryce opened a shutter and stared out the window, saying nothing. Bryce had a lot on his mind. Now, he had more.

"She only cares about herself." Bryce turned his gaze to her. "Be careful about sharing too many secrets with her. A leopard never changes their spots."

Neve thought about her mother pretending to be someone she wasn't for the last twenty-three years. As soon as she returned to SX, she slipped back into her former habits. Her mom glided around town as a Salem as effortlessly as if she'd never left. After spending half a lifetime in Iowa and raising a family, Maggie Noble resumed being Jackie Salem overnight. Bryce might be right. People don't change.

Neve grabbed the edge of the drapes. "I don't trust many people in SX. That's why I need you. I know you're busy, but I can't trust anyone else about this."

"Sounds serious."

"Maybe. I need your take."

Neve drew the curtains back, revealing her list.

1. *Why did Damien Halloweather kill Domino Salem?*
2. *What is the real reason behind the Dark Summer kidnappings?*
3. *Who kidnapped the Juliets and why?*
4. *What is the Iblīs family up to?*
5. *Who is Conner Graham?*
6. *Why did Helen Ryan switch the babies at birth?*
7. *Is there an ancient map to lost treasure?*

Bryce took time reading the list. She watched as he skimmed the questions, some several times over, before he reread the whole list one last time, top to bottom. He gazed out the window again as if longing for anyplace other than SX. Did he regret coming home? Was he imagining being gone again, run off like he had ten years ago?

Neve continued, "We have a good handle on these questions. The team is making headway on the list. We meet again in a couple of days to update our progress."

"The only thing on the list I can offer unique insight into is Conner Graham. Conner's father is Julian Graham. Julian Graham is my grandfather, but I've never met the man. He left during the great Graham exodus, and my mother hasn't seen him since. Like Martin Montgomery or Nolan Salem, Julian spread wild oats across the Florida peninsula."

"Julian," Neve repeated. She added an item to the list. "I want to talk about Julian Graham."

8. *What is Julian Graham up to?*

Bryce frowned. "Grandame disowned Julian. The family has been shattered and scattered for thirty, forty years."

"What if I told you Julian Graham was at the Graham Manor earlier? I overheard him talking to Conner."

Bryce was genuinely surprised. Usually reserved and able to keep his feelings incognito, shock registered in his eyes. Then, a shadow drew across his face. With all the people coming back to SX lately, Bryce himself and Neve's whole family among them, he seemed inexplicably perturbed by the return of Julian Graham.

Neve elaborated, "It was an intense conversation. Julian said there was a plan. He said the Grahams were going to rebuild SX their way."

"What does that mean?"

Neve shrugged. "Julian told Conner that the other families have ruined this town for too long."

"It took all six families to get us into this mess. If my grandfather hadn't run away like a coward all those long years ago, the Grahams might've been able to help before things got so bad."

Neve nodded. The sanctimonious tone in Julian's voice irritated her the more she thought about it. He sounded like a stereotypical cowboy riding in on a white horse to save the day, but maybe the town wouldn't need saving if the Grahams hadn't turned their backs on SX for decades. She was glad Bryce shared the same reaction. She had not liked the tone of Julian and Conner's conversation.

"Have you ever heard of someone named Kennedy?" Neve curiously asked.

"First name?"

"I assume it's a Graham."

"Male or female?"

"They referred to the person as 'her.'"

Bryce frowned while thinking, tapping his foot. "I don't think so."

"Whoever Kennedy is, Julian doesn't want him or her near Jax."

"What does Jackson have to do with this?"

"He was with Cin. Somewhere. Conner said Kennedy returned to town with Jax and Cin. Julian was more interested in Cin. He wanted Jax out of the picture."

Bryce paced back and forth in front of the board. "How did Acindina get mixed up in all this?"

"How does Cin get mixed up in all the shit that happens in this town?" Neve said with an exasperated smirk. "That girl can find trouble in a nunnery."

"We need to talk to Cin and learn more about this Kennedy person. If Kennedy is another Graham, my relatives are becoming legion."

"Julian said most of the players are already in SX. A lot of Grahams have returned in the last few weeks. Conner's return must connect to Julian crawling out of the woodwork." Neve extended her pointer to count off one.

Bryce pivoted to face Neve and lifted two fingers to add to Neve's. "My mother showed up, as well. Tomás, too."

"My dad."

Bryce met her gaze. "Me."

"You're not on my list of suspects, Bryce."

"But maybe I should be. I came back and ran for mayor. Won in a landslide. Took over the town. If Julian is planning some kind of coup in Salem Crossing, it makes sense to take control of the mayor's office. How do you know I'm not a pawn in my grandfather's mad scheme?"

Neve folded herself into his arms, and they embraced. "Because I trust you with my heart, my soul, my everything, Bryce Graham. I would know if you were planning some nefarious takeover."

Bryce squeezed her tightly. "What if I don't know I'm a pawn?"

Neve snuggled closer. She had burdened him with even more things to occupy his mind. She felt she had to hold him tightly so that Bryce didn't shatter into pieces. How many directions could one man be pulled before he broke apart? Neve needed to learn more soon because the questions were becoming overwhelming while the answers remained elusive. The list of mysteries for the Crossing Guard to address kept growing, and they weren't removing anything from their list.

Neve had enough of conspiracies for tonight. "That's enough about the Grahams for tonight. I'll track down Jax and Cin as soon as I can. Until then, you were talking about handcuffs?"

Her head rested against his chest, and she felt his mischievous grin on the top of her head. His hand slipped down to her waist, and he pulled her against him. She moved her head so her mouth could find his lips. They kissed. The detour had led them right back to where they'd left off. After a while, Bryce scooped her into his arms and carried her into the bedroom. He drew a badge on her naked breast with an erasable marker he'd brought from her whiteboard listing multiple mysteries. That was enough to certify her in using handcuffs, which she proved to be a natural at using to maximum effect.

Chapter Fifteen

ARIEL ÁLVAREZ

Ariel used to watch cop shows with her cousin Rico when Rico's mother babysat on evenings when her mother worked late. Rico would watch intently, trying to figure out every procedure the detectives employed to solve mysteries and catch the bad guys. Ariel couldn't help but wonder how boring the whole process seemed, and she watched because there was usually a romantic subplot that made her swoon.

Now, she was stuck in a bad cop show with no chance of a romantic subplot. Juliet Salem certainly was pretty, blonde, and had the perfect bod for an officer's conquest, but she wasn't Ariel's type. And while Ariel had all the requisite body parts to attract Juliet, it was no secret that Juliet would rather romance a Lamborghini than Ariel Álvarez. They were here for a stakeout, not an unexpected meet-cute.

"Fuck, Ariel, this is boring as shit." Juliet turned to face her in the seat. "Why didn't you ask someone else?"

"I did ask someone else," Ariel snapped, not taking her eyes away from the motel. "I left a message for Sammy, and she blew me off."

"That's cuz she's pissed at you."

Ariel gripped the steering wheel angrily. "Why the hell is she mad at me? I didn't do anything to her."

"Do I look like I'm privy to Samantha Montgomery's secrets? Ask Bryce."

Mention of Bryce took the edge off her percolating anger. "Bryce is too busy. I asked him to do this stakeout before I asked Sammy, but he didn't have time."

Juliet's perfect blonde brows bunched along her tanned forehead. "So, I'm your third choice?"

Ariel didn't want Juliet storming off in the middle of the stakeout. "Well, you are still a great choice because you have experience with stakeouts. I'm sure you learned something when you helped Delilah spy on Tom Graham."

Juliet frowned. "That wasn't me. That was Naomi."

"No, I'm pretty sure that was you."

Juliet fumed. So much for defusing the situation. "I was fucking deceased at the time, Ariel. I was baking cookies in Iowa and trying to say 'pop' instead of 'soda.' I wasn't on a stakeout with Delilah. Besides, I don't have the patience to sit in a car with Lilah for more than five minutes. She would've ended up dead."

"Hell, then I meant to ask Naomi, not you."

Juliet shook her head, exasperated. "Jesus Christ, I didn't even need to be here. You're lucky I felt so bad for making you think I was dead, or I would've ditched you like Sammy and Bryce did."

"I could've asked JZ," Ariel stated. She wanted to follow up on Juliet Zhang acting weird lately. She needed to run her concerns by Juliet Salem. "Have you noticed lately she's been acting str—"

"There." Juliet pointed ahead, out the heavily tinted windshield that no one could see inside. "Someone's coming out."

Leira stepped out of room 112. A man emerged from

111. He faced Leira, with the left side of his face in profile toward Ariel and Juliet. Scars ravaged his flesh—the auburn tone turned a murky, muddy color, with ropes of ruined skin from his neck to his crown. His scalp was shiny, and his ear was mostly a hole featuring slight ridges like a fossil of something long gone. But the left eye was fine, and Ariel thought she recognized something familiar.

Leira and the dude from room 111 started talking to each other, the scarred man leaning on the wall in a blatant attempt to woo her. Ariel tried to read Leira's lips. She picked out a few words—"Hallie," "birthday," and "holidays."

"Damn, Ariel, I don't remember Leira looking like she could be your long-lost sister. You sure Maria didn't have twins, and she shipped one off?"

Ariel held back a physical response, preferring to avoid a catfight in tight quarters. Instead, she retorted through gritted teeth, "You said the same thing when we were sixteen, Juliet. I told your white ass back then, we don't all look alike just because we're Latina."

Juliet ignored the insult. "Without the pink hair, piercings, and tats, Leira looks more like you than Cin does. Maybe you're sistehs from different misses?"

Ariel rolled her eyes. "Please don't talk anymore."

"You're pissed because you might secretly be siblings, and Bryce dated her and not you."

"I see dying didn't cure you of being a bitch," Ariel said, angry she'd accidentally picked Juliet instead of Naomi. At least Naomi was still depressed about her boyfriend dying and mostly remained mute.

"Bitch is what we both do, Ariel. You and I give the Caesars an edge."

"Sometimes you're over the edge, Juliet." Ariel watched the couple flirt. Then the guy turned toward where Ariel and Juliet were spying. He couldn't see them through the tinted glass, but it revealed his entire face. Only half his head featured scars, like a villain from one of the comic books Rico used to read during commercial breaks while watching the cop shows. The undamaged right side was handsome, full of luxurious black hair, and smooth, unblemished brown skin. Ariel wasn't sure what she was seeing. Then he turned again, showing the scars.

"Did you see that?" Ariel asked Juliet.

Juliet studied the dude like an abstract painting at an art museum. "He's half scarred, half fine as fuck."

"Didn't he look like...like Bryce?"

Juliet tilted her head to one side as if trying to make sense of the idiosyncrasy. "Is that Conner? The one you fucked?"

Ariel stopped herself from backhanding her Caesar sister. It wouldn't be the first time she slapped the hell out of Juliet Salem, but it probably wouldn't be a good idea to break the bitch's nose on a stakeout.

"You don't need to elaborate on which Conner you're talking about, Juliet. And that's not him. Conner didn't have scars. But the undamaged half of this guy looks more like Bryce than Conner."

Then Leira and the scarred stranger turned, spinning around so Leira was closer to room 111. The damaged doppelganger faced the other way, his marred side hidden, and it looked like Bryce was talking with Leira, the couple who had been the bane of Ariel's existence ten years ago, now time-traveled to torment her present. Even the way he smiled mirrored Bryce.

"Now that's fucking freaky," Juliet said like the scene was an impressive special effect in a sci-fi film.

The women watched the two young people across the street perform the familiar mating dance that's been around much longer than SX. Ariel felt like she was watching an alternate-world version of her life. A universe where Ariel

Álvarez and Bryce Graham found a happily ever after. Her heart raced at the thought, as she watched the Bryce-twin lean in and kiss Leira, their initial embrace turning steamy. Ariel wanted to keep watching, as if she could create a memory of herself that had never really happened. Instead, Leira led the Bryce-twin into his motel room and closed the door behind them.

"Show's over," Juliet said, stretching like a cat who'd gotten its fill of sun. "That kinda revved my engines. Take me home to my wife. Juliet might be in for some afternoon delight."

Ariel wasn't ready to gloss over the idea of multiple duplicates of their Caesar brother suddenly appearing around town. "What do you think this means? There's another Bryce lookalike in SX."

"I don't think you'll mistake that guy for Bryce with those scars, Ary. Keep it in your pants. I'm sure it's a coincidence."

Ariel wished she'd brought anyone else along. Even Delilah would have offered more thoughtful insight. "Someone who looks like me with someone who looks like Bryce? Together? A coincidence?"

"This town has been inbreeding for a hundred years. We have a limited gene pool. I'm surprised we don't all look like Bryce," Juliet dismissed.

Ariel started driving toward the Ryan section of town. The Juliets rented a lovely condo that avoided any hurricane damage. They couldn't stay along Salem Shores or in the Zhang neighborhood, as neither family accepted the Juliets' unholy union. Millie Zhang and Tessa Salem agreed on one thing: their daughters shouldn't be married. Not even their fake deaths and subsequent resurrection could erase the animosity over their marriage.

"Everything okay with JZ?" Ariel asked, returning to the subject Juliet had ditched before.

Juliet frowned as if someone had accused her of something she had done and was trying to play it off with feigned ignorance. "What do you mean?"

"She's been acting off since she rode back into SX on a motorcycle."

"I think of Delilah when you say 'acting off.' She doesn't act like Lilah."

"I said 'off,' not batshit fucking crazy," Ariel said. "She's not the same as before."

Ariel pulled up to the condo as Juliet got a rare introspective look in her eye. "None of us are, sis. We're all changing, all the time. You don't want to still be the same sixteen-year-old girl who swore to wait for Bryce to love her, do you? How many years would you want to lose for a guy who doesn't love you back? Things might be shitty right now with Rob, but you married him. Your life progressed. You changed, Ariel. Juliet is no different."

JZ *was* different, though. Ariel couldn't explain it. Some fundamental part of Juliet Zhang had flipped after she died and came back. Like a zombie with the same looks and clothes but devoid of the spark that made them who they were.

"You would know better than I, Juliet," Ariel said, then repeated, "No different."

Juliet wore an expression of a woman who didn't believe her own bullshit. Instead of elaborating on JZ's normalness, she exited Ariel's car. Ariel watched her pseudo-sister disappear inside before she drove off. Her next destination would take her full circle to where she'd been when her life fell apart.

Ariel had a fondness for Graham Manor. The Caesars had been inseparable in their youth. Despite age-old animosities between the families, the seven pseudo-siblings found every opportunity to be together when they were kids. The warring factions of SX waved the white flag regarding the Caesars and townsfolk, who weren't involved in the multiple feuds, frequently instigated to facilitate playtimes for the kids. There were certain safe havens across SX where the Caesars could spend time together without parental interference. Under the watchful eye of Grandame Graham, the Graham Manor was one such place.

Grandame didn't answer the door. Instead, Ariel faced Neve's younger brother, the Iowan, who had returned to SX with his Graham father and Salem mother. His name was something Greeky and new-age—Parthenon? Zeus? Cyprus. Cyprus was skinnier than Ariel liked a man, with black wiry hair that reminded her of Bryce's, skin a shade darker than hers, and dark brown eyes that seemed to scan her from head to toe.

"You're a Caesar," he said.

"Is that an accusation or an observation?"

Cyprus shrugged bony shoulders. "I just haven't met you all yet. We'll be at the wedding together, after all."

"Right," Ariel said, her stomach flip-flopping as she thought about Bryce and Neve getting married. "Save me a dance, kid."

Cyprus raised an eyebrow. Most people were intimidated by Ariel's abruptness and sharp beauty, but Cyprus shrugged it off, looking more intrigued than annoyed. Ariel fumed. She hated that her superpowers didn't work on these Iowan transplants. Neve had never been intimidated by Ariel, either.

"Are you here about wedding plans?" Cyprus asked.

"I was wondering if Conner was here?"

Ariel watched as the corner of Cyprus's mouth curled upward. So, he knew what had happened between Ariel and Conner. Half the fucking town must be in Ariel's business. A woman couldn't screw a man outside on a picnic table in a hurricane without rumors spreading like wildfire.

"Yeah, come in," Cyprus invited, stepping aside. "You know where the workout room is?"

"I've been here more hours than you, kid. I can find my way."

Ariel left Cyprus in the foyer and headed down the main corridor. Returning after all these years dredged up a youthful hopefulness for a brighter tomorrow. She dreamed of being Mrs. Graham and spending holidays with Grandame under this roof. She'd wished that she and Bryce would inherit the manor one day and fill the rooms with a dozen beautiful kids. She had envisioned a very different life from how things turned out.

She quickly found the place Cyprus called a workout room, significantly transformed since the days of her youth. Fifteen years ago, the Caesars used it as a playroom. There had been a Ping-Pong table, a Foosball game, beanbags for chillin', and an old treadmill in the corner. The treadmill remained, now accompanied by a rowing machine, weight bench, elliptical trainer, and a punching bag.

Conner was on the treadmill, and the image transported Ariel back to when Bryce would run for miles on it while Ariel watched with a dreamy glaze over her eyes. Conner was sweaty and flushed, but he flashed that Bryce-Graham grin as Ariel entered the room. Ariel knew she'd made a mistake as soon as their eyes met.

"You remember me?" Ariel asked, standing beside the treadmill as he paced himself nicely.

"Seems you were wetter the last time we were together. Less clothes," Conner said, ogling her from head to toe.

"The storm left a lot of ruin in its wake. Seems my marriage was one of the casualties."

"I'm sorry," Conner said, not sounding sorry. "I didn't know you were married."

"Yeah, that's on me." Her stomach fluttered. *I want something else on me.* Conner's shirt was sweaty and clinging to his sculpted chest. He worked out more than Bryce. One of the differences was that Conner was more sculpted than Bryce. Bryce was too busy to work on his deltoids and quads. Conner had perfected his glutes.

"From what I've seen of the Ryans, you can do better than that bore you married. Tom brought Delilah around. What a complete nut."

"Lilah is Lilah. She's like a sister to me."

Conner slowed the treadmill to a walking pace. "Right. The famous Caesars. Like fucking royalty in this town. A bunch of princesses."

"And one prince," Ariel added.

Conner wrinkled his nose at the mention of Bryce's name. "I've spent enough time with Bryce since I've returned. I think you're all princesses."

"You didn't treat me like a princess in that motel room," Ariel said, remembering their hours of debauchery.

"You said you wanted it dirty," Conner replied with a flirty smirk.

Ariel started to feel warm at the memory of their moments together. "I admit that was a new experience. Rob is definitely more traditional in that department."

"Well, anytime you want to make things a little spicier than the missionary position in your marital bed, I'm not the kind of guy who lets a wedding ring stand in the way of a good time."

Conner turned off the machine. The treadmill stopped. He leaned on the rail, breathing heavily. The scent of exertion and masculinity wafted off him, not unpleasant, but rather a primal smell that made Ariel quiver. She had come for information, but she was repeatedly making the same mistakes.

"I'm not here for sex," Ariel said, although it felt like a lie as soon as it left her lips. She was hot and suddenly horny as hell.

"But since you're here, why not have sex anyway?"

Ariel was tempted, but she focused on the reason she came here. "I want to know what's going on in SX."

Conner still wore that sexy smirk. "That's a little vague. Seems like there's all sorts of drama in this town."

"Why are you here?"

"My family and SX are inexorably linked, just like yours. This is my destiny."

"Space-age trippy fate shit? You sound like Bryce's sister."

"Zephyr isn't wrong about everything."

Conner was so close that Ariel had trouble organizing her thoughts. Why did she think Conner had the answers she wanted? Was she making an excuse to see him, or did she think it was suspicious that his return coincided with JZ acting weird, Leira Gemini coming back, and a new guy in town who looked even more like Bryce than Conner did?

Ariel had to keep this conversation on track, or she might end up getting screwed on a treadmill. "I saw someone today. He looked like Bryce."

"I think that's what got you into trouble the last time. I hope you controlled yourself," Conner said, moving even closer. His face was within kissing distance.

"I can control myself fine, Conner Graham," she snapped, although she felt like she was losing the reins on her passions in the moment. "His face was scarred. Right down the middle, half and half."

"Which side looked like Bryce?" Conner teased.

He was making a joke. He didn't know anything about Leira's boy toy. She had come here for no reason. She exhaled, making a fist. That wasn't true. There was a reason. She had made a mistake betraying Rob by screwing Conner in the rain and again in the motel repeatedly. Now, she was on the verge of making the same mistake again.

The story of Ariel's life.

"You're no help," Ariel said breathlessly.

"I'm not here to save you, Ariel Álvarez. I'd rather join you in making some really bad choices."

Ariel's heart was racing, her blood boiling, her mind fogging with desire. She could lose control and do sinful things on the treadmill...and the rowing machine...and the weight bench...and maybe against the wall in the corner. Instead, she remembered something Bryce said in this very room when they were kids and Juliet tried to twist the rules in a Ping-Pong match against Sammy, "Cheating never works out in the end. You always know in your heart that you failed."

Cheating never works out in the end.

"I gotta go," Ariel said, tearing herself away with herculean effort. She wasn't going to discover the identity of the scarred man who looked like a villain in a comic book, but maybe Ariel could act like a hero for once. She left the workout room, turned down the hall, and got the hell out of Graham Manor before she cheated again.

Chapter Sixteen

JACKIE SALEM

Jackie worked late in her makeshift office above the SX Club lounge. She had stacks of papers covering every flat surface in the room. The living area surrounded a retracting portal that led down a spiral staircase to the currently empty nightclub. The club needed repairs before it could pass inspection and reopen to the public, but the red tape tangling emergency funds still restricted access to government money. Alistair hadn't received insurance benefits yet, either. Everything for repairs was at a standstill. Things became stressful.

The creditors were coming for the Salems.

Jackie worked eighteen hours a day. She coordinated efforts between the Salems, who had returned to the family fold to work in shifts, sifting through the piles of paperwork that seemed to multiply like rabbits every time she turned her back. The volume of applications invigorated the avalanche of denials.

"More rejections, Jacquelyn. These were delivered today," Tessa said as she ascended the spiral stairs through the aperture in the glass floor. She carried a stack of financial applications.

Jackie exhaled in exasperation. “Impossible. We’ve filled out everything exactly as requested. Dotted every ‘i’ and signed on all the dotted lines.”

Tessa looked grim. If Jackie had been sleeping four or five hours a night, Tessa was down to two or three. Bags swelled under her eyes, lines showed on her temples, and she even had a blemish on her chin. Always glamorous and flawless, the rigors of reconstruction were taking as much of a rough hit on Tessa as the hurricane had on their properties.

Tessa flipped through the stacks and stacks of paperwork piled everywhere. “It’s sabotage. There are agents in the government working against the family. Our enemies have stymied us at every turn.”

“Who? Why?”

Tessa threw up her hands. “The suspects could be anyone who has ever lived in Salem Crossing. We have made enemies for more than a hundred years. The bloodlines extended through every echelon of the government—Montgomerys, Zhangs, even an occasional Álvarez or a bitter Ryan who wants revenge. Enough over all those years to thwart our applications for assistance.”

“Don’t we have assets in those same branches of government?”

Tessa’s expression turned dark, dolorous, like someone trapped behind enemy lines without a map to find a way out. “Salems have gone into business and finance. Government work has never been our forte. We’ve always been able to buy our way out of a jam, but now everything got fucked at once.”

“What about Alistair and the insurance companies? Zhangs and Montgomerys can’t block access to our claims there. The insurance companies are in the business sector.”

Tessa sighed. “That’s a slow process. I don’t think there’s anything nefarious about the insurance company options.

Alistair assures me that he is making progress. We need access to those funds very soon."

"Or else?"

"Or else the creditors will start repossessing Salem property along the coast, one by one."

Tessa left things there. She dropped the bomb on Jackie and then retreated. Tessa added more pressure to what Jackie needed to do, but how could she fight the process if there was a cancer eating it from the inside? That was why Tessa told her. Jackie was expected to figure it out.

"The princess sits alone in her tower."

His voice didn't startle Jackie. He stood on the spiral staircase with his torso visible. She hadn't expected him, but he was often on her mind, so his appearance didn't surprise her. Jackie worried her shortcomings in securing funding for restoration had derived from her constant preoccupation with Martin Montgomery. At least Aunt Tessa's terrible news had suggested the forces against her had nothing to do with Jackie's carnal distractions.

"We've got to stop meeting like this," Jackie teased, thinking back to their passionate romp a few days before.

Martin's face fell like she'd somehow insulted him.

"That's what I'm here to talk about, actually," Martin said, ascending the staircase the remainder of the way.

His tone suggested he wasn't there for an evening booty call. Jackie had pictured him standing there without pants, his concealed bottom half bare and aroused, ready for spontaneous lovemaking. Disappointingly, he wore Brooks Brothers slacks, although the bulge in his pants indicated that intercourse may still be on the table. Or the floor. Maybe the bed. Then, in the shower.

"That doesn't sound like we'll have fun tonight."

Martin zigzagged across the room to avoid stumbling over the reams of documents stacked on the floor. Jackie stood to meet him if passions overtook evil tidings and they could prevent imminent bad news. He stopped so close that he could've swept her into his arms, kissing her passionately and carrying her to the bedroom, leaving the complicated mess of their lives lying among the clutter in the living room and her discarded clothes.

But, no...

"Magdalene knows about us," Martin said.

Jackie fumed. "Neve told her?"

Martin shook his head. "I don't think so. Someone else got to her. They told Magdalene about everyone I've ever had an affair with." He'd been confessing everything to Jackie's feet but paused and met her eyes. "She told me that Bryce Graham is my son."

Jackie took a step back. "She's lying."

Martin shrugged. "She claims to have proof. I haven't confronted Bryce with it. Has Neve told anyone else about you and me?"

Jackie hadn't seen her daughter in days. She knew Neve carried more secrets about SX than Jackie ever did. Between Bryce and Nevada, the pair was privy to too many sources of information. Did Neve know Bryce was Martin's son? Jackie recalled the revulsion on Neve's face when she caught Jackie and Martin in the act, but hadn't Bryce also indicated an elevated level of disgust? Like he, too, had walked in on a parent in an intimate moment?

"I don't think so. She would've warned me before telling Gil. I don't think Neve would tell anyone besides her father. Someone else must have discovered our affair and told Magdalene. We haven't exactly been careful."

"I have trouble thinking clearly when you're near," Martin said in a husky voice.

Jackie moved closer again, and she was inside Martin's personal space. If they were supposed to keep their hands off each other, it was unwise to get so close. She knew he couldn't resist her.

"So, this is it? Magdalene gave you an ultimatum? Monotony or me?"

"I think the word's monogamy," Martin corrected, leaning in, face to face.

"No, it isn't," Jackie said, her lips so close they brushed against his.

"This is the last time," Martin said.

"Then make it fucking count," Jackie replied.

Martin grabbed her waist with his strong hands and pulled her against him, kissing her. Jackie wrapped her arms around the back of his head, losing all sense. She felt every part of him yearning for more, but he kept a slow pace, like a death row inmate savoring his last meal. He could take his time at the all-you-can-eat Jackie buffet.

Clothes started flying. The scattered outfits and underwear soon draped over the stacks of papers, making the room look like an antique house where someone concealed vintage furniture with dust covers. Jackie pushed him back for a second, her sweaty hands on his bare chest, panting like a runner who'd just finished a marathon. The actual workout had not even begun.

"Say it," she said, looking him in the eye.

She saw the answer swimming in his brown pupils, sparking like lightning behind his mournful gaze.

His reply seemed to cause physical pain. "I can't."

"I gave you the chance all those years ago. Before I left for Iowa with Neve. I told you to say it."

Martin's face twisted, conflicted. "I couldn't."

Jackie continued, her voice cracking, "And I left. We lost twenty-three years."

She was naked before him, her breasts heaving as she tamped down her lust and the feelings she'd buried for so damn long. Martin didn't conceal the mutual attraction, undeniably standing tall between them. It would be so easy to mount him right there and merge their bodies for one last time. She wanted him in a final coupling more than almost anything. But she wanted one thing even more, and she wanted him to say it. She would walk away if he didn't tell her the magic words.

"You already know it. Words won't make it true," Martin tried.

"Say it," Jackie repeated, "or never say another damn thing to me ever again."

Martin stared. He tried to move in for a kiss, an attempt to gloss over her wants by using her needs, his cock touching her right where it counted and almost making her surrender to him. But she managed a tenuous grip on self-control. She turned and started walking away.

Martin grabbed her arm. She stopped and turned around.

"I love you," he said.

"I love you, too," she replied.

Martin took her right there. He grabbed her by the ass and lifted her, his dick slipping inside as quickly as a hand into a favorite glove. Jackie groaned like she had never felt anything so fine. With both fists full of her flesh, Martin held her up until he managed to get her against a wall. Jackie smashed herself against him as Martin moved faster and faster. She worried he was pumping too vigorously and it would be over too soon, but he managed to stave off a finish while she rode her first orgasm.

Between highs, he managed to get her into the bedroom and flat on the bed. Martin must've gained immense stamina from his proclamation of love—their session felt like it lasted for an eternity. He brought her to climax twice more, and they finally finished long after midnight. Jackie wondered if she'd be able to walk in the morning.

Jackie used the bathroom to clean up and exited an empty apartment. Martin's last words had been, "I love you." Better than "Goodbye." Or "I'm sorry." She preferred it that way. She wandered back into the living room. His clothes were gone. It was one a.m. What would Martin tell his wife about his nocturnal activities? Jackie didn't care. Magdalene had won. She took Martin away from her.

Jackie opened the aperture and descended the spiral staircase. She hadn't grabbed a towel, blanket, or robe as she crossed the deserted SX Club without anything covering her. She stopped beside the infinity pool where this affair had begun during the hurricane. Jackie crossed her arms under her breasts and looked out at the sea.

The Atlantic lapped at the shores, illuminated by soft moonlight. Anyone meandering in the surf would have seen her fully exposed, but no one strolled along the beach at this late hour. The volunteers cleaning the coastline had all retired to the least damaged resort rooms along Salem Shores. She wouldn't give a shit if anyone saw. Jackie felt defeated. Empty. She hadn't realized how much she loved Martin until he was gone. Again.

She put a palm against the floor-to-ceiling windows and leaned her forehead against the glass. Tears fell at her feet, splattering on her toes, dripping from her chin onto her heaving breasts. Her sacrifice, spanning more than two decades, had come to this.

A knock on the outside of the pane startled her. She looked up, not bothering to cover herself. Gil stood on the other side of the window, an inch away, gazing at Jackie without anything covering her from head to toe. He had seen her naked a thousand times, but never like this.

Jackie walked to the beach access door and unlocked the deadbolt. Without asking what was wrong, Gil took her in his arms. Before she knew it, he kissed her, and she let him. If he smelled sex on her, it didn't stop him. He led her up the spiral staircase to the same bed she'd been in with Martin. Then Gil was on her, in her, making her forget the last few hours, the last few days, the last few weeks. He made everything feel like it had in Iowa. Mundane, predictable, and suddenly, she was dead inside all over again.

Chapter Seventeen

JACKSON MONTGOMERY

Jax had played this game before. When Cin avoided the law because the SXPD suspected her of murdering Domino Salem, he kept Cin hidden at Manny's Motel in Old Mat. Now, Jax had another room reserved at the end of the same establishment, where the parking lot lamp remained eternally burned out, and the room next door was usually vacant. This time, the person he concealed at Manny's was virtually a stranger and posed no threat of romance.

Jax went on a food run because Cin and Kennedy were hungry. He left the newly revealed half-sisters alone and drove to Sammy's food truck. He parked his red Jaguar in the lot that once served Aunt Edna's hair salon before Hurricane Marlena destroyed the establishment. The remains of the parlor had been tarped like a corpse fallen victim to the deadly storm.

The storm also trashed Sammy's truck. She had managed to gather enough friends to right her food truck, which had been blown onto its side by the tornado-like gusts, and get it back on four flat tires. The engine was toast, and the waiting list for repairs stretched longer than Jax's cast of sexual conquests, so Sammy fixed the kitchen and the back half enough to make food and serve customers. The truck had remained parked in Aunt Edna's hair salon since the hurricane. Instead of traveling to various locations throughout the week, her customers came to Sammy, supporting her until she could refurbish the rest of the truck. Jax approached the ordering window as the noon lunch rush wound down. Most customers had food and sat around Edna's parking lot, eating overflowing plates of comfort food. Sammy and her coworker served the last stragglers in line.

Nevada Noble was the last person in line.

Jax walked up behind her and rested a hand on her shoulder. Neve instantly jabbed backward, driving her elbow into his breadbasket. He bent forward and exhaled loudly. Neve turned with a clenched fist, ready to finish him with an uppercut, when she realized who it was.

She gave him the stink-eye. "Don't fucking sneak up on me like that ever again."

"Right. Never," he groaned.

Sammy appeared beside Neve with her hands on her hips, frowning at Jax like she had spent her whole life disappointed by his decisions. "What'd you do?"

"He snuck up on me like a little bitch," Neve said. "He's lucky I didn't turn around and knee him in the balls. I didn't know if it was a guy or a girl, so I went for the gut."

"Damn, girl. They teach you moves like that in Iowa?" Sammy said, impressed.

"They need to teach that move to all young women everywhere."

Sammy put up her hand, and Neve gave her a high-five.

"Hell, yeah. I used to grab this one by the ear and bring him to his knees."

"You're used to being beat up by the ladies, huh, Jax?" Neve teased.

"You two are savage," Jax said with a steadier voice. He eyed the last couple of customers in line for Sammy's truck. "Can we take a walk?"

Sammy picked up on Jax's serious tone.

"Cammie can handle the rest. Let's go down Walker Avenue. Most of those residences are still empty," Sammy suggested.

Jax followed the women, the view of Neve's ass a distraction from the lingering ache in his stomach. He might be all in on Cin, but that didn't mean he didn't have a pulse. Besides, the view recalled more entertaining times with Neve than when she elbowed him in the fucking gut. Still, after a glance, guilt turned his eyes away from her pert posterior. There were other ways to bring Jackson Montgomery to heel than twisting his ear. He didn't want to disrespect Cin by lusting over anyone else. As they turned the corner and found themselves alone along the deserted street flanked by storm-ravaged homes wrapped in caution tape and tagged with warning signs, Jax finally started walking like a normal human being.

"You know I'm starving," Neve said, rubbing her belly. "This had better be pretty damn important."

Sammy nudged Neve playfully. "You'll get anything you want from the truck as soon as we get back, sis."

Jax was glad they got along so well. They would need to act like family once the secrets in SX surfaced. Sammy meant the word "sis" as a play on the Caesar connection, but it meant more than that. Neve would soon become Jax and Sammy's actual sister-in-law.

"What's this about?" Neve directed at Jax.

Jax caught up with the girls, with Neve walking between him and Sammy. He looked at her and noticed her tone of voice. Neve asked like someone guilty of concealment and fishing for information on whether everyone else knew the secret. Neve had been involved in every crazy thing that had happened in SX over the last few months, so he wouldn't be surprised if she already knew about Bryce's true parentage. Did she also know about Kennedy?

"You wanna tell her, Sammy?" Jax asked.

"Bryce is our brother. My father had an affair with Amanda Graham," Sammy blurted.

"Mmm," Neve replied, keeping her pace without missing a step. So, she knew. "Who told you that?"

"My mother found out. Can you believe my mom found out that juicy bit of gossip before I did?" Sammy said.

Neve frowned. "You're not pissed about it?"

"That my pseudo-brother is actually my real brother. Hell, no."

"Your father cheated on your mother. That's okay with you?" Neve asked incredulously.

Jax noticed a pained tinge in Neve's voice that Sammy didn't. Sammy might be Neve's best friend, but she hadn't slept with Neve. Jax had been in love with her for months. Maybe he still was, but things had changed. His feelings had transformed. Jax liked what he had with Cin. But still, his connection with Neve made him notice that Sammy's nonchalant reaction to their father's adultery troubled her.

Sammy shrugged off the ramifications of their father's infidelity. "Marty has cheated on my mother with a lot more women than Amanda Graham, Neve. I have siblings out there that I'm much less fond of than Bryce."

"Like me," Jax said.

Sammy reached across Neve and punched Jax in the arm. It hurt entirely less than Neve's elbow to his belly.

"Like Damien Halloweather," Sammy stated.

"Your mother found out about Damien, too?" Neve asked.

Jax added, "And Sweetheart Salem. Everything came unglued at our family gathering. It was a bloodbath."

"Any other mistresses on the list?" Neve asked. Her tone was less teasing and more fishing. Did Neve know about someone else on his father's list of conquests?

Sammy's forehead furrowed with concern. "You didn't sleep with my dad, did you, Neve?"

Jax's aching midsection flip-flopped at the thought of Neve and his father. The fact that Neve was engaged to his half-brother was terrible enough, but even the thought of Nevada in bed with Martin hurt him worse than any elbow.

"Of course not," Neve snapped.

Sammy grinned. "I was kidding. Sheesh. Everyone's touchy today."

"There's a lot of shit going on, Sammy. This isn't the time for jokes," Jax scolded.

"What else is going on, Jax?" Neve asked.

Just as Jax had intimate knowledge of Nevada Noble, she also could sense when he was hiding something. Their connection went both ways. He wouldn't discuss Kennedy until he learned more about the young woman who claimed to be Cin's sister. A few weeks ago, he would never have considered keeping something from Neve. Now, he shook his head. Neve knew it was a lie but didn't press the subject. Both had things they didn't want to talk about right now.

Instead, Neve blurted out a confession. "I knew about Bryce. He was going to tell you right after the election. He didn't want Martin to find out before then."

"Too fucking late. Why does everyone have to keep these goddamned secrets all the time?" Sammy said, finally irritable. She didn't like that neither Bryce nor Neve told her.

Neve eyed her future sister-in-law suspiciously. "And you aren't keeping anything a secret from us, Sammy? Nothing at all? No hurricane hush-hush you want to come clean about?"

Sammy's eyes got big. Neve had hit on something. Jax was in the dark. He wasn't going to start pressing for answers. Jax was hiding things of his own. He needed to grab some food and get back to Cin and Kennedy.

"Now we're one big, happy family. I'm starving. Secrets make me hungry," Jax said, smiling, and then turned around.

"I'm surprised you have any room after your stomach took that elbow," Neve taunted.

"You're going to fit right into the family," Sammy said, already forgiving Neve for keeping Bryce's secret.

Whether she would forgive Bryce so quickly was a question for another day.

Before they returned to within earshot of Cammie and the last customers, Sammy added, "You've got Zhang-Álvarez-Salem blood in your veins, Neve. And Bryce has Graham-Montgomery genes. Your babies are going to represent SX better than anyone else in this town."

The thought of Neve and Bryce making babies had once sent Jax into a jealous frenzy, but now it merely reactivated the dull ache from Neve's assault. Neve was his past—Cin was the future. A future he needed to return to before she called him up to check on the food, loud and hangry.

He left the ladies at Sammy's after his sister handed him three portions and asked, "Who are you shacking up with this week, Jax? Some volunteers from Virginia who haven't heard about your reputation?"

Jax took a circuitous route back to Old Mat to ensure no one was following. Kennedy was very paranoid that she would be in danger if the wrong people found out she was in SX. Jax walked in on Cin and Kennedy in the middle of an intense conversation.

"You're telling me that my father chose to stay away from me because he thought it was in my best interest? I was fortunate to grow up without a man in the house?" Cin shouted as her legendary temper dialed to eleven.

"Dad wasn't exactly father of the year," Kennedy said, holding up both hands in case Cin started throwing punches.

She might.

"I wouldn't know. I had to go to the daddy-daughter dances with Uncle Carlos," Cin spat.

"Our dad doesn't dance, anyway."

Cin stepped forward with her hands balled into fists, and Jax inserted himself between them. Looking at them facing each other, Jax couldn't help but notice the resemblance. They had different mothers, but he noted similarities around the mouth, in the shape of their noses, and the fire flickering passionately in their eyes.

"Let's rewind. I think I missed something," Jax said.

Cin stomped around the tiny motel room, flailing her hands in the air. "She won't shut up about being a Graham. I chased Bryce like a lost little puppy for most of my life. That means I spent my entire adulthood wishing I could marry my fucking cousin."

Kennedy lifted one finger like she needed to make a point. "Maybe not the best adjective."

"You annoying bitch," Cin said, grabbing for Kennedy as if to throttle her.

Jax wrapped Cin in a strong hug, and she immediately calmed. They had gone so long without touching each other that such a tender gesture was transformational. Cin shrugged into him, eager for a loving embrace. Jax cuddled her as she shuddered, accepting the truth.

Niles Graham was her father.

Tom Graham was her half-brother.

"Niles raised you as his daughter? He claimed you as part of his family?" Cin asked, her voice a little gentler.

"My mother gave me up," Kennedy said, sounding wounded by the thought.

"Your mother is Elizabeth Halloweather?" Cin asked, circling back to their conversation when Jax left for food.

Kennedy nodded. "My father found out she was pregnant, and she told him she was going to abort the child. She said I wasn't part of her plan. Dad discovered that she'd changed her name. Like my brother, he was in the FBI and had used his connections to learn she was an Iblīs. He promised not to tell if she carried me to term and gave me to him. She signed away all rights. He never told her secret, not until after Tom and the rest of you uncovered the Halloweathers' true ancestry."

"I'm a Graham," Cin said, slumped in Jax's arms.

Kennedy nodded, as if being a Graham was some kind of prize. "And you're not the only one. I'm back for a reason. Me and Tom and Conner. Now we have Willow and Cyprus Noble, who are Graham nepo babies. Bryce. There's a reason we've all returned right now."

"You're telling me this is some sort of a grand master plan? I'm supposed to believe there's a method in this madness?" Cin asked, sounding tired.

"You'll see, Cin. Our grandfather is returning to SX soon. He will reveal everything. Keep me safe until he can set the final plans in motion, and the truth will come out," Kennedy promised.

"More conspiracy theories. More secrets and lies. More vague drama. I'm through with all of it," Cin muttered.

"We need you, Acindina."

"Fuck you," Cin said, taking Jax's hand and pulling him toward the motel room door. "Fuck Niles. Fuck all you Grahams. In fact, I hope the rest of SX fucks itself into the ocean. I'm done."

Cin climbed into Jax's Jag. She leaned on his shoulder

and softly cried as he draped his arm over her. He could start the engine, turn north, and drive until they found snow. They might be safe from anyone in SX if they retreated into frozen winter lands. But that wouldn't solve any problems. Jax knew they couldn't fix this by running away. Cin knew it, too. They would stay. They would see it through.

A chill ran up Jax's spine despite the tepid December night. He worried that once they crawled across the finish line of this shit show of a situation, they wouldn't be a "they" anymore.

Chapter Eighteen

Neve knew where to find Jax Montgomery when she needed to. He had been unable to keep secrets from her since the first moment he saw her, and their one night together had bonded them in a way that she carried in a special place in her heart. She wasn't in love with Jax, nor was it a sibling kind of bond, but they shared something unique. A one-of-a-kind ESP different from her connection to Bryce or her relationships with Cyprus and Willow. When Jax ordered three servings from his sister's food truck, Sammy accused him of having a threesome with some out-of-state coeds. Neve knew better. As surprising as it was, Jax was in love with Acindina Álvarez. He wasn't screwing around, but he was hiding something. Neve could sense it.

Neve believed Jax was hiding someone. She overheard Conner Graham talking with his father, Julian, and they said someone named Kennedy had come to SX with Jax and Cin. Conner and Julian said she's part of the "plan."

Neve knew exactly where Jax would stash someone if he had become embroiled in another clandestine operation. After eating with Sammy, Neve drove to Old Mat and rolled past Manny's Motel. Sure enough, she spotted Jax's red Jag at the far end of the shadowed parking lot. She hid her vehicle between two large trucks in the driveway of the laundromat around the corner and snuck back to Manny's in time to spy Jax and Cin exiting room number two, with Cin angrily cursing over her shoulder at someone still inside.

Neve circled the tree line and watched from the edge of the lot. She felt guilty spying on Jax like that, but he hadn't been honest about his activities, and Neve needed to know about this Kennedy person. She could only see shadows through the tinted windows of the Jaguar, but she felt uncomfortable intruding on the intimacy between Jax and Cin. In silhouette, Cin appeared upset as Jax comforted her. Eventually, Jax started the engine, and they drove away.

As soon as the car disappeared around the corner, Neve walked up to room number two's door. She knocked and stepped back. No answer. She tried again. Nothing.

"This is Nevada Noble. I want to talk to you about Julian Graham," Neve said through the door.

Neve saw a shadow appear through the peephole. Then, she listened as the deadbolt disengaged and the chain dropped against the door panel. The knob rattled. The hinges squeaked as someone opened the door from the inside. When fully open, she saw a silhouette in the dark interior outlined by the curtained windows behind the occupant. Neve noticed another shape in the outline, pointing at her face.

The woman had a gun. Aimed between Neve's eyes.

Neve stepped backward. "Jesus Christ. Point that fucking thing somewhere else."

"I'm going to pierce your tongue with a bullet if you don't quit yelling about Julian Graham."

Neve raised her hands as if the stranger were robbing her. "Okay, okay."

"Get the hell in here and close the door behind you."

"You want me to step closer to the gun pointed at my head?" Neve asked, still reaching for the sky.

The woman pointed the gun at the floor. "Shit, lady, get in here and quit making a goddamn ruckus."

Neve had been in more dangerous situations than this. This woman sounded tough, but the threats felt empty. She didn't give off killer vibes. Neve had stared down Damien Halloweather. A pacifist Graham wasn't going to scare her. If the occupant was related to Bryce, she would be part of Neve's extended family after the wedding. A new cousin, or aunt, or sister-in-law? Hell of a first impression.

"I don't know how you aren't dead already with your big mouth," the woman complained, turning on a desk lamp as Neve locked the door behind her. "Just keep me from getting killed, will you?"

"Are you Kennedy?" Neve asked.

"Well, aren't you a snoopy bitch?"

"You weren't even on the list of things I was trying to solve. Or, at least, I didn't think so," Neve said.

"What kind of detective follows the clues on the wrong case?"

"I'm not a detective. I'm trying to make sense of SX. To help Bryce."

Neve looked around the motel room. Half-full bags of chips, empty cans of energy drinks, and a pile of shorts and tank tops in a corner, typical of someone from the North, like Neve, who thought highs in the seventies still meant summer weather. The scene reminded Neve of her college dorm room. Kennedy had to be closer to Willow's age. She placed the gun on the table beside her phone. The two essentials for any single woman in SX.

Kennedy sighed. "So, you're the infamous Nevada Noble."

Neve eyed the gun still within Kennedy's reach. "You've heard of me? Then you know I'm not your enemy."

"I know you're trying to make things better around here. My brother vouched for you a long time ago. He thinks you and Bryce are good shit. But I only see the shitty part, nothing good. You always seem to be getting people into trouble."

"I want to help people, not make things worse!"

"Tell that to Auberon Fox. Domino Salem. Anthony Mascolo. Neil Halloweather," Kennedy rattled the names pointedly.

"I didn't cause their deaths," Neve snapped.

"Some of them wouldn't be dead if you hadn't come to SX. Maybe all of them."

Neve recoiled, stung by this stranger's accusations of being an accessory to multiple tragedies. Those events weren't her fault. SX was fucked up long before Nevada Noble arrived in town. Kennedy acted like Neve was the spark that ignited the powder keg, and things had exploded as a result.

"We don't even know why Damien Halloweather killed Domino."

"His name is Damien Iblīs. And that bastard is my half-brother," Kennedy stated.

Neve paused and studied Kennedy. Dark hair, meticulously shaped thick eyebrows. She hadn't bothered with a bra, and dark areolas showed through the light blue material of her tank top. She had a juicy booty with cheeks hanging out of tiny shorts. She could see some resemblance to Britney. Kennedy was half Iblīs and half Graham.

"Liz Iblīs is your mother?"

Kennedy nodded.

"Your father is a Graham?"

"My dad is Niles Graham. Tom is my brother."

"Tom is Liz's son?" Neve asked, wondering for a horror-stricken moment if Tom had shot and killed his own brother.

"No, no, no. Tom is my *half*-brother. Tom's mom died when he was young. She had no association with SX."

Neve looked around the motel room, the scene reminding her of a safehouse where cops kept an informant in a mob movie. "Why all the cloak and dagger bullshit? Why are you hiding at Manny's Motel?"

Kennedy exhaled and sat on the edge of her unmade bed. "Because dangerous people are descending upon SX, Neve. You don't understand half of what's happening around here."

"And you do?" Neve countered. "How long have you been in town?"

"This is the first time I've ever been to Salem Crossing. And I've been hiding in this motel room since I arrived. But I still know more than you."

Neve considered the Crossing Guard and her list of outstanding concerns involving SX. Was she so far off-base on what was really wrong with this town, or did Kennedy assume Neve was a naïve outsider with her head up her ass? Did this young woman, who came from nowhere and claimed to know everything, actually have her finger on the pulse of Salem Crossing more than Neve and her cohorts?

Hell, no.

"I'm investigating multiple mysteries on a dozen different fronts, using capable agents to uncover answers to SX's most pressing problems, Kennedy. Why did your half-brother kill Domino Salem? What's the full story behind the Dark Summer kidnappings? Why did Helen Ryan replace me with Clover Black? Who kidnapped the Juliets? What's your mother's family up to? Why is Conner Graham back in town? What does Leira Gemini want? What does Julian Graham want?"

Neve didn't mention the secret treasure map. If Kennedy knew about that, she would bring it up herself.

Kennedy stared in silence as Neve paced the room. Kennedy was the naïve one. She might only be a couple of years younger than Neve, but she hadn't experienced the nature of SX. Neve had only gained an understanding of how these six families lived together in some kind of tenuous incest through experience. Neve had become a part of it, while Kennedy judged from the outside, making assessments based on stories and legend. Kennedy might know things, but she couldn't understand them.

Neve didn't know this woman from a stranger off the street. Cin seemed pissed at Kennedy, but Jax thought she was valuable enough to keep safe at Manny's. Kennedy was Elizabeth Iblīs's daughter and the half-sister of the insane Damien. Yet Neve felt like she could trust her.

"Shit. You've pegged a lot of it, Neve. No wonder Bryce wants to marry you. You're making me kinda hot right now."

"I think you can help me with some of those answers. What do you know about the Iblīs family?"

Kennedy grabbed one of the unopened diet colas from the tabletop by the gun and cracked open the can, taking a swig. "Not a goddamn thing. My mother wanted me dead."

"Conner Graham? What's Julian up to?"

"Those are great questions. And you'll get the answers soon enough. I need to stay safe, and my grandfather will reveal everything."

"Stay safe from what? Damien? Martin Montgomery? The Salems? The Zhangs?"

Kennedy drained the rest of her diet soda and tossed the can toward the trash bin in the corner like Angel Reese going for a three-pointer. It bounced off the rim and landed among a field of five other missed shots scattered on the floor.

"You're not focused on the most important questions, Neve. The top two are on your list."

Neve ran down the list in her head. What would a woman who had never been to SX know about the answers to all the crazy things happening lately? Neve dismissed all items concerning the current events in SX. That left one crucial question that someone who had been away from the city all her life might know something about—the arrival of another person who had been away for most of her life.

"You know why Leira Gemini's here?"

Kennedy pointed to her nose and smiled. The expression reminded Neve of the dreamy grin Tom wore around Delilah.

"You're afraid of Leira?"

Kennedy shrugged like it was normal to be leery of one's fellow citizens. "Leira and her friends. There's a whole gang of them. And they mean trouble."

"How so?"

"We don't know the specifics yet," Kennedy admitted. "But we all need to be prepared."

"You said two of my questions were the most important. Do you know something about why Helen Ryan traded Clover and me?"

It was the only other event centered beyond the perimeter of Salem Crossing. Why did Helen switch Neve so that Clover ended up in Boston instead of Iowa?

Kennedy lifted a hand for a high five. Neve looked at it with a raised right eyebrow, then played along and smacked her palm. The girl was both scared and strange at the same time. How did she fit into the Graham/Iblīs dynamic? She was an oddball unto herself.

"Julian Graham is Amaya Montgomery's father. That means Clover's grandfather is a Graham."

"Shut the fuck up." Neve was shocked.

Kennedy shrugged as if secrets like this were commonplace in her family tree. After navigating the tangled underbrush of the forest of SX entanglements, Neve ought not to be the least surprised at the latest bombshell revelation.

"Amaya's mother died when Amaya was very young. Jefferson Montgomery raised his sister's daughter as his own. When Amaya became pregnant with a Halloweather bastard, Julian realized his grandchild would be part Montgomery/part Graham/part Iblīs. He knew Amaya had asked Gil to take her baby far away from SX and Neil Halloweather. As Gilbert Graham's father, Julian couldn't stay close to Clover with another Graham in the picture. Julian asked Helen Ryan to switch infants, then inserted himself into Clover's life in Boston. Julian has been Clover's martial arts instructor for the last fifteen years."

"My God. Julian messed with all of our lives so he could keep tabs on his grandkid?"

"Clover is an important piece of the puzzle," Kennedy said, standing and peering through the curtains to check the parking lot.

"I need to know what puzzle, Kennedy."

"Soon, Neve, very soon. As long as you don't lead Leira and her buddies to my doorstep."

Neve and Kennedy stared at each other for a long minute. The young woman refused to give up her information. She was a soldier carrying out orders, and Julian acted as the general who could instill more fear than some bitchy outsider behind enemy lines. Neve would have to wait for the answers until Julian wanted to reveal them. In the meantime, Neve had gathered valuable information she needed to share with the Crossing Guard.

"It looks like Jax is protecting you. He's not going to let anything happen to you."

"I can take care of anything that comes my way. My dad and my brother are both lawmen. I know how to defend myself," Kennedy said, picking up the gun.

Neve nodded. "I see that."

"If you can distract Leira and her goons until my grandfather is ready to reveal the master plan, I would appreciate it. No one needs a shootout on the streets of Old Mat."

"I'm working with some other people who can help. Including Tom," Neve said, stepping toward the door.

"Tom already knows Leira. He was supposed to spy on her a while back. Instead, he fell for her."

"I heard. The black widow caught him in her web, huh?"

"That's about right," Kennedy said, stepping between Neve and the door. Neve noticed the gun still in her hand. "Can you leave through the bathroom window?"

Neve blinked. "You want me to squeeze out the back way?"

"If anyone saw you come in, they'd be beating down my door already. I sure as hell don't want anyone to see you walk out. I'm keeping a low profile here, and the future Mrs. Mayor isn't exactly incognito."

Secrets. Skulking. Skullduggery. Neve longed for a dull, mundane moment like her life back in Horton, on a yawn-inducing date with Patrick, and home in time to binge-watch a rom-com before bed. Now, life was sexy, exciting, dangerous, and mysterious. And exhausting. After this was over, she needed to take Bryce on a vacation to the Midwest and shack up in a small town for a week of banality.

"I feel like I'm in high school all over again, sneaking out of my bedroom to go to a party." Neve squeezed through the small bathroom window, with Kennedy pushing her backside from inside, and plopped on the ground along the concealed rear stretch of Manny's Motel. High school had never been this thrilling.

Neve headed back to her car without anyone noticing her. She needed to call a meeting of the Crossing Guard ASAP. She'd gathered new information about at least some items on the list and needed to amend the questions regarding a couple of others. Kennedy had added a new layer of urgency to finding the answers.

Chapter Nineteen

HOLIDAYS WITH THE ÁLVAREZES

It was Christmas Eve.

Ramón Álvarez watched relatives gather at tables, crowd into corners, squeeze into the kitchen, and fill every seat in the house. The sounds of dozens of overlapping conversations filled the home with a bass that reminded Ram of riding his bike up and down Route 1. He was too large to plow through the packed crowd, so he stayed at his post, near the front door and out of the way, a corner to himself. Despite his hulking stature, he managed to blend into the background, black leather and tattoos camouflaged against Maria's palm-tree wallpaper.

Every holiday, the bits of banter and changing faces always reminded Ram of visiting his abuela after church every Sunday afternoon when he was a kid. She would play taped episodes of her afternoon soaps in the background as she baked for hours in the kitchen and chatted with visitors. Ram never talked much, so he would frequently glance at the television. Ram could never figure out who was married to whom, who was dead or back again, who was friends or enemies, and whether the leading actor played the hero that week or his evil twin.

The Álvarez holidays were like that. He hardly recognized half the people in Maria Álvarez's small home, overflowing with everyone from close relatives to distant cousins. He spotted Acindina whispering to Alicia in one corner. Cin hadn't spoken to Ram much since Jackson Montgomery interrupted their last tryst. Ram tried to figure out if she was happy. If Jax broke her heart, he would break every bone in that son of a bitch's body.

Ram recognized other distant relatives, mostly cousins several times removed, like Cin and Alicia. Their common ancestor might go back generations, as the original Álvarezes arrived in SX more than a century ago. The branches of this family tree compared to the great oaks farther inland that had lived long before the first settlers ever came to SX. Ram saw Carlos from the bar with Jack and Jake. Ram's parents had disappeared somewhere in the throngs of relatives. His abuela worked in the kitchen with Maria.

"Ram?"

Ram slowly turned so his broad shoulders wouldn't knock some of the chattering folks crowded around him on their asses. Rico stood at Ram's elbow, a beer in one hand and an empanada in the other. He wore a smile, always the happy peace officer, even out of uniform.

"Someone is asking for you at the back door," Rico said.

Ram frowned. Who would be looking for him at a holiday party? By the time he thought to ask, Rico had disappeared into the crowd. Ram started making his way through the sea of people, carving a path like a cutter through rough waves. Cin smirked as she watched little Álvarez offspring scatter before him like rats scurrying from a tomcat. Ram gave her an aww-shucks shrug and turned toward the back door.

He opened the dented metal door that needed a fresh coat of paint, a new doorknob, and some oil for the hinge.

Standing outside on the concrete square, Willow Noble looked up at him with those big brown eyes. He loved her nimbus cloud of black hair floating around her adorable face. Her lips were big and kissable, even if she hadn't shown interest in a second night together after they'd had a threesome with Cin weeks ago.

Willow arched her eyebrow in a way that pointed to the person beside her. Ram hadn't even noticed Neve standing beside her sister. He wondered if he'd missed a text about a Crossing Guard meeting but knew he hadn't. He'd been checking for any contact from Willow all day. They'd been investigating the Dark Summer since Neve made the list. Ram told Willow he had a Christmas Eve thing, but she could text him if needed. It was the longest sentence he'd said to her since they started investigating together.

"Ram, I need to talk to Cin," Neve said.

"I don't think Cin likes you."

Neve flicked her hand like dismissing a silly idea. "I know she doesn't like me, but she's hiding something at Manny's."

"Does Jax know?"

Neve stared at him. People assumed Ram didn't understand what was happening because he spoke so little.

"You know about Cin and Jax?"

Ram nodded.

"Yeah, Jax knows," Neve said.

"Why don't you ask Jax then?" Ram asked.

Again, Neve paused. Did she think Ram didn't know Neve and Jax had had a relationship? Everyone in SX knew about the brief fling that happened before Neve Noble chose Bryce instead. Ram knew Neve and Jax still had some remnant of a connection. The feud between the Montgomerys and Álvarezes hadn't been the only thing keeping Cin and Jax apart for so long. Jax carried a torch for Neve long after Neve chose Bryce.

Neve appeared impressed with Ram's insight. Most people underestimated Ram. He was used to it.

Neve said, "I don't think Jax has the answers I'm looking for. You know my mother is an Álvarez?"

"I heard," Ram replied.

"Well, this is Álvarez business. Not Montgomery business."

Ram looked at Willow as if asking her for confirmation. Willow nodded. She gave him a little smile that said, "I'll vouch for her," without saying a word.

Ram stepped backward, leaving the doorway open. "Come in."

"Ramón, I need your help opening this jar of jalapeñ—" His abuela paused midsentence. "Who is that sneaking in the back door, hijo?"

He moved aside and revealed Neve standing in the doorway, as Willow tried not to bust a gut laughing at Ram's grandmother's choice of words concerning sneaking in and the back door. Not that Ram had entered Willow's back door, but maybe if she offered an invitation...

"Hello, Mrs. Álvarez. I didn't know if I'd be welcome," Neve said.

Ram's abuela pushed Ram aside, as if he were a coat rack rather than a brick wall, taking Neve energetically by the hand and pulling her inside. "Welcome, welcome, welcome. We accept everyone at the Álvarez holidays. We did not turn your mamá away even as she made her terrible choices. Yet she still ran off and never looked back. Her daughter is always welcome here. Ram's novia may come and eat as well."

"I'm not his girlfrie—" Willow stuttered. "We're not togeth—"

"I think you are," Ram's abuela disagreed with a genial smile.

"No, he and I aren't..."

"Sure, you are. You'll see," Ram's abuela insisted.

Willow gave up. Neve smiled at her sister's defeat. Ram's abuela led them through the sea of people. If Neve had hoped for a quick powwow with Acindina and a subtle retreat without much fanfare, she would be entirely mistaken. The Álvarez family greeted her like a rock star as she passed card tables and TV trays filled with festive relatives wishing her a merry Christmas. People 'round SX liked Bryce Graham and considered Neve to be the kind of queen-in-waiting.

Ram's abuela shooed away a quartet of teens at a corner table who'd finished their meal. Ram took two spots on one side of the table as the sisters sat opposite him. Ram's abuela disappeared to retrieve a plate for each of them. Neve looked around the room crowded with Álvarezes, waving friendlily to everyone. Willow sat stunned beside her like she'd taken the wrong turn down a dark alley and found herself in a fantasy realm.

"They like you," Ram said.

"They like Bryce." Neve nodded at Ariel, who glared at her across the room. "And not everyone likes me, Ram."

Willow marveled at the scene around her. "How many people have they squished into this house? It's like how I imagine one of those clown cars at the circus when twenty of them pop out, only this is a house, and there are a helluva lot more than twenty."

Ram's abuela returned with three more Álvarezes in tow, all carrying plates and drinks. They set identical, overflowing portions before each guest, with a full beverage at each station. The girls' eyes widened at the sight of the piled plates, and Ram's belly growled hungrily.

"For Nochebuena, we serve a traditional dish called pernil con moros y cristianos. I added a helping of yucca with garlic dressing, fried plantains, and a salad. The drink is called crema de vie, a Cuban eggnog that will definitely warm your spirits. Enjoy, enjoy, enjoy! You are now a part of the family."

Willow did enjoy it. Her appetite for food was as voracious as her eagerness in bed. The woman had a verve for life that Ram found both appealing and daunting. Cin had always been a spitfire with a spirit that wanted to go anywhere but here. Endless energy directed entirely toward escape for years and years. But Willow hungered for new experiences right here in SX. She ran toward instead of away.

"Is that Ariel and Cin?" Neve asked, pointing with a fork to the portrait on the wall beside her table.

Ram cranked his head. The picture featured the sisters when they were young, maybe about four and eight years old. He nodded with a mouthful of plantains and chased the bite by drinking half of his cup of crema de vie. He remembered kickball with Ariel and his other distant cousins every holiday in the empty lot behind his abuela's home.

Maria, the woman of the house and hostess for this year's Nochebuena, arrived at the table. Ram knew Maria as a no-nonsense woman who forced food on anyone within reach. She would pass out torticas de morón to all the youngest Álvarez children running around Old Mat as they passed her house.

"Nevada Noble. Welcome home," Maria greeted.

"Your family is certainly making me feel welcome," Neve said.

"I heard of your kindness toward mamá before you even knew she was tu abuela. I know she pushes everyone away, yet you persisted. I am impressed. You are a good match for Bryce," Maria complimented.

Ariel glared daggers across the room. She understood her mother's dig at her daughter. Everyone in SX, including Maria Álvarez, knew damn well Ariel had loved Bryce since they were babies. When Ariel was young and sneaking around Old Mat with the other Caesars, Maria treated Bryce like the son she never had. Bryce Graham was the only one who penetrated the hard exterior of Maria's heart. Now Neve received the windfall from Maria's endearment toward Bryce.

"We are lucky to have you in the family," Maria said.

Neve waved a hand at the packed interior of the festive home. "I've felt something was missing my whole life. Now I know what it was."

"We believe you and Bryce will improve Salem Crossing for everyone."

"We're trying," Neve said.

Maria bustled off with much to do, as the three of them squeezed around the square card table, finishing their plates. Neve cleared the table and went off to thank Ram's abuela and Maria for their hospitality. She instructed Ram and Willow to confront Cin. Ram found her standing in a hallway. He remembered enough from past holidays that the corridor led back to Cin and Ariel's childhood bedrooms. Ram bulldozed Cin into the first doorway down the hall.

"What the fuck, Ram? We aren't repeating the last time we were together in this room," Cin said through gritted teeth.

"This isn't about sex," Willow said, then looked from Ram to Cin and back. "I mean, I don't think so. Not with us, anyway."

"Who else have you been throupling, Will?" Cin asked with a dirty smirk.

Willow shamelessly replied, "Leira Gemini. And she's up to no good."

"No shit. She's all kinds of trouble."

That wasn't Cin's voice. Someone else stood in Cin's bedroom doorway, listening to the conversation. Ariel had her hands on her hips, and Ram saw the resemblance between the sassy sisters. The look on her face suggested that

Ariel wanted answers, and no one would survive any attempt at an exit without talking.

"Leira made my life hell ten years ago. She cockblocked my last chance with Bryce," Ariel said, stepping into Cin's childhood bedroom and pointing her index finger at Willow.

"You never had a chance with Bryce," Neve said, reappearing and taking Ariel's place in the doorway.

The small bedroom was getting pretty damned crowded.

Ariel looked pissed at her proximity to Neve. "Why are the Noble girls crashing my family's Christmas party? Neither Cin nor I can stand either one of you."

"We want to know about Kennedy," Neve said, addressing Cin.

Cin stared at Neve. The two shot dark, smoldering looks at each other across the short distance. It wouldn't be the first catfight to disrupt an Álvarez get-together. It wouldn't even be the first fisticuffs to involve Acindina Álvarez. But icy glares defrosted to cool animosity as Cin exhaled, ending the tense standoff.

"She's my half-sister," Cin replied. Ariel's mouth dropped open. "But you already knew that, Neve. You're always sticking your nose where it doesn't belong. Coming in like a damn wrecking ball and making a mess."

"You never had a chance with Bryce, either, Cin," Neve tossed back at her.

"I don't want Bryce anymore. Maybe I should thank you for taking him out of circulation," Cin said.

"You can thank me by explaining what Kennedy is up to. She won't tell me what she's doing in SX," Neve said, now standing in the way of escape. She might be as intimidating as Ariel.

Cin shook her head, astounded. "So, you found her. You better have been fucking stealthy, Neve. Leira is a big problem. Kennedy is worried about her."

Neve shrugged dismissively. "Leira's a bitch, but she's about as scary as Owen Zhang."

"Leira's not alone. She's got a partner," Willow said, turning red. Ram knew how she knew. He didn't like thinking about that.

Ariel frowned. "She's got more than one partner. I spotted a couple of guys with her at the Riverside Inn. A girl named Hallie is in the picture. Leira came to SX with a whole goddamned entourage. Aren't they here to help clean up the town?"

Neve shook her head. "I think there's more to it. And I need to know everything you know about Leira Gemini."

Ariel looked from Neve to Cin, to Ram, and then to Willow. "I'll tell you everything I know about that whore. But someone else might know more than we do about Leira."

"Tom?" Neve asked. "We already talked to him."

Ariel shook her head. "We need to ask Juliet Zhang some questions."

Chapter Twenty

Neve and Ariel formed a tenuous alliance to investigate what the hell was wrong with Juliet Zhang. Neve had noticed that JZ seemed different since she returned to Salem Crossing, but the woman had been gone longer than Neve had known her before the Juliets' fake deaths. Besides, Neve understood how much Iowa could change a person. She had the Jekyll-and-Hyde situation with her mother as proof.

Neve and Ariel met at Neve's bungalow after sundown on Christmas Eve. Still hovering in the seventies, even at twilight, with waves crashing in the background, the holidays felt as far removed from her past life as her relationship with Bryce felt different from her former engagement to Patrick Moulder. Instead of snow and cold for Christmas, the warm wind carried a salty scent.

Bryce was working late at City Hall, so she wouldn't need to explain this clandestine mission to him until after it was finished. Neve preferred to avoid any interaction between Ariel and Bryce if she could. She still didn't like Ariel lusting after her future husband whenever Bryce was nearby. Neve watched Ariel as she focused on something other than unrequited love, as Ariel dialed into this mission with laser focus.

"There's something weird going on in SX," Ariel said as she paced back and forth in Neve's living room.

"Is that new? This place has reminded me of a reality show since I got here."

Ariel paused and glared at Neve, old animosities diluted but not gone. "You're the reason for a lot of that drama."

"I think there's enough blame to go around," Neve said, thinking about the crazy events that had her fingerprints on them since she arrived. Ariel wasn't wrong. Kennedy had accused Neve of the same thing.

"The timing of Conner Graham's appearance is strange. Why did he come to SX right before a hurricane?" Ariel asked, staring at question five on Neve's list of local mysteries, ignoring the fact that she screwed the guy as soon as he got to town.

Neve closed the curtain to cover her list. They weren't here to initiate Ariel into the Crossing Guard. "There are a lot of Grahams that have returned since Bryce moved back. Kennedy Graham is the latest arrival. She said something about pieces of a puzzle."

Ariel frowned and shook her head. "There might be another Graham in SX. I saw someone with Leira. He had scars on his face, but the uninjured parts looked like Conner...and Bryce. He must be another Graham. The three men could be triplets separated at birth."

"More mysteries tied to Leira," Neve said.

"I knew that bitch was trouble. I should've broken the cunt's nose," came a voice from Neve's foyer.

"Jesus, Lilah. I get what Caleb's talking about with your dirty mouth," Naomi said, entering the room behind her Caesar sister.

"That's coming from someone who cusses like a sailor," Ariel quipped.

Delilah plopped down on Neve's sofa. "Quit being a pussy, Naomi. If we're going to confront JZ, you need to grow a pair of balls."

Naomi glared at Delilah. "My sister-in-law isn't colluding with Leira. This is all a misunderstanding. You'll see."

"I don't know, Naomi. I saw JZ order a poppyseed muffin at Kenny's Koffee just a few minutes after Leira did. They both said the pastry was for someone else," Ariel said skeptically.

"You believe Juliet and Leira were getting a treat for the same person?" Naomi asked.

Ariel shrugged. "I don't believe in coincidences, Nay. And there's been a lot of weird shit going on around SX lately."

Naomi sighed. "Well, JZ told my twin that she was taking their Christmas baskets around SX tonight. Juliet doesn't have the energy to run all around town yet, so JZ is delivering them herself."

Delilah smiled big. "It's gonna be a sting operation."

"We're getting some answers. It will exonerate Juliet Zhang, and then we can focus on the rest of the mysteries in SX," Naomi said, sounding like someone trying to convince herself as much as the others.

Delilah was shifting her legs in the air over Neve's sofa like she was riding an invisible, floating bicycle. "Maybe JZ is working undercover to catch Leira doing something illegal. Something to send Leira to prison. Then that motherfucker can get beat up by bitches up and down the cell block."

Ariel nodded in agreement with her quirky sister. How nice the usually combative pseudo-sisters could find common ground in attacking the woman who'd dated both Delilah and Ariel's beloved men.

Ten minutes later, Neve was in a group of women she never would have imagined being a part of, even a few weeks ago. Since falling in love with Bryce, she understood one major hurdle would be ingratiating herself into the tight-knit unit called the Caesars. Neve and Sammy had quickly become fast friends. Her relationship with the other Caesars came over the last several weeks. Delilah had recently become one of Neve's closest confidantes. Naomi was a trusted teammate on the Crossing Guard.

Neve never thought she'd win over Ariel, but now Ariel was riding shotgun while Delilah and Naomi sat in the backseat. They shared a common enemy in Leira, and both harbored suspicions about the goings-on around SX. Neve didn't trust Ariel enough to invite her to join the Crossing Guard, but their goals aligned for this particular mission.

Neve thought she knew Juliet Zhang well after working alongside her at City Hall and keeping her secret for long weeks, but JZ had been acting strangely since she returned after the hurricane. She was neither the same person who had been Neve's boss, nor the woman who enlisted Neve to help her escape Florida and start her new life with her true love in Iowa. Those plans had come to ruin, and JZ seemed to have changed from the Juliet who had left SX.

"There," Ariel said, pointing ahead at the tinted windshield of the car Delilah had borrowed from Tom so JZ wouldn't recognize their vehicle. "She's delivering the fruit basket to the SXPD. She's following the route JTS gave us."

"Isn't your twin going to tell her wife you asked for her route, Naomi?" Neve asked.

"I stopped by right after she took her meds for the night. I told her we wanted to surprise JZ and help deliver the baskets. She was sawing logs before I even left her bedroom," Naomi answered.

JZ exited the precinct and hopped into her car. Neve had

become oddly proficient at spying over the last few weeks. She followed JZ at a distance as she zipped through SX. The four women inside Tom's vehicle looked at each other, stunned, when JZ pulled into the parking lot of the Riverside Inn.

"What the hell is she doing here?" Delilah asked.

"This is where I saw Leira," Ariel said as JZ got out. Juliet Zhang was not carrying a Christmas basket. She had a gift wrapped in paper imprinted with the words "Happy Birthday" repeated in a pattern. JZ knocked on the door to Room 112. The door opened, and JZ stepped inside. Neve couldn't see who let JZ in. "Leira was staying in that room."

"Aw, shit, this is bad," Naomi said in a distraught tone.

"There could still be a plausible explanation. We need to know what's going on," Neve said.

Delilah opened the car's back door. "Let's bust this bitch."

Sheesh, these Caesars were volatile. Neve got out and jogged to keep up with Delilah, who strode toward the motel room like a badass action star marching into a nest of Nazis. Ariel and Naomi followed at her heels. Delilah was knocking when Neve, Naomi, and Ariel arrived at her side. No one answered immediately. Delilah pounded on the metal surface, shaking the door in the jamb. For a moment, Neve pictured Juliet in high heels and a power suit sneaking out the bathroom window like Neve had done in Kennedy's room at Manny's Motel.

Instead, JZ herself opened the door. Delilah was surprised it wasn't Leira and retreated a step. The look on Juliet's face was fierce and pissed. They had busted her, but she seemed more offended than ashamed. It was just like Juliet Zhang to tackle confrontation head-on rather than skulking out a secret exit.

Ariel stepped forward, elbowing the ambushed Delilah aside.

"What the hell are you doing here, Juliet?"

"I could ask you the same thing," JZ countered.

"We followed you. Why are you hanging out with Leira Gemini on Christmas Eve?" Ariel challenged, unintimidated by JZ's cool confidence.

"We go way back. You remember, she stayed in SX for a couple of months when we were teenagers," JZ said, knowing full well Ariel recalled how Leira ruined the Caesars' last summer.

"I don't recall you and Leira exactly becoming pen pals after she left," Ariel said.

"You seem to forget that you're married, and that happened only a few weeks ago," JZ snapped.

Ariel turned red. Neve worried she was about to be ring-side for another catfight here in the Riverside Inn parking lot, the main event after the pre-match bout between Delilah and Leira at the ballroom in Graham Manor. Neve slipped between the Caesars and pushed past Juliet, bursting uninvited into the motel room. Leira stood by a table with the unwrapped gift Juliet had been carrying. It was a bag of roasted pecans. The nuts felt specific and personal to Neve. Behind Leira, standing by the ensuite bathroom, a tall, muscular African American man watched the scene cautiously.

The man was handsome and still. He reminded Neve of Jax in a way. But something about his eyes and lips resembled Sammy. She saw hints of Bryce in his profile. Did Martin Montgomery have another bastard child?

"It's your birthday?" Ariel asked Leira, following Neve inside, with Delilah and Naomi next, followed by JZ.

"Christmas Eve birthday," Leira confirmed, eyeing the Caesar entourage with suspicion.

Ariel stopped in front of Leira, looking the punk eye to eye. Neve realized the resemblance, minus the cosmetic differences, was uncanny. "A lot of birthdays lately. I saw you buy a poppyseed muffin for someone named Caid. You mentioned that Mr. Tall, Dark, and Handsome here recently had a birthday too. I overheard you talking about celebrating a birthday for someone named Hallie the other day. Now, there's you."

Leira shrugged. "Yeah, we call ourselves the Holidays. We were all born within a few weeks of each other."

"Seems strange," Ariel said.

"The Caesars share a single birthday. That's stranger," Leira said.

"Why did you follow me?" JZ asked, irritated and on the offensive.

"Because Leira is our archvillain, and you're sneaking around with the enemy," Delilah said.

JZ didn't balk at Delilah's aggressive interaction. "Leira and I were friends ten years ago. I couldn't say anything because Ariel was bonkers with jealousy. I spent a lot of time with Leira. She was more interesting than most of you. We've stayed in touch over the years."

"Et tu, Brute?" Delilah muttered, stepping back and glaring at JZ.

Naomi wasn't so easily miffed. "That doesn't explain sneaking around now. Juliet doesn't know you're here."

"You've been acting weird since you got back to SX," Ariel added.

"We couldn't let anyone else know what we were up to," Leira said. She looked at JZ, and JZ nodded. Leira stepped closer, eyeing Delilah in case the volatile Ryan attacked. "We've been discussing Neve."

Neve blinked, staring because she wasn't sure she heard that right.

"Me?"

Leira glared at Neve. "I dated Bryce ten years ago, and I've never stopped loving him. I think I'm a better fit for him than you are."

"What does that have to do with you, Juliet?" Ariel asked.

"I agree with her," JZ said.

Neve felt like someone had punched her in the gut. She cared more for JZ than most of the other Caesars. But the sentiment was obviously not mutual. Juliet Zhang conspired with Leira to steal Bryce away from Neve.

"You lied to Bryce about my death," JZ said.

"To protect you," Neve cried.

JZ dismissed Neve's reason. "You chose a stranger over your own fiancé. Leira would never do that."

"Never," Leira agreed smugly.

"Let me knock out those smiling fucking teeth," Delilah said, hands balled into fists.

JZ stepped in, a woman commanding the room. "I think you need to go. You have your answers. Now, leave me alone. I'm disappointed in all of you."

Ariel wouldn't be bullied by JZ. "Don't talk down to us, you condescending bitch. You've changed, Juliet."

"I grew up, Ariel. I don't believe in fairy-tale endings and happily ever afters. Love requires hard work and commitment. It takes a steel backbone and unwavering trust. Neve has treated Bryce like an afterthought instead of a trusted partner." JZ walked up to Neve, stared her in the eye, like the badass Caesar she always was. "Does Bryce know you're here right now?" JZ looked at the line of pseudo-sisters. "Any of you?"

No one answered.

"How about Tom? Juliet?" JZ asked.

No reply.

"Get the hell out before I call the cops. Most of the ones in charge share my last name. You don't want to explain why the police arrested all of you for harassing your fellow Caesar and Bryce's innocent ex-girlfriend," JZ said, turning her back on her sisters.

"And the former flame of Tom Graham," Leira chimed in.

Neve waited for Delilah to fly across the room like a wildcat. The big guy by the bathroom appeared poised to intervene. But Delilah managed to control both her body and mouth. Naomi had taken her hand and restrained her like a rabid dog.

"We're done," JZ said.

Naomi exited, pulling Delilah along. Neve noticed Ariel studying JZ. Something puzzled Neve's former archenemy. Neve would circle back to it later. Not today. She followed Delilah out, Ariel at her heel. They had suffered a smackdown. They were defeated. Kennedy Graham's accusation that Leira was dangerous proved true. Neve had more to lose from Leira than even Kennedy did. Leira plotted to steal Bryce.

Before they reached the car, while Naomi was distracted, they calmed Delilah so she wouldn't come back with a crate of Molotov cocktails.

Ariel leaned and whispered in Neve's ear, "Juliet Zhang is lying."

Chapter Twenty-One

ARIEL ÁLVAREZ

Ariel didn't believe a goddamn word that had come out of Juliet Zhang's mouth. Maybe Neve had connections to learn more about it, but Neve wasn't the only one with resources in SX. And Naomi, Delilah, and JZ weren't the only Caesar sisters. One of them who hadn't joined their little bitch hunt was perhaps the one with the best resources to find the truth in this cesspool town.

Ariel ditched the others immediately when they returned to Neve's bungalow. She didn't like spending time in a house where Neve regularly fucked the man she loved. Besides, despite Delilah clucking like a plucked hen and Naomi grumbling in disappointment about her sister-in-law, only Neve realized something more was going on with JZ's story. If anyone could corroborate Juliet's reimagining of their last summer with Bryce, it would be the Caesar who always had to stick her nose in everyone's business. Sammy would have known if JZ was covertly spending time with Leira a decade ago.

Ariel parked in front of Sammy's house. She could see her pseudo-sister's silhouette through the front window's drapes as Sammy paced in front of the lit interior. She held a phone to her ear, and the conversation seemed intense. Ariel watched as Sammy waved a hand, always wildly gesticulating when her emotions ramped up.

Ariel knocked. Sammy answered with a surprised look. Or was it guilt? Guilt about what?

"Ariel, I wasn't expecting you," Sammy breathed, exhaling like she'd just finished biking ten miles.

"That's because I didn't call first," Ariel said, frowning. Since when did she need to make an appointment to see Sammy? Of her Caesar sisters, she had always gotten along best with Sammy. Usually. JTS had said Sammy was pissed at her for some reason. "You okay?"

"Oh, yeah. Yeah. Getting ready for bed," Sammy said, biting her lip.

Sammy still wore the apron she used when working her food truck. Ariel knew every year she offered a complimentary Christmas Eve feast for folks around SX who couldn't afford home-cooked meals. She probably got home right before Ariel pulled up. Sammy didn't look anywhere near ready for bed.

"Who were you talking to on the phone? I saw you through the window."

"Oh, that. That was Neve," Sammy stammered. Sammy thought Ariel wouldn't know if that was a lie because Ariel hated Neve and avoided her like a sunburn, but Sammy was a lousy gambler. Neve was probably planning with Naomi and Delilah and not taking calls.

"What were you talking about?"

"Aw, nothing. Y'know. Bryce. Stuff."

"Right," Ariel said, letting it go. If Sammy lied to Ariel, she might feel guilty enough to rat out JZ about the Caesars' last summer together. If she called out Sammy's bullshit, she might have clammed up about the past and sent Ariel packing. "Can we talk?"

Sammy shrugged and stepped aside to let her enter. Ariel noticed her pseudo-sister's nervous tick, her fingers drumming notes on her hip. Sammy had played flute in high school, and now her nervous tick showed up in a tap-tap-tap. She was snoopy as hell and loved knowing other people's business, but she couldn't keep a secret worth a shit.

"I followed JZ tonight. She went to see Leira Gemini," Ariel said. She didn't name her coconspirators.

Sammy frowned. So, Sammy thought this was as strange as she did.

"Juliet said she spent a lot of time with Leira when she was here during Bryce's last summer. Do you remember that?" Ariel asked.

Sammy wrinkled her nose like something stunk. "Hell, no. JZ didn't like Leira at all. She didn't think she was good enough for Bryce. She's got good judgment, because she felt the same way about you."

"JZ's working to get Bryce to dump Neve for Leira," she said, ignoring the insult.

"Bullshit. Juliet adores Neve. She said so a dozen times before she faked her death," Sammy said, shaking her head as if a conman were trying to get her to take a deal.

Ariel raised her eyebrows. "It came straight from the horse's mouth."

"That doesn't sound like JZ."

"She's been acting strange since she came back."

Ariel disliked the change in her fellow Caesar's personality. She was never a fan of Juliet Zhang, but they were as much sisters as Ariel and Cin. Things were strange in SX. Everything felt sideways. People were acting oddly. Even her own predictable husband had cheated on her. Ariel looked at Sammy. She knew a lot about what was happening in SX. Maybe she knew?

"Who's Rob been sleeping with?" Ariel asked.

Sammy's fingers tapped against her hip, nervously playing a tune. She opened her mouth to answer, then closed it again. Sammy was a terrible fucking liar. She'd been talking to someone on the phone, then lied about who it was. Juliet Salem said she was mad at Ariel, but JTS didn't know why. Was Sammy pissed because Ariel cheated on Rob? What did Ariel's marriage have to do with Sammy? Why would she care if Ariel had an aff—

"Oh, hell, no. You didn't," Ariel said, the truth dawning like the awful stench of rotted fish carried on a sudden sea breeze.

Sammy offered a stammering explanation, "He was devastated, Ariel. You broke his heart. He came to the Montgomery offices during the storm, devastated. I didn't mean for it to happen, but it just...we..."

"I don't want your excuses. How could you do that to your own sister?" Ariel spat, rage filling her heart and tears blurring everything in Sammy's house. Was she more upset about Rob's betrayal or Sammy's?

"I've loved him for as long as you! He deserves better," Sammy hollered. Ariel blinked away the tears, stunned. Sammy had been in love with Rob all these years?

"You backstabbing whore. I ought to stuff my fist down your fucking throat," Ariel said through clenched teeth.

Sammy's face changed instantly, and Ariel took a step back. She had forgotten that she could push Samantha Montgomery too far. Half of her DNA came from her father. Ariel had heard rumors of her brothers' capacity for violence. Carver had spent time in prison. Ariel shouldn't set her off. But Ariel knew karate, and she could defend herself if needed.

"Try me, bitch," Sammy countered.

Ariel almost threw a punch. An angry Álvarez was probably a match for a murderous Montgomery, but Ariel wasn't willing to risk her life for goddamn Rob Ryan. No, Ariel had a better way to get revenge. Without another word, Ariel spun around and exited Sammy's house, slamming the door behind her loudly enough to wake the neighborhood.

Ariel climbed into her shitty blue Toyota and sped away in a huff. As she angrily drove out of the Montgomery neighborhood, she spotted Sammy's food truck in its permanent place on the outskirts of the neighborhood. She came to a stop, her headlights illuminating the little truck parked in the dark lot of a hair salon damaged during the hurricane. Citizens had evacuated the entire neighborhood, and the buildings stood empty for several blocks in every direction. Ariel stared at the truck through tear-streaked eyes.

No one was watching. Ariel checked her seatbelt. She slammed the gas pedal to the floor, sped across the parking lot, and hit the side of Sammy's truck at thirty miles an hour. She felt the box truck's side cave in to cushion her blow. The seatbelt tightened across her chest, driving the air from her lungs. Her forehead missed the steering wheel. The airbag didn't even deploy, so it was probably defective all along. Ariel checked herself and was mostly unhurt.

The door was crushed and crammed against the sidewall of Sammy's truck, so Ariel climbed over the seat and exited through the shattered back window. The Toyota was totaled. Sammy's truck looked like a soda can someone had stepped on in the middle. Ariel listened for a siren for several long minutes. Nothing. No one drove by. Ariel started walking. She didn't know what she'd tell the police when they found her Toyota crashed into Sammy's truck. She could deal with that tomorrow.

The edge of the Montgomery neighborhood bordered a section of the Ryans' territory. She found herself wandering toward Rob Ryan's house. The home they'd once shared before the hurricane and before Ariel lost control during the storm. Sammy revealed that Ariel wasn't the only newlywed to cheat that night. Rob slept with Sammy. Sammy loved Rob.

That cruel cunt.

Ariel stopped before the walkway leading to Rob's front door. His car was in the driveway, but no lights were on. The hour was close to midnight, on the eve of Christmas Day. Ariel started removing her clothes on the front lawn. It was the holiday season, and Ariel loved unwrapping a gift. This gift was for Rob. And it would act as coal in Sammy's stocking.

She knocked on the door and waited. Would Rob be expecting Sammy for a midnight rendezvous? Maybe Sammy told him she'd confessed, and so he expected an angry Ariel ready to rip him a new asshole. He definitely didn't expect his estranged wife to be standing outside on his doorstep, as naked as on their awkward wedding night when she fantasized Bryce was consummating their marriage instead of Rob.

The door opened.

"Ariel," Rob said in that husky voice of deep wanting.

"Merry Christmas," Ariel said with a sultry tone in her voice.

"You look like an angel under the stars," Rob said, not blinking once.

"An angel needs to top a tree. Got any wood?" Her Cheshire smile was filled with revenge and sexual desire.

Rob looked up and down the street. The neighborhood had survived the storm better than some. However, everyone was either asleep at this hour or was busy finishing the last preparations for Christmas morning surprises. Ariel was more interested in something between the sheets than under the tree. Bryce would never be an option; Conner proved to be a poor substitute, so Ariel would be damned if she was going to let Sammy steal her husband.

If Rob thought about Sammy and their relationship, if he

considered what they discussed on the phone, if he worried about Sammy's feelings if he slept with his wife again after everything she had done to him and everything Rob did inside Sammy, he didn't show it. Rob swept her into his strong arms and pulled her naked body against him.

He led Ariel inside, deadbolting the door behind him. He pulled off his T-shirt, tossing it on the table in the foyer. As they kissed, he removed his sleeping shorts, one hand yanking down the waistband as the other groped her bare ass. When his phone fell out of the pocket of the shorts, face up, silenced, vibrating, and dancing on the hardwood floor, Sammy's name and face appeared as an incoming call. Rob didn't glance at the phone, mesmerized by her tits.

Ariel kicked at the phone, her heel connecting and sending the device sliding across the floor under a cabinet against the wall. She wrapped her hand around his dick and gave his engorged cock a practiced stroke, just like they did in high school when they only ever practiced hand jobs and oral. Now, it was the prelude to something else. Ariel wanted wild, fucking revenge sex.

"Take me...against...the wall," she groaned breathlessly as he fondled her in their hallway to the bedroom. "I can't wait...for the bed."

He lifted her with a firm hand on her backside, his strong arms able to move her around like a marionette. She spread her legs as he aligned himself with her opening and lowered her onto his thick cock. He wasn't as devilish or rough as Conner Graham, but this was as wild and lustful as Ariel had ever seen Rob.

Maybe he'd finally get her to an orgasm.

Rob fucked her against the wall. Her shoulder blades dug into the picture frame that held their wedding photo as her ass bounced against the wall. He moved with hard, deep thrusts, making her breasts bounce like a pair of flotation devices bobbing in the surf. She kissed him, releasing a passion that she didn't know she had. Was it because she finally let go of Bryce and had some genuine feelings for Rob? Did his urgent lovemaking rouse her? Or did Ariel get off on wrecking the happy ending Sammy wanted with Ariel's husband?

Ariel didn't know if the reason was revelatory or a revenge story, but he brought her to the first climax Rob had ever managed. Conner had smashed her so hard that she experienced multiple orgasms in their night together, but she'd never come with Rob. Her noises made Rob somehow harder and more eager, and he carried Ariel into their bedroom, managing to bring her to a second climax.

"I love you so much," Rob mumbled into his pillow beside her, and then Ariel recognized the familiar breathing of slumber.

Ariel lay on her back for a long while, thinking about Rob and Sammy. Ariel was sure he'd never thought about her once. She remembered crashing her car into the side of Sammy's food truck. She considered Leira's motivations, trying to steal Bryce away from Neve by any means necessary. Vindictive bitch. Ariel had always thought the two looked eerily similar, and now Ariel wondered if she and Leira might act the same, too.

Chapter Twenty-Two

JACKIE SALEM

Was this how Superman felt?

Jackie wasn't hiding a superhero suit under her professional blazer and business skirt. She couldn't tear open her button-up blouse to reveal a red and yellow "S" on the sexy costume she wore to save the day. Her glasses served a purpose rather than to conceal a secret identity. Jackie's eyes were tired and her vision blurry after weeks of poring over the fine print on endless documents. Jackie *did not* feel like a superhero.

But she was a woman living with two identities. Since returning to SX, she had relished being Jacquelyn Salem again. She felt like her old self for the first time in over twenty years. Maggie Noble had been a fictional alter ego used to protect baby Neve. Neve wasn't a baby anymore. Jackie could quit pretending.

Yet, fantasy had become reality in Horton, Iowa. Parts of her life, as Maggie Noble, were as genuine as her past as Jacquelyn Salem. She had two beautiful children with Mark Noble, and they'd shared a caring, comforting, and safe marriage. Jackie had lived a fairy-tale life since she was barely into adulthood, and most women would have traded the sun and beaches for a good man and hot breakfast every morning for two decades any day of the week. But Jackie fully embraced her true identity as soon as she hit Salem Shores, and her life as Maggie Noble washed away like the rough surf eroding the most fantastic sandcastles.

Mark Noble had never been any different from Gilbert Graham. Gil only changed his name, not his personality. Jackie Salem couldn't survive in a quiet marriage in the suburban Midwest, so she had to craft a persona as a dedicated wife, a domesticated family woman, a doting mother, and a disciplined teacher. Upon reclaiming her old name, she reasserted her old personality. Jackie Salem was wealthy, confident, decisive, independent, adventurous, and a little bit bitchy. Like a pair of comfy sweatpants after a day dressed for business, Jackie felt like she could let loose and be herself.

But Jackie now wasn't the same as the Jackie who'd lived here before.

She had become an amalgamation of the Jackie from SX and the Maggie of Horton, Iowa. Mackie. Or maybe Jaggie.

Jackie confronted Alistair earlier on Christmas Eve, standing in her office above the SX Club, reviewing the latest slew of documents. "The numbers don't add up. I hit a dead end with government assistance, so I decided to focus my efforts on supporting your insurance claims. That's our only way out right now. We're out of time. However, the docs I see don't jive with what we have on the books. It doesn't make any sense."

"No offense, sis, but you've been out of the loop since I was in diapers," Alistair said. He held out his arms to indicate the stacks of papers around him. "Look at this. It looks like a museum in here. We keep records electronically nowadays, you know?"

"I prefer physical copies to review. You can print anything, Alistair."

"You must've spent half the renovation budget for the club on printer supplies."

"It's easier to connect the dots when they are in neat little stacks."

Alistair narrowed his eyes. "What dots? Are you pulling at some loose thread, Jackie? Trying to unravel the whole thing?"

"Not unravel. Reveal. I think there's something you're not telling me."

Alistair stared at her coolly. He had been Tessa's right-hand man since he was old enough to look respectable in a business suit, so Jackie knew her brother could wear a poker face and lie like a politician. She couldn't believe a word coming out of his mouth on his perfectly handsome face. He could stand before her in the office along Salem Shores and swear it was snowing outside.

Alistair inhaled sharply and icily replied. "You're a schoolteacher from Iowa. You weren't even the math teacher. You taught history. If I need a lesson on the saga of the Miccosukee tribe in central Florida, I'll sign up for your PowerPoint presentation."

Jackie pointed her finger at her younger brother. "Listen, you cocky little punk, I'm trying to help save the family from financial ruin here. We're on the edge of bankruptcy, and you're making quips about my presentation skills. You said you had a handle on the insurance claims, and it looks to me like it's a giant shit show. I think you're in over your head, and the whole thing is about to blow up in our faces."

"You don't know what the fuck you're talking about. I have everything under control. The insurance money will come through at any moment. Take a goddamn Xanax and chill out. Everything's going to be fine," Alistair retorted. She remembered the same little toddler before she left—temperamental, spoiled, and stubborn.

"Santa Claus is going to bring a big fat check and leave it in my stocking tonight? I don't believe in fairy tales, Alice."

Alistair bristled at her pet name for him. She knew he didn't like that.

"You've been living a lie in your white picket fence castle with Gilbert Graham in the 'burbs with a family, a book club, and probably a pet terrier."

Alistair was wrong about the terrier.

He stormed out, offended by Jackie's insinuations, but for her, it was a performance, and his exit was more of an escape. She returned to poring over the records, looking for a way out of this crisis. The creditors might have given the Salems a brief reprieve for the holidays, but they were like sharks circling as she treaded in the choppy surf, and they didn't consider Jackie a friend. She was chum in the water.

"Merry Christmas."

Jackie looked up from piles of documents spread across the table. If she had felt like Superman playacting in a business suit, her Lois Lane had arrived to offer support. As Gilbert shuffled nervously from foot to foot like a man unsure if the prom queen would agree to a dance, Jackie couldn't help but think of the confident and assertive Martin Montgomery, who would cross the room and ravish her rather than wait for Jackie to make the first move. What happens when Superman lusts after Lex Luthor instead of Lois Lane?

"Christmas? What time is it?" Jackie asked, blinking. The world outside the window was dark and hourless.

"After midnight. You missed Christmas Eve," Gil said.

In Iowa, Christmas Eve had been a night of food, song, and gifts. Neve had made her signature eggnog for the family for the past ten years. Last year, Cyprus spiked the bowl, and Neve's former fiancé, Patrick Moulder, had gotten inadvertently intoxicated and passed out in the light-up nativity scene on the front lawn. Willow could never wait to open a present and begged to start distributing gifts every ten minutes. Gil insisted on singing a round of holiday songs around the piano before anyone touched anything under the tree. And they would watch an animated Christmas special after supper every single year.

Until now.

Until they returned to Florida and everything changed.

Until everything went back to the way it was.

Like Superman leaving Smallville, Kansas, and returning to live on planet Krypton.

But Krypton had exploded. There was no going back. Jackie thought about SX, the Salem properties in ruins along the coastline. The lenders would repossess the entire row of buildings along Salem Shores, changing names, razing others, and making the entire stretch of beach unrecognizable. Maybe there was never any going back.

"What have you got there?" Jackie asked.

Gil held a gift in his hand. He reminded her of a shy suitor waiting for a prom date, holding a corsage and being nervous about giving it. Wrapped neatly with a red bow, she recognized Gil's handiwork. He was meticulous about everything, including wrapping presents. A tag dangled from one side, and Jackie could see what was written on it—"To Maggie. From Mark." He was still pretending.

"A little something," Gil said.

"I'm sorry. I didn't know we were exchanging gifts this year. I've been so busy with all this," Jackie said, waving her arms at the endless reams of paper around her. "I didn't get you anything."

Gil smiled an aw-shucks grin that was more Clark Kent than Jackie's self-image. While Jackie spent twenty-three years acting like someone she wasn't, Gil had been more comfortable as Mark Noble than he ever did as Gilbert Graham. He had never liked Salem Crossing. He hadn't been playing a part. Gil had discovered his true self up in Iowa. He was a husband, father, and Midwestern man.

Jackie preferred metropolitan and badass.

Jackie took the gift, cleared a spot on the table, and sat down to unwrap it. She worried it would be something sentimental, and she'd have to pretend to like it, emoting over a memento she didn't want to remember. Or maybe it would be something romantic, and he would expect the night to end in the bedroom. Jackie wasn't in the mood to avoid fantasies about Martin Montgomery while making love to her husband.

It was neither sentimental nor romantic but rather enigmatic.

She extracted a cylinder made of a light metal. It featured markings with letters and symbols. Dials occupied the entire length, allowing one to turn the markings to align with other letters to spell a word or short phrase. The engravings were intricate, and the artifact appeared antique. Jackie didn't understand what she was looking at. She glanced at Gil with furrowed brows.

"I don't get it."

"It's a puzzle box."

"I don't have time for puzzles, Gil. Is there something inside?"

Gil shrugged his shoulders. "I don't know. I've never been able to open it."

Jackie frowned. "Then what's the point if you can't open it?"

"That is the point. That you can't open it."

"A puzzle that you can't solve?"

"There isn't an answer for every problem out there in the world. Some things we have to take on faith," Gil said.

"You want me to pray that the Salems avoid money trouble and duck repossession of all our property?"

"That's the idea."

Jackie shook her head. "I don't think God gives a damn about rich people's problems. In fact, I seriously hope the Almighty has better things to do than save our wealthy asses from the repo men."

Gil approached cautiously, like a wrangler trying to get close enough to lasso a calf without spooking her or wrestle a gator without losing an arm. He took her by the elbows, like he used to in Iowa after she had a rough day at school, or when she felt sad thinking about home, or when the kids had some sort of problem that worried her. It was sweet, intimate, and nostalgic. All the things she didn't need right now. She really wanted someone to fuck her hard and make her forget about everything for a while.

"Leave the puzzle, Maggie. Let it go for a while."

She wasn't Maggie. She was never Maggie. Gil didn't understand that she had been faking it her whole life. As a teacher, as a mother, as a wife, and especially as a lover. Jackie had never been Maggie Noble. And she never wanted to go back.

"Call me Jackie," she said, unbuttoning the blouse she'd been wearing all day.

Gil apologized as she dropped her top on the floor. "I'm sorry. I called you Maggie for so many years..."

"I'm not interested in the past." She unclasped her bra, letting it fall, standing topless before him. "Call me Jackie."

"Of course. I'll call you whatever you want," Gil stammered, staring as she unzipped her skirt.

"Then call me Jackie," she said, sloughing off her underwear and revealing herself completely.

Gil pulled her into his arms, burying his face in her breasts. She fumbled opening his pants, shucked off his bottoms, and released his dick, hard and ready. She shoved him back onto a davenport worth more than Gil's yearly salary and mounted him like a rider swinging a leg over a saddle. Jackie hovered over him, the tip of his cock at the entrance to her pussy. She stared down past her hanging breasts and looked him in the eye.

"Call me Jackie, damn it."

"Jackie, please. Give it to me," he said, begging like a trained dog.

"That's it. Say it again," she said, rubbing herself against the head of his cock.

"Jackie," Gil moaned, reaching up and fondling one breast, the other hand trying to coax her ass to descend on him. She'd never heard him more urgent or desperate in her twenty-three-year marriage. "Jackie, Jackie, Jackie."

She lowered herself slowly on his erection, making him groan like a starving man ravishing his first meal in weeks. She didn't think about whether she was Jackie or Maggie. She didn't consider whether the man inside her was Gil, Mark, or Martin. She gave herself over to experience and let the sensation take her on waves of pleasure, like the current pulling her out to a sexual sea. Her mind went to a place where she didn't have to solve any problems, like Gil had suggested about her puzzle of a present.

"Jackie, I'm gonna—"

"Don't you fucking dare." Jackie put a hand around his neck and squeezed a little. Not enough to hurt, but enough to give the threat some meaning. She was riding him hard, and she wasn't quite there. She wouldn't let him finish until she was done with him. "You wait for me, motherfucker."

And he did. Somehow. Maybe it was the hand on his throat or the way she called him a vile name, but he managed to stave off ejaculation for a few more moments. Jackie kept her hand around his throat, his Adam's apple bobbing against the palm of her hand. She smashed her pelvis against his body as the flood arrived, and she came hard and long. Somewhere in there, Gil finished, too. He was softening by the time she came back to her senses. Jackie realized she still had one hand under his chin, as he gasped for air. She loosened her grip and dismounted.

Gil watched as she grabbed a cigarette and started smoking. She stared at the puzzle on the table beside the davenport. It wasn't meant to be solved. She looked at the letters and symbols up and down the length as she puffed. Eventually, Gil drifted off to sleep. Jackie finished the cigarette.

She picked up the puzzle. Twisted it. Turned it. Stared and studied. Of course, there was an answer. Everything had a solution. She could solve any problem with the correct key. Jackie simply had to find the right way to think about it. She picked up the puzzle and started manipulating the cylinder.

Chapter Twenty-Three

JACKSON MONTGOMERY

Jax used to wake up early on Christmas morning, in the middle of the night. Back when he still believed that Santa was real and magic could make miracles. He'd wake Riley, and they'd creep downstairs to see the presents overflowing from beneath the tree. He would try to catch the old man in the act, but he never stumbled upon Santa stuffing stockings. They would look at the presents labeled "To: Jax, From: Santa"; "To: Riley, From: Santa"; "To: Samantha, From: Santa"; "To: Carter, From: Santa." They would shake them and wonder what was inside.

Turned out Santa ought to have delivered a few more presents under the Montgomery tree: "To: Bryce, From: Santa"; "To: Damien, From: Santa"; "To: Sweetheart, From: Santa."

Jax later wondered, after he'd come to believe magic was as mythical as true love, precisely when his mother had time to wrap their gifts and slip them under the tree. Maybe it was when his dad was out sleeping with Elizabeth Halloweather, Amanda Graham, Makenna Salem, and God-knew-who-else. Parents weren't only sneaking around SX playing Santa

Claus; some tiptoed into houses to deliver a different type of package.

Wouldn't the world be better off if fat, jolly men with enchanted reindeer bringing gifts could solve all the problems? Jax preferred believing the lie over accepting the truth. Reality offered nothing particularly remarkable. Love equaled problems, a family brought drama, and Christmas delivered only danger and the possibility of death. He awoke at five a.m. on Christmas morning for different reasons in adulthood than when he was nine.

A phone roused Jax instead of the promise of presents under the tree. Lately, the only thing delivered was terrible news. He grabbed the glowing device with lightning-fast reflexes, his heart sinking as he saw Cin as the caller and the time an ungodly hour. Cin was a night owl but never an early riser. A call when she should be sleeping meant trouble.

"Intruder. He's inside my house," Cin whispered hoarsely as soon as he answered. Jax sat upright, fully awake, skills honed after years of living on the edge of the law.

The line went dead. Jax moved instantly. He had been staying at Kennedy's room at Manny's Motel, sleeping in a chair across from the bed, as he had when the cops wanted Cin for murder (minus the sexual tension), fully clothed and ready for action. Kennedy had been afraid of Leira Gemini and her entourage, worried they meant her harm. It turned out Jax might have been protecting the wrong woman.

"What happened?" Kennedy asked groggily from bed as Jax slipped on his shoes and disengaged the security chain on the door.

"Lock up after me," he barked as he opened the door. He sprinted away.

Luckily, he was already in Old Mat, and Cin lived only a few blocks away. He'd parked his red Jag at the far end of the lot, but by the time he started the engine and drove off, he could run to Cin's just as fast. Besides, he didn't want to alert Cin's intruder that he was on the way. The roar of the Jag's engine in the middle of the night would wake the whole neighborhood.

That could get Cin killed.

He reached Cin's mobile home three minutes after she called. He slowed, surveying the scene before barging in. Recklessness could cause someone with a gun to shoot unnecessarily. Jax had to scout the situation before charging forth. If he got this wrong...if his mistakes resulted in Cin getting hurt or...or worse...then he'd never forgive himself.

He told Carver not too long ago that his relationship with Cin wasn't like Romeo and Juliet. He told his brother that he wouldn't kill himself in the end. But if his screw-up tonight resulted in a funeral for his one true love, Jax couldn't go on. He could never live with the guilt of failing Cin. He'd been trying to protect Kennedy, but Cin had been the one in danger all along.

Jax crept to the end of the trailer house, staring at the window of Cin's bedroom. That would've been where she was sleeping if the intruder had arrived while she was in bed. Had Cin had time to retreat? The window wasn't open, so she hadn't exited that way. The back door was around the rear side of the mobile home.

Then, a cry behind him. To any nine-year-olds up at this hour in Old Mat, checking if Santa had delivered the goods, they might mistake it for any one of the dozen wild nocturnal animals prowling about the neighborhood. But Jax knew Cin had made the sound. His heart could translate what his ears might have missed. The sound came from the overgrown preserve behind Cin's place, which had been undeveloped since the founding of this town.

Jax used the light on his phone to illuminate Cin's backyard, sure she had already escaped into the wilds. Or maybe the intruder had dragged her away. He noticed signs someone had crossed the lawn—something the size of a person had disturbed the dew in the grass. Maybe more than one person. Jax followed the trail into the overgrown foliage, pushing blindly through thick underbrush and even denser darkness. The light from his phone was the only illumination through the dense vegetation, but it also made Jax a target if anyone was waiting for him ahead. Luckily, there seemed to be only one navigable path through the overrun bushes, downed trees, moldered detritus, and abundant vines. Jax followed the single route through the scrub.

Had Cin safely escaped through the wooded area? Was a pursuer following her? Or had a kidnapper nabbed her and dragged her off through the underbrush?

"Hands off, motherfucker," Jax heard ahead, maybe thirty yards, depending on how much the thick undergrowth muffled Cin's voice. But it was definitely Acindina. And she had to be talking to someone. "I'm going to tear your goddamn balls off."

A gruff voice replied, "Shut up, or I'll knock your teeth down your throat. Now move your ass."

Jax turned off the light on his phone and moved purely by instinct. He followed the source of the sound. He prayed Cin would say something else to keep him on track. Jax listened as he moved as quietly as possible. A long minute passed.

"This how you killed Domino Salem? Dragged her out into the middle of nowhere and murdered her?" Cin asked, now closer, maybe ten yards ahead.

Domino's murderer? They thought Damien Halloweather was the killer. Damien had kidnapped Cin? Oh, shit, things just got much more dangerous very quickly.

"This is different. No one's going to ever find your body," Damien said.

"I won't tell. You can have the fucking thing. I won't say a word," Cin promised, her voice strong and defiant.

Damien chortled. "I know you'll run right to your big boyfriend. I don't need Ram Álvarez on my ass. He already hates my family—he blames my uncle Neil for what happened to his little Salem friend on Nightmare Island."

Jax felt a pang of jealousy and pushed it away. Damien thought Cin was with Ram? The idea made him queasy. He wanted to punch the asshole even harder for that asinine comment.

"You have what you came for. I gave it freely. You can have it," Cin said, now maybe ten feet away.

Damien didn't sound amenable to negotiation. "You can't give me what I already stole. And you can't forget what you've already learned. Unless maybe I bash your brains in. I could leave you a drooling vegetable instead of feeding you to the gators."

Jax burst into a clearing. Damien and Cin stood less than ten feet in front of him, framed by a backdrop of stars. Behind them, the Madonna River ran in a serpentine fashion, leaving them nowhere to go but down the embankment to the water below. Water that is filled with hungry reptiles.

Jax was fast, but Damien was quicker. Half-brothers, they must have both inherited quick-draw genes from Martin Montgomery. They aimed their guns at each other. With his free hand, Damien grabbed a fistful of the front of Cin's T-shirt, which she wore as pajamas, and swung her outward until she dangled precariously over the riverbank. Cin had her feet planted at the edge of the precipice, leaned out forty-five degrees over the edge, hanging over a fifteen-foot drop into the river below, suspended only by Damien's grip on the thin cotton of her top.

"No! Stop," Jax shouted, holding his free hand out with his palm faced to Damien.

"What the fuck are *you* doing here? I was worried about Ram. I figured she'd called him when her phone showed 'Romeo.' I knew I'd hear him coming after me like a bull in a china shop. Never figured 'Romeo' was a half-brother I never wanted," Damien snarled.

"Let her go, asshole," Jax said.

Damien dropped his fist holding Cin's T-shirt a few inches and jarred her to a halt again. Jax heard the seams begin to tear. Cin grabbed Damien's wrist and held on tightly.

"Awful thin material. Might rip right off," Damien said with a grin.

"Reel her in, you sick bastard," Jax said through gritted teeth.

"Shoot me, and she falls. She might survive the gators. Might not," Damien warned.

Jax's face was burning, blood pumping, more angry and scared than he'd ever been his whole life. "She dies, and I will hunt you down and make you suffer. I'll make you beg for death before I give you an end. You'll want that bullet by the time I pull the trigger, you son of a bitch."

"You'll save me, right, Jax? You good enough with that gun to shoot in the dark?" Cin asked, dangling by the thinnest of cotton.

Damien warned, "He pulls that trigger and you're gator food, you stupid cu—"

Cin moved faster than Damien could counteract. Bending her knees caused her angle to strain the shirt, and more tearing sounds made Jax's heart stop. She looked over her shoulder to the plunge beneath her, leaned over the precipice at a steep angle, and then planted her soles against the edge of the drop-off. Her hands still gripped Damien's wrist, anchoring them together. When she extended her legs again and pushed off from the cliff's edge, Damien toppled over the brink with her.

Cin used Damien's momentum to swing him over her head like a sledgehammer raised in a heavy arc. Damien flew farther out toward the river, whereas she dropped more straight down from the edge. It looked like some cheerleading move or a couple of acrobats performing at a circus. Damien tried to keep his grip on Cin, but she let go when Damien reached the apex of his trajectory, and her T-shirt ripped away. The thin cotton top flapped like a flag of surrender in Damien's fist as the two separated.

In a panic, Jax rushed to the edge of the river channel. The starlight above illuminated Damien's flailing dive, and then splashed into the river ten feet from the shore.

Below, Cin landed on the steep embankment, and her momentum carried her closer and closer to the river's edge. She slid on the steep, sandy incline toward the water, grabbing at weeds, roots, and tree limbs along the shoreline in an attempt to slow her descent. She managed to seize a fistful of vines near the water's edge and stopped with her legs curled near her chest and her ass right where the water lapped ashore from the waves made by Damien's plunge.

She scrambled up the steep, sandy wall as Jax scanned the waterway. He hoped any reptilian predators would go for the easier prey splashing in the water, trying to swim to shore as the current swept Damien downriver. Yet he glimpsed a snout as a gator emerged from the surf behind Cin, a big fucking monster maybe eight feet long, mouth open and aimed at her legs.

"Cin," Jax shouted as the gator lunged forward.

She was in his way, and he couldn't get a shot. Cin dove sideways as the gator came within chomping distance, and Jax got a bead on the bastard. He fired off one shot, taking out the beast's right eye. The jaws clamped shut on empty air, and then the tail whipped around, nearly taking out Cin as it made a hasty retreat. It missed her by inches. One splash later, the beast was gone.

Cin clambered up the side of the riverbank, reaching close enough to grab Jax's outstretched hand. He hauled her up and set her beside him on the safe shoreline. She knelt while catching her breath. Jax watched Damien flailing in the water, trying to swim against a strong current that pulled him away as several dark shapes closed in on him in the darkness. His half-brother disappeared around the river bend. That would likely be the last they'd see of Damien Halloweather.

Cin was shivering. He didn't know if it was from fright or from being topless in the cold December night. Jax pulled off his shirt, the black AC/DC tee he always slept in, and Cin pulled it over her head. He couldn't help but notice how beautiful she'd looked topless by moonlight, but she somehow looked just as sexy in his AC/DC shirt. He held her until she stopped trembling.

"This trail leads along the river and back around to Old Mat," Cin said, getting up and walking away.

"What the hell did he want from you?"

"The map. The map I had under my mattress all these years. He said his family has been looking for it for a long time."

"The map Bryce gave you before he left?"

Cin nodded.

"Why?" Jax asked.

Cin shrugged. She looked irresistible in his shirt. He noticed her glancing frequently at his bare abs illuminated by the starlit sky.

"Whatever it was, he thought he needed to kill you to keep it secret?"

"I don't think Damien needed much of a reason to kill somebody. I think he likes it."

“Not anymore. He’s a midnight snack right now. How did you learn that move? You swung him around and launched him like a shot put,” Jax said, impressed.

“Ariel is a blackbelt in karate. She might’ve taught me a move or two.”

“Ariel saved your ass, huh?”

Cin shook her head. “I guess so. Who’d have thought?”

They found the trailhead leading back to Old Mat. There were still a few hours before dawn.

“Home?” he asked.

Cin looked at the dark sky through the canopy of trees, a bright star directly overhead. “Take me to Manny’s with you.”

“I don’t think Damien’s coming back.”

“I’m not scared,” Cin said, a smile touching her lips. “I want to wake up with you on Christmas morning.”

Jax thought back to rousing in the middle of the night to see what Santa had brought. The excitement of that moment was a special part of childhood, but now Jax felt that old exhilaration again, just as he had when he was a kid. He no longer expected or believed that Santa delivered gifts by magic, but this year, Jax would get exactly what he wanted on Christmas morning—to be with Cin.

He reached out and took her hand. They laced their fingers together.

“Merry Christmas, Jackson Montgomery,” Cin said.

“Merry Christmas, babe,” he said back.

Chapter Twenty-Four

Neve woke on Christmas morning to music from the kitchen. She stared at the ceiling, blinking, concentrating on the tune and trying to determine if it was the original version of the holiday jingle about ole Kris Kringle or some new version. Classic rotation marinated over decades, or forgettable confection that would last a while and fade into obscurity? Some things left an indelible mark on the world and became enshrined in infamy, while others disappeared after a brief fling.

Neve considered the settlers of this town and how the secret deal and illicit relationships that started more than a century ago still reverberate today. The ramifications of events from the nineteenth century affected Neve's present and would shape the course of SX's future, and perhaps her own. These people's lies and affairs nearly derailed her marriage and threatened her plans for a happily ever after.

The song was the classic version. Neve could picture her father hanging tinsel on the tree, wearing a floppy Santa hat, and singing along to the same version of the song. She smiled and rolled out of bed. Neve took a shower, humming happily in harmony with the faint sounds of holiday music. She wore a bamboo cotton blend pajama top featuring Santa and his reindeer, barely long enough to cover her hips. It was Christmas morning, and yoga pants and a sports bra didn't fit the occasion. She headed for the kitchen.

There was a fully decorated tree on her dining room table, with blinking red and green lights and big, shiny silver bulbs.

"Merry Christmas, sweetheart," Bryce said from behind the cooktop on her kitchen island.

The omelet in the frying pan smelled of shallots and green peppers, making her mouth water. Bryce had squeezed fresh orange juice into two glasses. He wore a chef's apron without a shirt underneath. Neve had a dirty thought that perhaps he wasn't wearing anything under the apron's bottom half. She tingled from her center to her toes.

"What's this?" Neve asked.

"I worked at the hospital overnight to give some of the staff time off with their families. We closed City Hall for the holidays. All agencies paused recovery operations today. With the whole town on pause, I wanted to pause with you," Bryce said.

"I want your paws on me, too," Neve said flirtatiously, arching her back enough to emphasize her bralessness beneath the caricatures of Blitzen and Vixen.

"Skipping breakfast and right for dessert?" Bryce asked with one eyebrow raised.

"Don't we have all day?"

Bryce smiled widely. "We do." He turned off the stove burner. "Maybe an appetizer to start things off." He grabbed a carafe of orange juice and two wine glasses. "What would you like to unwrap first?"

Bryce came around the table. She'd guessed right. He

wasn't wearing anything under the apron. The material was tented in front of him. The front said, "Kiss the Cook." She knew exactly where she wanted to plant her lips.

"First, a toast. Sit," Bryce said, handing her a glass.

Neve couldn't wipe the smirk off her face, but she nodded. She sat at the table with the Christmas tree on it, six feet tall, a star at the top brushing the ceiling. Sitting there, she felt the holidays were an umbrella over her life.

"What's with the tree?"

"That's part of the toast," Bryce said, smiling ear to ear, and clinking his wine glass filled with OJ against Neve's. "To being each other's Christmas present."

Neve remembered her thoughts while lying in bed about how the past affects the future. But the present was here and now. Bryce was across from her, in the moment, her one true love, nice and close on Christmas Day. He thought like she did. They were together, in love, the perfect pair at this perfect moment. They were each other's present.

Under the tree.

Bryce reached up and poked something hanging from the lowest branch, mere inches over Neve's nose. Mistletoe. He leaned in, and she kissed him. Her whole body buzzed at the touch of Bryce's lips. Her mind went fuzzy, and the desire inside her surged, overtaking her like a person possessed by a horny ghost.

He thought mistletoe was clever? Neve was going to use it in the spirit that the holiday intended.

Her dining room table was six feet long and four feet wide, and Bryce had placed the artificial evergreen in the center. The lowest branches afforded two feet between the tabletop and dangling ornaments. Neve slid herself onto the surface like helping set the table for Christmas dinner. She supposed someone would be snacking very soon. She slid under the tree until her hips settled near the edge of the top, the mistletoe dangling directly above the center of her pelvis.

Right over her pussy.

Neve had put on an old pair of underwear she'd had since before she left her teen years behind. They were pink, cute, and comfortable. She'd had them so long that she even had a name for them, the Flamingo Pair, because the thin straps on each side reminded Neve of a flamingo's neck, while the part covering her bits curved like the beak. She knew what Bryce intended as his chin hovered between her thighs, and his hand grabbed a handful of the delicate underwear's straps like a hunter about to wring a bird's neck.

"Do it," Neve said.

Bryce ripped them in a quick, strong jerk, tearing the waistband like tissue paper, unwrapping the surprise like someone excited on Christmas morning. He didn't take out his new toy and play with it right away. No, he studied the shape, size, and purpose. Maybe he was trying to decide if it needed batteries, how to play the game, or whether to start easy or go hard.

The mistletoe decided it.

He kissed her right on the lips.

Neve groaned, bringing her hips up and grinding her pelvis against his face. She pushed her cunt into his mouth, and he slipped a tongue inside, darting deep within her, sending her brain to a place where visions of sugarplums danced in her head. Something was stirring inside her, a creature who would take over and ride Bryce Graham like a fucking reindeer.

Neve tangled her fingers in the curls at the back of Bryce's head and pulled his face harder into her. His mouth expertly worked her pussy, as his lips and tongue made out with her melted center. She moved her hips against him as he licked, prodded, and suckled at her swollen clit. One hand slid up her body and fondled a breast as his teeth lightly nibbled her swollen nub.

"Fffuck," she managed, then she let go.

She came hard. Neve arched her back until her pointed nipples brushed against two smooth, cold metal hanging bulbs on her tips. She made sounds like some unintelligible yuletide song where the sentiment seemed familiar but the lyrics were indecipherable. When she finished, there was a puddle beneath the mistletoe and stars in her eyes.

"Damn, why didn't Santa ever bring me anything like that?"

"You weren't ready for it before. You needed the right man for the job." Bryce helped her slide out from under the tree.

Neve grinned, noticing the satisfaction on his face. When truly quenched, Neve had that stoner look about her that indicated a man's job was well done. Bryce looked pleased with himself. He should. She'd remember that climax every time she saw mistletoe, or a Christmas tree, or her table. But now, it was Santa's turn to get his milk and cookies.

Bryce sat on the dining room chair, grinning like a boy who'd just licked the world's best candy cane. Neve ripped the "Kiss the Cook" apron away as quickly as he had dismembered her underwear. His cock was rigid and ready, standing at attention as faithfully as Cupid and Comet. She wanted this vixen to donder her cunt, giving it the full blitzen, making her insides dance, dashing toward another orgasm. Neve aligned his cock with her wet lips. The words of the old poem, "'Twas the Night Before Christmas," returned as the need peaked again in her nether regions. He spoke not a word but went straight to his work—he entered her pussy with a quick little jerk, and laying his fingers aside of his dick, and giving a nod, up the chimney he rose.

Neve was on top. She modulated their acceleration toward the finish line. She started slow, getting a handle on the instrument, making sure she knew how to handle the sweet ride. Luckily, she knew how to drive a stick. Bryce handled her curves like a professional, his hands moving along her hips as she started going faster and faster. Her chest was at the level of his face, so she peeled off the festive pajama top and leaned in. He nibbled her nipples. She shifted into overdrive and opened her up, humping him like a speed demon slamming the pedal to the metal. She zoomed toward the checkered flag at the finish line. She would either bring them both to a satisfying end or break the fucking chair.

The chair survived.

His erection did not.

"Come all ye faithful, eh?" Neve managed between ragged breaths.

"You made me a believer, Nevada Noble. I'm having a very happy holiday," Bryce said, dreamy and drained.

Neve panted like a puppy who'd run too hard to fetch the ball, settling down gradually. She eventually dismounted, his spent member slipping from her, and the satisfying feeling of being joined into one entity faded a little as they decoupled. Yet she felt closer to him every time they made love, a connection that remained even when he wasn't inside her. Neve felt like she carried a part of him constantly, no matter how far apart they were.

They shared a quick rinse-off before they returned to the kitchen, and Bryce finished making breakfast.

While Bryce hummed holiday tunes and restarted their omelets, Neve watched him work. He'd donned a pair of gym shorts and a sleeveless shirt cut down the sides to reveal his toned abs when he stood in profile. She'd pulled on loose sweatpants and a T-shirt advertising Imelda's Donuts that

Imelda herself had passed out as a promotion for her business's anniversary in October.

Neve pondered asking Bryce about Leira Gemini, but the day was too perfect to invite any kind of bad juju. Leira plotting with Bryce's Caesar sister to break up Bryce and Neve was too much drama to inject into an enjoyable holiday. Neve wanted to enjoy their first Christmas together without worrying about all the crazy commotion across SX. She preferred to hold off dealing with the endless shitstorm until tomorrow.

After breakfast, they sat on the lanai. A cool December breeze off the ocean necessitated a blanket, and they snuggled together on her loveseat, sharing each other's warmth. On Christmases past, sitting outdoors on December 25th in Iowa would have been avoided. It was usually freezing, often snowy, and sometimes brutally cold. She couldn't have staved off the chill with a blanket and body heat. Dad usually started a fire in the hearth while the younger Nobles fought for pole position on the sofa to sit nearest the flames.

Neve sighed contentedly. "Our first Christmas together. It's perfect."

"Of all my holiday memories, this one is my favorite so far," Bryce said.

"Tell me another. I want to know more about your life before we met."

"Did any of my pseudo-sisters ever tell you about the best Caesar Christmas?"

Sammy had told her some tales of their youth, and Delilah liked to reminisce, but neither had ever mentioned a holiday story. Neve shook her head.

"We were thirteen. I don't remember what precipitated it, but the families were all at war, vowing not to let us see each other again. That happened pretty regularly growing up, but never worked out. We would always find a way to sneak around until things cooled down again. Some parents, like Millicent Zhang, Martin Montgomery, and sometimes Nolan Salem, would frown upon mutual interaction. Still, we usually had advocates like Maria Álvarez or my mother, who let us hang. I don't think Jonathan Ryan ever cared what Delilah was up to, but we always had to escape Caleb's ubiquitous eye.

"We exchanged presents every year since we were old enough to make crafts with clay and decorate pictures in a coloring book. As we got older, we started saving money throughout the year to buy actual presents for the holidays. At thirteen, the girls were mostly into boy bands and makeup, and I remember getting a lot of comic books. Ariel gave me a necklace with our birthstone in it. I suppose it was her way of giving me a hint, and one that I didn't understand until years later.

"The annual gift exchange almost didn't happen. We had a way of sending messages to one another through Mariah Ryan. The Ryans were the most neutral of the families and central to life in Salem Crossing. Everyone had a stake in the church, so Mariah would pass messages between Caesars at services if we asked her to. No matter how fractured the families were at any given time, they came together every Sunday on neutral ground at Our Lady of Faith, even if no one looked at each other. Mariah would pass our notes to one another as she mingled among the factions.

"Juliet Zhang decided to cancel our annual tradition. Her mother had threatened to lock her up until summer if she tried to see her fellow Caesars. The other families were nearly as strict in keeping us apart. Nothing Mother nor Maria Álvarez could say would sway the naysayers. For the first time that any of us could remember, we wouldn't see each other on Christmas Day."

Neve found his hand under her blanket and squeezed. "That's awful, Bryce."

"Well, 'tis the season for miracles, and magic happened that holiday thirteen years ago. Another message accompanied Juliet's cancellation. An invitation was tucked in with the note. Anonymous. Anyone able to get away on Christmas morning was to meet at Crockett's Pond at the end of Briar Trail. Of course, no one thought we'd be able to sneak away under the watchful eye of most of the town. But on Christmas morning, before the sun even started to rise, sirens sounded off all over SX."

Neve raised a black eyebrow. "A hurricane in December?"

Bryce shook his head. "Fire alarms. The whole town came out to see what the ruckus was about. Someone had set fire to the Founders' Tree in Memorial Park. The massive oak burned like a big birthday candle across from City Hall, black smoke covering the coastline, flames flickering so high one could see the inferno from almost anywhere in Salem Crossing."

Neve frowned. "I've never heard of the Founders' Tree. There's no oak in Memorial Park."

Bryce explained, "Not anymore. By noon on Christmas Day, only char and ash remained. It had stood since before the first settlers arrived on the Florida coast. Each of the six original citizens had carved their initials into the trunk. It served as a symbol of unity for more than a hundred years. Then, thirteen years ago, someone burned it to the ground."

"Someone desecrated the tree as a distraction? So that you could have your Caesar Christmas?"

Bryce nodded. "Seems so. The whole town showed up to watch it burn. The tree symbolized unity, but it hadn't been an effective symbol in decades, if ever. It was an insult to allegory. It served better as an effigy."

"One of the Caesars did it? To give you cover to meet?" Neve asked.

Bryce shrugged. "Probably. We all met at Crockett's Pond at the end of Briar Trail while the rest of the town watched the fire. We exchanged gifts outside under the warm morning sun. It was magical because it almost didn't happen. That was a holiday miracle."

"Courtesy of a yuletide arsonist," Neve said. "No one ever confessed?"

Bryce shook his head, the ghost of a wistful smile appearing. "But I'll never forget that Christmas."

Neve leaned into him. "You Caesars are badass."

"We can be. When we work together," Bryce agreed.

Neve thought about JZ and how she preferred Bryce to be with Leira. Other Caesars stood opposed. They weren't working together at the moment when SX needed them most. But Neve didn't want to think about that. She preferred to make more memories with Bryce. She wanted their first Christmas to be unforgettable.

Neve let go of his hand and moved her fingers down to the waistband of his gym shorts, sliding down his front, and finding his cock. She gripped the hefty member and squeezed, the flesh hardening as Bryce gasped, surprised. Neve kissed his neck, his dick turning into an iron rod in her fist. She slid her hand along his thick length as he moaned. They were covered by the blanket but otherwise under an open sky, feeling the cool winter breeze.

Bryce moved his hand between her legs. She was already wet. He inserted a finger, massaging her swollen clit. Neve started moving her fist faster, and Bryce plunged deeper into her aching cunt. They were each writhing under the hand of the other, Bryce coaxing her to a quick orgasm as Neve pumped furiously at his rigid erection. They came again, simultaneously, under a sunny sky, the cool breeze wicking away their perspiration.

Neve smiled. *We exchanged gifts outside under the warm morning sun. It was magical because it almost didn't happen. That was a holiday miracle. The past was the present.*

It might not be a burning Founders' Tree, but things were hot despite the tepid air temps.

It was only ten in the morning, and they'd already crossed the finish line twice. Neve knew this would be one unforgettable first Christmas together.

Chapter Twenty-Five

HOLIDAYS WITH THE RYANS

Christmas Day was a big fucking deal at the Ryans'.

Mariah's father, the esteemed Reverend Saul Ryan, began the Christmas dinner by telling a nativity tale about an innkeeper giving Mary and Joseph a place to stay for the night. He tied it to the present day, hosting a holiday gathering at the rectory to celebrate the birth of baby Jesus. Her father spoke about the glory of Christ's arrival and the commune between angels, shepherds, commoners, and kings. Mariah could swing a leather whip all around the room and not hit a single wise man.

Saul Ryan loved to talk about the Christ child. He delivered a lengthy sermon right in the same dining room where Mariah once declared she'd won first place in the state's debate tournament, revealed that she had become class president at her university, and told her father about being personally honored by the president of the United States for her efforts volunteering for the Global Literacy Initiative. Reverend Ryan gave her passing acknowledgment for her accomplishments, but her father could talk for days about the single feat of simply being stuck in a manger overnight. Fuck, she loved Jesus as much as the next bitch, but he only managed to doody in his diaper at this point in his life.

But on Christmas, it was the baby this, the baby that, the baby, baby, baby.

Mariah Ryan watched her relatives each act as though they were more pious and Christian than the next. Mariah didn't need to bother because everyone in SX had already seen her S&M video. She might purport salvation, but that was a load of bullshit. She'd played dominatrix to Owen Zhang a few weeks ago, blackmailing him to get on her side and whipping him, literally, into submission. Now, Owen was one more pawn in her wicked game of chess.

The rest of the assholes at the Ryan holidays were mostly sanctimonious hypocrites. Nearly all of them put on fake faces and kissed ass, pretending piety while talking smack behind everyone's back. David and Esther Ryan ran a commune north of SX, but Mariah knew it functioned as a front for a psychedelic drug trade. John Ryan had been a neglectful father to Delilah and Caleb after his wife died. She heard Rob cheated on Ariel after Ariel fucked that Graham from out of town, an eye for an eye of sorts. Leah Ryan abused alcohol. Her sister, Hannah, regularly shoplifted from the tourist shops along Salem Shores. Mariah's dad cared more about the Bible than his wife, so Mariah's mother cheated on him, then ran off and left them when Mariah was only four. Yet they all sat around watching their language, collars buttoned over cleavage, acting like God was a rockstar, ignoring their sins like buzzing gnats flitting around their heads in pesky halos.

Mariah only considered two Ryans to be honest about their scruples: her cousin Delilah and Aunt Rebecca.

Rebecca was a confident elder who didn't take any shit from anyone, not even Mariah's revered dad. She sat on the Ryan couch, her impressive girth taking up half the surface, talking to Edgar Ryan, an old coot who was Mariah's grandfather's brother. The old man had said something about Mariah's mother being an Álvarez bastard, and Rebecca promptly ripped him a new one.

Delilah was pure chaos. She didn't have a duplicitous bone in her skinny body. She was 100% authentic, with no filter between her head and mouth. The clout of being a Caesar afforded her a certain celebrity status that not even the piety of the Ryan reputation could diminish. Caleb followed her around, trying to get her to speak like a Christian, act like a child of God, and mind herself like the great women of the Bible, but Delilah continued storming through the house, dropping four-letter words like a sailor out at sea. She didn't give a solitary fuck about Caleb's admonishments. In fact, Mariah wondered if his badgering made Delilah's salty language worse.

But Tom Graham currently occupied Delilah's full attention. Tom somehow managed to handle dating Delilah. Mariah thought that would equate to being in a relationship with a circus clown. The whole situation seemed ridiculous. If Delilah wasn't bonkers, Mariah had never seen evidence for it. When Mariah used to pass secret notes between the Caesars at church when they were kids, she would label Delilah's note as "From: Daffy." But even crazier than a loon, at least Delilah was completely genuine.

Melvin Dobbs, a man in his sixties who'd married Mariah's grandfather's widowed sister, still diddled various single retired ladies at the Restful Meadows retirement home. He cornered Mariah while she waited to speak with her dad. Reverend Ryan was currently consoling Cara Cochran, formerly Cara Ryan, whose husband hadn't left the ICU since the hurricane, when a tree branch fell on his head during his attempt to film the tornado ripping up Salem Shores to post on social media. Dumbass.

"The election is only a week away, Mariah," the balding older man said, as he lowered his forehead conspiratorially, with snowy, bushy eyebrows like a puppet's accessory. "Have you got the votes to torpedo Martin Montgomery?"

Melvin had no more influence within this family than Mariah's mother. A common trait among pious pricks was a penchant for prattle. They used gossip as a way to make their own personal sins seem less scandalous. If a two-faced asshole like Melvin could find out something more immoral about someone else, it made his own moral flaws feel less serious.

"The people of Salem Crossing will pick a repentant sinner over an irredeemable villain any time, Melvin. The city will be in good hands when Bryce and I work together to rebuild," Mariah said.

"Redemption. That's a catchy hook that could land that ass in the mayor's seat," Melvin replied, the smile crossing his face both knowing and creepy. *Did he watch the video?* Mariah was confident he had.

Did he wagggle those unruly white eyebrows when he mentioned my backside? Jesus, she caught some serious dirty-old-man vibes off this motherfucker. Mariah nodded politely, as she needed every vote on election day. She retreated to the kids' table, where several Ryan teens devoured Grandma Judith's holiday sugar cookies. As Mariah approached the table for a reprieve, the three boys facing her sprouted identical grins. *The little bastards have also seen the fucking video.*

"I can punch these little shit stains in the face if you need me to, Mariah."

It was Delilah. She cracked her knuckles as she approached, acting like she was ready to break some noses. The three teens must've heard enough stories about crazy Delilah Ryan because they scrambled over each other and scurried through the back door faster than one of Mariah's subs after she unlocked the handcuffs.

"God, you're scary," Mariah marveled.

"Let me know if you need security after you win on Election Day," Delilah said.

"I need a brother who will take a bullet for me. Like you do."

Mariah watched Caleb corner an obviously uncomfortable Tom Graham. Caleb hated Tom. Mariah caught the waves of jealousy every time Delilah was closer to Tom than her brother, and Caleb did everything he could to insert himself between the two. As creepy as Melvin Dobbs appeared in their awkward conversation, he had a long way to go to be in the same league as Caleb Ryan.

"You only have a half-sister who doesn't seem to like you very much," Delilah said, referring to Nevada Noble. "But I'm on your side, Mariah. I mean, I wouldn't jump in front of a gun for you, but I want you to win next week."

"Thank you, Delilah. Most of the Ryans abandoned me after I embarrassed the family."

Delilah rolled her eyes dramatically. "Sheesh, most of these douchebags have as much dirty laundry as you, Mariah."

"Well, they don't think their shit stinks."

"Shit always stinks." Delilah raised her voice and shouted across the room, "Isn't that right, Hannah? About shit?"

Their cousin Hannah had been talking to Mariah's grandfather, Solomon, by the little sandwiches Mariah had catered in from the deli. Hannah stared blankly for a moment, then her face scrunched, wondering what the hell Delilah was talking about. Her mouth moved silently, like a fish flopping out of the sea and gasping for air on the beach. Maybe she did know what Delilah was talking about.

Delilah leaned in and whispered to Mariah, "She's got a scatological fetish. Her boyfriend does some crazy shit in the bedroom. Literally."

"Jesus, Lilah," Mariah said with a wicked grin.

Delilah shrugged. "I know things. Like, I'm not the craziest one in this family."

Mariah pulled Delilah into a corner while Caleb had Tom trapped.

"You really want to help me?" Mariah asked.

"I sure as hell don't want Martin Montgomery running SX with Bryce."

"I'll take care of Martin." Mariah considered his blackmail threat about releasing her relapse into S&M after she promised to be a better Christian. She had to deal with that before Martin and Riley decided to post the video to the world. Martin may have been distracted by something else. Most likely, he bided his time until right before the election to get Mariah out of the way. If he destroyed Mariah's redemption storyline right before election day, there would be no time for anyone else to take her place on the ballot. Martin would sail to victory unopposed.

Mariah leaned close to Delilah and whispered, "I'm worried about other candidates coming out of the woodwork."

"Isn't it too late for that?"

"Someone could launch a last-minute write-in campaign. The right candidate could ride a surge of support into office."

Delilah waved her hand dismissively. "The last time anyone tried to run against you and Martin, it was like auditions for town clown. I wouldn't be concerned about Elizabeth Halloweather or Carl Tillman."

"I'm not worried about those two. Have you talked to your Caesar sister lately?"

Delilah frowned. "Which one? You'll have to zero in a bit. I was down to only three, but then the others came back from the dead. Now, I've got five again."

"Juliet," Mariah said.

"Still fifty-fifty."

Mariah clarified, "Juliet Zhang. Does she want back in City Hall? Is she trying to get her old job back? Does she want it to be her and Bryce teaming up to save the day?"

Delilah frowned. "You think she'd start a write-in campaign?"

"A resurrection tale trumps my redemption storyline. Juliet came back from the dead. She'll win if she runs," Mariah said, thinking about her father's Easter homilies—almost as long-winded as his Christmas sermons.

Delilah grew serious and completely sane. Mariah had never seen such gravity affect her cousin's face in all her life. Delilah looked to make sure no one was watching. No one paid any attention to daffy Delilah Ryan. Even so, she leaned in closer and said quietly, "Juliet Zhang has other things on her mind. She doesn't give a damn about running the show anymore."

Mariah frowned. Owen seemed confident Juliet would want to reclaim her place in the government. Delilah, who knew her better than Owen did, disagreed.

Mariah nodded.

Daffy Delilah departed and squeezed between her boyfriend and brother. Mariah watched a bit, but the situation was more awkward than Melvin Dobbs's pervy comments or the trio of teen boys who had watched their relative in a viral online S&M video. Using a litany of four-letter words, Delilah told off her brother and stormed away, Tom following on her heels, Caleb looking like he wanted to cry.

"She needs some serious Jesus in her life."

After speaking with everyone in the room, her father came to converse with his daughter. Although Mariah portrayed herself as the poster child for seeking forgiveness and symbolizing second chances, falsely, as she'd already returned to her wicked ways with Jax and Owen, her father still seemed ashamed of his only daughter. Mariah supposed that the thought of his offspring, in black leather, expertly whipping a man, might cause discomfort. Still, she suspected his shame as pastor of SX's largest congregation was worse than the indignity he felt as a father.

"Delilah's a little rough around the edges, but she's a better person than most people in this room," Mariah said.

Her father put his hands together in prayer like a pious prick. "I suppose a sinner can cuss like a sailor and still be pure of heart. She could tame it a little on Baby Jesus's birthday, though."

"The baby wouldn't know what she was saying anyway."

"Right. Innocence unblemished," he agreed.

"Innocence unblemished," Mariah repeated.

They could at least agree on something. They spoke for a while longer about the nativity, the miracle of God in man, the magnificence of Christ's birth, and blah, blah, blah. He moved on, and Mariah felt a bit like Hannah Ryan or Melvin Dobbs, a waypoint along Pastor Ryan's duty to speak to everyone in the room.

Mariah headed to her old bedroom, the place where she had grown up and learned life lessons. She had to discover everything about becoming a woman on her own, without a mother to be found anywhere or a father who cared to give her guidance. Maybe she'd learned about being a dominatrix as a mechanism to gain control over a situation where she felt helpless, lost, and scared.

Mariah thought about her father constantly going on about a miracle baby. An unexpected gift for the world. Her father could talk for hours about God's greatest gift —the baby, the baby, the baby.

Mariah stared at her reflection, as she had so often in the past. She'd watched herself become a woman in this room, staring at the changes brought on by puberty during her youth. Boobs. Body hair. Pimples. Hips. She transformed from a kid to an adult in this bedroom, measured over the years in the reflection of this mirror.

Her body was changing again.

Mariah was pregnant.

Chapter Twenty-Six

Neve and Bryce spent the remaining daylight hours of Christmas Day like they had throughout the morning. The two of them, naked more often than not and oftentimes engaged in copulation. As the memorable daytime ripened into the evening, they showered off the lingering aura of frequent fornication and dressed to go out. Had Neve ever been so reluctant to put on underwear?

"You're okay with spending the rest of Christmas Day with the Caesars?" Bryce asked as they drove through the quiet streets of SX.

"Tus hermanas son mis hermanas," Neve said, window down and enjoying the temperate December day. She wished she could feel the breeze on her bare breasts. Their day of decadence had left her in a state of heightened sensuality. "Besides, we had our Noble get-together last night while you were on your shift at the hospital. Today is all about you and me, baby."

Bryce reached over and took her hand, smiling.

"The Caesars haven't all been together at Christmas for a decade," Bryce said.

Neve marked the homes along the route where cars gathered in small clusters, a household hosting friends and family after the last hellacious few months in SX—murder, disappearances, drama, hurricane. The holidays were a time to renew focus on positivity and progress. The sentiment of the day offered fresh hope and great promise that good things were on the horizon.

The Caesars agreed to meet at Weisheng Manor. Juliet's grand home had weathered the storm better than many structures in town, and the Zhang neighborhood was more accommodating than the Salem section of SX or the Montgomery district. Neve said nothing when Bryce revealed their destination, but she was concerned about walking into the lion's den. Juliet Zhang was actively attempting to break up Neve and Bryce so Bryce could be with Leira Gemini.

"Tell me about the last summer before you left SX. I want to know about Leira," Neve said.

Bryce looked perplexed. "My summer fling?"

"She's back. Causing trouble."

Bryce sighed. "I've heard she's clashed with some of the other Caesars. The girls never did like Leira."

"Not all of them were against her."

"What do you mean?"

"She had a friendship with JZ that summer. It sounds like they teamed up to sideline Ariel and clear the path for you and Leira's relationship. And now she's returned, stirring up trouble again."

Bryce frowned. "What kind of trouble?"

Neve didn't want to sound like a conspiracy theorist chasing every oddball theory down a rabbit hole. "I'm not sure. She's hanging out with a group of shady outsiders. They're connected, somehow. I get the idea that they're up to no good."

"I knew Leira a long time ago, Nevada. I'm sure she's changed just as much today as I am different from the boy who knew her back then."

"Did you know she dated Tom Graham?"

"Delilah loudly mentioned it," Bryce said.

"Leira is up to something in SX."

"It would be strange if she didn't have ulterior motives. Doesn't everyone in Salem Crossing have secrets?"

Neve felt a pang of guilt. Bryce likely meant the remark as a generic statement on the morality of SX, but the comment reminded Neve of her subterfuge in keeping the Juliets' plan under wraps, letting Bryce think his pseudo-sisters were dead for weeks. After they reconciled and barely saved their relationship, they promised each other that they wouldn't keep anything from one another anymore.

"Bryce, I need to tell you something about Juliet before we get there."

"Zhang or Salem?"

"JZ," Neve said. "Have you noticed anything different about her? Since she's been back?"

Bryce considered the question as they passed shuttered homes and businesses still boarded up from the storm. Everything was different after the hurricane—not just Juliet Zhang. The storm had forever transformed the town. Nothing would ever be the same. Like many structures around SX, maybe JZ had suffered damage and simply needed repairs.

"Perhaps you're seeing her differently since you've learned she's your half-sister?"

Neve had hardly considered it. She'd been so distracted with her duties to Salem Crossing and the mysteries plaguing the Crossing Guard that she'd pushed reconciliation with her relatives to the back burner. Besides her visit with the Álvarez family, she had not explored her SX roots.

"I'm not the only one who thinks so. I went to see Juliet last night with Delilah, Ariel, and Naomi. Things got pretty heated," Neve said.

"About what?" Bryce asked, confused by the turn of the conversation.

"Juliet thinks Leira would make a better partner for you."

Bryce looked perplexed. "As co-mayor? It's too late for anyone else to get on the ballot."

Neve clarified, "As a cohabitant. She still thinks you ought to be with Leira. In a relationship. Rather than me. They're plotting to get rid of me and hook you up with Leira."

"What? Juliet and Leira are working together to sabotage our relationship?" Bryce burst out, aghast.

Neve nodded. "It seems insane, but I saw the crazy with my own eyes last night."

Bryce glared at the road as they approached Weisheng Manor and muttered. "Wait till I get my hands on her..."

As they entered Weisheng Manor, Bryce stomped like a kid who found out someone else was playing with his toys. Neve followed nervously at his heels. The sounds of a war already in progress came from within the walls of the house. The vulgar name-calling echoed down the main hall to the entryway, a string of four-letter words as inventive and insulting as the most graphic mob movies. Delilah Ryan had the same idea as Bryce and unleashed a barrage of invective missiles.

Neve noticed the juxtaposition of the angry energy between the Caesars and the idyllic holiday decorations around the home. Juliet Zhang's gathering room resembled a scene from a Dickensian Christmas tale, and she half expected Tiny Tim himself to serve wassail and figgy pudding. The tree looked as if it had been transported from nineteenth-century London, and the nativity scene featured gilded ceramic on a one-eighth scale.

Among immaculately wrapped gifts and glamorous adornments, the Caesars confronted each other in a rage antithetical to the celebration of Christ's birth. Delilah stood in the middle of the room, red-faced and ribald, giving JZ a piece of her mind. Juliet Zhang leaned against the mantle lined with stockings, each bearing the name of a Caesar, with a flickering fire in the hearth. She looked bemused to be the target of Delilah's diatribe. Juliet Salem hovered near her wife, appearing sleepy and bored, probably eager to count the diamonds she received from Santa last night. Ariel glared at JZ from the east wall, holding a sip of whiskey in a lowball. Naomi curled on a window seat along the west wall, staring at her own feet, as if she were a million miles away. Sammy stood near Naomi, fists clenched, armed and ready to join the Caesar war.

"You faked your fucking death, lied to all of us for weeks, and made us mourn and miss you," Delilah shouted.

"You'd do the same thing for your sweetheart," Juliet Salem drawled, sounding ready for a nap. She was mainly back to her old self, cool and bitchy, but Neve figured the slur was maybe an effect of strong painkillers or something else medicinal. "I mean, imagine if you wanted to marry Caleb and the whole town cried 'incest.' You'd move to Iowa, too. Where they're okay with incest." She looked at Neve with a blonde eyebrow raised, daring Neve to say something.

"Not paying anyone to laugh today, Juliet? Not even your wife cracked a smile," Delilah sneered.

"It wasn't a joke," Juliet Salem clapped back.

Delilah glared but moved on. Caleb wasn't someone she could use to gain sympathy from the other Caesars. "Then JTS shows up, and we dread the news that maybe first you lied about dying, and then you actually ended up dead. But hell no, you ride into town after the hurricane on a motherfucking motorcycle. You're back, and all is good...until you start meddling with Bryce's relationship."

"Yes, why are you sticking your nose into my love life, Juliet?" Bryce interjected.

Juliet Salem defended her wife as JZ remained mute. "Get over yourself, Bryce. We've been manipulating your decisions since you were a kid. If we didn't shove you out of the nest, you would've never left SX in the first place."

"That's not how it happened. We didn't want him to leave," Ariel said, perking up as the convo shifted to include Bryce.

"Of course we didn't want Bryce to leave, but leaving was what was best for him ten years ago. You wouldn't be convinced, Ariel, but the rest of us knew that Bryce had to go to school. We had no right to stand in his way," Sammy argued, joining the fray.

Ariel jabbed a finger toward Sammy. "I'm not talking to you."

"You don't get to play holier-than-thou with me, Ariel Álvarez. You're lucky I didn't press charges for wrecking my food truck."

"You're lucky I didn't wreck your face for fucking my husband."

The room fell silent. Growing up, Willow and Cyprus had gotten into legendary fights around the holidays. As teens, the belligerent twins even occasionally had a few choice words with their mom. But this fight between the Caesars was wilder and more awkward than the worst Noble family gathering.

JZ finally spoke up, "This isn't about who's sleeping with Rob Ryan, although it appears easier to narrow down who isn't sleeping with Rob Ryan."

"Leave my husband out of this."

Sammy looked stung by Ariel's use of the word "husband." Sammy stepped closer to Ariel, and Neve braced for things to turn physical. Ariel was a black belt, but she might not be a match for an angry African-American woman.

"You fucked a stranger in a hurricane, but we're not talking about that because you say we're not talking about that. Just like always. Ariel Álvarez always has to get her way," Sammy hollered, nose to nose with her Caesar sib.

"Who gives a damn about Rob and Ariel right now, Sammy? Their relationship has been shit from the start. What Bryce and Neve have is a good thing, and JZ is trying to break them up," Delilah snapped.

"Why do you think Leira Gemini is a better choice than Nevada?" Bryce asked JZ.

Juliet didn't even back down from Bryce. "Don't act like you two have some kind of fairy tale romance out of a kid's storybook, Bryce. Neve lied to you for weeks. Her family is more fucked up than the Halloweathers. She's the daughter of Mariposa Álvarez, who ditched Mariah as a kid. I've never seen anyone who meddles more in everyone else's business than Neve does. Hell, she even slept with your half-brother."

"My relationship with Jax happened before I ever started dating Bryce. Don't accuse me of infidelity, Juliet," Neve said, getting angry, too.

"Adultery is more of an Ariel thing," Sammy interjected.

"Oh, bitch, don't you dare talk about cheating," Ariel said, seething.

"Enough," Bryce finally roared. Neve had rarely seen him so agitated. Only when she lied about his sisters being alive had he previously raised his voice. "We didn't come together for Christmas for the first time in ten years to fight like a bunch of schoolyard kids. This is supposed to be fun...like it used to be."

"The last time we were together, we were too young and

naive to understand that life can be pretty fucking rough," Naomi muttered.

Naomi had watched the circus silently, her arms crossed and expression nonplused. Neve suddenly felt small inside the big room. Here they were, all arguing about adultery, instigations, and backstabbing each other, when Naomi had lost the man she loved weeks before. She was a woman who'd suffered actual loss, and the Caesars were fighting about problems all their own making. Her words shut everyone up instantly.

"I'm sorry, Nay," Sammy said.

"Me, too. You've had a rough year," her twin added.

Neve approached her with Bryce, Sammy, JTS, and Delilah. Juliet Zhang and Ariel stayed on opposite sides of the room. Ariel had warned Neve that she didn't trust JZ, but Ariel didn't like Neve, either. JZ preferred Leira for Bryce and kept her distance. The room's temperature was freezing cold.

"This doesn't feel like Christmas to me," JZ said. "Party's over."

JTS looked over her twin sister's shoulder at her wife, but Juliet Zhang's expression remained resolute.

"This isn't the time for us to hash this out, Juliet, but there will be a reckoning," Bryce said.

"Some things can't be repaired," Ariel said, staring at Sammy.

"Y'all need to get the hell out of my house," JZ said.

The Caesars left except for the Juliets. JTS looked sad to see them leave, something finally breaking through her resolute loyalty to JZ. Juliet Salem hadn't wanted the afternoon to end like this. Neve, Bryce, Sammy, Delilah, Naomi, and Ariel stood on Weisheng Manor's front lawn, admiring the lights and decorations that made the front look festive, and wondered what the hell had happened.

"There's my ride," said Ariel as a plum-colored Mazda

pulled up to the curb. The darkened windows concealed the driver, but everyone knew what kind of car Rob Ryan drove.

"Is that...?" Sammy asked, voice wavering.

Ariel wore a smile like a cat with a bird in its mouth. "I texted him five minutes ago when things started going south in there. Rob and I are working things out."

"But you cheated. And you'll cheat again," Sammy spat.

Ariel walked toward the car, grinning triumphantly over her shoulder. "He picked me. He'll always pick me."

Ariel climbed onto the passenger seat, and the car sped down the street. She was going home with her husband.

Sammy ran toward her car, sobbing.

"I'll go after her," Neve said.

Delilah raised a hand. "I got it. This is your first Christmas together. You two need to make some happy memories." Delilah chased after Sammy.

Naomi looked back at the house where she'd left her twin sister. "This gathering was not about making happy memories. I'm not going to cheer anyone up. You two go on. I'm going to walk a bit."

"You going to be okay, Naomi?" Bryce asked.

Naomi nodded reluctantly. "Eventually. But not today."

She hugged Bryce and threw an arm around Neve, including her in the embrace. She managed to stay dry-eyed as they walked away, waving back as Naomi started walking toward the sea. Bryce got behind the wheel, and Neve assessed his reaction to the last half hour. He looked stunned at the turn of the holiday.

"Are you going to be okay, Bryce?"

"I was gone too long. I left them, and everything broke into a million pieces. I did this, Nevada. But I don't think I can put it back together."

"It's not up to only you. Everyone needs to work for it."

"Family isn't easy."

Neve thought about her mother. How she had spent the holidays angry at her instead of trying to find a way to fix things. Everyone needed to put in the effort to make it work. "No," Neve agreed. "It really isn't."

Chapter Twenty-Seven

ARIEL ÁLVAREZ

Ariel woke the morning after Christmas beside Rob Ryan. Typically, someone married a few short weeks wouldn't dread the idea of her husband next to her in bed. Still, she hadn't wanted this wedding, didn't particularly care to remain married, and was now with Rob simply to spite her cheating whore pseudo-sister. The look on Sammy's face when Rob picked her up from Weisheng Manor the previous night was almost worth the weird grunting noises he made as he slept.

Ariel couldn't tell if Rob was awake or asleep. If she thought she could sneak out of bed, she'd quietly slip from the bedroom, pull on some yoga pants, and go for a morning run that might take her someplace else, far from anyone with the last name Ryan. But if he was already awake, she would play dead and hope to God he would get up and leave. Maybe he had to work. She could make a run for it if he got into the shower. Or she might even have enough time if he took a long pee.

He wasn't making the grunts. The goddamn grunts would've clued her in on whether he was conscious or not.

As she debated between playing dead and sneaking out

like a cat burglar, Rob rolled and cupped her breast. He fondled her sleepily while groaning—at least it wasn't a grunt. Rob snuggled closer, and his morning wood pressed against her ass. The last thing she wanted to start her day with was enduring a pity fuck just to get away from her husband.

"Sorry, Rob. I forgot that I have a holiday thing. With the family." Ariel slid out from under his arm and escaped his probing prick before he managed to start humping something.

"You get together besides on Christmas Eve?" Rob asked sleepily, sitting up in bed. He wasn't wearing a shirt, and Ariel had to admit he looked good. Not pity-fuck good, but second-glance good. "I didn't know anyone in your family liked each other enough to drag it out longer."

"I promised Mama I would help clean up the house after she hosted the family festivities. I think a hundred people went through that place. Worse than the hurricane," Ariel lied, pulling a sweatshirt over her sleeping tee and tugging on a pair of Rob's sweatpants, cinching them tight so they didn't fall to her ankles.

"Need another pair of hands?"

Rob's hands were what she was trying to get away from, along with everything attached to them. She caught the suspicion behind his gaze as he waited for an answer. Ariel didn't like how he doubted her every word since she cheated on him. She had been in love with Bryce Graham throughout their relationship, and Rob never questioned her lies and deceit. Now, he didn't trust her to use the bathroom alone.

"Cin's going to meet us. We'll be fine," Ariel said, building up a story that could fall apart in countless ways.

Rob offered, "Take my car. I'll ride my bike today."

Ariel left Rob's place before he could protest further. He wasn't going to follow her to her mother's with a hard-on, so she had a head start before he attempted to spy on her. She stopped at her place for a shower and changed clothes, then arrived and parked Rob's plum-colored Mazda around the corner at her mother's house. She wasn't going to help her mother recover from the Christmas Eve party. Mama would've worked all Christmas Day putting the place back together. Ariel had another endeavor in mind.

The scene between JZ and the rest of the Caesars the previous day weighed on her mind. Ariel believed Juliet had acted weird since she rode into SX on that bike. Something was off. JZ's chummy relationship with Leira Gemini, the mysterious group of birthdays surrounding Leira's friends, and Juliet's sudden desire to push Neve out of the picture. Juliet Zhang had changed.

Nostalgia blinded the judgment of the other Caesars. Some were concerned about JZ's strange antics, but they wanted things to return to normal, so they overlooked these eccentricities. Ariel had always been the black sheep of the Caesars, lacking the intimacy the others shared. Her personality had always been prickly, and she only really wanted to be around Bryce. Ariel endured the others. At least, that's what she'd always told herself.

Why had she kept the Caesars at arm's length? She had spent as much time with her pseudo-sibs growing up as any of the Caesars, yet Ariel remained the Pluto of the group—the planet that wasn't always a planet. She had always believed that Bryce was the only reason she ever showed up. But this thing with JZ bothered her more than Sammy sleeping with Rob. She needed to know the truth.

But why did she care why JZ was acting like a bitch?

Because Ariel did care. She had always cared. She couldn't admit that she needed Delilah, Sammy, Naomi, and the Juliets as her sisters. They were as dear to her as any Álvarez. She had lied to herself for twenty-six years because of Bryce. If she considered the girls separate from her real sister, she could see Bryce as a lover instead of a brother.

Damn. Revelation.

Ariel had to find a way to fix the Caesars.

Instead of staying at her mother's house, she walked to the Riverside Inn. To remain inconspicuous, she pulled the hood of her pullover over her head to conceal her identity from anyone watching in Old Mat. She had spied on this place before, on the stakeout with Naomi, and again when they confronted JZ inside, communing with Leira. Ariel wouldn't stop short of getting the whole story this time. She wanted to know exactly what Leira and her birthday buddies were doing in SX.

Ariel didn't start at Leira's motel room. Instead, she knocked on the guy's door in 111. She wasn't sure if he or Leira were still at the Riverside Inn or even in SX anymore, but she thought maybe she had a better chance of getting answers from a stranger than from sneaky Leira. It was eight o'clock in the morning, so she waited a while before the occupant answered, yawning and obviously freshly awake.

"I don't need room service," he mumbled.

Ariel was too busy admiring his sculpted, naked chest to be offended by his assumption that she was the maid because she was what, Cuban, like everyone else who worked in Old Mat? His light brown flesh was damn near perfect from his neck to where his shorts rode low on his hips, revealing the beginning of his line of black pubic hair. Muscles rippled as they woke up after the long night. Ariel felt warm despite the cool December morning.

She could see precisely why Leira had seduced him the other day.

From the neck up, he looked like Bryce smooshed with a burn victim. The scarred left side of his face featured smooth flesh in a murky clay color. His ear was mostly melted away.

His eye was milky and damaged, and he had no left eyebrow. His hair on that side of the puckered scalp grew only in thin tufts. The right side was identical to Bryce.

"I'm not the maid. I want to ask some questions," Ariel said.

"Aaron, ask the maid for towels. We're out again," came a voice from within.

Ariel tried to lean into the doorway, but Aaron's large and beautiful body blocked her view.

"Who is that?" asked the voice inside.

"It's not the maid, Caid." Aaron frowned at Ariel. With her back to the early morning sun, Ariel mainly remained hidden in shadows as he tried to peer inside the hoodie. "Who are you?"

Caid. When Ariel spied on Leira and Booker, they bought a poppyseed muffin as a birthday surprise for someone named Caid—the same guy in Aaron's room. Then Juliet Zhang also got a poppyseed muffin. It had to be for Caid. *Who is this stranger?*

Ariel pulled down her hood and revealed herself. She knew she looked enough like Leira to shock Aaron. With his mouth hanging open, Aaron took a step back, and another man stepped beside him. He must be the one who'd asked for a towel. His hair was wet, and he wore gym shorts mottled with drips. Shirtless, the condensation made his smooth torso glisten as the morning light dappled over his body as sculpted as Aaron's. He'd obviously gotten out of the shower and pulled on clothes without a towel to dry himself first.

"She looks like Leira. If Lay was like...boring," Caid said with a dazzling smile.

Ariel couldn't even get mad at the insult. Caid was blond and drop-dead gorgeous. His blue eyes glowed like they were android props. His face was flawless, with lips turned up in an adorable smirk that could make girls' panties drop. She stared at him without blinking. Was this asshole hypnotizing her somehow? He reminded her a little of Alistair Salem, but not quite.

Caid put his arm over Aaron's shoulder in a manner that was more than friendly but less than romantic.

"You two...roommates? Or more?" Ariel asked.

"Sometimes. Depends on the mood," Caid replied teasingly.

"I'm looking for Leira. She was here with you before," Ariel said, looking away from Caid with great difficulty and addressing Aaron, who at least had a scarred side to detract from his dreamy half.

"She's here sometimes. Sometimes it's Caid. Or Booker," Aaron said.

"Or Hallie?" Ariel asked.

"You know a lot, Ariel," a voice said behind her. Ariel turned to face Leira. "Too much. We can't have that."

From behind Ariel, one of the men grabbed her and slapped a hand over her mouth. She knew a dozen moves that would result in him in a heap at her feet, but Caid poked the sharp point of a knife in her side. A long enough blade would pierce her kidneys. Leira stepped into Room 111 as Aaron dragged her backward. She attempted to bite the palm slapped over her mouth so she could scream, but the hand was strong and holding her jaw from opening. The tip of the knife bit deeper, poking like the sting of a wasp. Leira closed the door, trapping Ariel inside.

"You yell, and I'll break your teeth. Then no one will think we look alike," Leira warned.

Ariel glared but nodded. The hand withdrew. Aaron stepped around to face her, elbow to elbow beside Leira. That left Caid with a knife, threatening to slice her tender flesh. Ariel wished proximity to the blond Adonis were under different circumstances. This particular situation seemed especially ominous.

"Why did you bring her in here?"

Someone else was inside the room. A voice Ariel was very familiar with, although her presence in the motel room at this hour didn't make any sense. The other two people in the room were men, one in pajama bottoms and the other who looked like he'd just gotten out of the shower.

"Juliet?" Ariel said, confused.

JZ sat on the edge of the bed with her hands crossed over her lap, wearing a man's T-shirt without a bra and loose sweatpants. Her expression had a sanctimonious way of appearing both regal and bitchy at the same time. Ariel thought she would've made a great queen in Victorian England. Ariel wanted to slap the smug smirk right off her face.

"What the hell is going on, Juliet? Who are these people?" Ariel looked again at the strangers around her. Leira could be a distorted mirror image of herself with a pink mohawk, prolific piercings, and scattered tattoos. Aaron might've been the nightmare version of a scarred Bryce. Caid looked like Alistair and Domino made the perfect incestuous baby, or maybe if JTS and Naomi had a triplet brother. They all resembled Caesars. Why?

Leria took satisfaction from Ariel's shock. "I told you, we're the Holidays. We're not quite as cool as the infamous Caesars."

Ariel tried to make sense of it, but it was like a mystery with no clues. "What's that have to do with you, JZ? We were born in March."

"She was born on December 26th. Today's her birthday. Did you bring a present?" Caid whispered in Ariel's ear from behind her.

Ariel frowned, stunned. This didn't make sense.

Ariel felt like everyone was speaking in riddles. "What are you talking about, Juliet? Did you hit your head while kidnapped?'

JZ smiled wickedly. She stood and wandered closer. "No one kidnapped me, you silly fool. I'm not Juliet Zhang. My name is Jasmine. Jasmine Gemini."

What was Juliet saying? Was she brainwashed? Did she have some sort of dementia? Had she gone stark raving mad? Or did Ariel fall down a rabbit hole, and this was some kind of fucked up SX Wonderland where everything was topsy-turvy?

Last name Gemini?

"You're related to Leira?" Ariel muttered, her own words sounding like nonsense.

"As much as you're related to Bryce," Jul—Jasmine said with a scandalous grin. She was a carbon copy of Ariel's Caesar sister, but there was something different about her. She wasn't Juliet. A clone? An evil twin? "That's why we can share everything with each other."

Jasmine kissed Aaron in front of Ariel. The woman looked exactly like Juliet, making out with a guy who, from his good side, looked a hell of a lot like Bryce. Jealousy, confusion, fear, and anger swirled into a sick emotion that made her lash out again, trying to break free. Caid pushed the knife forward, the point piercing flesh and making her stop.

Someone knocked. Ariel prayed Rob had followed her here against her wishes. Or maybe Juliet Salem was out looking for her wife, missing early in the morning. Ariel would settle for that snoopy bitch Neve sticking her nose where it didn't belong. She didn't want to be stuck in this madhouse anymore.

Aaron opened the door. Delilah Ryan stood outside. She wore vertical rainbow stripes that made her look taller. She'd teased her hair into some kind of ginger cloud. Delilah wore sunglasses bedazzled with purple rhinestones, glittering in the sun as it rose higher in the sky. She had her hands on her hips like she was Superman here to save the day.

"Run, Lilah. Get help. We're in danger," Ariel cried.

"Danger's my middle name, boo," Delilah said, stepping inside.

"These people are nuts, Lilah. Get Bryce!"

Aaron closed the door behind Delilah. Her stance, with hands on her hips, still showed confidence, but her demeanor shifted, making her look less like a superhero and more like the principal assigning detention. Her attention, however, seemed centered on Ariel instead of the mob of maniacs.

"We're not ready for Bryce quite yet, Ariel." Delilah pulled off her sunglasses. Ariel had spent the last twenty-six years getting damn good at reading her pseudo-sister's crazy eyes, but the light behind Lilah's gaze appeared totally sane. And infinitely dangerous. "And please don't call me Lilah in polite company. My name is Hallie."

"Wha—" Ariel choked on her words, tears welling. A fake Delilah. A false Juliet. "Where are my sisters?"

Hallie grinned wickedly. "I can't keep track of them all. But Delilah..."

Jasmine walked to the closet and opened the door. Propped inside was a bound and gagged Delilah Ryan. The real Delilah. Her eyes were bulging and pleading at the same time, and as crazy as ever. Ariel could read them without trying. Delilah was scared to death.

Chapter Twenty-Eight

JACKIE SALEM

Jackie twisted the puzzle this way and that. She had been working on it for hours since Gil gave it to her. She hated questions without answers. Jackie was determined to solve the damn thing, even if it took until Easter.

The holiday reprieve was over. The creditors pushed at the gates, louder and hungrier than before. Despite reinforcements submitting endless, ironclad applications with all necessary addenda, official letters repeatedly denied emergency funds from every government agency. Jackie and her fellow Salems had exhausted every effort to keep their debts from being called in. Jackie was at a loss. Their only hope resided with Alistair and his attempts to get insurance money.

"We're facing utter ruin, and you're playing games?"

Jackie's blood ran cold. Tessa had put Jackie in charge, and she had nothing to show for her extensive efforts but utter failure. The devil had sent her on a mission, and Jackie had come up empty-handed. What would this demoness do to Jackie if Tessa's entire world collapsed on her horned head?

Jackie gritted her teeth and replied tersely, "Every puzzle

has a solution, Aunt Tessa. I know there's a way out of this problem."

"The American bureaucracy has provided the way, Jacquelyn, but apparently, your sharp skills are no match for red tape."

Jackie slammed the puzzle on the tabletop. She crossed the room to where Tessa stood with that pompous look on her face. Somehow, in the face of financial ruin, Tessa Salem wasn't as terrifying as she'd been when she owned the whole damn world. Jackie stood her ground and refused to back down.

It probably helped that they were on Jackie's territory instead of Salem land. She'd been staying with Gil the last few nights in one of the Graham guest homes, expecting creditors to foreclose on the SX Club at any moment. She didn't want to endure the walk of shame as hired security guards escorted her out of the building when the lenders came to repossess the property. Instead, she went crawling back to her husband's bed.

"I've been back in Salem Crossing for a few short weeks. Alistair and Domino have been your lieutenants for years. If you're feeling pissed, then I suggest you take it out on my brother," Jackie snapped.

"And where is he? I haven't seen him in days," Tessa countered.

"I'm not his babysitter. I'm barely his sister." Jackie was tired of taking the blame for all the shit coming down on the Salems' heads right now. "Try complaining to Domino. At least you know where she is."

Tessa didn't appear to be bothered by the jibe. The ice-cold bitch didn't flinch at the reference to her dead daughter, buried in a plot at Peaceful Pines cemetery. Tessa might look older, more tired, and less fabulous than Jackie had ever seen her aunt, but she hadn't substituted money for compassion.

Jackie regretted her words. She should still be afraid of Tessa Salem. Money comes, money goes...and money replenishes.

"They came for the resorts today. They evicted everyone," Tessa said. A lesser woman would've crumbled, but Tessa squared her shoulders and held her chin high.

Jackie paused. Tessa wasn't her foe. The real enemy had arrived to attack her family. Jackie asked in a softer tone, "The SX Club? The Salem Inn? Salem Heights?"

"Everywhere."

All at once? Jackie wandered through the stacks of bills arranged around the workspace, reams of notices making a labyrinth of her office. The Salems owed dozens of different creditors. The money holders would have had to coordinate such a surgical attack.

"What's left to try?" Jackie asked.

"My lawyers have filed for bankruptcy to delay any major moves for a short time. The lenders want to raze the resorts along Salem Shores. They'll put up new buildings with corporate sponsors on every marquee. Hell, they'll probably rename the city after the highest bidder."

"There's still the insurance claims. Alistair assured me that he has it under control."

"He has failed me infinitely worse than you, Jacquelyn. There is no insurance money. His incompetence created huge gaps in our coverage. We are not getting any settlements. He managed our policies cheaply, and as a result, there are loopholes for exceptions to hurricane damage. I cannot find Alistair because he knows that if I do, so help me God..."

Tessa's permanent veneer of preeminent calm cracked. Her hands became fists, and she shook with rage. Tessa could manage the disappointment in Jackie's failure, but the anger at Alistair's ineptitude consumed her. Her eyes burned with a fury no salve would ease. Alistair had brought about the downfall of the entire Salem empire.

"You came to deliver news of hopelessness and defeat? Is there no Salem moxie to stave off the creditors and secure a last-minute reprieve?" Jackie asked.

Tessa stared at Jackie, standing among the labyrinth of paperwork. "You like puzzles. How many routes usually get one out of a tangled maze? Isn't there generally one exit that leads to an outcome? Every turn I can conceive now leads to ruin, Jacquelyn," Tessa said, turning away to leave.

"What now?" Jackie asked.

"We are at rock bottom. We start to climb," Tessa said, leaving Jackie alone in the Graham guest house.

Jackie stared at the puzzle on the tabletop. Sometimes, there wasn't an answer. Tessa had tasked Jackie and Alistair with saving the Salems after the disastrous storms, but she couldn't save the day. Alistair had mismanaged affairs to the point that the family had no safety net. Someone used the government bureaucracy to block the Salem family's access to federal and state emergency tax dollars. Utter financial failure was a problem that had no solution. The Salems were bankrupt.

Jackie wanted life to be like she'd never left. When she returned to SX, she believed she could act as if the last twenty-three years of her life had never happened. She returned to the family and pretended to fit right in. But decades as a Noble changed her. She couldn't ignore her time in Iowa as a teacher, a mother, and a wife. As much as she wanted to pretend that she'd never left, the world moved on without Jacquelyn Salem, and that young girl who'd escaped with a baby and Gil Graham didn't belong in this world anymore.

Then where did Jackie fit?

"Mom?"

Neve had entered the room, and Jackie didn't even notice her arrival. She blinked blankly at her daughter, almost as if trying to remember who Neve was. The intermittent years between then and now flooded back in, and Jackie felt a reset, a new becoming. She finally accepted that she was no longer the Jackie Salem she'd been when she left nor the Maggie Noble she'd playacted as through all these years, but rather some amalgamation of the two, like Jackie Noble.

"I'm sorry, honey, I was working through a problem," Jackie said, planting her thoughts firmly in the present.

"Which one? SX has no shortage of crises."

"Salem problems. There's no Salem Crossing without the Salem name."

"They can call this beach town by another name tomorrow, but it will still be the beautiful, broken community it is today. It was called New Matanzas before SX, and things were no different then as they are now."

Jackie disagreed. "Our family has come a long way since the beginning of New Matanzas. We went from the poorest citizens to the biggest badasses in this town. We climbed up the food chain to the top of the heap."

Now, circumstances had once again knocked the Salems down. According to Tessa, the family name was worth no more now than when they founded this place. The Salems had risen from nothing to become the controlling family over the last hundred years. If they did it once, then by God, they could do it again.

Neve didn't come to discuss the Salem financial calamity. She probably didn't even realize how bad things had gotten. Neve was only one-quarter Salem and had as much interest in the Álvarez family and twice the stake in the Zhangs. She was about to marry into the Grahams. And yet, Neve still acted like a Noble.

"You're staying here? With Dad?" Neve asked. Of course, she'd already heard. Cyprus and Willow also occupied the guest house, and neither could keep a secret for shit.

"You're not here to discuss my relationship with your father, Nevada. Are you here to convince me to tell him all my secrets?"

Neve shook her head. "It looks like you've got a full plate. You need all the help you can get. I saw Tessa Salem leaving as I was coming in. She looked royally pissed."

"She's something more dangerous than angry, Neve. She's desperate."

"The creditors are moving in?"

"They've taken over Salem Shores. Evicted us from properties with our names on the buildings. Tessa said the family lost everything."

Neve appeared to ponder solutions, like Jackie hadn't been wracking her brains over it for weeks. "Too bad no one can find the treasure the families have been after for decades."

"You know about the treasure?" Jackie asked.

Neve nodded. "Seems people are looking again. Some have been searching for decades."

Jackie knew the story of a ship full of gold and jewels that sank off the coast of Florida shortly after leaving shore. The original families had paid the Miccosukee tribe for the land with tons of valuables, only for the entire fortune to sink off Salem Shores. Jackie's Uncle Mason had disappeared years ago in search of investors to finance a recovery effort for the lost riches. A treasure like that would be priceless. It was the kind of Deus ex Machina that could catapult the Salem family from piss poor to living in a penthouse once again.

"We've discovered that Neil Halloweather and Andre Mascolo orchestrated the whole Dark Summer kidnappings to retrieve the pieces of a secret map leading to the treasure. Apparently, each family has a section of the map showing the location of the sunken fortune, but it seems no one wanted to part with their portion in exchange for their child's life. Or maybe the parents of the kidnapped victims didn't know where to find their piece of the puzzle after all these years."

Jackie imagined Tessa deciding between the fate of her sons or the key to a fortune.

"Did it work? Did Neil Halloweather find the pieces to the map?"

"We don't think so. We're still investigating," Neve said. She looked at the puzzle box Jackie had been pondering when Neve interrupted. "There is no shortage of mysteries festering in SX right now."

Jackie nodded and exhaled. "I'm glad you came by, Neve."

"I'm glad to see you on Graham property instead of at one of the Salem buildings or even at Mar—"

Neve stopped, but Jackie knew the next word she was about to utter. Jackie thought about Martin. He had made it perfectly clear that things were over between them. Jackie had too many other things on her mind to consider what her heart wanted. Jackie's love life was secondary to staving off the ruin of the Salem family. She couldn't promise herself or Neve that things with Gil would work out.

Jackie opened her arms. Neve stepped forward into a motherly embrace. "I'm not going anywhere right now, Neve. We have a wedding to plan. A future to build. You don't need to worry about anything else."

Neve nodded, but they both knew it was a lie. Jackie had been away from SX for a long time, but growing up here, she had honed her opinion of Salem Crossing. Neve had only been here for a few months, but she was the woman Jackie raised. Both knew the endless possibilities of twists and turns throughout this troubled town could shape their futures.

"I don't want to fight anymore," Neve said, snuggled in Jackie's arms.

Jackie felt more like Maggie Noble right now than she

had since returning to SX. She still needed to figure out who she was now that Jackie had shed her disguise of twenty-three years, but at the same time, she couldn't forget who she'd been in Iowa. She was really Jacquelyn Salem, but she was also a mother. As for the rest, a teacher, a wife, middle class—well, she'd see about that.

"I don't want to fight, either," Jackie said.

Neve kissed her on the cheek, as she used to in Horton, and left for the night to return to her place, or, earlier, as a teen, when Neve would head off to her bedroom. Neve moved toward the door, pausing to look back at Jackie before she left. "Are you going to the Snow Ball?"

Jackie hadn't even considered it before. Her entire focus had been on avoiding the Salem foreclosure, with a little distraction from Martin Montgomery in the mix. The Snow Ball was the biggest event of the year in SX. She supposed a Salem couldn't avoid making an appearance. Besides, she wanted to see her children dressed up and happy. New Year's Day was Jackie's birthday, and what better way to celebrate than with a lavish party?

"I'll be there," Jackie said.

"See you then," Neve said and left.

Jackie stared again at the puzzle on the table beside her. She picked it up and turned it around. Gil advertised it as a mystery meant to remain unsolved. The point was that some puzzles had no solution. Jackie squeezed it so hard that it would have crushed under her strength if the shell had been less sturdy. The granite tabletop was tougher. Jackie grinned, lifting the box into the air, then slammed the puzzle onto the surface, smashing it against the stone. It shattered like tempered glass.

A billion shards scattered across the floor, with a few tiny slivers of debris in a pile on the small table. A piece of folded paper peeked out from beneath the remains of the shattered puzzle. Jackie grabbed and unfolded the paper. She recognized Gil's writing. The message was short and straightforward: "You always find a way."

Hell, yeah, she did. And Jackie would again. She had no intention of giving up. She would find a way to preserve the Salem legacy.

Chapter Twenty-Nine

JACKSON MONTGOMERY

Jax moved their base of operations out of Manny's Motel. He couldn't trust keeping the women safe in a place with so many people coming and going. Tourists looking for a spot for illicit activities, locals trying to sneak around to commit sins, and so many suspicious, shady people made Jax start imagining anyone who checked in as dangerous.

Besides, the motel room was too small for the three of them. Jax wouldn't let either of the women out of his sight now that Damien had attacked Cin. Damien's dead body hadn't turned up half-eaten on the shores of the Madonna River, so Jax worried the bastard had somehow survived and was plotting to finish the job he started. Cin could testify that Damien attempted to murder her. His evil half-brother wouldn't leave a witness roaming around SX.

Jax needed help keeping Kennedy and Cin safe. He'd had to recruit two improbable allies for aid.

Jax found Ram at his motorcycle shop two days ago. He entered enemy territory with Cin and Kennedy flanking him. The last time he saw Ram, he had cockblocked the jealous bastard before tying the biker up and leaving him trussed.

Ram might want to break Jax over his knee. As New Year's was only days away, Jax hoped the dangerous dude would let bygones be bygones in the spirit of Auld Lang Syne.

Ram looked from Jax to Cin, barely acknowledging the other girl.

"I'm keeping her safe, Ram. But I know when I need to ask for help," Jax stated.

Ram grunted.

"Damien Halloweather has Cin on his radar. He's a right mean motherfucker," Jax continued.

Ram nodded his huge cinderblock head. "I know. He murdered Domino Salem."

"You think so?" Jax said, surprised the monosyllabic dude could put two and two together.

"Willow thinks so," Ram said in his booming baritone.

That made more sense. Sort of. Someone else was doing the math, but what did Ram have to do with Neve's younger sister?

"I might have valuable information about Damien to share with you. Something Willow would find useful. But I need a favor," Jax said.

Ram agreed. Jax traded what they knew about Damien's quest for a secret map to the sunken treasure in exchange for Ram's services in escorting Cin to and from work at Laverne's and staying through her shift to ensure she remained safe. Ram was one of the few people in SX whom Jax would trust to protect Cin during her shift.

Jax tried to get Cin to take a leave from Laverne's, but she insisted her uncle Carlos had given her enough leeway these last few weeks. Cin refused to let him down over the hectic Christmas break. So, during Cin's shift at work every day, she left Jax alone to babysit her sullen and sassy half-sister.

The second favor came from Mariah Ryan. Cin didn't want Jax to have anything to do with the temptress, but she reluctantly acquiesced after Jax couldn't think of any other place to keep Kennedy safe and secret. They trusted Ram not to say anything, since he didn't talk much anyway. But most people would gladly betray a Montgomery or an Álvarez. They wouldn't find many who wouldn't side against one family or the other.

Cin didn't like that he had slept with Mariah, even though it had been a one-night stand and meant nothing to either of them. It was during a low point for him, and he and Mariah needed solace the night of the election. He hadn't been optimistic about his life at that moment. He certainly never pictured himself with Cin. Happy and looking forward to forever.

Jax remembered when he was about eight. His mother told him to fetch Sammy after church one Sunday. Jax had searched and searched for his older sister. He finally heard her voice behind the church. Mariah showed Sammy her playhouse, a converted garage that Reverend Ryan had transformed into a princess castle out of guilt for putting the congregation before his only daughter, which manifested in occasional grand gestures. Everything in the playhouse was pink and satin, looking like something out of a cartoon.

Jax left Cin and Kennedy with Ram for a while and went to see Mariah alone. Cin seethed but stayed behind with Kennedy. She had to trust Jax. Jax knew damn well he would never sleep with Mariah Ryan ever again.

"I didn't expect to see you," Mariah said as she answered the door. "I thought that thing was a one-time-only deal."

Jax rocked from foot to foot. "It was. I'm not here for that."

Mariah raised one strawberry-blonde eyebrow, studying Jackson like she could read him like a book. "Come to endorse my mayoral run?"

She knew that wasn't possible.

"My dad would torture me much worse than you could manage."

"I don't know. I only showed you a few of my toys," Mariah purred.

Like saying "pretty please" to a schoolyard bully, Jax forced out the next words, "I need a favor."

Mariah smiled like a cat playing with a defenseless mouse. "Why do I owe you a favor?"

"I suppose I'll owe you one. I need a place where someone can lay low for a while."

If she had paws, Mariah would have batted him on the nose. "Do I strike you as someone with safehouses situated around SX?"

"Did your princess castle survive the hurricane?" Jax asked.

Then, her Cheshire grin turned into something more innocent. Wistful. Her posture changed from savage to sentimental. "Popcorn Palace? You remember that place?"

"I came to get Sammy when we were kids. I thought you were the most spoiled damn girl I ever saw."

Mariah had a sparkle in her eye as she reminisced about a more innocent existence, when she preferred princess castles to sex dungeons. "I guess you never hung out with Salems or Zhangs when you were a kid. The Salem twins had their penthouse suites at beachside villas, and Juliet Zhang moved into Weisheng Manor when she was sixteen."

"Can we crash there for a few nights?"

"We?" Mariah asked, lips pursed, trying to deduce the who. Then, she answered her own question. "Someone special."

Jax thought he detected a hint of jealousy. Their night together hadn't meant a damn thing to either one of them. Had it?

"A couple of friends who are in trouble," he said, keeping it ambiguous.

Her eyes softened into something...friendly. "You better not do anything kinky in my princess bed, Jackson Montgomery."

He gave her his megawatt smile. "You did something kinky in your princess bed, didn't you, Mariah?"

She didn't answer. Mariah gave him the key and reminded him he owed her one.

"Jax," Mariah said as he was walking away.

Jax paused and turned back. Mariah had a look on her face different from any he'd seen before. Timid? Scared?

"What is it?" Jax asked, his blood turned cold for a minute.

They stared at each other for a few seconds until the silence became awkward. Mariah finally shook her head.

"Nothing."

Strange. But then, in a family that included Delilah and Caleb Ryan as members, being an oddball was par for the course. Jax nodded, turned, and didn't look back.

Jax picked up Cin and Kennedy. He left his car at Manny's after dark and led the women to the mid-sized building behind the church. No one saw them slip inside. Besides Mariah, no one used this small garage. This would be a safe place to stay.

Mariah had kept the Popcorn Palace pristine. She'd stocked the pantry with canned goods and several boxes of microwave popcorn. A miniature kitchen featured a small fridge and a microwave. After her first shift at Laverne's, Cin brought back some fresh food with Ram. They stocked up enough for a week.

The Popcorn Palace was basically an efficiency apartment, with one room and a half-bath in the corner. The kitchenette provided food. The bathroom had functional toilet facilities.

The sink gave Jax and the ladies a place to wash up daily, a quick rinse to stay fresh. There was one single bed, which Jax graciously offered to the women. He slept fitfully in a beanbag chair in the corner.

He always kept his gun within reach.

Now, Cin had her first day off since they moved into the Popcorn Palace. The three of them spent the entire day together in the confined space. Jax and Cin discussed the map Damien had stolen and debated whether he was working with someone else. Between Damien hunting for Cin and Leira after Kennedy, Jax had enemies on all sides.

"We've been stuck in this pink, perfect hell for days," Kennedy complained for the tenth time that hour. "I would kill both of you just to get a shower."

"We can't risk going to Manny's. Or my place. Or Cin's. Deal with it and shut up," Jax said.

"I feel like swamp ass. I want to rinse off," Kennedy grumbled.

Kennedy had taken the princess motif too damn seriously. "You know who doesn't feel like swamp ass? Dead people."

Kennedy turned his own comments back on Jax. "You know who fits right in at the Popcorn Palace? A drama queen."

Cin rushed to Jax's defense. "Jax is trying to protect your stanky butt, Ken. Maybe show a little appreciation."

"Sorry, the smell is making me cranky, sis. You get to shower at Laverne's after work every evening," Kennedy retorted.

Luckily, Laverne's had a small locker room for waitstaff who pulled a double shift, or for someone who needed a rinse and a change of clothes after a drunken coed spilled beer all over a server. Cin recounted rough nights when she'd been the victim of an over-intoxicated lightweight unexpectedly vomiting all over her.

"At least you two are used to your own smell," Cin said.

"We smell?" Jax asked, suddenly embarrassed. "Both of us?"

Cin shrugged. "It's been a few days, Jax. This castle is a little ripe."

Kennedy offered a suggestion. "The neighbors are gone. I saw them roll their luggage out this morning when I was bored and spying through the crack in the blinds. I saw airline tags on the handles. It appears they'll be gone for a while."

"The Lancasters have a guard dog inside their house. Killer will eat your face off if you try to use their shower," Cin said.

Kennedy smiled smugly. She had a plan. "They have a backyard pool. Like a big fucking bathtub."

Cin looked from Kennedy to Jax. "It's too dangerous."

Jax peeked out the window. They could climb over the short wall, and he could pick the lock to their gated pool enclosure. Jax didn't want to bypass a guard dog to take a shower, but disabling the alarm system was a piece of cake. He could also turn off the automatic lights over the area. They could easily get in and out without anyone noticing. It was less dangerous than Cin's daily shifts at Laverne's.

"I don't want to stink," Jax said.

"I like you ripe or fresh, Jackson," Cin said, embracing him. She kissed him, a surprising expression of intimacy. Jax kissed her back.

"Get a room," Kennedy said. Then quickly added, "Oh. Right."

"We don't need a room, Ken. But we can use the pool," Cin conceded.

The trio ducked through the shadows behind Mariah's Popcorn Palace. Jax boosted Kennedy over the wall surrounding the Lannister's backyard first, then Cin. Jax went over last, quickly clambering over the border. He found the wires entering the property, bypassed the perimeter alarm system, deactivated the automatic lights over the pool, and picked the lock to the enclosure.

Kennedy stood at the pool's edge, grinning in the dim light like a person discovering an oasis after trekking through the Sahara. She peeled off her grimy clothes. Jax couldn't give her privacy because he couldn't let her out of sight. So, Cin's sister stripped right in front of him, tearing off her underwear before Jax could avert his gaze.

Without access to grooming, Kennedy had a cloud of black between her legs. Her areoles were dark and small, like Cin's. The December cold puckered her nipples, standing out from her small breasts like twin points. Fit and svelte, she didn't have an ounce of fat to stave off the winter's chill, gooseflesh covering her chin to shins. Kennedy descended the steps until the water covered her to her chin.

"C'mon in, the water's fine," Kennedy said quietly, teeth chattering. None of them wanted to alert the neighbors and get caught trespassing.

Jax looked at Cin for permission. He'd been naked in front of other people with Cin around, even after they started to acknowledge their feelings for each other. Kennedy had met them while they were skinny dipping. But that had been an ambush, and this was a choice. Jax also knew now that Kennedy was Cin's half-sister. Would a naked evening in the pool make for an awkward family Christmas dinner by the following holidays?

He liked the idea of being together for an entire year.

Cin started shedding her clothes. She had showered at Laverne's the previous night, but she wasn't going to stand around and watch Jax swim naked alone with her sister. Jax watched her strip, a tease worthy of a professional on a stage.

Her breasts were fuller than Kennedy's. Her nether region was shaved smooth and sultry. Jax wanted so badly to take her right then and there. Cin knew what he wanted, so she turned, giving him a view of her pert, round, juicy ass. Cin went to the steps and joined Kennedy in the pool.

Jax peeled off his shirt and ditched his jeans. Cin was watching, but Kennedy wasn't shy about enjoying the show. Jax and Cin had someone between them for nearly their whole relationship. They weren't in a place where things could be different yet. Jax removed his underwear and headed for the edge. His cock was hard and aching, but he knew the cold water would put a damper on his urges as soon as his toes touched the surface.

Not so. Jax's erection managed to defy the cold water. Kennedy eyed his submerged manhood as he hovered near Cin. The only thing stopping him from ravishing Cin's beautiful body was the presence of her sister ten feet away. Jax wanted their first time making love to be something special. An intimate moment when they would be alone.

"You've got balls, Jax. I know because I can see them," Kennedy said in a low voice.

"Keep your eyes above water, Ken," Cin scolded in a hoarse whisper.

"Nothing I haven't seen before. Jax had his dick in the water the first time we met. Now, here we are again. It's getting to be a regular thing," Kennedy replied.

"It isn't going to be a regular thing," Cin hissed.

"So, abstinence? You two aren't fucking?" Kennedy asked, changing the subject, her quiet volume making it sound shameful.

Cin whispered, as if they were sharing secrets. "We're waiting until life is a little more settled before we take the next step. I don't want to start a relationship while we're running from killers and hiding from crazy bitches."

"Does that mean you're moving away from SX? 'Cuz that kind of seems on the regular around here."

"We're going to make a nice life here in Salem Crossing. What we have together is stronger than the forces trying to keep us apart," Jax insisted.

"That would be beautiful if this were a nineties rom-com starring Julia Roberts and not a soap opera with everyone either trying to murder everyone else or sleeping with them," Kennedy taunted.

"You'll see. This is going to work," Cin whispered.

She sounded more comfortable than Jax felt. Cin was assured. Defiant. Strong. Jax swam closer. Their eyes locked on each other. Closer and closer. Nothing between them but swirling water. The neighborhood streetlights faintly illuminated the pool area, casting silver reflections on the water and shadowy skin. Cin exhaled, and Jax inhaled. She was close enough to kiss. The situation begged for romance. Jax's body yearned for satisfaction.

One kiss. Jax could steal one kiss.

They were so close. Jax could feel the heat of Cin's body through the inches of water separating them. The thought of her submerged nipples close enough to possibly brush against him made his erection throb like a muscle having a spasm. Her tongue slipped along the length of her lips. Her dilated eyes indicated desire. An aura of inevitability urged them forward. A kiss would be the key to unlocking their passion.

One kiss would lead to a helluva lot more.

"It's not the right time," Jax sighed, panting like a dog in heat.

"It's not the right place," Cin murmured, reminding Jax of the third person in the pool.

With great effort, Jax retreated. Cin moved to an opposite corner for a moment to cool down. After they regained control, they swam for a while, then got out. The three of them lay naked on the poolside chairs for a few minutes to dry before pulling on their clothes. Jax could smell the stink on his shirt that Cin was talking about. How long would they be able to hide in Mariah's Popcorn Palace before Jax needed new laundry?

Jax opened the door to the Popcorn Palace, and someone was sitting on Mariah's princess bed, the pink canopy over the mattress shielding their identity. Jax had his gun, ready and aimed, before the silhouette waiting for them even flinched. With his body between the intruder and the women, Jax advanced. He kept the pistol trained on the target.

"Don't shoot," said the intruder. A familiar voice. It sounded a little like Bryce. The trespasser pushed aside the pink veil hanging over the bed. The outline of curls around his head resembled Bryce's. Jax moved close enough to see more details. The intruder's face even looked like Bryce's. Why would the mayor track them down here?

"It's Conner. It's okay. He's a Graham. He's family," Kennedy said.

Jax didn't like this. No one should know they're there.

"How did he find us?"

"Kennedy told me where you were. The day you moved from Manny's," Conner said.

"Jesus Christ, Kennedy. Why did you say anything? This should be a secret," Cin snapped.

Kennedy dismissed the sisterly scolding as if it were nothing. "The next phase of our plan was imminent. I needed someone to notify me when Julian Graham was ready. Conner promised to get me when it's time. I need to go."

"You're sure he's safe?" Cin asked.

Jax had heard what Conner did to Ariel during the hurricane. He hadn't been safe for Rob and Ariel's marriage.

"I trust him more than I trust you two," Kennedy said.

Cin shook her head and rolled her eyes. She pulled Kennedy into a hug.

"Be careful, sis," Cin said.

"Julian will protect me from now on. I'll be fine," Kennedy promised, hugging back.

Kennedy punched Jax lightly on his biceps. "Thanks for keeping an eye on me the last couple of weeks, dude."

"That's what family is for," Jax said.

Kennedy grinned. "Speaking of what things are for, I want you and Cin to have the bed. Stay another night. Give it a good test."

Kennedy left with Conner. Keeping only Cin safe now would be easier without worrying about Kennedy. Damien might still be out there, so SX continued to pose a danger to Cin. They would have to stay a little longer until they figured out what happened with the maps.

That was okay with Jax.

They were going to be alone.

Together.

In a princess palace.

He supposed he could spend a little while living the royal life with his future queen.

Chapter Thirty

Neve gathered the Crossing Guard for their final meeting of the year. The following day would be Mariah and Martin's New Year's Eve debate, and the Snow Ball would be the day after that to ring in the new year. She needed to address any topics with fresh data and set her investigators up for success on the potential fertile opportunities for snooping as everyone in SX gathered for the big year-end events.

All members attended. Neve noticed that Willow sat very close to Ram. Her sister would surely tell her if something had kindled between them, but maybe Willow didn't even realize her feelings for the big guy. Simmer noshed on a platter of cheese and crackers Neve had thrown together for the meeting. Tom leaned against a corner, looking tired but wearing a satisfied expression. Naomi was getting back to her old self, standing near the whiteboard and studying the questions.

1. *Why did Damien Halloweather kill Domino Salem?*

2. *What is the real reason behind the Dark Summer kidnappings?*
3. *Who kidnapped the Juliets and why?*
4. *What is the Iblīs family up to?*
5. *Who is Conner Graham?*
6. *Why did Helen Ryan switch the babies at birth?*
7. *Is there an ancient map to lost treasure?*
8. *What is Julian Graham up to?*
9. *Who is Leira, and what does she want?*

"Alright. Let's see where we stand on our mission," Neve said to start the meeting.

Naomi appeared frustrated. "Every answer begs another question."

Neve tried to stay positive. "But each clue has led us in the right direction. There is a destination at the end of the route for every one of these questions. We're getting closer, Naomi."

"I feel like I'm chasing the rainbow. The closer we get, the farther away it moves." Naomi wasn't convinced.

"We'll take it one at a time. Why did Damien Halloweather kill Domino Salem? Ram and Willow are chasing leads on that one." Neve prompted Willow.

Surprisingly, it was Ram who answered. "We have new information. Jax came to me."

"Jax came to you?" Neve repeated. She knew Jax and Ram had been having issues about Jax running around with Acindina. "That's a twist."

"He needed help. We traded favors," Ram said cryptically. Neve wondered if it was a new mystery or about something already on their radar.

"He had information about Damien?"

Ram nodded. "Damien abducted Acindina. Jax intervened. Things got ugly. Jax thinks Damien might be dead."

"We haven't seen Damien since Christmas. Jax might be right," Willow added.

"He was looking for a piece of the map. That might be why he killed Domino," Ram said.

"Cin had a piece of the map?" Neve asked, surprised.

Ram nodded his huge square head. "She didn't know what it was."

"We need to visit the Halloweathers. Maybe Liz or Brit will roll on Damien. If he's gone, they won't have a reason to protect him anymore. Or fear him. Maybe Cy can get info from Clover," Neve suggested.

Willow shook her head. "I already tried. The Halloweathers are circling their wagons. They're really leaning into their Iblīs identity."

"Yes, they've petitioned a legal name change. They've filled out the paperwork with the county court," Neve said.

"Liz and Britney don't trust anyone since Neil's death," Will said, glaring at Tom, who had shot Neil. Not that he had any other choice. "Cy got a trickle of info from Clover. Clover hasn't seen Damien since Christmas, either."

"Alright, keep on it. Maybe try another tactic. Damien is our number one suspect, but I find it hard to believe he acted alone. He's about as sharp as a dildo."

Willow smirked, as that was one of Neve's sayings from Iowa. She nodded in acknowledgment.

Neve continued, "Next. What is the real reason behind the Dark Summer kidnappings? We know Neil Halloweather was blackmailing citizens to get the pieces to the map."

"And Damien carried on the mission after his uncle died. Damien has the answers we need...if he's not dead," Willow appended.

"Acindina may also be a lead. You said Damien came to her for a piece of the treasure map. Maybe she knows something else," Neve hypothesized.

Ram nodded. "We'll ask."

Neve tabled question two for the moment. They had no definitive answers thus far. "Next question. Who kidnapped the Juliets and why? Naomi and I have had a few run-ins with Juliet Zhang. She's acting very weird."

"I think something happened while she was missing," Naomi said with concern.

Neve was worried about her, too. "Everyone thinks she's different. Maybe your twin has some insight?"

"She's been reluctant to talk. But I'll try again," Naomi promised.

Neve poked her marker down the list. "The next one on the agenda might tie into some of the other questions. What is the Iblīs family up to? I think some of them have their hand in half the shit going down in SX."

Simmer took the lead on the topic. "I've been investigating the family. After combing through research covering the last decade, I found evidence of the Halloweathers lurking at the edges of some of the biggest scandals to hit SX over the years. They were never directly involved in the spectacle but often drama-adjacent. I never connected the dots because they were always such a boring family. They always kind of faded into the background. But I think they've been exacerbating local hostilities for years."

"We need to get one of the Halloweathers to spill the beans," Neve said sternly.

Simmer wore a conniving grin. "Blackmail. I'll find something they want to keep secret and bargain for answers."

Neve nodded and wasted no time moving from topic to topic. "Conner Graham. Who is he?"

Tom answered. "I'm digging into this one. My grandfather, Julian, is Conner's father. But I haven't found out who his mother is."

Neve considered the Fallout Shelter. "I can do some more research as well."

"Why did Helen Ryan switch the babies at birth?" Tom read off the board.

Neve revealed, "That one is solved. Julian Graham is Clover's grandfather. He wanted to keep an eye on his grandchild while Clover was growing up. Julian couldn't do that with his son, my dad, around. If he let Gilbert Graham and Jackie Salem fulfill their promise to take Amaya Montgomery's baby out of SX, he wouldn't have been able to be a part of the kid's life. Mariah Ryan didn't know Julian Graham from Samuel Montgomery. By switching babies, Julian could mentor Clover in Boston anonymously."

"My grandfather has been manipulating things in SX for decades," Tom said.

Naomi stared at Tom and observed, "You look tired, dude. You finding out that being in a relationship with Delilah Ryan is fucking exhausting?"

Tom smirked. Something Naomi said was funny?

"She's definitely keeping me busy," Tom said with a glimmer in his eye.

He was talking about sex! Was Delilah sleeping with him? The dedicated virgin cast off her vow of chastity? Neve caught Naomi's eye. Naomi was as surprised as Neve.

"Well, try to squeeze in some time to spy on your family," Neve teased.

Willow spoke up. "We're getting answers to the next couple of questions. Is there an ancient map to lost treasure? Yes, we have evidence. Naomi has the Salem section. Other people are looking, too. Like Damien and whoever's the brains behind stealing a section from Cin. Neil Halloweather and Andre Mascolo kidnapped the boys during the Dark Summer to hold them hostage in exchange for the pieces of the map."

"We need to find out who else is searching," Neve said.

They all nodded.

"What have you found out about Julian Graham?" Neve asked, moving to the next question.

Ram replied, "Jax is hiding Julian's granddaughter in SX. Someone wants to hurt her."

"Damien again?" Neve asked.

Ram shook his massive head. "I don't think so. Damien attacked Cin because of the map. Jax is protecting the Graham girl from someone else."

"You know anything?" Neve asked Tom.

Tom didn't look tired anymore. The glow of new love had entirely evaporated under the spotlight of this new direction in the discussion. He looked pale and worried.

"Is there something we need to know about Julian Graham?" Neve asked.

"The girl is Kennedy Graham. She's my sister," Tom revealed.

"You know what this is about," Neve accused.

Tom looked like a Lothario caught climbing out the window of a married woman's bedroom.

"After decades in exile, my grandfather has returned. Julian Graham arranged for other family members to reassemble in SX. I don't know what it's about, but he will make an announcement on New Year's Day at the Snow Ball. We'll have answers about Julian soon. Then we can find out how it connects to other mysteries in Salem Crossing."

"How long have you known?" Neve said, feeling betrayed by one of her Guard.

Tom confessed, "A while. It's a Graham thing, not a Crossing Guard thing."

"Does Bryce know about this?" Neve asked.

Tom shook his head.

"We discovered what Leira is up to. She wants to break up

Neve and Bryce," Naomi interjected, changing the subject and tackling the last item on the list.

"What? Why does she care about you two getting married?" Willow said. Willow had spent a night with Leira and one of her companions a few weeks ago.

"Because she was in love with Bryce ten years ago. Juliet Zhang is helping her," Neve said.

Neve and Naomi shared a look. That would be an issue for the Caesars to address.

The answers trickled in slowly, like watching the tide come in throughout an afternoon, inching closer with each wave. Neve was frustrated that the secrets plaguing SX were stubbornly institutional, infecting every facet of the community. Uncovering the truth could lead to a new era of prosperity and cooperation once she could root out the treachery and cancer.

The Crossing Guard began to take their leave. Tom left first, eager to get back to Delilah, the look of a man who'd recently been introduced to a new flavor and couldn't get enough.

Naomi whispered to Neve as she left after Tom, "I can't believe Delilah gave it up. I thought she'd save that virginity until at least marriage. Maybe even till after her first divorce."

Ram and Will left on Ram's motorcycle. Neve gave her sister a wink as Ram started the rumbling engine, and Will scowled even as she mounted the bike behind Ram, until her glower broke into a scandalous smirk.

That left Neve alone with Simmer. Simmer wore a scarlet hooded cloak that made her look like a cross between an evil Jedi and Little Red Riding Hood. She stopped on Neve's front step and looked her up and down.

"Y'know, I've got most people in this town pegged, but you're different, Nevada Noble," Simmer said. "Everyone else in SX has an agenda. The push and pull between families is like the moon's influence on the sea. It's a gravitational shift that constantly changes and sometimes wreaks havoc."

"Well, I'm not from around here. I have Midwestern sensibilities."

"Yet your sister, Willow, is caught in the current of shifting SX alliances. And your brother, Cyprus, has been swept up in Clover Iblīs's drama."

"My father seems to stay above the fray. Gil Graham is a good man."

"We'll see," Simmer said with a coy smile. "We both know he's in for difficult times ahead."

Neve caught Simmer's eye. Did she know about her mom's infidelity? Did Simmer know who Jackie was having an affair with? Would she publish the juicy details in *Simmer Salem's Scandal Sheet*? Simmer was part of the Crossing Guard, but her devotion to Auberon Fox's sacrifice had an expiration date. Eventually, Simmer would turn on Neve and betray her. Neve wanted some answers before Simmer became an enemy.

"Maybe I'm not like everyone else in SX, Simmer, but I'll protect my family. Leave the Nobles out of this," Neve warned.

"The Nobles are fiction, Nevada. I deal in dirty truths."

Bryce pulled up in his Jeep and watched the two women curiously as he made his way up Neve's walkway. His tie was loose, and his shirt was disheveled. He'd been working since early that morning before the sun was up, and now it was the end of his very long day.

"Simmeron. How are you?" Bryce greeted.

"Still trying to turn over a new leaf, Bryce. Taking a walk on the side of the angels and all that shit."

"That sounds good."

Neve detected from his tone that he wouldn't believe Simmer Salem if she told him the sky was blue and her hair was blonde. But Neve had to trust that people could do the right thing under the right circumstances. Simmer said she wanted to honor Auberon Fox's sacrifice to save her life by doing something to help SX. If Neve could trust backstabbing Simmer Salem, then maybe she could have faith in the six families of Salem Crossing to find a prosperous future.

"I was telling Nevada that she's special. Like Pluto. A planet, but not really. She orbits the same sun as the rest of us, but she's far enough away from the center to avoid getting burned."

"She is special. She's immune to Salem Crossing," Bryce agreed, taking Neve's hand.

"That's it," Simmer said, pointing a finger at Bryce like he nailed an observation. "SX is a disease, and she managed to avoid infection."

"Yes, this town is sick."

"Good thing we know a damn good doctor. If anyone can cure this septic city, it's you, Doc," Simmer said, turning toward her car.

Simmer drove off. Bryce watched until she disappeared up the point like he didn't trust her enough to let her out of his sight. He also stayed silent until her car disappeared behind the line of palm trees, as if he thought she might hear him if he started talking about her.

"I don't trust that woman."

Neve grabbed his loose tie and led him inside her home like a dog on a leash. "Good thing you're not sharing her bed."

Bryce kicked the door shut behind him as Neve wiggled her butt, glancing over her shoulder with a playful wink.

"I don't think we're making it to the bedroom," Bryce said.

They didn't. At least, not for the first few minutes. They started foreplay in the foyer, stripped in the hall, paused in the shower for a lot of lather and sexy suds, making love in the doorway between her ensuite and the bedroom, and finished on the mattress sometime after midnight.

Chapter Thirty-One

HOLIDAYS WITH THE SALEMS

Alistair Salem hosted the family's annual New Year's Eve holiday party at the island resort. Britney adamantly opposed the idea, but Alistair concluded any risk was minimal. Bringing the family to the resort would reassure progress, illustrate the setbacks caused by Hurricane Marlena, and divert suspicion from the mysterious isle. What could be a better way to hide one's secret lair than in plain sight?

Brit criticized the plan up to the day before New Year's Eve. "What if one of your snoopy relatives wanders around and finds the holding cells? You've got quite the roster of intriguing prisoners locked up there now."

"The only way to navigate the overgrown interior of the island is through the tunnel. I control all access to the entrance on either end," Alistair assured.

"You don't think your cousin Simmer is snoopy enough to suspect something hinky is going on? Or intrepid Naomi? She found the Dark Summer kids at Nightmare Island. And you know she's working with Neve Noble on some secret investigation. Bryce's little princess is nosy as hell."

Brit wore a summery dress as thin as gossamer, despite

the winter temps. The offshore breeze chilled, causing her nipples to perk. Alistair missed the days before he learned Britney was his half-sister, and when a lascivious gaze wasn't knowingly incestuous. He averted his eyes, staring across the sea toward SX.

"There will be plenty of drama and intrigue at the party without people worrying about seeking adventure elsewhere, Brit. The family is in financial ruin, and everyone is on edge. They'll be like a pack of sharks with chum in the water. They'll eat each other alive before they finish with hors d'oeuvres."

Now, on New Year's Eve, with Britney at his side in a decidedly less distracting evening gown, stunning without being overtly sexy, they greeted guests as SX citizens arrived by ferry throughout the evening. Strictly a black-tie affair, the recently bankrupted Salems dusted off their finest attire to attend an extravaganza worthy of rich people in ruin, no less opulent than before their bank accounts registered in the red.

Nevada arrived with Bryce on her arm. The mayor and his fiancée were the most famous citizens in SX right now. Neve was a beautiful thorn in his side. When she arrived in Salem Crossing, he'd considered wooing her before his intuition cautioned him that she was bad news. The alarm bells had warned him away from seducing his cousin. Alistair had lately resisted dating anyone in SX for fear they would turn up in the Salem gene pool.

Alistair greeted them as they entered. "I'm glad you two could make it to the party."

"Wouldn't miss it. Who could resist a preview of the world-famous Salem resort?" Neve said, surveying the room like a sleuth looking for clues.

"Yes, well, there have been setbacks. The far side of the island took the brunt of the storm. Major damage," he repeated, the refrain of the evening to all the attendees. Neve might not be like his other guests, but she was still a Salem.

Bryce assessed the condition of the opulent resort. "At least this building looks to have withstood Marlena better than any structures along Salem Shores. Any headway with the insurance claims?"

"Still problematic," Alistair lied.

The issue wasn't the insurance companies being unreasonable. Alistair had carried inadequate coverage on the Salem properties. He had purposely authorized policies that wouldn't cover the Salems in case of a weather-related event. Alistair had been biding his time for a hurricane for the previous two years. He had several contingencies for his family's financial ruin, but Marlena arrived and delivered the perfect storm for the Salems' downfall.

"If you need help cutting through the red tape to access disaster dollars, I have contacts in the federal and state governments willing to assist," Bryce offered.

Alistair turned to Neve. "Your mother, the Salem one who ran off to Iowa and not the bio-mom who ran off to Boston, is captaining the efforts to secure emergency funds to stave off the creditors. You ought to check with her. I know she was struggling with all the bullshit."

"Mom hates paperwork," Neve stated.

Alistair affixed a grimace to support his false frustration at the bureaucracy. "I don't think she's any fonder of it here than up north. The wolves are at the gates, Neve."

"Neve, Neve, Neve, Neve, Neve!"

A cloud of black curls the size of a beach ball burst through the sea of blond hair. Sweetheart Salem ran into Nevada, practically knocking her over in the middle of a black-tie soiree. Neve managed to stay on her feet, chuckling appreciatively at the girl's enthusiastic greeting and returning the child's over-the-top embrace with a warm hug.

"Sweetie," Neve exclaimed while holding the girl at arm's length and looking over her princess outfit. She resembled someone from a Disney cartoon. "You look so lovely."

"Willow helped me pick it out."

"Well, my sister has good taste," Neve said.

Sweetie's smile lit up the room. "She's really cool, but not as cool as you."

"I've been telling her that since we were little."

Bryce and Neve continued into the party with Sweetie.

"Thank God. A babysitter for the night. Parties and parenting don't fucking mix." The voice came from behind Alistair.

Makenna was drinking something stronger than Alistair's ginger ale. He thought she'd been clean again since her bender during the hurricane, but one glance told him she was both drunk and high. Domino had believed she could clean up Makenna and bring her back into the family fold, but people never changed. Most will never pass up an opportunity to disappoint.

"You're trashed, Mack."

"I've seen the tourists you pick up on the beach with your flirty little jogs. That's trashy," Makenna slurred.

"There are guest rooms upstairs. Go sleep it off," Alistair suggested.

"And miss the most lavish holiday bash of the season? Not a chance. You have an open bar."

Makenna attempted elegance and only succeeded in looking like a debutante who'd been manhandled in the back of the quarterback's hot rod halfway through prom, then stumbled back in for the last dance. Her makeup was smudged, and the edge of her red bra stuck out over the top of her dress. If she intended to take someone home tonight, she'd forgotten that she was either related to these partygoers or they were already married to a Salem. Besides, they were on an island, and Makenna could only get home by boat.

The crowd parted like a packed room at the office party, giving a wide berth to the boss's arrival. Aunt Tessa crossed the room and headed toward Alistair, with Alistair's father on one side and his sister, Jackie, flanking the other. The trio looked like the horsemen of the Apocalypse had arrived to portend doom.

"That's my cue to get the hell outta here," Makenna said, disappearing like a rabbit in a magic trick.

"Pretty fancy party for a bunch of broke-ass Salems," Jackie observed.

Alistair had prepared defenses. "Funds supporting the island resort fall under different financing than the rest of Salem Shores. All assets currently frozen by repossession arrangements are in Tessa Salem's name, whereas the island project falls under my personal LLC. I've already tapped federal and state emergency funding for repairs, and the insurance company has approved all claims."

Jackie hadn't come to party. Tessa led an ambush. "You were also responsible for the insurance claims for the resorts on the mainland, and you failed to get a single dollar for those properties. None of the policies on our coastal properties cover storm damage."

Tessa glared at Alistair like she wanted to kill him in the middle of his own party.

"Domino arranged those policies a long time ago. I've been untangling her mess for weeks. If you want to accuse someone of a mistake, I suggest you try a séance," Alistair said. It was a lie, but no one could prove the dead woman didn't do it. Alistair had brokered the policies but commissioned Domino's signature on the forms. He'd always planned plausible deniability if anyone discovered the shortcomings in insurance coverage.

Jackie jabbed a finger at Alistair's chest. "Your responsibilities included ensuring the policies protected our investments, Alistair."

Alistair countered the accusation with indignation. "I've been searching for loopholes since the insurance companies started denying claims."

"It looks more like you've been ordering hors d'oeuvres and designing swag bags," Jackie retorted, her raised voice attracting a lot of attention.

"Don't act like you know how to run a billion-dollar company, Mrs. Noble. You were passing out pop quizzes to high schoolers a couple of months ago," Alistair snapped.

Jackie leaned in, nose to nose. "I know what I'd grade you on business acumen."

"Yet, I'm currently the only one who can afford to throw a party like this," Alistair said, holding out his hands and indicating the expensive celebration. "I'm the last chance at saving this family's reputation."

Jackie had spent a lifetime hearing students make excuses for late homework and shoddy grades. She wasn't buying Alistair's bullshit. "You've failed this family. This resort belongs to all of us."

Alistair stood his ground, unwavering. "You'll find the paperwork states otherwise. You'd better start being nicer to me. All of you. Because the fate of the family is now in my hands."

His father interjected, "Alistair Alexander Salem. You will not speak to us in that manner. Show some goddamned respect. You were born with a silver spoon in your mouth. Alistair Salem wouldn't own the beach blanket cabana outside Salem Tower if it weren't for the advantages of being born into this family. You might be on the deed, but the last name is still Salem."

Nolan Salem might've thought putting his foot down

would mean the end of it, but instead of nodding along like a good son, Alistair stepped forward and faced his father eye-to-eye.

"I built this place on my own." Alistair pointed at the marble tile surrounding the fireplace with roaring flames. "I personally descended into the South African quarry to pick out the perfect tile for that mantle." He nodded toward the chandelier overhead. "I almost got killed by the Mexican cartel when traveling to Guadalajara to secure that fixture." Alistair glared at his father. "I had to sleep with the daughter of a wealthy collector from Bulgaria to get the Renoir hanging in the foyer, and she wasn't going to win any beauty contests, Father."

"We've all worked hard for this family, Alistair."

"Yet you're broke and homeless, and I have my own island," Alistair replied savagely.

Tessa finally spoke, her cold tone always able to turn anyone in her presence into a shivering, quivering mess. "Listen, you little bastard, I made this family. The family made this. Thus, it's as much a Salem property as any other assets we own."

"What other assets? You've lost everything else," Alistair answered, unintimidated.

Alistair turned and walked away. No one ever turned their back on Tessa Salem. Alistair knew the confrontation was coming and relished the impending fight. He had been planning this battle for years, and Tessa had never even known she was the enemy all along. Until now. Alistair had taken the first shot, and now the war had begun.

Alistair slipped into a corridor leading to the commercial kitchen and the back stairway to the second floor. He paused beside a grandfather clock that blended in with the charming décor of the resort, looking both ways to make sure no one had followed him. Alistair was alone. He stared at the clock's hands, face to face. A scanner behind the Roman numerals verified retinal identification, and the grandfather clock swung outward on a hinge. Alistair had seen it once in a comic book and thought it was a perfect secret entrance for his personal lair.

A long tunnel led underground beneath the overgrown center of the island. Soft lights illuminated the concrete path. The corridor stretched two hundred yards, ending in another passageway with redundant security features. Alistair opened the locks with biometric identification and emerged from the tunnel.

The other end of the passageway opened outside into a small courtyard with a tiled overhang to protect it from the weather. On Alistair's left was the building where he kept his prisoners. The collection of guests was getting a little crowded. More would be arriving within the next few weeks. Their comfort was not his top priority.

The Rocco Chateau was on his right, a comfortable but accommodating cottage that served as a guest house for Alistair's leading partner in crime. He entered through the back door. All the lights were off inside, and Alistair wondered if the occupant had already retreated to bed.

"Fun party?"

The voice floated from the shadows inside the living room.

"I threw down the gauntlet against Aunt Tessa. The war has begun," Alistair said.

The figure hidden in the shadows turned on a lamp beside the sofa. The pale light illuminated the man's features. He looked a lot like Alistair, only with twenty-five years added and a grizzled glint that indicated he'd seen some real hardship in his half-century of existence.

"Good. It's time to start asserting power."

"The pawns are all in place, Uncle Mason. The Salem fortune is gone. We have them backed into a corner."

Mason had an eager expression, like a man at the cusp of achieving his goals. "Now, we need to find the last pieces of the map and recover the lost treasure. Once we've secured the sunken gold, we will reclaim this town as our own. No more Tessa Salem."

"The dawn of a new day," Alistair said, feeling the pull of destiny.

Mason had two glasses of champagne poured and on the coffee table in front of him. He handed one to Alistair and raised the glass.

Mason toasted, "To the new year. Tonight, we herald the beginning of a new Salem Crossing."

Alistair would toast to that. Mason was right. This would be the year when everything changed. Alistair was about to get everything he wanted.

Power. Influence. Adoration.

Chapter Thirty-Two

Neve and Bryce arrived early for the New Year's Eve debate. Neve wasn't sure if they scheduled the strange event at nine p.m., only hours before midnight, to ensure everyone was drunk and impressionable during the presentations, or if this was how SX liked to party. The Salems were mostly out at Alistair's resort. Naomi had ferried Neve and Bryce ashore from Alistair's island, and they had come straight from the Salems' party to the debate.

The SX Board of Elections held the event at City Hall, one of the few neutral locations outside Our Lady of Faith. Because the debate could potentially provoke outraged violence from audience members loyal to either candidate, Reverend Saul refused to host the event, leaving City Hall as the only remaining impartial venue. The debate was held in a large auditorium called Mellon Hall, named after Georgina Mellon, the only mayor who had never been a member of any of the six original families. She was the very picture of neutrality.

"Look, there's Sammy with Jax and Riley. Let's see what she thinks about all this," Neve said, spotting Bryce's half-siblings across the auditorium. "I bet this thing is going to be a shitshow."

Bryce hung back when Neve tugged his hand. She raised a dark eyebrow and shot him a piercing look. They could already read each other's body language. She interpreted the expression on his face. Sammy had discovered she was Bryce's biological half-sister, and Bryce had known about it previously. He was nervous to discuss it with Sammy.

"Sammy doesn't hold a grudge," Neve said.

"She still punches me in the arm whenever someone mentions her little baby doll named Hippolyta that she had when we were kids. I threw it in a retaining pond by the park when we were six because I was sick of her coddling it, and a gator instantly popped up and swallowed Hippolyta whole."

"Alright, but this is good news," Neve said, dragging him behind her.

"She hits really hard, Nevada," Bryce muttered.

Neve noted the awkwardness as they arrived. The three Montgomery offspring eyed their illegitimate brother. Jax sized him up as he used to when both men competed for Neve's affections, but now Jax was checking if he thought Bryce measured up to being a Montgomery. Riley stared like someone trying to find some kind of resemblance. And Sammy scowled, as if she were six and someone had taken away her doll.

Then Sammy's frown turned upside down, and her brilliant smile split her face. She threw herself at her fellow Caesar and half-brother, hugging Bryce so tightly that he might've understood what Hippolyta had endured in the jaws of the gator.

"Welcome to the family, Bryce," Sammy said happily.

"Hrn," Jax grunted.

"This is going to be interesting," Riley said.

"So, everyone knows?" Bryce asked after Sammy released him from a bear hug.

"Mom laid it out in no uncertain terms. She gave Dad until the Snow Ball to settle all his affairs," Riley answered, more intrigued by the salacious details than the other two.

Bryce frowned. "Settled? His relationship with my mother happened nearly three decades ago."

"Funny, Dad wasn't surprised by Sweetheart or Damien. You were the only bastard offspring he didn't seem to know about. You sure your mother got the right guy?" Jax interjected.

Sammy hung onto Bryce's arm. "It's true. I've always felt more of a connection with Bryce than with the other Caesars. I mean, Ariel was fruit loops in love with him, but the rest never had that link." She tapped her temple. "We're related by more than a birthday. We're kin by blood."

Bryce circled back to Jax's comment. He couldn't seem to let it go. "He admitted to the other affairs? Makenna Salem. Elizabeth Halloweather. He confessed to affairs with those women?"

Jax fidgeted uncomfortably, looking like he'd rather discuss almost anything other than his father's infidelities. "He didn't deny it. He only refuted the accusation about Amanda Graham."

Bryce frowned but didn't say anything.

"Mom told him to end any extramarital adventures by tomorrow, or she would take the story to the press right before Election Day. I think Dad was seeing someone recently," Riley said with a wicked grin. Jax was embarrassed by Martin's infidelity, but Riley seemed to enjoy her father's adulterous activities. Neve considered Riley's homewrecking past with Owen Zhang, and she decided the coconut didn't fall far from the palm tree.

Neve looked at Bryce. They both knew that Martin Montgomery had been sleeping with Jackie Salem.

"You think it's over? His philandering?" Neve asked.

Sammy sounded more conciliatory about their father. "He'd do anything to keep Mom. He might cheat on her, but they've been together since they were teenagers."

"He'd do anything to keep his reputation," Riley corrected. "And Mom has his balls in her court."

"Anything?" Neve asked, the idea sparking something related to her Crossing Guard investigations.

Jax met her eyes. He was always honest with her. He couldn't lie to Neve. Even if Jax moved on and pursued Cin, he still had a thing for Neve. He always would. She could see it in the way he looked at her.

"He'd do anything to survive. There's no one more important to my father than Martin Montgomery," Jax said with a bitter tone.

Neve saw the truth flicker across the faces of Sammy and Riley. He wouldn't put his children's safety above his own interests. If someone blackmailed him for his piece of an ancient treasure map by bartering the life of his eldest son, Neve believed Martin wouldn't give up the secret for Carver's freedom.

Neve turned to Sammy. "Can you get me backstage? I want to ask your father something."

Sammy shrugged. "Sure. Karen Keene is supposed to keep people out from backstage, but if I start talking about my recipe for collard greens with smoked turkey, she wouldn't notice the whole SXHS marching band comin' through."

Bryce lightly touched Neve on the elbow in a way that sent sparks through her entire body.

"I'd better not tag along, Nevada. I don't want to seem like I'm showing more interest in one candidate over the other," Bryce stated. "In fact, I should engage the Ryans to make a show of remaining neutral between the contenders."

Bryce followed Neve and Sammy until he spotted Rebecca Ryan closer to the stage, then parted ways. Delilah hovered nearby, looking like a bright rainbow among the otherwise monotone crowd.

Sammy distracted Karen Keene, as promised, with talk of collard greens. Neve slipped by and crept backstage. The debate would occur on the main dais, where the mayor typically addressed constituents, citizens proposed ordinance changes, or performers entertained during City Hall functions. For the office Christmas party a week prior, a magician from Orlando had dazzled employees with feats of illusion.

Neve approached the large curtain separating the debate stage from a prep area with a table, chairs, and refreshments. She heard voices, and the tone was tense as two people argued back and forth. Neve stopped when she was close enough to eavesdrop but far enough not to be seen. Mariah and Martin engaged in a conversation in hushed, fervent tones.

"You say one word about the rumors floating around SX about my family, and I'll bring up every salacious scrap of scandal regarding your sex dungeon."

"You wish I would give you an excuse to talk about my sex dungeon, Marty."

"Leave my personal life out of this debate, Mariah, or I will bring your private affairs back into the public discussion."

"Listen, I'd prefer to talk about the issues affecting SX rather than the fact that you can't keep your dick in your pants around all these women who aren't your wife."

"And I would rather debate policy than what type of nipple clamps you use to torture your subs."

"The crowd probably isn't ready for Martin sowing his wild oats or Mariah's BDSM bedtime stories," Neve interjected, stepping out of the shadows. "Glad you two can keep it civil."

Mariah rolled her eyes. "Miss squeaky clean Iowa approves of playing nice. How droll."

Martin scoffed. "She's not so innocent. She helped cover up the Juliets' scheme to fake their deaths. This city official falsified the public record, and the mayor's office overlooked the incident without an investigation. That ought to be something the new mayor looks into."

Neve glared. "You want me as an enemy, Marty? Really? We're practically...family."

Martin clamped his mouth shut in a hurry lest Neve let slip that Martin would soon become Neve's father-in-law. Mariah might not be able to keep that particular juicy story under wraps if she learned Bryce was Martin's illegitimate son. Mariah looked from Neve to Martin, sensing something unspoken. As Neve's secret sister, she had information she wanted to suppress. She couldn't afford to have Millie Zhang learn that Mariah's mother had conceived an illegitimate daughter with Millie's husband. The fallout from such a war would sink Mariah's chances on election day.

Mariah noticed the icy silence between Neve and Martin, took note, then changed the subject. "You're not supposed to be backstage, Neve. I know you're used to sticking your nose where it doesn't belong around SX, but you need to butt out. Let the people hear us out and make an informed vote. You can annoy whichever of us wins after the election."

"I need to borrow Martin for a moment. I have a question about Salem Crossing's history."

"Tonight is about the future, not looking back on the past. Give your incessant meddling a rest for one night, will you?" Mariah argued.

But Martin held up a hand. He wanted to build a bridge to Nevada Noble because she would soon be part of the family. If Mariah won the election, she would have to serve as co-mayor with Bryce and, therefore, would need to navigate SX politics alongside Neve as the first lady of Salem Crossing. Mariah realized resistance was futile and refusal was foolish.

"I need to use the restroom before we go onstage anyway. You've got a couple of minutes," Mariah said, heading out the way Neve came in.

After Neve was sure Mariah was gone, she leaned over to Martin to whisper. She had easily eavesdropped from the shadows and didn't need anyone else in SX to hear what she had to say.

"I've been looking into the Dark Summer. I have questions."

"Neil Halloweather's confession should have cleared up any lingering concerns, Ms. Noble. That is all in the past," Martin replied quietly.

"Little happens in SX that isn't rooted in the rotted history of this town."

Martin looked irritated. "You've already gained greater insight into SX than most people who've lived here their entire lives. But I don't have any additional information to offer about the evil actions of a deranged man."

"Neil was a descendant of the Iblīs clan. They go back to the origins of SX. There's more to it than a lunatic kidnapping a bunch of kids. He had a method to his madness."

Martin held her gaze. He could lie with practiced ease. "And you think you understand Neil Halloweather's motivations?"

"I do," Neve said. "He wanted pieces of an ancient map."

She saw the truth flicker in Martin's eye, but his expression remained unchanged.

Martin shook his head. "Old legends. SX Urban myth. There are tales of secret maps up and down the treasure coast.

Neil Halloweather was just an evil bastard who kidnapped a bunch of boys."

"I'm not stupid, Martin. I know you're not stupid, either. Neil teamed up with Andre Mascolo to abduct those kids for a reason. Madmen don't team up like supervillains trying to trap Batman. So, why did they do it? They didn't molest the boys. They didn't torture them. They didn't extort SX for ransom money. They had a reason."

"They killed a kid. It could've been my son they murdered. They're monsters," Martin hissed, showing real emotion. Maybe he cared more than she gave him credit for.

Something flickered in his eye. Regret? Realization of his own dark side?

"They wanted the map to the sunken treasure lost off the coast of Salem Shores more than a century ago. Each family kept a piece of the map. Did you have the Montgomery piece, Martin?"

He stared hard into Neve's eyes.

"It's the past, Miss Noble. Let it go," Martin said coldly.

"The history of this town is rotten," Neve restated.

Martin stared at Neve. She was certain he wouldn't tell her anything. He was stubborn and expert at keeping skeletons buried. Maybe Neve shouldn't be trying to push Martin Montgomery too far, but she needed answers to the questions on the Crossing Guard's list. SX couldn't survive with all these secrets eroding the town's foundation.

Martin unexpectedly confessed, "There is a map. I don't have the piece. I...tried to get it. I needed to trade it for Carter. Someone refused to give it to me."

"Who in the hell had the juice to tell Martin Montgomery no? You're the patriarch of the family—the scariest son of a bitch in SX."

Martin looked pleased at the sentiment. "You don't seem afraid of me, Miss Noble."

"Maybe I should be."

"Well, there are worse than me. Do not pursue this any further. Some people wouldn't hesitate to keep the secret, even if it meant eliminating a future granddaughter-in-law," Martin warned.

Neve inhaled deeply. Jefferson Montgomery. Martin's father. Someone who instilled fear in even Martin.

"Looks intense," Mariah said, reentering the backstage area and interrupting the apprehensive atmosphere. "But enough clucking like a pair of old hens. You ready to do this, Marty?"

"I'm gonna whip your ass," Martin said.

"If there's one thing I've had a lot of practice at, Marty, it's whipping asses. But don't worry, I always make sure there's a happy ending." Mariah gave him a lascivious wink.

Neve retreated as the curtains opened and the candidates approached the podiums. She returned to Bryce's side as the debate began. Mariah and Martin went at each other hard but never brought up personal stuff. In the end, Bryce said he was impressed with both candidates. Neve hardly registered a word. She had a lead. A clue. Let the mysteries plaguing SX begin unraveling.

Chapter Thirty-Three

ARIEL ÁLVAREZ

Ariel dreamed.

She'd been dreaming a lot for days, slipping in and out of consciousness. They were drugging her, keeping her sedated, while she fought like a wildcat and hollered like a banshee every time she could summon the strength. Maybe they were afraid she would injure herself, but they were probably more worried she would hurt one of them. They kept her in a hospital wing, strapped to a table and hooked up to an IV. As a result, she had spent her time as an abductee in a fugue state where reality and imagination bled into each other.

The Holidays had brought her to an island off Salem Shores. Hadn't this same story already been told fifteen years ago during the Dark Summer? This time, no one would organize a search-and-rescue party comprised of nearly every citizen in SX to find Ariel Álvarez. She'd watched Leira Gemini write a letter in Ariel's handwriting telling Rob she was leaving SX forever. The Holidays surely took Rob's Mazda and made it disappear.

No one would come looking. Everyone would believe Ariel ran away from her problems rather than stay and clean up the mess. She had talked about leaving SX for years. But that was to go off and try to woo Bryce. Now, Bryce was back. She would never leave SX as long as Bryce stayed. Not by choice.

Whenever Ariel regained consciousness, she pulled at her restraints and howled like a trapped wolf. Maybe someone across the ocean in SX would hear her cries. Instead, her masked captor routinely pumped her full of drugs again until she slipped into a deep sleep.

She dreamed Bryce found her. He burst into the clinic and pulled off her straps. Ariel threw her arms around her hero, weeping with joy.

"I should've never let you go, Ariel. And I'll never make that mistake again," Bryce said in the dreams.

They kissed. Ariel melted. All her fondest wishes came true.

Then, the dream turned into a nightmare.

She woke.

The room was dark, per usual, but this time nothing restrained her arms or legs. Ariel sat up and tried to see in the blind surroundings. The darkness pushed in from all sides. She felt like the blackness was trapping her, although she couldn't discern the wall from the shadows. She stood, walking forward with her hands extended until she touched something. Round. Steel. Bars. Ariel was in a cage.

A prison.

The darkness wasn't complete. Staring, Ariel spotted a red LED light, the glimmer of some small electronic screen in the distance, the faded green glow-in-the-dark that might've been a few inches away or a hundred yards, and the unmistakable reflective sheen of someone's eye.

"What the hell?" Ariel muttered.

"Hell, indeed," came the reply inside the dark. "Welcome to the motherfucking party, Ary."

Ariel remembered the woman bound and gagged in the Riverside Inn closet. "Lilah?"

A dim light flicked on when Lilah pressed a button, enough to illuminate the way to a toilet and cast Delilah in a faint glow. She sat on a bed, locked in the cell adjacent to Ariel. Delilah's wild hair looked even more chaotic than usual, orange curls sticking up in every direction. Dark circles under her eyes appeared positively black against her pale complexion. Each freckle presented as cancerous, as shadows danced around her face. Her fellow Caesar looked like death warmed over.

"What is this?"

"A prison."

"I get that," Ariel snapped. Delilah was irritating even when they were in mortal danger. "But why? Where? Who?"

"We're still trying to figure that out," Delilah said gloomily.

"Who's we?"

"You think you're alone in there?" Lilah asked.

Ariel gazed around the perimeter, searching the shadows inside the jail cell. She saw a stool in a partition in one corner, like Lilah's, a single stall from a public restroom replicated in the jail cell. There was a sink and a mirror outside the stall. A pair of chairs. And the bunk bed where Ariel had awoken moments ago.

A ghost appeared in the top bunk like the specter of death rising from a grave.

The woman swung her legs over the side of the upper bunk. She leaned forward enough to catch the soft glow from Delilah's nightlight before the illumination flickered off on a timer. Ariel had been staring at someone she had started to worry she'd never see again.

"Juliet!"

Arms grabbed her and pulled her into an embrace. Had

Juliet Zhang ever hugged Ariel in her whole life? Had any of the other Caesars besides Bryce ever shown Ariel genuine affection? Yet the self-proclaimed big sister of the Caesars now held Ariel steady in the darkness, squeezing her so tightly that Ariel could barely breathe.

The moment triggered a memory Ariel had long suppressed. Bryce Graham had so consumed her youth that she'd forgotten the moment until now. The Caesars were eleven and having a sleepover at Our Lady of Faith for a Bible camp. Other kids attended, but the seven of them gathered in an exclusive group like normal. She recalled Bryce in a dapper button-up shirt his mother had forced on him, looking handsome. At some point, Juliet Salem had savagely taunted Ariel about not knowing her father's name. Ariel remembered the tears welling and fighting to hold them back. Juliet Zhang intervened, shutting JTS up with a word, taking Ariel's hand, and holding it tightly.

Her moments with the Caesars extended beyond just scenes with Bryce. Ariel simply focused on those memories and feelings. She had forgotten that she and Juliet had been like sisters for a very long time.

Ariel was crying. Positively blubbering. After putting on a brave front for so long, she finally crumbled.

"Shush now. Your loud mouth is what got you drugged for this long in the first place," Juliet said in a firm, kindly way.

Ariel sniffed and stopped her tears. "I remember someone bringing me to an island far from Salem Shores. Why does it matter if I scream my fool head off? Can you even see SX from here?"

Delilah answered in a laden tone, "There was a party. The Salems hosted a New Year's soirée. Our captors couldn't risk anyone hearing your caterwauls, so they kept you unconscious until the guests came and went."

"They didn't keep you sedated, Lilah?" Ariel asked into the darkness.

"I learned a long time ago with Caleb that there are hardships one may overcome, and there are agonies one must endure," Delilah replied.

"It's no use fighting. I've been here a very long time. There is no escape," came another voice on Ariel's other side.

Delilah pushed the timed nightlight again. The feeble glow barely carried far enough to illuminate an older woman through another set of bars in a cell on the opposite side of Delilah's. She resembled JZ in a way, but Ariel couldn't put her finger on a name. Her face displayed exhaustion, defeat, and the pallor of sickness.

"I've escaped worse."

The words came from Delilah's cell, but Delilah's lips, uncharacteristically, didn't move. Instead, Anna Álvarez stepped into the faint glow of Delilah's dim nightlight, looking haggard and angry but entirely determined to get the hell out of there. Ariel's cousin was a survivor of the Dark Summer, and now she was once again a prisoner on a nightmare island.

"Anna?" Ariel exclaimed, reluctantly leaving Juliet's embrace to step closer, blinking to ensure she wasn't hallucinating. "We all thought you died during the hurricane."

"I was at the wrong place at the wrong time."

"Someone saw you out at the docks during the peak of the storm. Everyone thought the storm washed you out to sea. The authorities declared you dead. We had a funeral," Ariel said.

"More than half of us have had funerals without being dead."

Juliet could have said it, but the words came from the old woman in the next cell.

"Who is that?" Ariel whispered to Juliet.

"This is my grandmother, Lula," Juliet introduced.

"The mayor who died during the summer when Bryce left?" Ariel asked.

"She wasn't dead at all. She has been held prisoner out here all this time," Juliet said.

"Why do the Holidays want us locked up on some remote island?" Ariel asked.

Juliet gave a despondent sigh. "Yes, the Holidays. They aren't the ones instigating this whole thing. They're merely the minions doing the menial tasks as the evil plan ramps up. This has been going on for a long time."

"I've been here ten years," Lula reminded Ariel.

"The Holidays would've been sixteen at the time. They could hardly be the masterminds behind such an ambitious endeavor," JZ said.

"Someone else has been running this thing a lot longer than the Holidays have been in town," Delilah added.

JZ pointed through the bars down the line of cages. "There's someone else locked up in here. A man in the last cell at the end."

"Who is he?"

Lula shook her head. "I don't know. He was here when they took me from SX. He never speaks. I never see him. They take me to the clinic for treatments, but I never pass his cell. He never leaves."

Ariel grabbed the bars, gripping the steel like she could bend them open like Supergirl and escape. "Why? What's all this for? What are they planning for SX?"

The timer on Delilah's nightlight ran out again, plunging them into darkness. Ariel reached for Juliet in the pitch black, and her Caesar sister found her hand, grasping it tightly. They had each other. Together, the Caesars had survived in a city that might have otherwise suffocated them in the terrible tides pulling at Salem Crossing. Now, the three had to lean on each other to get through this crisis.

Juliet's voice sounded weak and anxious in the dark. "I'm worried about the doppelgängers. Delilah told me about Leira's cohorts. Someone named Hallie, who is a dead ringer for Lilah. And a woman named Jasmine, who has already taken my place in SX. They're up to something terrible."

They took Ariel away at the worst possible time. "Leira wrote a note telling everyone I left town and signed my name. No one will think it's a fake after the mess I made over the last few weeks."

Even Delilah had concerns. "The rest of the Caesars are in danger. Jasmine has already convinced everyone she is you, JZ. Hallie will take my place."

"Lilah said Jasmine fooled even JTS," Juliet said darkly.

"I think she has her strung out on pain meds," Ariel said.

"Do you think Hallie will trick Tom?" Delilah wondered aloud.

Ariel offered a little hope. "She didn't dupe everyone. I managed to uncover the truth."

Lilah replied despairingly. "But now nearly half the Caesars have been taken off the board, Ariel. Bryce has his head up his ass with hurricanes and wedding plans. The knock on JTS's head left her halfway hopped up on meds most of the time. Sammy will be distracted by your husband's dick, Ary, especially now that you've 'left town.' Naomi is wallowing in grief. No one is paying any attention."

Sammy would swoop down on Rob like a hawk in Ariel's absence. Was Ariel more concerned about their potential relationship, or that Sammy would be too busy fucking Ariel's husband even to consider it strange that Ariel left SX so soon after Bryce came back?

"Nevada," Ariel said, tearing her thoughts away from Sammy. "We might not like her, but she's an honorary Caesar now. She's trying to figure out all the weird shit going on in SX."

"We like Neve just fine, Ariel," Juliet said.

"We like her better than we like you," Delilah added.

"I'll like her a lot more if she can rescue our asses from this prison," Ariel said begrudgingly.

"Someone will find us. I believe it," Anna said, offering hope. She'd been rescued once before, on Nightmare Island.

"I've thought the same thing for fifteen years," came the voice from down the line of cells at the far end of a row of barred cubicles. "No one is coming. This is your fate, and no one escapes fate."

"That voice. It's...the sound of a ghost," Anna whispered. Lula had said he never spoke.

Delilah pressed her nightlight, but the illumination could not penetrate down the row of cells to the end.

"Who is it?" Ariel asked.

"Someone who's supposed to be dead," Anna said.

The stranger continued, a thin voice floating out of the darkness, "Lula Zhang. Anna Álvarez. They declared you both deceased, right? I heard you talking about the funeral for Juliet, but she's not dead, either. My story is the same." A dry laugh sounded haunting in the faint light from Delilah's cell. "We should start a club."

"But you're really dead. It can't be," Anna replied, her voice breaking.

"Reports of my murder were entirely exaggerated," said the person beyond the edges of Delilah's dim light.

"Who is it?" Ariel asked Anna.

"The only Dark Summer kid who never made it off the island," Anna answered in a hollow tone. "Sean Salem."

Chapter Thirty-Four

JACKIE SALEM

Jackie remembered her last Snow Ball—the day she turned eighteen. Less than two months before she would leave SX for twenty-three years. Jackie's relationship with her mother was tense. She'd been seen around town running with the Graham boy who rode the motorcycle, the one who'd been staying at Grandame Graham's since summer. Jackie's friendship with Marilyn Danvers became strained after she told Marilyn she was madly in love with a married man. Marilyn disapproved, refusing to let Jackie come to the Danverses to prepare for the ball. At her father's house, Jackie's stepmother could barely contain an active two-year-old Alistair and the rambunctious three-year-old twins while Jackie tried to get Daphne's help with her makeup.

Jackie always pretended the Snow Ball was her personal birthday party. Her parents were always too busy fighting, then preoccupied with divorcing, then focused on new beginnings to ever pause to celebrate the day of Jackie's birth. Maybe they couldn't find a reason to arrange any fanfare if the City of SX would do it for them.

It had been many years since her birthday had coincided

with such celebratory commotion. Decorators had transformed the ballroom at the Graham Manor into a white wonderland that reminded her of the snowy Iowa winters she'd endured for the last twenty-three long years, only without the painfully bitter cold that dried her skin and caused uncontrollable shivering for five months each year. Strangely, unexpectedly, Jackie felt a pang of nostalgia at the sight of the wintry scene.

Things may have been banal and predictable in Horton, Iowa, but at least they were also loving and stable.

Chaos ruled SX.

Enemies packed the room from wall to wall. Jackie caught a glare from Chief Zhang across the room, whispering something to his sister, Millie, who looked at no one and everyone at the same time. Someone had invited Carl Tillman, already half drunk and leaning beside the punch bowl, giving Jackie the stink eye even though she didn't recall doing anything in particular to the drunken blowhard. He simply hated all Salems, and the rest of her kin were in short supply at the Snow Ball. Britney Halloweather murmured in Armando Álvarez's ear as they danced. A couple of Ryans had their heads together, gossiping while glaring at Jackie. Juicy chatter about the fall of the house of Salem dripped off every forked tongue.

Jackie marveled at the waste of resources committed to this party. The Salems were usually known for senseless opulence, but the Grahams outdid themselves this time. Someone had put the strange Ryan girl in charge of the décor, and she transformed the formerly formal and stuffy Graham ballroom into a snowy scene from a Disney movie. Something resembling snow covered the floor, right down to how it twinkled in the soft lighting, but it was neither fluffy nor slippery nor cold. Blue cloth draped all the tables, recalling the color of the icicles that bordered the edges of every roofline back in Iowa. Large snowflake mobiles dangled from the ceiling, spinning slowly and emitting incandescent light. Snowballs on turntables rotated like small satellites strewn across the Milky Way. Sculptures of ice placed around the room represented wintry scenes like sledding, building a snowman, and a skier. The Grahams cranked the A/C to maximum, so some attendees wore furs, hats, and a few even sported mittens.

"An evening dress in this icebox, Jackie. A bold choice for the ball."

Jackie turned. Her father wore an expensive ski jacket that he would never wear again, designer boots, and leather gloves. His ears burned red from the chill. He wouldn't have survived an hour in Iowa during a cold spell.

"This is a walk in the park compared to a northern blizzard, Dad."

"A shame I was never invited to visit Iowa all those years. In fact, I wasn't sure you weren't in Bali all this time," Nolan Salem scolded.

"I sent a card on your birthday and a gift on Father's Day," Jackie said. "We spoke around the holidays every year, and I texted news about the twins as they grew up."

"I didn't meet my grandkids until they were old enough to make me a great-grandfather," he said.

"If you wanted to dote on grandkids, Father, Britney has two sons."

Her father scowled and leaned forward, whispering, "That is not common knowledge around town."

Jackie rolled her eyes. "Your niece may have kept it out of *Simmer Salem's Scandal Sheet*, but that doesn't mean the whole town doesn't already know. Luckily for you, it's a drop in the ocean of juicy revelations percolating in the community. That's not one of the more salacious stories floating currently around SX."

Her father looked almost offended that his philandering didn't outrank some more sensational surprises revealed in Salem Crossing lately. His cheating was old news in SX.

"Well, the birthday girl looks stunning," he said, changing the subject.

Jackie wore a red evening dress that was more stylish than any clothing she'd worn in Iowa for over two decades. She'd opted for soccer-mom couture in the Midwest, but that was Maggie Noble's taste. Jackie had been playing the part of a family woman, schoolteacher, and community leader. Now, she felt sexy, powerful, and confident. Her evening wear featured a plunging neckline and a slit that nearly reached her hip. Her diamond necklace was worth more than the Nobles spent on Neve's college tuition.

"But you must be cold," her father added.

"I eat cold for breakfast," Jackie said with a grin.

She hadn't been around her father for twenty-three years, but it felt like old times tonight.

"A hardy northerner. My ice princess is going to melt come summer."

"Not a princess anymore, Dad. The Salems have lost our castle."

"Temporarily."

Jackie leaned in, fully aware of the stares and scuttlebutt from one end of the ballroom to the other. "Everyone's talking about us."

"Let them gawk at the Salem scandal tonight, Jackie. By the next Snow Ball, we will be back on top."

Jackie wanted to believe her father's optimism, but he was simply foolish. She was privy to the facts on the ground, and Nolan Salem was in denial of the reality of the situation. The family was royally fucked.

Her father moved on, mingling among the crowd, while Jackie searched for one specific face. Martin had told her it was over, and Jackie was sure he'd pick his wife over his mistress. She'd always known he would choose Magdalene over her any day, but she still wanted to catch a glimpse. Instead, she found herself counting how few Salems attended the ball. No Tessa, no Alistair, no Naomi. Juliet Salem stayed beside Juliet Zhang. Micah mingled with Dalton Zhang and Rob Ryan. Simmer stood out in her red cloak. Secret Salem Britney Iblīs spoke with her former sister-in-law, Juliet Zhang.

Jackie approached the hostess of the ball. Grandame Graham looked resplendent in white fur. She wore an ushanka that made her look imperial, a shawl that gave her a regal appearance, and boots that took twenty years off her age to appear a sprightly eighty. Her hands disappeared into a furry muff she tucked under her bosom. Her bright, perceptive eyes observed the entire scene.

"Quite a gathering, Grandame," Jackie complimented. "Impressive feat, considering most of the city is still recovering from the hurricane."

"The people of Salem Crossing needed an escape from the problems plaguing the city. There are many hardships. People need a distraction from their trying endeavors. The Salems are having especially challenging times, are they not, Jacquelyn?" Grandame said.

Jackie had to carefully navigate the conversation with Grandame Graham. Unlike Gil and her naïve future son-in-law, Bryce, Grandame's apparent feebleness of age or fogginess of mind did not fool Jackie. She understood that no one could survive a century in Salem Crossing without being shrewd and ruthless. Grandame was as calculating as Tessa Salem and even more dangerous because most considered her a stoic figurehead rather than an active player in a nasty game.

"Salem Shores took the brunt of the storm," Jackie

admitted. Public knowledge was that the Salem properties had been devastated by the hurricanes. "We will rebuild."

"Restoration takes money. I've heard your family has had difficulty securing funds."

"The Salems will persevere, Grandame. We have been at the top of the food chain in SX for many years and will remain so."

Granddame tutted doubtfully. "I disagree. History does not bode well for you. The Álvarez family was once the preeminent force in SX until tourism trumped farming, and the tides changed in the Salems' favor. We Grahams had power until my husband left with most of the family, undermining decades of success. Just a few short weeks ago, the Zhangs monopolized City Hall, and now they've been exiled to political purgatory. The ebb and flow of control in SX is as predictable as the tides, my dear, and the Salems' influence in this town is receding."

"We'll see about that."

Jackie wouldn't take advice from some old bat with one foot in the grave.

"That," Grandame replied witheringly, turning and shuffling off, "we agree on."

Jackie vowed to prove her wrong. Grandame had been around twice as long as Jackie, but it was Jackie's birthday, and she was due a wish. That was her wish—to return the Salems to glory in SX. And like a much younger Mavis Graham, Jackie was ambitious and merciless.

A voice behind her interrupted Jackie's thoughts.

"Happy birthday, Mom."

Jackie turned around at the sound of Willow's voice, but all of her children stood in a row. She had been working so hard the past few weeks that she didn't realize how little time she'd spent with her family since arriving in SX. Seeing the three of them standing together at the Snow Ball brought a flood of emotions, memories, and feelings within Jackie.

She opened her arms, and they piled on like a Golden Girls group hug. People on the dance floor looked a little different from the four Nobles swaying to the beat among the tables and chairs surrounding the nucleus of the party. She recalled homemade cards, flowers from Horton Market, and a clay ashtray Cyprus made at school, even though Maggie Noble didn't smoke, and this moment equaled any of her former gifts.

Neve reminisced. "Remember when we rented the cabin in the Smoky Mountains for the holidays when I was ten? We stayed through New Year's so you could celebrate your birthday somewhere other than Iowa. You stared at the snowy scene and said that was your favorite birthday, but now you're back in Florida. Better than Tennessee, Mom?"

"We got home, and I ended up in the hospital with pneumonia because of the mountain cold," Jackie said. "A beachside birthday beats a winter wonderland any day of the week, kids."

"I don't think I've ever worn shorts on New Year's my whole life," Cyprus said.

Jackie frowned at her son's attire. "It isn't appropriate today, either. Just because you can doesn't mean you should, Cyprus. You better not let Grandame see you dressed like a bohemian at the finest party of the year."

Cyprus gazed across the room at Clover, who had migrated to where Britney retreated to visit her mother. Jackie knew he had a crush on the kid from Boston. The one Mariposa mistakenly took north to raise as her child. It couldn't be easy being the offspring of a killer and kidnapper, so Jackie understood why Clover retreated to be with an aunt and cousin. Plus, Cyprus had told her how he'd tricked

Clover to learn more about Mariposa in Boston. Clover probably felt betrayed.

Cyprus looked forlorn.

Jackie could sympathize because she wished Martin would appear, if only to see him for a moment.

"Go talk to Clover. You won't know if you can salvage things unless you try," Jackie said to her son.

"I don't think I should," Cyprus said.

Intrepid Willow, never one to back down, took her twin by the elbow and steered him across the room toward confrontation. "C'mon, you coward. Let's find out if Clover Black can forgive you."

Jackie watched Cyprus and Willow cross the room and caught another volley of hateful glares. Álvarezes gawked at her as if the Salems had received delayed justice for decades-old offenses. The Montgomerys appeared satisfied that circumstances had humbled the mighty family. The Zhangs gloated over the possibility they might ascend in the power vacuum created by the Salems family's misfortune. Ryans commiserated in their predictably condescending manner. Everyone was talking about the Salems' troubles.

"Fuck 'em," Neve said.

"Nevada," Jackie admonished, defaulting to mom mode. "Crudeness is unaccep—"

She sounded like Maggie Noble, a supermom and dowdy schoolteacher. That personality was extinct, as archaic as the Salem stranglehold on the city. The world had evolved in the last few months, and the relationship between Jackie and Neve was entirely different.

Jackie exhaled. "I'm sorry. I don't have any right to scold you."

Ava Álvarez pointed and sniggered as she muttered to her son, Hector. Dr. Conners and his wife, Janice, smirked as they shared comments while watching Jackie. Jasper Meeks and Lewis Buchanan were drinking heavily and cracking jokes about the Salems loud enough for Jackie to overhear. Margo Zhang sipped wine from a full glass, a smug grin on her commonly sourpuss face as she made eye contact with Jackie.

Jackie finally retreated, heading toward the back of the ballroom, familiar enough with the Graham properties to know the quickest way out. She hadn't realized it, but her momentum had snowballed so much that she was practically running in her elegant red dress by the time she reached the ballroom's back door. Her hasty withdrawal looked like a sign of defeat.

She managed to stave off a breakdown until she reached the parlor, where, once upon a time, Gilbert Graham proposed they rescue Amaya Montgomery's baby and escape to Iowa. How did her affection for Amaya's brother, Martin, influence her decision? Did she agree to Gil's grand gesture to impress Martin, a payoff twenty-three years in the making and then so short-lived that it encompassed only a few weeks? Jackie's long-denied love affair ended abruptly. If her reason for helping Gil had been to help Martin's niece, Jackie had been protecting the wrong person all along.

Tears flowed, unstoppable. Her return to SX had been an unmitigated disaster. Her dormant affections for Martin had reignited before Magdalene Montgomery promptly doused any continuation. Reclaiming her rightful place as scion of the Salem fortune lasted briefly before they lost everything. Her return to the family fold had resulted in failure and ruin. Scorn and ridicule greeted her reintegration into SX society.

What a fucking birthday.

A hand touched her shoulder. Her heart leaped as she turned, hoping for Martin to be there. It wasn't. Neve stood before her with sympathy in her gentle gaze and open arms. This wasn't the time for an illicit lover. She needed her family. Jackie collapsed into her daughter's loving arms and felt safe.

Maybe being Maggie Noble wasn't so bad.

Chapter Thirty-Five

JACKSON MONTGOMERY

Jax and Cin had remained hidden inside Mariah's Popcorn Palace for a couple more days. They'd shared Mariah's princess bed as Kennedy suggested, though cuddling and a little kissing were as far as it went. The most impressive display of restraint Jax had managed in his twenty-five years. One morning, when he woke before Cin and watched her sleeping, it took every last erg of self-control not to ravage her in the early morning sunlight dappling through the Palace window.

Jax decided to depart the Palace, declaring Damien Halloweather no longer a mortal threat. He hadn't shown up since he vanished in the Madonna River, surrounded by alligators. Nor had his body washed up along the riverbanks. Maybe Damien was completely eaten in a feeding frenzy or was mortally wounded enough to crawl into the foliage somewhere along the river and die, or his body washed out to sea, or maybe he survived, map in hand, with no reason to return and finish off Cin now that she'd had days to tell her story anyway.

Jax still arranged for Cin to be observed 24/7. When he couldn't keep an eye on her in Old Mat without drawing suspicion, Ram Álvarez watched over her. There had been no sign of danger. Jax started to relax when Cin asked if they were going to the Snow Ball, and he couldn't bring himself to say no.

Jax had arrived early. He mingled through the crowd of elegantly dressed attendees. This was the biggest event of the season, and Jax had fond memories of flirting with girls and ogling the rich and fancy guests. They always served elaborate hors d'oeuvres on silver platters carried by waitstaff dressed better than Jackson. An open bar offered complimentary flutes of champagne, giving a brief insight into being a Salem. The event always made Jax feel both intrigued and gross.

Jax paused to chat with Nevada and Bryce. The pang of jealousy watching them together still existed, now more like the last vestiges of an echo that had almost disappeared. Neve was beautiful in a simple white dress that fit her perfectly, accentuating her form. The dress was simultaneously elegant, sexy, and sublimely Neve. She swept her eyes across the ballroom and then raised a black eyebrow at Jax. She wanted to know where Cin was, and Jax ignored her silent inquisitiveness.

Jax moved on to other guests he could stand to engage in conversation. The list was short and sweet. He exchanged pleasantries with Tom Graham for a while, but Delilah Ryan was all over him. She was so overtly sexual in front of Jax that it made him uncomfortable. Tom had unleashed some dormant volcanic tigress from that awkward, abrasive, virginal shell that had previously been Delilah. Jax noticed Caleb glaring jealously from the sidelines. The vibe made Jax claim a sudden bout of diarrhea, and he retreated. Moments later, he watched Delilah and Tom exit, her hand deep down Tom's front pocket.

Millie Zhang glared at Jax across the ballroom. While conversing with her family, she shot daggers at Jax over her husband's shoulder. In the past, that was her way of flirting, and when their paths crossed during previous community social engagements, it often led to sex in the guest suite behind the Zhangs' family home. Jax had broken off their affair weeks ago. Now, he wondered if her intense stare was a warning, or loathing, or simply the same old same old. Jax wasn't revisiting past bad habits.

Maybe Millie knew if Damien Halloweather survived the Madonna River incident. Millie had a harem of consorts who pleasured her whenever something distracted Corden Zhang, and Corden was always looking the other way. Damien was another of Millie's young conquests. Jax couldn't think of a sneaky way to ask her the question, and he worried that she might mistake interaction for incitement to excitement. Then Jax noticed Millie paying more attention to Greg Dean, who was dancing provocatively with his wife, Raven. Greg was yet a third member of Millie's harem. Greg smiled as Millie caught his eye. Jax was glad someone else had become the target of Millie's illicit lust.

Jax made the mistake of getting something from the complimentary bar at the same time as Rob Ryan. Jax immediately regretted his situation when he noticed that he was half-drunk and bleary-eyed. Certainly, the tumbler of whiskey on the rocks wasn't his first drink of the night. Cin already told Jax how her sister, Ariel, had split town, leaving a note and ditching the mess she'd made in SX. Cornered, Jax listened to the devastated Rob list his many regrets about marrying an Álvarez. Of course, he didn't know Jax was in love with an Álvarez. Rob was so intoxicated that he probably didn't realize he was at the Snow Ball. Finally, Chastity Ryan, wearing a provocative top in sheer nylon showing the shadows of nipples (one pierced through with a bar) and a skirt short enough to show ass cheeks, collected her brother and snuck him through a side door that looked like it led deeper into the mansion.

The orchestra played beautifully. The center of the ballroom featured a dance floor, and Jax watched for a while. Neve and Bryce captivated the room, and even Jax had to admit they represented everything good and promising about Salem Crossing. Grandame Graham took a turn with her grandson, Conner, to the respectful applause of the audience. Gil Graham danced with his wife, Jackie Salem. Riley took turns gyrating wildly with a rotation of young SXers. Big Ram Álvarez, both imposing and impressive in a black leather suit, danced one number with Neve's sister, Willow. Everyone was having a lovely time.

Jax searched for his family. Riley was on the dance floor, Carver wasn't healed enough for a ball, and his parents decided to sit this event out despite his father's political proclivities and the election mere days away. Jax circumnavigated the room, searching for Sammy, and found her entering through the same door Chasity had exited with Rob a few minutes prior.

"Where were you?" Jax asked, startling his sister as he approached from behind.

"Since when do you care what I'm doing?" Sammy asked.

"Rob Ryan is trouble, Sam. Guy's a fucking mess," Jax said.

"I repeat, since when do you care what I'm doing?"

"Am I really such a bastard that you think I don't care?"

"You've been my brother a helluva lot longer than you've been a lovesick puppy, Jax."

Jax clammed up. Sammy would push back on Jax's tender parts if Jax persisted in poking at her. There had never been peace between the two. Of the Montgomery children, the middle two—his mother's middle two—since his father apparently had kids all over SX, egged each other endlessly and would razz one another to the point of becoming supremely pissed.

"Snow Ball truce?" Jax asked.

Sammy held out a hooked pinky finger. It had been their thing since they were little. When their battle royales got out of hand, once Riley, maybe twelve at the time, had been caught in the crossfire and suffered an absolute pummeling of pellets from Jax and Sammy shooting at each other with paintballs, so much so that she looked like a tween with a bad case of oversized pox, they eventually called a ceasefire.

Jax hooked her finger, and they shook on it.

"Did you see Delilah?"

Jax wished he could unsee what he'd witnessed. "Shit, she couldn't keep her hands off that boyfriend. I was afraid she was going to give him a blowjob behind the punch bowl while I was trying to get a drink."

Sammy shook her head. "She waited twenty-six years to lose her virginity. It's like the freaking floodgates opened up."

"I hope Tom Graham brought a snorkel."

"He's going to need a goddamned submarine."

The siblings sniggered in the corner. How many years had Jax and Sammy stood at one of these community functions mocking the pretentious assholes meandering about the room? Lovesick fools tripping over themselves for a chance at a Salem. Álvarez family drama that spilled over into fisticuffs in the street out front. Mariah Ryan sneaking through the side door with one of the Zhang boys. First Lady Britney Zhang took a turn on the dance floor with her husband, the mayor.

Britney.

Jax swept his gaze across the crowd and found her talking to her mother in the opposite corner of the ballroom. Britney had finalized her divorce from Owen Zhang and returned to using the last name, Halloweather, although, technically, she was an Iblīs. Her bright red dress featured a plunging neckline that exposed a belly button pierced with a small golden ring. Jax couldn't explain how she kept her impressive chest covered under the wide-open collar.

Britney would know if Damien Halloweather survived the Madonna River. Her brother would've come crawling back to his mother even if he were missing limbs. And Jax knew Britney, as they had carried on a short, steamy affair after she separated from Owen Zhang, a series of revenge fucks that had blown Jax's mind. Rumor had it that Owen wanted her back, and after a few steamy sessions with Brit, Jax understood why.

"Excuse me, Sammy, I need to talk to Brit."

Sammy grabbed her brother by the arm. "Be careful of that family, Jax. They're trouble."

Jax looked her in the eye. "More trouble than the Montgomery family?"

Sammy smiled. "Hell, no."

Jax nodded. "Right."

Elizabeth Halloweather glared at Jax as he approached. She hated everyone involved in her brother's death. Jax had only been a bystander at the scene, and technically, Jax should be the one pissed, as Neil Halloweather had shot Jax's brother, but Jax ignored the daggers coming from Liz. He focused on Brit. Not hard to do, as she was a vision in the red dress, her deeply tanned skin contrasting with the color, wearing his most dazzling smile to charm and disarm her.

"What do you want, Jackson Montgomery?" Brit asked with a bemused smile on her face.

"A moment of your time," he said, suggesting Liz scram. Brit nodded at her mother, and Liz moved toward Clover Black, standing like a wallflower near a convenient exit.

"I'm not going to dance with you. I don't need any

rumors about us printed in *Simmer Salem's Scandal Sheet,*" Britney said curtly.

Jax smirked. Brit had an attitude that never quit. "There's enough juicy gossip going around SX without mentioning us. Besides, I think our story was over a long time ago."

Britney accentuated Jax's statement. "That *was* a long time ago. I'm moving on."

"I've moved on, too."

"I'm sure," Britney dismissed. She didn't care who Jax was sleeping with any more than Jax concerned himself about who Brit was seeing. "Then to what do I owe the interruption?"

"I'm looking for Damien. You seen him lately?"

Britney's expression didn't change. Jax needed to remember never to play poker with her. She was stone-cold.

"What do you need him for?"

"Family business. He's my half-brother, too, after all," Jax reminded her.

"He's not here," Brit said vaguely.

Jax tried to read her. He'd been intimate with her, but Britney was otherwise a perfect stranger to him. The same went for Millie Zhang. Zephyr Graham. Raven Dean. Mariah Ryan. Even Neve Noble. He'd had all these conquests, but he didn't know any of those women like he knew Cin. They had gotten to know each other better over the last few weeks than he'd ever known any woman. That was something a helluva lot more important than anything physical.

Did Britney know about Damien's mission to get the piece of the Álvarez map? His abduction and attempted murder of Acindina? Was it some kind of evil Iblīs agenda? Jax tried to gauge her reaction to the conversation, but the Iblīs family had lied for decades about their entire lives.

"Can you tell me if you've seen him lately?" Jax asked.

"Not for the last week," Britney said. "Why, do you know something?"

Jax knew Damien might be alligator shit along the Madonna River. No less than he deserved after murdering Domino Salem, trying to kill Cin, and whatever other evil deeds that motherfucker did over the years.

"No," he lied.

"I guess this conversation is over then," Brit said, turning and walking away.

Then, she arrived on Rico Álvarez's arm, dressed in full formal SXPD attire, with his pistol holstered on his hip, reassuring Jax that he was one of the few men he trusted to keep Cin safe. The first glimpse of Acindina Álvarez took his breath away. Jax thought about knowing her for so long and the deep feelings that had developed—this was true love. He had ridiculed lesser men for falling for a woman so completely that they ignored all reason, but here he was, as smitten as a teen with a crush. More than that. This feeling was the stuff that writers used as fuel for timeless poems.

Cin wore a voluminous dress that reminded Jax of the color of a bright, ripe watermelon. The bottom skirt poofed in multiple pleats, causing her to cut a swath through the crowd at least four feet wide as she crossed the busy ballroom floor. Her top was a tight corset that lifted her chest and showcased her distracting cleavage. Delicate, see-through lace connecting the top and the skirt revealed her stomach from the bottom of her breasts to just below her belly button. Her hair was up, so the space between her bustline and jaw showcased her smooth brown shoulders and long, elegant neck.

Every eye in the room followed her.

Jax and Cin snuck around SX incognito for weeks. They agreed that their families would be apoplectic if they knew they were in love. They promised to keep their affair quiet until they were ready for battle or consigned to retreat. The mysteries plaguing SX were too many to escape, so they resorted to tiptoeing around and hiding in places like the Popcorn Palace.

He saw men gathering up their courage to approach Cin and ask her to dance. Rowly Crawford licked his lips, screwing up the nerve. Kendall Bradford straightened her suit and slicked back her short hair, looking ready to make Cin fall for a woman whether she wanted to or not. Conner Graham rocked back on his heels, eager to join the hunt. Jorge Álvarez was distantly related to Cin, probably no closer kin than Ram, and he wore an expression of a man calculating how related is too related. Jake Conners was old enough to be Cin's father but had recently divorced and appeared about to jump back into the dating pool with both feet.

Cin had tried to show she was ready to reveal their relationship when she came to the hospital after Neil Halloweather shot Carver, but Jax hadn't been able to face his father yet. He saw what happened to the Juliets. The whole town would be against an Álvarez dating a Montgomery.

Jax noticed the attention of every single man at the Snow Ball recentered on Acindina, as well as several men with a woman on their arm. And a few females, too. Jealousy percolated, but he had navigated that already as it pertained to Cin. He'd dealt with his envy when he prevented Ram from fucking her and barely lived to tell the tale. This time, the emotion triggered something other than possessiveness and anger.

Jax felt the chains of this society break and fall away.

He didn't give a damn what SX thought about who he decided to love.

Jackson Montgomery crossed the ballroom floor, cutting off several other suitors making a beeline for Acindina. He passed Rowly, hip-checked Kendall into the punch bowl table, elbowed Jorge in the ribs, and beat Jake Conners to the dance floor. They all wanted the first chance with the belle of the ball. A hundred pairs of eyes watched Cin as she pulled men toward her like the moon tugging the tides. She was a celestial body, as beautiful as anything in the sky.

Jackson shoved Jasper Meeks out of the way as he arrived at Cin's side. Jasper was a wildcat and would've retaliated but for Ram on the sidelines, grabbing the feral suitor by the scruff and holding him back.

Acindina looked at Jackson like an apparition of someone long dead manifested before her eyes, as if she couldn't believe it was true. A brilliant smile bloomed. Anyone watching would know how Cin felt about Jackson Montgomery.

"Dance with me?" he asked.

"You're sure?"

"I can't think of a single thing I've been more certain of in my entire life."

He offered his hand, and she took it.

He spun her onto the dance floor and pulled her into his arms. The rest of the world faded away. It was Jax, Cin, and the music. He put his hands on her waist, fingers brushing the lace covering her middle, their eyes locked. Everyone else in attendance had retreated as if shocked by the combination of Montgomery and Álvarez as the royal court of the Snow Ball. Never before in history had a Montgomery publicly wooed an Álvarez.

They glided around the dance floor like the prince and princess of Salem Crossing, deferring only to Neve and Bryce in esteem and envy. The whole world would know they were together after tonight. Neither of them could have faked the look of affection on their faces. These were two young people in love.

They danced until the orchestra stopped for a break.

Before the crowd could ask a question, they dashed out the exit together. They crossed the backyard, laughing brightly, and the rest of their lives were suddenly scary, surprising, and exciting. Jax wanted to take Cin away from SX, anywhere, someplace where they could be alone and finally be together like they'd wanted all these long weeks. They were ready to make love.

"Jax, wait," came a voice behind them.

Jax paused. He knew that tone of voice. It was the tempo of someone about to deliver news that would change everything. *She's dead, I'm sick, it was an accident, I didn't want it to happen this way.* Jax paused halfway across the Grahams' backyard, his fingers still intertwined with Cin's. They both turned, looking back toward Graham estate. One person stood outside with them, bathed in the back porch light.

Mariah Ryan.

Her face wasn't smiling. She didn't look prepared to wish two young lovers a happy future.

"I thought you should know before you ran off with an Álvarez," Mariah said darkly. "I'm pregnant, Jax. And I think you're the father."

Chapter Thirty-Six

Neve danced with Bryce as the evening drew to a close. The crowd thinned after the big dance number between Jax and Cin. They had outed their relationship to the entire citizenry at the Snow Ball. The new couple would be the talk of the town over the next few days, at least until the runoff election. Had a Montgomery and an Álvarez ever overtly demonstrated their love for each other in the history of all Salem Crossing?

Fake snowflakes fell on the remaining attendees during the last dance. The orchestra played a selection from Schubert's Winterreise as the white shavings of ice cascaded from above. Neve felt like she was dancing in a snow globe. Bryce wore a broad smile as he whisked her across the ballroom floor. She couldn't recall if there was ever a more lovely memory of her dancing in her whole life. This could be a scene in a holiday romance movie.

Neve gazed upon the other remnants of the party in the Graham ballroom. Grandame watched from the sidelines. Tom and Delilah had disappeared, surely for a quick romp somewhere private, and returned for more revelry. Greg and Raven Dean pawed one another in the darkest corner of the room, almost masked by the snowfall. Riley hung on to a Ryan whom Neve couldn't name. Willow slow danced with Ram for the tenth time. Cy stared across the room at Clover through the blizzard. Britney ground hard on Rowly Crawford, while Owen glowered miserably in the shadows.

"This is magical," Neve said.

Bryce smiled brightly. "Snow in Central Florida. It's a miracle.

"Yet it really happened once, against all odds, in the winter after the original settlers founded this town. January 1, 1898. The six families came together then to memorialize the surprising phenomenon. They continue to celebrate that moment every year."

Nevada considered all the descendants of those six bloodlines, seven if she counted the Iblīs clan, who had gathered here tonight without one fight or feud. The only dramatic moment was when the members of two different families reached past the animosity between the contentious factions of Salem Crossing.

"Positivity connects the past to the present," Neve said.

"You and I, Nevada, we're the snowfall in Salem Crossing. We will be the change that affects the next hundred years."

"I plan to live long enough to see it, Bryce. Right at your side."

"Rocking chairs on the porch at the point of the cape, watching the tides come in and go out."

Nevada smiled. Bryce twirled her around as the orchestra reached a crescendo. As the last note played, Bryce dipped Neve low, and she could see the world upside down. She spotted her parents on the dance floor, applauding the orchestra as they held the last note. Neve was glad to see them together again. Jax and his siblings had said Magdalene put the kibosh on her husband's philandering, so Neve chose to believe that her mother's dalliance with Martin was a brief fling, perhaps left in the past. Neve decided that it wasn't her place to tell her father about her mother's infidelity, as long as it was over.

"Helluva party," Neve said.

"It's not over yet," Bryce replied with a lascivious grin.

"You'd better get me home before my clothes end up on the dance floor in a snowbank," Neve said with a twinkle in her eye.

The hour was past midnight, but one of the few remaining guests at the ball was Grandame Graham, spry as a perpetually energetic Willow despite the ungodly hour. Bryce led Neve toward Grandame to say their goodbyes. Neve wanted to return to her cottage and take their last dance horizontally. A quick hasta la vista, and she was lista para follar.

Instead of a quick goodbye, Grandame met Bryce and Neve's eyes and simply said, "Come."

Grandame led them into the adjacent parlor, where a fire crackled in the hearth. Someone had dimmed the soft lights in respect for the late hour. The room was already quite crowded. Willow and Cyprus flanked Bryce's mother in a corner featuring a map of Salem Crossing on the wall behind them. Zephyr and Tom shared a small divan, looking exhausted after the long evening. Conner leaned on the fireplace mantle, and Grandame took a seat beside him. Her parents followed Neve and Bryce inside.

There were mainly Grahams in attendance, and those intimately connected to the Graham family, such as Neve and her mother. Clover Black lingered in one corner of the room. Neve knew Clover was Julian Graham's grandchild. Newcomer Kennedy Graham leaned against the wall near Conner, with her pink hair, tats up and down each arm, and several piercings around her face, black lipstick accentuating her cocky grin.

Neve couldn't understand why Acindina Álvarez was there without Jax, looking totally out of place among the Grahams, a princess without her prince. Bryce gravitated toward Cin, who looked lost and confused.

"I thought I saw you leave a long time ago with Jackson," Bryce said.

"Yes, well, something came up before we left the Graham grounds. Mariah stopped us before we escaped. She had something to say to Jax," Cin said darkly. Neve had discovered that Jax slept with Mariah after he lost the election. Had that come back to haunt him? "Then, Tom interrupted and said Grandame needed to see me. Jax insisted on accompanying us, but Grandame kicked him out before all these people started showing up. He's waiting in the library, probably curled up with a good Victorian romance."

"Really?" Bryce asked.

Cin frowned. "Of course not. Things might be different in SX lately, but Jax hasn't become an Emily Brontë fan."

"Did Tom or Grandame mention what this was about?" Neve asked.

"I assume it has something to do with him," Cin replied, nodding at a man with his back turned to the crowd.

Neve had missed him before. Conner's broad shoulders had concealed the man. The stranger had graying hair, still full and curly, a thin frame, and was taller than Conner. He wasn't dressed for a ball but instead looked like a cowboy pondering tracks in the pasture. Neve wouldn't have been surprised to see a handlebar mustache or a Marlboro sticking out of his mouth when he turned, but he was a plain old man in his seventies who was obviously a Graham.

Clover Black stepped forward, open-mouthed, and a stunned expression. "Sensei Julian?"

Julian Graham was behind some shenanigans in SX. Neve had him on the list for her Crossing Guard to figure out. Willow and Tom looked at her across the room. They were finally going to get some answers. This excited her.

"You know this man?" her mother asked Clover.

"I've known him all my life. He's my instructor at the dojo in Boston," Clover said, dumbfounded. "What're you doing here?"

"I can explain everything. Or, more precisely, she can," the older man said.

The door between the parlor and the library opened, and Neve glimpsed Jax inside, trying to see into the parlor to make sure Cin was okay. Jax's eyes found Neve's, and reassurance passed between them. Neve gave him a thumbs-up. Jax nodded, looking relieved.

Helen Ryan entered and closed the door behind her.

Neve had a million questions for the woman. Helen's rash decision to switch Amaya's infant for Mariposa's changed the course of Neve's entire life. She had experienced a wonderful upbringing, but it was a mistake. Gil Graham and Jackie Salem had upended their lives to inadvertently kidnap Corden Zhang and Mariposa Ryan's bastard child.

"Clover, you know your biological father was Neil Iblīs, an awful man that we needed to protect you from," Helen said. "We managed to get you away from SX, where Neil could never find you."

"By switching babies without anyone knowing about it," her mother accused with an angry glare directed at Helen Ryan.

Helen didn't flinch away from Jacquelyn Salem's ire. "It was necessary. We needed to watch over young Clover. Gil would've noticed his father skulking around, keeping an eye on Clover. So, I switched the babies. Mariposa Ryan wouldn't know Julian Graham from Ricky Martin."

"You had no right to play God with the lives of so many people, Helen," Jacquelyn spat.

"I had to protect Clover. I promised Julian I would safeguard the bloodline," Helen said without a hint of regret.

Julian Graham was Gilbert's father, Bryce's grandfather, a Graham who had been missing from SX for decades. Now, he had returned and revealed himself as one of the architects behind Helen switching Neve and Clover as infants.

"What the hell are you talking about? What do I have to do with the Graham bloodline?" Clover asked.

Helen unloaded secrets she'd been keeping for decades. "Your mother was Amaya Montgomery. Her mother died in childbirth, and Jefferson Montgomery raised Amaya as his daughter. Julian is Amaya Montgomery's biological father... your grandfather, Clover."

"I'm...a Graham," Clover stuttered. Cyprus exchanged a distraught look with the stunned Bostonian, further romance now permanently off the table. "Impossible."

"I assure you, I know more about what's possible in SX than anyone else in this town," Helen said.

Helen had been the purveyor of public records before Neve took over the job. She had access to the Fallout Shelter in City Hall, which kept secret records of everything in SX. Neve had no doubt that Helen knew more dirty secrets than the top brass at the FBI. Her story verified what Kennedy Graham had told Neve about Amaya Montgomery's parentage. Neve noted Cyprus's devastated reaction. She had hoped Kennedy was wrong.

Bryce stepped forth and interjected, looking weary of secrets and lies, "What's this about, then? Why are we all here? To show that the Grahams are back after leaving the bulk of the responsibility on Grandame alone for the last fifty years?"

"The Grahams are back," Grandame reiterated. "But I've not been alone all this time, dear Bryce. Julian has been planning our resurgence for decades."

Grandame handed the floor to her son, Julian. Everyone moved away from the hearth, leaving the aged man as the sole focal point. Julian looked over the whole crowd. Neve wondered what Cin was doing among the Grahams. She said Tom specifically invited her here and purposely excluded Jax. Then, she considered Acindina's parentage. She knew Maria Álvarez was Cin's mother, but Neve didn't know the identity of Cin's father.

Julian Graham started speaking like an actor debuting on Broadway. "The stars are aligned. For too long, this city has relegated the Grahams to the sidelines, excluded from influencing the fate of Salem Crossing. We brought some of this on ourselves. Most of the Grahams decided on a self-imposed exile decades ago. But even before, we stood by while the Zhangs, Salems, and Montgomerys shaped this city. Look at what has become of our home. Ruin. Scandal. Chaos. No more."

Julian paced in front of the fireplace, the light from the flickering flames dancing across his animated expression adding drama to every word. He looked like a classic actor delivering a Shakespearean soliloquy with ambition for a Tony award to place on the mantle above the hearth. Julian was passionate, articulate, and convincing. Neve felt like a soldier ready to fight, but who was her enemy? The rest of SX?

Was Julian the leader of the Graham cult?

"Come forward," Julian said. Kennedy stepped to Julian's side. Conner joined them. Julian nodded at Clover, who reluctantly came forward. "Tomás. Willow and Cyprus. Bryce and Zephyr. Acindina. Will you also come up here?"

Bryce gave Neve a concerned look, then wandered forward, joining Zephyr beside Tom at the front of the room. Five people on Julian's right and four on his left. Neve stared at the line of SXers as if they were the cast of a local production of Hamlet, trying to figure out who was playing whom.

"These young people are the future of SX. They are each a part of the puzzle that will reunite the seven families of Salem Crossing," Julian declared.

"What does Acindina have to do with this?" Jacquelyn asked. She wasn't a Graham, but she was more vocal about this strange ceremony than anyone else in the room.

"My father is Niles Graham," Cin declared. "Tom Graham is my brother."

Kennedy added, "And mine. Niles is also my father. My mother is an Iblīs. You know her as Elizabeth Halloweather."

"That is the solution to bringing this community back together, and these nine young people are the key. Acindina, representing a Graham and an Álvarez. Kennedy with connections to the Iblīs family. Willow and Cyprus Noble are both Grahams and Salems. Clover carries both the Montgomery and Iblīs bloodlines. Tomás is half Graham and half Zhang." Murmurs of surprise issued through the crowd. Neve wondered who Tom's mother was. "Conner is my son with Helen Ryan." Gasps hissed at the reveal. Julian and Helen had made an offspring who looked a damn lot like Bryce. Speaking of Bryce. "Some people in this room already know, but others may be surprised to know that Bryce, our own mayor of Salem Crossing, is part of this reunification puzzle. Bryce, why don't you tell the folks? We're all family here."

"My father is Martin Montgomery," Bryce said aloud. Most of the room already knew. The ones who didn't were so few that Cin and Conner's reveals significantly outdid Bryce's.

"What about me? What am I doing up here?" Zephyr asked.

Neve wondered the same thing. The others embodied all

six families of SX. Kennedy represented even the Iblīses, and they were a tangential part of the SX web at best.

"Zephyr Graham is the daughter of Amanda Graham. Her father has been a mystery for her whole life. It is time for me to reveal that mystery."

Zephyr looked at Bryce. Bryce grabbed his sister's hand.

"His name is Austin Black," Julian announced.

"Austin Black? My adopted father?" Clover stuttered.

The man who married Mariposa in Boston? What the hell did he have to do with Salem Crossing? He might've been Neve's stepfather if Helen Ryan hadn't switched babies.

Julian explained, "Austin Black changed his name when he moved to the northeast. His real name is Austin Fox. He is a member of the Miccosukee tribe. Zephyr represents a connection to the original inhabitants of this land."

Neve's mother appeared imminently impressed. "Scions of every family with claims to this town. What do you plan to do with these kids?"

Julian grinned mischievously. "Why, my dear Ms. Salem, we plan on taking over the place. It has been in the wrong hands for too long. These young people will transform it into something better. Something to make our ancestors proud. These nine people are the future of this city."

Neve looked them over. Her fiancé. Her siblings. Her friends. These people can transform Salem Crossing into something new. But it will not be easy. The challengers from every family will be against them. And Leira and her ilk are out for blood. Neve believed in the people charged with forging a new tomorrow, but it will not be fun. It will be war.

Epilogue

HOLIDAYS WITH THE HOLIDAYS

Aaron was the baby of the Holidays. His birthday came the day after New Year's and technically ruined the group's name, but they based their entire identity on being "almost," so none of the six Holidays made a fuss about Aaron being born a few days late. Aaron was as much a part of the hodgepodge half dozen as the rest of the clones.

Clones. Leira would recall when they were little, scampering around the laboratory, and the boys always thought it was some kind of extraordinary origin story, like they were superheroes ready to put on costumes and fight crime. The lab was a kind of superhero lair. But it turned out no one made them to rescue anyone. The sole purpose of the Holidays was to bring ruin. They were supervillains.

Leira was okay with that. The bad guys were always cooler than the fucking heroes.

Alistair Salem announced that their diabolical plans were entering a new phase. This morning, he moved the Holidays from the Riverside Inn to the penthouse suite at the iconic Salem Inn. The historic hotel was scheduled for repossession and had remained uninhabited since the hurricane. Fortunately, Alistair acted as innkeeper for the Salem family's oldest resort property until the creditors took physical possession.

Any respectable supervillain group had a wealthy benefactor.

"This place is fucking balls," Hallie said.

She wore a wild blouse with pink and neon red zigzags and a pair of billowy pants featuring laughing jalapeños to resemble that crazy Ryan bitch. Hallie teased up her usually straight and sleek hairstyle into a rat's nest of curls. Leira had seen clown costumes with more subtlety. Hallie went all in on her impersonation of Delilah Ryan. So much so that she'd thoroughly convinced her foolish Graham boyfriend.

"You've still got Tom wrapped around your finger?" Leira asked.

Hallie gave Leira a lascivious grin. "It's got nothing to do with my fingers, Lay. That man can't get enough. We're doing it like twice a day. I haven't had this much dick since Booker was accidentally taking the doc's ED pills instead of his ADHD meds."

The doc. The doctor was a mad scientist...because what supervillain group wouldn't have one of those? Plus, a group of six clones didn't magically manifest. There had to be some science behind it. No one else but one of the senior physicians at Salem General Hospital could've stolen blood samples from each of the legendary Caesars on the night they were born. Only a diabolical genius could've cultivated their genetic material into viable specimens, artificially inseminated them into paid surrogates, and created a group of lookalikes.

The experiment wasn't completely successful. Leira looked similar to Ariel Álvarez but not enough to pass as an identical imitation. She sufficiently resembled her donor so that Bryce's nostalgia for a young woman who looked like one of his forbidden pseudo-sisters had made him fall for Leira during his last summer in SX. Since she couldn't convincingly pass as Ariel, she dyed her hair, pierced herself, and lately even added tattoos to set herself apart. If she couldn't be a substitute, then she didn't want to be a shadow.

Booker was Samantha Montgomery's clone and obviously popped out the opposite sex. The same thing happened with the Salem twins' clone. Caid resembled Alistair more than Juliet or Naomi, although he had a more feminine softness in his features except where it counted—Caid packed a punch beneath the belt.

Aaron had been a success story. The doc groomed him to replace Bryce. The doc's boss —the real mastermind behind this whole damn thing —sought to switch Bryce with Aaron during the plan's implementation, but then Aaron had the accident. The boys were running amok inside the doc's lab, and Aaron spilled a bottle of acid all over the side of his face. Of the Holidays, Aaron actually looked like a supervillain, scarred and angry all the time.

Only Jasmine and Hallie turned out perfectly. Hallie could easily pass for Delilah Ryan, and as Juliet Zhang's clone, Jasmine might've been her identical twin. Not even Juliet Salem had noticed someone had replaced her lover. The snoopy Ariel Álvarez managed to figure it out, and the intrepid Delilah learned the truth in the end, but they were now both imprisoned on the sinister isle where the villains kept their main evil headquarters.

Maybe Leira should get a cat. Like Blofield in those spy movies that the doc used to watch when the clones were growing up. A cat would be a nice touch.

Most of the Holidays were in the corner hot tub of the primary suite inside the penthouse apartment. Jasmine was screwing Aaron while Leira and Hallie chatted about fooling

Delilah Ryan's unobservant FBI agent boyfriend. The waves became intense as Aaron approached his climax. He finally finished with his signature grunt of ejaculation, and the splashing stopped.

"Happy fucking birthday, Aaron," Jasmine said.

Jasmine stood up in the tub, resplendent in wet nakedness, and stepped out of the water. Booker tossed her a towel. She wrapped it around her body, sitting across from Caid at the small table filled with fruit.

"Change of pace from the last few weeks, Jas?" Caid asked.

"You know I don't mind a woman now and again, and Juliet Salem knows how to properly eat some pussy, but I needed that," Jasmine sighed. "Comes a time when I really need a good dick."

One thing about the Holiday men: they were all hung like kings. Leira had never gone far enough with Bryce to know how the original compared to the carbon copy, but if he was anything like Aaron as a lover, then Leira needed to break up Neve and the mayor so she could have Bryce to herself. She was sick of sharing these three studs with her fellow Holidays.

The door to the penthouse suite swung open, and Alistair Salem strolled in. Leira had acted as the de facto leader of the Holidays ever since they were fifteen, and she'd taken on the mission to infiltrate the Caesars during Bryce's last summer in SX, so she got out of the hot tub and sauntered over to discuss strategy with Alistair. Alistair was as fine as Caid but with the added gravitas of a lot of cash. He was also integral to this diabolical plan, twenty-six years in the making. Therefore, Alistair possessed a kind of power-broker vibe that turned Leira on. She was supposed to seduce Bryce Graham, but Alistair Salem had always been the guy who revved her engine.

"Come to join the birthday party, Alistair?" Leira teased, fiddling with his designer tie.

"I can't keep track of all your festivities, Leira. Seems there's a birthday among you lot every time I turn around," Alistair said.

"It's kind of our thing this time of year."

"Makes me think the Caesars got it right when they wrapped it up on the same day."

"The Caesars didn't get anything right. We perfected the form," Leira purred, leaning in close enough that her buxom chest pressed against Alistair's expensive suit. She wore a tiny bikini, and her soggy swimsuit left wet spots on his tailored coat.

"Mmm. There are certainly improvements to some of the models," Alistair said, looking right at her impressive cleavage.

"You should see my new piercing," Leira said, leaning in closer to whisper in Alistair's ear. If it remained covered by the scant material of her swimsuit, Alistair could guess it could only be in a very intimate location. "Actually, it's better if you feel it."

"Mmm, mmm," Alistair moaned. "Unfortunately, something came up."

"Sounds like I should be fortunate that something's up."

"It isn't the fun kind of something."

"Trouble in paradise?"

"Gather 'round, Holidays. Change of plan," Alistair said, loud enough for the whole room to hear.

"Another disaster in SX?" Jasmine asked, coming closer.

"A new wrinkle," Alistair said.

"Speaking of wrinkles," Aaron said, standing in the hot tub. His skin had become as rubbery as his prophylactic during his long session in the water. He joined the Holidays in a semicircle around Alistair. His naked body was a work of art topped with a defaced half of a head. Sexy and disfigured at the same time. "You brought bad news as my gift? Most people bring a muffin."

"Do you want to put something on?" Alistair asked.

"It's my birthday," Aaron said. "This is my birthday suit."

Alistair raised a blond eyebrow at the naked man. "Right."

"What's the trouble, Alistair?" Leira asked, steering the conversation in a productive direction instead of Aaron's already reactivating erection. She needed to wrap this up before Aaron was ready for another session. One Holiday tradition was that the birthday boy or girl could get as much "cake" as they wanted—"cake" was the Holidays' cute term for fucking. Hallie had already called dibs the next time Aaron wanted a slice, as she wanted to try the whole body shower in the primary bath while Aaron pounded her from behind.

Alistair looked grim. "The Grahams jumped into the competition. Apparently, we're not the only ones playing the long game. The Grahams have been making plans for decades."

"They have their own Graham clones?" Aaron asked, sounding jealous.

Alistair shook his head. "No, nothing science-fictiony about their efforts. They're trying a take over the old-fashioned way. They have natural-born offspring who are half Graham and half every other family."

"Graham-Álvarez?" Leira asked.

"Graham-everybody. They have a member in every facet of Salem Crossing society," Alistair said.

The entire purpose of the Holidays was to take over SX. Without a reason for existing, they would only be cheap knockoffs of the original Caesars. Leira wouldn't let that happen. They had a destiny to fulfill. Leira needed motivation to be here.

"What are we going to do, Alistair?" Leira asked.

"Well, Holidays," Alistair said ominously. "We're going to kill them all."

The End...For Now

THANK YOU FOR READING

Did you enjoy this book?

We invite you to leave a review at your favorite book site, such as Goodreads, Amazon, Barnes & Noble, etc.

DID YOU KNOW THAT LEAVING A REVIEW...

- Helps other readers find books they may enjoy.
- Gives you a chance to let your voice be heard.
- Gives authors recognition for their hard work.
- Doesn't have to be long. A sentence or two about why you liked the book will do.

About the Author

Antonia Church left the great white north for the sunny, sandy beaches of Florida. Salt air and the sound of crashing waves sure get the creative juices flowing. After growing up in the upper Midwest, a thousand miles from the nearest coast, she's found a place where her spirit matches her surroundings—a place to call home. Settled in central Florida, there is plenty of opportunity for hiking green trails and walking the sandy shores. The bright and exciting vibe of the Orlando scene had inspired a new series of novels set on the beautiful beaches of the nearby Atlantic coast.

antoniachurch.blogspot.com

 facebook.com/antonia.church.33

Also by Antonia Church

WITH SATIN ROMANCE

Salem Crossing Series

Riptide

Sandcastles

Driftwood

Hurricane

A Day at the Beach

www.ingramcontent.com/pod-product-compliance
Lightning Source LLC
Chambersburg PA
CBHW020933020726
47495CB00002B/476

* 9 7 9 8 8 8 6 5 3 4 6 3 4 *